SIX

ALSO BY M. LUKE MCDONELL

The Perfect Specimen (prequel to the Optima System series)
The Bear Box

SIX

A Novel

M. Luke McDonell

Bang and Pound

Six
Copyright © 2025 by M. Luke McDonell

This is a work of fiction. All events portrayed in this book are fictitious and any resemblance to real people or events is purely coincidental. All rights reserved including the right to reproduce this book or portions thereof in any form without the express permission of the author and publisher, except in the case of brief quotations embodied in critical articles and reviews.

Published by Bang and Pound
2180 Bryant Street, Suite 208
San Francisco, CA, 94110
www.bangandpound.com

Cover art by Patrick Farley

ISBN: 978-0-9912153-4-8

This book also doesn't exist without you, reader.
Thank you for your curiosity and eagerness to look into the future.

Chapter One

Han Corporate headquarters occupied a very secure building on a very insecure planet, so working there had its advantages and disadvantages.

If a fast-moving dust storm swirled in and pounded the city with 300-kilometer-per-hour winds and fist-sized rocks, shutters would slam shut, air purifiers switch into overdrive, and all the employees would be safe. If one of the millions of poisonous insects native to Victoria made it past the lasers and into a breakroom, tiny drones would vaporize it. If bad actors tried to access the network—from within or without—the AIs would know within milliseconds and shut down the connection and locate the culprit.

It also meant it was often hard to do normal things like get a cup of coffee, convince a smart toilet to flush, or even walk through the front door. The technology protecting Han employees and the rest of the inhabitants of the newly colonized planet was nearly flawless; *nearly* being the key word.

Mia waved her hand through the spiderweb of blue lasers again, hoping the entry gate to the executive-floor elevators would open like it did every morning, but the cryptic message *Record Hold* remained on the screen and the gate stayed shut. She and the other social engineers begged the software security team to include follow-up instructions with error messages like this one, but they couldn't be bothered. *Try again in a few minutes* was the answer to every problem and truth be told, that usually worked.

The cavernous atrium echoed with the laughter and cheerful chatter of hundreds of employees arriving for work, but the woman behind Mia was not happy.

"I've got a meeting in five minutes. Would you mind?"

She snaked a chartreuse-nailed hand forward and Mia brushed it away.

"Give me a second." *Maybe sixty.*

After one final, futile attempt to gain entry, Mia stepped aside. The gate opened for the woman, who—though running late for a meeting—found time to tap her thumb and forefinger together in the "get bit" gesture.

Executive staff should know better than to do that in front of the cameras. Unprofessional behavior wasn't tolerated at headquarters. *She must be a new arrival.* Indeed, her skin sported the blotchy brown patches that appeared during the first few weeks of taking the required anti-UV medication. If she were lucky, she'd get a warning from her boss. If not—a fine.

Mia made her way to the back of the line. She, too, had a meeting in five minutes and might be late for the first time. Would her boss Erika even notice? Monday mornings were hit or miss for the woman. Some days she'd be sharp and demanding. Others, she'd hold up a hand when Mia entered and tell her to go away, she was busy putting out a fire or fighting a battle—some action-oriented metaphor to disguise her obvious hangover.

A sudden cessation of laughter and conversation interrupted Mia's thoughts. She followed the collective gaze to the executive-floor security guard stomping across the atrium's glossy floor. She'd grown used to these guards since her promotion, but some of the lower-floor staff had never seen an armature-enhanced suit nor an openly carried stunner, and they scattered before him as if blown by wind. This guard didn't belong down here. Why the break in protocol?

He stopped in front of her. "Miss Julian."

"Yes?" Mia couldn't fathom what this was about.

"Follow me." He gestured toward the row of small, windowless conference rooms used to meet with vendors from Earth or anyone without clearance to enter the building proper.

Had her boss scheduled something in the last minute that she'd missed? No. The calendar was clear until their usual 10 a.m. planning session. Curious as she was, there was no point in asking questions. Whatever this was, it would be confidential. She followed him across the lobby, her shoes clacking too loudly against the gleaming, imported Earth-marble floor.

The conference room was dominated by a glossy black table and eight chairs, none occupied. He gestured for her to enter, then closed the door and engaged the deadbolt, leaving her alone. Mia pressed the green unlock button, which did nothing but beep. She tried to contact Erika but her glasses couldn't connect to the network. Right. The room was intentionally shielded. She sighed and took a seat. This was pure Erika. The woman loved drama.

As if hearing her cue, Erika blew through the door like a winter dust storm, mouth compressed into a tight horizontal line.

Mia was the only one who ever saw her temper. Everyone else—the partners, the other social engineers, the admin assistants, delivery people—saw her charm. The woman did have charisma. She could shine her pie-plate-sized blue eyes on anyone and make them feel like the most interesting person in the city. She'd listen attentively, laugh at the right moments, then tell a secret in an intimate stage whisper—because you were friends. That was how she acted when she recruited Mia. Fun. Mischievous. A boss who wasn't really a boss.

A lot had changed in the last year.

Erika's normally exuberant swirl of blonde hair was gathered into a tight bun and makeup couldn't hide the puffiness around her eyes. She'd been out too late the night before and was too tired to bother with her usual beauty routine. Bad sign.

She slammed the door, took a silver half sphere from her pocket, and tossed it onto the table. A leaky-tire hiss emanated from the device. Why bring a conversation shield to an already private room?

"You were on the 187th floor Friday night." She spoke slowly, in her carefully-preserved Southern California accent, as if Mia might not understand.

Mia nodded. "Yes. I sent you my report. I was adjusting the color temperature of the night lighting. The partners complained that the red was too—"

Erika held up a hand. "You saw me."

"I did," Mia said.

"Who was I with?"

"Larissa Mills and a man I didn't recognize."

Erika shut her eyes and took a deep breath.

"Would you recognize him if you saw him again?"

Something told Mia the answer had to be no. Erika collected and hoarded information about the partners, saving it, Mia presumed, for the day it might be used as currency to secure the promotion she so desperately wanted. Han Corporation had moved its headquarters to Victoria 20 years ago, and careers were made here, not back on Earth.

Though Erika was ambitious, she was also vain, and Planet Victoria's intense gravity had not been kind to her. During the decade they'd worked together, Erika's visits to the mod shop had grown more and more frequent. Mia had no idea of Erika's age, but the skin on her hands and neck spoke of a number somewhere north of 60. Once she made partner, she'd transfer herself back to Los Angeles.

"I'm afraid not. I was at the other end of the hall and barely caught a glimpse."

Erika stalked toward her, and the sharp click of her heels, the dark suit, and rigidly styled hair brought to mind a scarra beetle advancing on its prey. She had a lot in common with Victoria's deadly insects.

"Tell me exactly what you saw."

Mia relaxed…a bit. This wasn't too different than their usual Monday morning meetings. Mia submitted her weekly reports Friday night, and by Monday, Erika had a thousand questions.

"I was on the floor, doing the lights, and the elevator chimed. I looked up. You and Ms. Mills got out. She was in a fuchsia cocktail dress, you, in all black. I guessed you'd been at the trade delegation reception. The man followed. I assumed he was a guard, probably new. He was wearing ridiculous, oversized glasses and a crappy suit."

She smiled, hoping to distract Erika with the topic of fashion, but it didn't work. Erika's brow furrowed, an expression Mia didn't believe was possible given the tautness of her skin.

"And then?"

"And then nothing. I went back to work and fixed the lights and wrote my report, like I do every week. What's the problem?"

Sure, she'd noticed more. Ms. Mills, a thin, boney woman with close-cropped black hair, glanced nervously left and right before she'd exited the elevator and hurried toward her office, Erika close on her tail. The man—tall, muscular, with dark gray hair and huge mirrored glasses—had taken a moment to get his bearings. His physique and wariness suggested a background in security, and he'd carried a silver, military-grade communications case. Many of the partners carried the same. It was virtually impossible for anyone but the owner to open them without destroying the contents. He'd taken a deep breath and straightened out of an almost imperceptible hunch before slowly shuffling after the women, all signs he wasn't used to the gravity.

Why was this Friday night different from any other night, or day, for that matter? Mia had one job and it was to improve productivity, not to monitor the comings and goings of entitled partners. She'd been the picture of discretion since she and Erika had been promoted last year, taking the contractual requirement to secure the partner's privacy seriously.

Erika took a folder from her shiny black purse. A paper folder.

"Read this." She tossed it onto the table.

Mia ran her hand across the smooth, beige surface of the folder before she opened it. Paper didn't exist at headquarters. It wasn't secure. People could write on it, and writing couldn't be erased as easily as data on glasses. They weren't technically in headquarters, though. Not in this conference room.

The folder contained a stack of twenty or so pieces of A4-sized paper, the first loaded with fine print. A Han patent application for a smart fishnet that captured large fish and let the small swim free.

She looked up. "You want me to actually read this? All of it?"

Erika nodded and took a seat across from Mia. "Read it carefully."

Mia sighed. Clearly this was one of Erika's side projects, maybe something a partner wanted, maybe something she was pursuing on her own. She'd learned not to ask questions; better that way.

The document was extremely technical, and Mia didn't fully comprehend most of it. She finished and arranged the papers neatly in the folder.

"I'm not sure I'll be able to help. I don't know much about nanotech."

"You know more now than you did twenty minutes ago." Erika smiled, red lips pulled back to reveal too-white teeth. "Han didn't get the chance to file this patent because a corporation on Earth beat us to it."

"You mean something similar?"

"No, exactly the same. Okafor Industries filed this exact patent, word for word."

"And, we're suing them? We must have proof that we developed the technology first."

Erika waved a hand. "I'm sure we are, but that isn't the important thing. The real problem is that the theft of this IP was an insider job. The partners want the thief uncovered and thrown out."

"You think I saw something suspicious during the past few months? Someone where they shouldn't be?"

"*You* were somewhere you shouldn't be. Supposedly adjusting lights in a partner office while really looking for this." She pointed to the folder.

Was Erika joking? Mia was a rule follower, often irritating others by refusing tasks that didn't adhere to Han policies.

"I would never steal from Han. You know that."

Erika did and yet here they were, and—

Oh, shit.

"It was you," Mia said before she could stop herself. "That's why you've got that paper file. I just read classified material and now if I'm given a veracity test, I can't say I've never seen it before."

"It wasn't me. You have close ties with senior management in the division at Okafor that filed the patent. Oh, and there's your bank account in Zanzibar with half a million credits. You could have gotten more, you realize. You aren't a very good negotiator."

Mia stood, light-headed, as if she'd been on a shuttle flight. "I don't have a bank account in Zanzibar, I don't know anyone at Okafor, and I've never violated my employment contract in any way. If you give me a veracity test, I can prove it."

She hated veracity tests, but in this case, it was the only option. Did Erika sell the document and need a scapegoat? Or, did she honestly believe Mia might have done this? Had she been tasked with finding the perpetrator and failed and needed someone to blame?

"There won't be a veracity test if things go as planned. The partners are in a bit of a bind. If they question people, they'll have to expose confidential information, and more importantly, reveal there was a breach. Our security system is flawless." Her boss winked, or more accurately, given that her cheek and eyebrow didn't move, closed one eye. "There's no way to smuggle unauthorized material out of this building. Everyone knows, so no one tries. I don't have to prove you did this, just show it was extremely likely. Then…" she waggled her slate-gray nails in the air. "You disappear."

She laughed at Mia's horrified expression.

"Not literally. You're dead to Han. Fired. Cut off. Done."

A spark of anger burned away Mia's fear. "There is no social engineering department without me." She preferred to stay under the radar, but this was no time for modesty.

Erika smiled coldly. "Let me guess. You do everything. It's all going to fall apart without you."

"It will. Fire me, and you'll be demoted before the end of the year."

Erika, an MBA, knew almost nothing about social engineering. Mia resisted the title of manager, but she unofficially mentored the staff of fifteen SEs—checking data, suggesting different approaches for stalled projects, and spending nights and weekends patching up shoddy work.

"*I'll* tell *you* how our department functions," Erika said. "Ninety percent of the job is politics. I handle that while you decide which hardwood flooring will save the company from ruin. You'd get nothing done without me running interference. Phoebe can take over your job and no one will notice you're gone."

"There's no way she can do my job. You don't see her draft reports—"

"You always know the best way to do every project. None of the junior SEs ever make the right decisions. None of them are up to your standards. You fiddle with everything, and I have to listen to your staff complain about how unempowered they feel." Erika shoved the folder back into her purse. "I'll be honest. I worried I might miss you, but I won't. You're a good social engineer but also an annoying know-it-all. Phoebe is much easier to deal with, and she's a loyal team player." She gestured to Mia's ID tag. "Would you mind?"

Mia covered it protectively.

Erika shrugged. "Doesn't matter. It's been deactivated. Keep it as a souvenir if you want." She turned off the conversation shield, returned it to her purse, then opened the door.

"After you," she said, gesturing to the sunlit lobby.

For a moment, their eyes locked, and Mia saw something strange in Erika's. Not anger or triumph, but walking-on-a-cliff's-edge panic.

Mia lowered her voice. "You know I didn't sell that data. You want something from me but I don't understand what."

Erika shook her head. "It's too late. It's done."

The same beefy security guard who brought Mia to the room appeared at her side. He looked pointedly at the nearest set of exit doors. Erika turned away.

This had to be some bizarre negotiating technique. She'd given Mia a good scare and would let her stew until tomorrow. Then her boss would call and ask who else got out of the elevator Friday. Was it the caterer known for serving fresh-off-the-ship interns to sleazy Dominique Wells? Or maybe, the admin assistant who brought quasi-legal drugs from R&D to what everyone laughingly referred to as the testing lab—aka Tadaki

White's office. Erika always pressed for details about partners and Mia always kept quiet.

But no one had gotten off that elevator after Erika, Ms. Mills, and the man. Not one chime in forty-five minutes—which was odd, now that she thought of it. Mia had finished her work in solitude, taken the employee elevator down to the twenty-third floor, grabbed a quick bite at the cafeteria, and headed home. She had nothing gossip-worthy for Erika.

Mia tried to walk purposefully across the atrium and ignore the guard, but all eyes were on her, and she tripped on a seam in the travertine, righting herself only thanks to a comical flailing of arms. That no one laughed said much about the gravity of the situation, given that gravity-related pratfalls were fair game for teasing.

She made it out the main doors and into the comforting heat of the deep plaza that buffered the high-rise from the whisper-quiet traffic of Ring One. Her glasses darkened to protect her eyes from the intense, yellow-green morning sunlight.

Tall, thin sculptures jutted from the paving stones like aggressive metal blades of grass and offered no respite from the heat and glare. She'd helped design this art installation. The plaza used to be covered with colorful fabric sails, a cool harbor in a sea of sand. A few months ago, Erika demanded Mia decrease employee's "pod-to-post" time by ten percent. But how? She couldn't control the speed of the elevators or eliminate the elaborate security procedures. The data showed only one soft spot. When employees exited the pods, they lingered beneath the sails, laughing and talking, relishing a few more minutes of freedom before the workday started. She tried to find another solution, but there was only one way to get people into the building faster. She'd hated herself for suggesting it.

She braved the sun and called Liling, an enthusiastic new hire in the HR department.

"Hey Mia." The woman's glossy, black hair framed her face like a tight-fitting helmet.

"Can you check something?"

"Sure."

"What's my access status?" Mia asked.

Liling arched one thin, painted brow. "Did Erika block you from the gym again? I warned you not to irritate her the week before the quarterly report is due. That woman is spiteful." She typed on a keyboard Mia couldn't see, then abruptly pulled away and held up her hands as if she'd been burned. "Shit! What did you do? Your contract has been terminated and you're Code 88!"

"What's that?"

Liling paled, a difficult feat given her artificially lightened complexion. "You aren't allowed on any Han Headquarters property—physically or virtually. You're trespassing with this call. Are you trying to get me fired too?"

Liling cut the connection.

A tap on her shoulder startled Mia.

"Ma'am." A different guard handed her a white plastic bin containing a red gym bag and potted cactus. Her personal property? Everything else in her office must belong to Han—even the awards.

The guard lingered, sweat running down her otherwise implacable face. Code 88. Mia was trespassing. The stream of brightly dressed employees traversing the covered walkway slowed, taking in the strange sight of a guard and a woman standing in the beating sun. A distant, logical voice told Mia to get out of there before she suffered further embarrassment.

She hurried across the plaza and threw herself into a recently vacated pod as soon as she reached the street.

"Home," she said.

An admonishing chime sounded after she scanned her hand. The text onscreen stated her corporate transport voucher had been rescinded.

"Uh…charge account 872296," she stuttered. She had no idea how much a pod ride cost, or how to pay. Han had picked up the tab ever since she arrived back from college. Was the number of her savings account what the pod wanted?

Apparently, yes.

The pod threaded its way through the dense traffic of Ring One and turned onto wide, straight Avenue E. The beautiful winter morning was dust-free. Residential towers—mirrored windows flashing staccato sunbursts—rose elegantly from landscaped gardens. A new type of bougainvillea thrived in the shade of the jessup trees in the center median, paper-thin pink blossoms somehow impervious to the afternoon wind. Well-dressed people chatted as they made their way down the sparkling sidewalks. Mia noted these details but couldn't focus on any of them for more than a moment. She was too unsettled.

The pod dropped her off in front of her building and she hurried inside, relieved that none of her neighbors were in the lobby. The box in her arms might raise unwanted questions.

The moment she opened her door, a low tone sounded, and a message window appeared on the living room wall.

The auto-payment account for the rental of this apartment has been closed. Which account would you like to use instead?

Then, scores more. Notice of termination. Health insurance cancellation. Maps with big red squares indicating where she wasn't allowed to go. Buzzy little NDAs, shaking and requiring she sign again.

She swept her arm in a wide arc, the text faded, and the art nouveau wallpaper pattern returned. She slumped down onto the couch, shut her eyes, and thought through her employment contract. Han could terminate anyone at any time for any reason. That they preferred to demote and fine poor performers had more to do with the expense of shipping workers back to Earth than any kind of leniency, but the worst offenders were always deported. They couldn't deport her, though. Born on Victoria in the early days of colonization, before birth control was required, she and a few hundred others were the only real Victoria natives. Was that why Erika had given her the Code 88? It was the nearest thing to a deportation she could pull off?

Mia straightened. No time for questions. If this was real, she was in real financial trouble. She'd worked for Han since graduation and had expected to be employed for life. The small savings account for an imagined vacation she never had time to take wouldn't last long. The dispassionate part of her personality—the one that took over late at night when she was exhausted and still had tons of work to do—kicked in.

"Show my monthly expenses."

A meter-square portion of the floral wallpaper vanished, and in its place, a sickeningly long list appeared. She ran her hand down the cool surface, dizzy at the thought of losing access to everything that made life tolerable, and horrified by the realization that if she didn't cancel most of these services right now, she'd be out of credits in less than a month.

Half an hour of slicing her finger through hair appointments, gym memberships, premium data access channels, spa treatments, VIP club passes, bar memberships, recreational drug deliveries, and many other essentials gave her enough credits to pay rent for four months. Cutting her mom's ImmersiveEx subscription would have given her another two… but her mom couldn't live without the fantasy worlds she buried herself in. Mia had tried to wean her from them multiple times and failed. She'd have to find a way to keep paying for that.

The living room wallpaper disappeared. She'd forgotten it was part of the 20th century art and design data pack she'd just unsubscribed from. The whiteness was overwhelming.

In the bathroom, she opened the drug drawer and dug her hand into the confetti of colorful foils and packages. She pulled some Baby Janes from the mess, popped one pill out of the silver six-pack, and swallowed it with tepid tap water.

She collapsed onto the dusty lounge chair on the balcony and waited for the drug to kick in. The quality of the view from her high-floor apartment varied with the light, and now, at noon, the mountains beyond the city limits of New Canberra were flat and featureless. A distorted reflection of Han Tower zigzagged down the windows of the building across the street. She'd trained her glasses to automatically erase the eyesore, but she wasn't wearing them.

The Baby Jane eased its way into her system slowly, an I.V. of warm honey. She sank into the soft cushions as her spinning mind slowed. She couldn't worry about her future now even if she wanted to, and she didn't.

Chapter Two

Mia jerked awake to the three descending notes of an incoming call, a sound she hadn't heard in weeks. What time was it? Midafternoon maybe. She pulled a cleanish shirt from a pile on the floor, threw it on, and raked her fingers through her tangled hair. She'd fallen into a strange schedule since she'd been fired, going to bed later and later until last night, she'd had to darken the windows against the dawn.

If this was a response to one of the many applications she'd submitted, she wasn't going to make a very good first impression. She doubted it would be, though. The job hunt was not going well. Recruiting for all but the most menial positions happened on Earth, with face-to-face interviews a mandatory part of the process. None of the Six corporations on Victoria were set up to hire senior staff on-planet.

The comm chimed again.

"Who is it?"

Crisp blue text appeared on the bedroom wall.

Claire Meyer calling, live image feed.

Claire, her college roommate from New Beijing University on Earth? They'd graduated ten years ago and hadn't spoken much since. A rush of gratitude and guilt flooded Mia. She still had a friend. A socially awkward one to be sure, but one who wasn't forbidden from contacting her. None of her "friends" from Han would accept her calls or return her messages.

"I'll take it."

A black square bled onto the wall. Claire sat in a dark room, barely lit by the glow of the screen in front of her. Oversized mirrored glasses covered the top of her face, and a shaggy, not-quite-professional haircut hid much of the rest.

"Hey."

Mia recognized the voice more than the nearly invisible face.

"Hey to you, too. How are you?"

"Okay," Claire said without conviction.

Mia waited for Claire to continue—patience was key to conversing with her—but when the silence had gone on too long, Mia filled it. "This is an amazing connection. Earth to Victoria calls usually have a delay."

Claire looked puzzled. "I'm here." She gestured around the room. "Here?"

"On Victoria. That's why the connection is good."

Mia examined the room more carefully, and yes, the space had to be on Victoria. The security panel near the front door sported a glowing, peach, honeycomb logo. Barricaid never exported that system to Earth. Still, it was impossible. Claire hated the idea of Victoria, calling it a police state where innovation was impossible. Even if she'd changed her mind, she couldn't have made it through the screening required for a job on this planet. Smart, but acerbic and impatient, she tended to alienate people— people like Victoria's polished, polite recruiters. She wouldn't have come here for vacation either; Claire hated travel and was mildly agoraphobic. During college, she hid behind her major of theoretical technology and interacted with the world remotely whenever possible, rarely leaving the apartment and never going home for holidays or summer breaks. When she took an underpaid research assistant job in Applied Tech at the university after graduation, Mia was sure she'd stay on campus forever.

"What are you doing here?"

"My boss from Itek, Lucas Dunn, is starting a business. He recruited me and a few others from our division in New York."

So, Claire did escape the university after all. Itek was a successful Earth corporation—nowhere near the size of any of the Six, but still respectable.

"What's the business?"

"Private security," Claire said.

Mia hadn't misheard—the connection was crystal clear—but Claire might as well have said she was building a factory to make sand. "There's no need for that. We have zero crime."

Claire smiled. Not the guileless grin Mia remembered. This one was thin and bitter. "Of course you have crime. You can embed every road and wall and streetlamp with sensors and have those silver things fly around, but crime still happens."

"We have no *physical* crime. Zero murders or muggings. This isn't Earth. It's safe. Data crimes may happen, but that's headquarters business and a private security firm would never be brought in. You won't get any clients."

Mia tapped the apartment wall to bring up the crime stats for the last ten years then remembered, as she did at least a dozen times a day, that the databases she normally referenced were property of Han and now off-limits. It didn't matter that she could recite them verbatim; Claire would want real proof.

"Of course we will," Claire said. "At the least, people need security unaffiliated with whatever sector they're in. If it's true that you have privacy in the home, which I doubt, there'll be domestic violence. You think nothing happens because it isn't made public. It's not like you've got a free press or court system here."

Mia breathed in slowly and kept her temper in check. She'd almost forgotten how much of freshman year was spent arguing with Claire about the lack of laws and rights on Victoria. Claire's point being there weren't any, and Mia's, made after plucking off Claire's glasses and dragging her to a window, was that rights didn't matter much when everyone lived in squalor on an overcrowded and polluted planet. After months of back and forth they both gave up and united in complaining about the smog in New Beijing and the guy living below them who was learning to play the trumpet.

"We don't give employment contracts to anyone who'd hurt another person. We've got ten thousand applicants for every job opening. We don't have to hire the brilliant scientist who's got anger control issues and an addiction to stims. We can pick the one who coaches a kid's soccer team and paints to relax and is great friends with her ex-boyfriends. Not only that, her parents are the same. Smart, driven to succeed, and totally stable."

"I'm surprised you're still spouting propaganda after they fired you."

"I wasn't fired, I was…wait, how do you know my employment status? That's HQ only."

The smirk was the first glimpse of the old Claire.

"I don't do theoretical work anymore. I was part of the intra-company crime team at Itek. A senior staffer like you gets fired from somewhere like Han? That generates a lot of data."

Of course it did. Mia's termination had been processed, gym membership canceled, health benefits cut off, pod voucher rescinded. Echoes of her failed career reverberated throughout the city. She shouldn't feel ashamed. She'd done nothing wrong.

"Let's meet tomorrow," Claire said. "Better to talk face-to-face. Can you be at the café on the roof deck of 360 Degrees at 10 a.m.?"

Claire's commanding tone was something new. As was her willingness to spend time outdoors.

"That's kilometers outside the city. You've got to take a pod, then the monorail, then an aerial tram. It's at least an hour trip depending on traffic. Can't we meet in town?"

The restaurant, perched on a mountaintop outside of Ring 20, had long ago fallen out of fashion with everyone but tourists.

"It isn't that far. New York City is—"

"Fine." Mia didn't need a lecture on the grandeur of Earth cities. Maybe Claire wanted to see the view. "I'll be there."

Claire cut the feed without a goodbye.

Mia got an early start, glad to have a reason to put on something other than pajamas and to get out of the house. She hadn't left the apartment in the weeks since she'd been fired. The official reason was to make sure she didn't spend credits, when really, it was fear of running into someone she knew. The bathroom mirror heard many convoluted explanations as to why she'd lost her job. The NDAs made it impossible to tell the truth. After innumerable speeches it hit her: no one would ask. Code 88 was a blank canvas that each person would paint with a different lurid deed.

No chance of running into anyone today. Her fashion-conscious ex-friends wouldn't be caught dead in the untrendy restaurant Claire chose.

The pod took her straight out Avenue C. Sleek, tall apartment buildings gave way to low-rise housing, then to tasteful manufacturing complexes, after which development thinned and landscaping disappeared. At Ring 10, the pod speeded up, turning the desert to a yellow-gray blur her eyes couldn't focus on. At Ring 20, the outermost ring road, the pod rolled to a stop in front of a covered platform, the terminus of the high-speed monorail covering the final eight kilometers to the base of the mountains.

Mia stepped out into the searing heat and took in the surroundings—flat scrubland, stunted bushes, and tufts of waxy, blue-green grass. After the whir of the departing pod faded, the silence was almost complete. She shut her eyes and breathed deep, catching the faint acidic scent of lemonbush, a native herb. Dare she pick some? Ten meters of rocky ground separated her from the nearest bush. The sidewalk and the land near it carried a mild electrical charge to repel bugs, but the bush was well out of that range, and she wasn't wearing stinger-proof shoes. So, not today.

The monorail, shimmering into existence out of a heat haze, was a dusty silver, thirty-years out-of-date vision of modernity, and Mia the only passenger. She took the front seat in the empty car, the same spot where she used to sit with Dad. Her parents were so busy during those early years of the city build-out that she rarely spent time with both of them at once. She and Dad loved the outdoors, so when he had a day off they'd hop on the monorail first thing in the morning and hike around the base of the Santana mountains before the sun burned its way over the peaks.

Five minutes later the monorail slowed to a stop at the base of the mountains. Mia stepped from the car onto a smooth plasticrete walkway. A strong breeze blew dried twigs and tiny leaves in swirls around her feet. She shaded her eyes and peered up at the looming peaks. Steep and jagged, they'd shrugged off large boulders throughout the centuries and she wondered when one would smash the aerial tram ticket booth. She thumbed for a ticket, surprised at the price. Everything suddenly seemed so expensive. Truthfully, she'd not paid much attention to the cost of anything until recently.

The aerial tram was a vertigo-inducing transparent sphere printed from a thick crystal alloy. Mia remembered attending the opening day festivities as a child and thinking this rainbow-creating bubble was the most beautiful thing she'd ever seen. Now, the floor was dusty, scratched, and littered with cups. Some industrious tourists carrying substances harder than diamond had etched their initials into the walls.

The door clunked shut and the slow ascent began. Mia relaxed on the bench and took in the breathtaking view. The mountain's layers of brown, yellow, and gray stone had eroded to beautiful imperfection. Why didn't she get out of town more often? Unspoiled nature was only a breath away, but she'd been too caught up in work to take the time.

As the tram whirred upward, the distant city morphed from a hazy brown and green smudge to narrow ellipses defined by the ring roads. From above, the city was twenty perfect circles growing from Center Park, the ripples of a stone dropped in a sand pond. The first seven rings were almost completely developed, seven to ten about half filled, and Ring 10 through Ring 20 mostly empty. She couldn't see the six wedges that defined the six corporate sectors, cutting the circle like pieces of pie, but they were ingrained in her memory. In elementary school, they'd been forced to watch "The Evolving City" holo at the City Museum every year. The 3D, animated display showed buildings sprouting from the tan ground like hyperactive spring bulbs, until, one hundred years in the future, the garden would be full.

The tram bounced as it slid into the semi-enclosed docking area at the summit. Mia alighted and peered into the window of the main restaurant. It was sparsely populated by a few groups, probably relatives from Earth visiting sons and daughters on Victoria who'd landed a ten-year contract.

The spiral staircase leading to the rooftop café was coated in dust, more proof of the unpopularity of this place. Sturdy red tables with yellow plasticrete umbrellas populated an expansive, round deck encircling a self-service food and beverage dispensing machine. No way a human server would work up here. It was only 9:30 and the temperature was already in the mid-thirties.

Mia walked to the railing, took a breath, and looked down. The restaurant overhung the peak, and standing here was like teetering on the end of a diving board above a thousand-meter-deep, empty swimming pool. Warm wind from the valley floor blew her hair upward, and excitement and terror filled her. A woman could tumble down, just like a boulder. She stepped back.

The distant city of New Canberra was dwarfed by the wild, uninhabited landscape surrounding it. Mountains to the north, the flat blue line of the Western Sea, and south, the plains continued until, beyond view, the wastes began. The city was designed to camouflage its own insignificance, and the ruse succeeded as long as you stayed in the inner rings. Most people did, but this was the perspective Mia needed.

From here, the high-rise headquarters of the Six were nothing more than tiny sticks. She'd been so impressed with herself for getting to the upper third of one of them, to the coveted executive floors. Now, she shut one eye, held out a thumb, and the city vanished.

The creak of the metal staircase pulled her from her musings. Claire shuffled across the deck with the wilted weariness of a recent arrival not yet used to the above-Earth-standard gravity, her progress was further hindered by a black case—obviously very heavy—that she hugged to her chest. The oversized brown shirt and thick gray pants she wore were completely inappropriate for the climate.

"Hey Mia. You're early." She panted more than spoke, and let the case slip to the ground where it landed with a solid thunk.

Knowing Claire, it was some exotic tech toy. Why bring it here? She could barely stand, let alone carry those extra kilos.

Mia leaned in to give Claire a brief hug, which she stiffly endured but did not return.

"Let's get into the shade." Mia gestured to a nearby table and reached to help her with the case, but Claire snatched it away.

"I got it." She dragged it the last few meters.

She'd always been protective of her gear. Mia went to the dispenser to get cold drinks.

By the time she returned, the table had been transformed into a freshman hardware seminar gone wrong. The case spewed a tangle of wires and lighted boxes from its black belly, and Claire fussed over it as if it were a sick baby.

"What's all this?" Mia asked.

"Conversation shield."

Such a mess compared to Erika's compact silver ball. "How long have you been here? On Victoria, I mean."

Claire, engrossed in wiring, didn't look up. "Two months."

Why hadn't Claire called sooner? To be fair, they'd barely communicated in the past few years, and moving here was a tough transition, mentally and physically. Earth native's bodies often mistook Victoria's heavier gravity for depression instead of the physical condition it was. The Six had a regime for new employees that Claire and her team might not know about. Mia made a mental note to send her the information.

"Which corporation sponsored your business?"

"Weber," Claire replied.

Weber developed and manufactured pharmaceuticals, including Mia's beloved Baby Janes. Why they'd sponsor a security firm was beyond her, but partners had their own, opaque reasons.

"Sorry if I sounded skeptical about your chances of success. It's an accomplishment to get a permit to operate here. There's a year-long waiting list just to apply. You must have a really solid business plan."

Claire shrugged. "Dunno. I didn't write it."

She gulped down half of her iced tea, then startled Mia by reaching forward and taking Mia's DV glasses from her face. Mia had them on mirror, which was rude during one-on-one interactions with peers, but the glare on the roof was intense.

Mia soon realized Claire wasn't enforcing social etiquette—she was a child irresistibly drawn to a shiny new toy. She peered through the lenses, flexed the arms, pulled out the tiny ear buds, and examined the discreet logo.

"Lucida 3300? We only have the 2000 series on Earth."

Claire's glasses were gray and utilitarian, and no brand Mia had ever seen. A thin, transparent cable ran from behind her ear down to something in her pocket. Strange to be hardwired like that. Paranoid.

"Are those custom-made?" Mia asked.

"Yeah. We've got a great hardware guy. Jason. He can transform a pile of junk into just about anything." She detached the cable and offered the glasses to Mia.

So like Claire to exchange tech instead of a hug.

The glasses didn't interest her, but Claire's bare face did. Her neutral expression lacked the almost combative excitement she'd exuded during college. Excitement to solve problems, to understand a malware attack, to prove her professors wrong. She looked older than she should have at thirty-four—furrows in her brow, lines at the edges of her serious brown eyes, and a pallor that had nothing to do with fashion. Stylistically seemed the same as before. No jewelry, no makeup, nails cut short, everything utilitarian. Her hair too short to pull back or style and too long to stay in place. She projected an almost aggressive disdain for her physical appearance. At eighteen, this had been quirky. At thirty-four, it read as unprofessional.

"How are you?" Mia asked.

"Fine." They exchanged glasses.

Claire gave her a critical once-over. "You look different."

"I do."

In college, Mia's scholarship barely covered tuition and lodging, so anything she earned at her part-time job went to food and data. She had no extra credits for makeup and clothes. Plus, she was hopeless with Earth fashion. The four seasons and their attendant changes in wardrobe flummoxed her. One day, a white jacket was fine. The next, it made the upper-crust girls around her giggle. She didn't have the time or inclination to attempt the elaborate braided hairstyles popular then, so she pulled her plain brown hair into a ponytail. What did it matter? She was there to get a degree and would never see most of her fellow students again. Earth was not a good look for her.

She was more attractive now, at least by New Canberra standards. Her hair was streaked with fashionable, rich auburn highlights, and what should have been her savings account draped and dangled from her body: Lucida glasses, Sandy Malone orange silk sundress, Talia platinum bangles, Benito Holmes boots, the latest PT bag in impractical white leather. She'd overdressed for the meeting—she knew it—but it felt so good to look nice for the first time in weeks.

While anyone in New Canberra would approve of her look, Claire wasn't anyone, and her expression delivered a verdict—guilty of frivolity and superficiality. Mia changed the unstated subject.

"How do you like New Canberra?"

Claire frowned.

"You have to admit it's better than New Beijing."

China's plan to upgrade Beijing began and ended with the addition of a prefix to the name. Claire hated the unstable infrastructure. Mia hated the crowding and the smells. Urine, sweat, rotting food, smoke, and other unidentifiable smells mixed in the damp air. Victoria's scent was clean, dry dirt baked to sterile perfection.

Claire deflated, dropping her chin to her hand. "It's not as bad as I thought it would be, but it still feels like being trapped in a huge shopping mall."

"I'm surprised you came. You always made fun of Victoria."

"My boss didn't give me much of a choice."

"I get that. If you wanted to keep your job, you'd have to move with it. How many people in the company?" Mia asked.

"Four."

"That's a bare-bones staff. If you're hoping to hire, you'll have a tough time. Everyone here from Earth is locked into contracts, and the number of native-born and unemployed is probably less than a hundred."

"You're unemployed. How'd you lose your job?" Claire asked.

The question she'd feared to hear from one of her former coworkers seemed perfectly natural as a non sequitur coming from Claire.

"I wish I could tell you. My contract is void, but most of the NDAs I signed are still binding. I can't talk about anything that happened at HQ."

Claire moved a few of the blinking boxes so they aligned perfectly. She was borderline obsessive-compulsive. "You fucked up."

"I didn't. I didn't do anything wrong. I'm…I was…the highest-performing social engineer at Han. I saved the company millions of credits and increased overall job satisfaction by twenty percent. The department won't make its numbers without me."

"So, what happened? You can speak freely. I didn't pick this place by accident. Those cameras…" She pointed to a cluster of corroded silver bulbs hanging limply from a pole atop the food dispenser. "Don't work. And this conversation shield may be ugly but it's highly effective. We might be in the most private spot on the planet right now."

The urge to defend her reputation was nearly overwhelming, an aching pressure in her chest. What could she tell Claire legally?

The answer was as obvious as the yellow umbrellas, and Mia wasn't sure whether to be embarrassed or elated she finally realized it. She couldn't talk about anything that had happened on headquarters property, but the room Erika took her to that awful day was technically *not* headquarters property. It was used to meet with outside vendors and others without clearance. What happened there wasn't covered by many of the NDAs.

"What is it?" Claire noticed her smile.

"I might have been framed." The heaviness in her chest vanished, as if the words weighed kilos each. "By my boss, Erika. She showed me a patent filed by Okafor Industries, an Earth corp. She claimed the tech was stolen from Han. She said I knew people at Okafor, and that I had a secret bank account in Zanzibar with half a million credits."

"Do you?"

"Of course not. I've barely got enough to pay three months' rent. I don't know if anyone from university went on to work at Okafor, but if they did, I'm not in touch with them."

"You think Erika sold the tech and needed a scapegoat."

Mia gnawed on her thumbnail, a nasty habit she hadn't indulged in since high school. "Maybe, but she might have just wanted to look good in front of the partners. She called the theft an unsolved crime. The whole encounter was so odd. She was all over the place, asking about work projects that had nothing to do with the patents, then accusing me, and going on about needing a team around her she could trust."

"What's with the Code 88?"

"How do you know about that? It's proprietary."

Claire snorted. "When did that ever stop me?"

True enough. Claire hacked into just about everything back in university days. Mia had wanted to be outraged, but she'd needed the pay-per-byte resources Claire provided for free.

"From what I can tell, it's a kind of catch-all to ban people from HQ properties. Possibly a way to handle security breaches because, as Erika pointed out, we don't have any. Not officially."

Claire, mercifully, didn't make a snide remark. "You never violated the terms of your employment agreement or sold company secrets?"

"No. You know me. I'm a rule follower. You made fun of me for always thumbing for tram fare at school when no one else did."

"I wouldn't call you a rule follower," Claire said. "More like someone afraid of getting caught. There's a difference. Give me your glasses."

"Why?" Mia asked, though she handed them over.

Claire pulled a translucent piece of film from the right temple of Mia's glasses and placed it carefully on one of her own screens.

Mia frowned. "What's that?"

"Part of this." She twirled a finger over the wires and boxes. "One of Jason's creations. Conversation shield, transmission jammer, and veracity detector. You didn't lie about anything important."

Mia stared at the mess on the table, which suddenly looked a lot less like a freshman science experiment and more like the contraption Claire built to siphon free data access from their apartment's network.

"You used a veracity detector on me without my permission?" Mia found she was standing, though she had no recollection of working her way off the half-circle bench. Unauthorized use of a veracity detector was illegal, and authorized use required obtaining consent. Mia had a special hatred of the devices. What little privacy she enjoyed on this planet was mostly in her own head, and no one trespassed there.

She snatched her bag from the bench. "Good luck with the gravity."

Claire's eyebrows rose. "Wait! Lucas wouldn't interview you unless I could prove you weren't a criminal."

"Interview me? What are you talking about?"

"I want Summit Security to hire you. We've got no clients, and you've got no credits. You can help…" Claire tumbled her hands around each other. "Get things going. None of us can figure out the bureaucracy here. Every form we submit gets kicked back. Lucas won't admit anything's wrong, but we need to get the business up and running. Soon."

Standing half in the shade of the umbrella and half in the blistering sun, Mia struggled to contain her temper and assimilate this new, untrustworthy version of Claire. She hadn't realized she *had* trusted her—until now. Their five years together in student housing started awkwardly but had settled into something comfortable and safe.

Claire began to disassemble the machine infesting the red table, nestling the pieces into the thick foam in the black suitcase, checking the placement of each three times. She did that whenever she was stressed. Pillows on the couch, fruit in the bowl, chairs around the kitchen table— all were subject to a ritual that calmed Claire before midterms and finals.

Claire was stressed. *Their business must be in trouble.*

Mia recalled the questions Claire had asked. Nothing inappropriate, though Mia regretted admitting she only had three months' rent. As much as she'd like to fling the suitcase over the railing and watch it shatter on the rocks below, she couldn't turn down a job interview. It was entirely possible Erika had somehow blacklisted her across every sector and no one would hire her—no one but an ignorant, newly-arrived, badly-conceived, private security firm from Earth.

"I don't know anything about running a small business," Mia said.

Claire stopped fiddling. "You know about Victoria and New Canberra. That's enough. Come to the office Friday. Meet Lucas. He can tell you more."

If Mia stood on principle, she'd be standing in the desert with all her belongings in boxes beside her when she was evicted.

"Fine. Send me the address."

Claire smiled and Mia noted that she still hadn't gotten her teeth straightened. A small thing, but it put her at ease. Maybe Claire hadn't changed as much as she feared.

Chapter Three

Mia was overdressed for the job interview.

She stood in the sun and dust in a hand-made burgundy suit—part of the wardrobe Erika forced on her after they were both promoted. The woman had thrown outfits at Mia like she was a shabby couch in need of a new slipcover. While most of them were dull and conservative—and suspiciously ill-fitting given her measurements were on file—this suit was perfect. She wore it today to feel powerful and in control.

Coveralls would have been more appropriate.

The dilapidated plasticrete warehouse in front of her was at least thirty years old, making it one of the older buildings in the city. The ten-meter-high flat façade was punctuated by strange porthole windows up by the roofline. Stains leaked from the round, rusted frames, giving the building a sad, weepy look. She couldn't believe Weber, the owner of this sector, hadn't fined the business and forced them to clean up, but development was sparse out here and the lots surrounding the structure were empty. Thus, no one to complain.

She picked her way carefully down the gravel path, hoping whoever designed the building had put in a bug-repelling perimeter. The front door looked to have been recently installed, a matte black slab of metal more substantial than the building itself. To the left of it, a blank screen flared to life and Claire's face appeared, shrouded in darkness as it had been when she called Mia's home.

"Palm the screen," she said. "I've still got your print from our old apartment."

Claire vanished, replaced by an outline of a hand.

Claire hoarded data, but had she really saved everything from their shared server in college? Mia pressed her hand to the glass and the door hissed open, expelling cool air. Apparently, she had. Mia would process the full implication of this later.

She entered, pausing to let her eyes adjust to the dimness. A long hall, sparsely lit by a few dangling overhead lights, led to another solid black door. It swung open and Claire appeared ghostlike in the gloom, beckoning her into a room no brighter than the corridor.

"Welcome to Summit Security."

A windowless office occupied what must have been the entire back half of the building. Drab, dark carpet covered the floor. The walls were bare plasticrete, one lined with black cabinets. The folding tables and chairs were cheap metal and plastic, something to be used once for a weekend event then recycled. Two tables, pushed together in the room's center, were covered in a jumble of wires and tools. Was this where Jason the amazing tech guy built the veracity detector Claire used to raid her thoughts? In the back, a four meter-square cube nestled into the right-hand corner, possibly a private office. The only redeeming feature of the cave-like room was the high ceiling—the full height of the building—though without proper lighting it was like standing at the bottom of a well.

"Nice place," Mia said.

Claire walked to the messiest table, sat heavily on the squeaky chair beside it, and hung her glasses on a charging rod. "You're still mad at me about the veracity detector. You might not be if you search your name." She typed *Mia Julian* into an unsecured window. "You were one of the top searches in Han sector earlier this month. No one knows what the Code 88 means, but that isn't stopping your colleagues from speculating. IP theft, property theft, improper use of company resources, drug dealing, and animal trafficking. That last one surprised me."

Mia gaped at the text, which Claire helpfully enlarged. She hadn't searched her name in years, not since a paper she authored was given an honorable mention in the New England Journal of Social Engineering. For a few weeks she'd edged out another *Mia Julian*—a woman's lacrosse coach from San Diego—then, to her relief, settled back into obscurity.

Now, she had a rush of the same primitive fear she experienced on the climbing wall at the gym—that the next handhold wouldn't be there, even though it always was. That's how the wall was designed. That's how her life had been designed, too. A tough upward climb, but if she stayed fit and alert and reached as far as she could, the next handhold would be there.

Not this time.

She was hanging, nothing above her, just a long drop down. Recruiters ignored her. Friends blocked her ID. They'd read all the search results Claire displayed. Did they believe it? Had some of them written it?

"There are photos as well." Claire pulled up a dozen puzzling images of Mia in bars and restaurants with men and women she'd never seen before.

"I don't—"

"I know." Claire cut her off. "They've been altered. All those people are senior execs at Okafor Industries, the Earth corp you were supposed to have sold IP to." Before Mia could respond, Claire revealed a photo of Mia holding a puffy, startled chicken.

"The Six don't allow birds here, right? You've allegedly been importing fertilized eggs and hatching chicks. That's courtesy of a guy named Phil. Says you had him over to your place and the chicken ran out of your closet."

This false memory transfixed Mia. She'd never seen a live chicken, let alone held one. The ridiculousness of it threatened to send her into a fit of giggles. Those weren't her hands. She'd never had laser nails. Did people actually hold chickens? Where was the background? It certainly wasn't her place, and Phil had never been anywhere near her apartment, despite pestering her for years to go out with him. Asshole was finally getting his revenge.

"Mia." Claire poked her shoulder with a stylus.

"Sorry. This is surreal." She pulled a chair over and sat beside Claire. "No one would believe I raised chickens or had drinks at Sticks and Stones with that guy. That's what I don't understand. Erika can't prove I did anything wrong. On the contrary. Anyone who reviewed my records could see where I actually was at those times." *The one advantage of living with twenty-seven-hours-a-day surveillance,* she refrained from adding.

"That's the clever part," Claire said. "I researched one of these composite images to figure out where and when it was supposed to be. You recognized the restaurant, Sticks and Stones. That's in Andaman sector. Erika would know it would be hard for Han to get images from bars in other sectors. Maybe what she does is search your calendar, find times you left Han sector, then finds out when executives from Okafor were in New Canberra, and—this is genius—she alters your records from your university days on Earth to give you ties to these people. Records on Victoria might be locked down but things are much less secure on Earth. You know him?" She poked to a grinning guy in a black and white suit.

"No," Mia said.

"Guess what?"

Claire rearranged the documents and Mia recognized a paper she'd written in sophomore year for a business ethics class. Now, bizarrely, it featured a co-author and read as if it were a team project.

"Who's Kelvin Moss? I never wrote a paper with him." She was viscerally angry in a way she hadn't been when faced with Erika's vague threats and accusations. Her university record was spotless and not a part of Victoria politics.

"That guy in the bad suit is Kelvin Moss, and I know you didn't write a paper with him. I've got a backup copy of our old apartment data storage unit, and," she grinned, "all your student records from New Beijing University. I grabbed a copy when they were upgrading the system right before we graduated. They left the default password active for a few hours. Wish I had more time. I got your records and mine before they locked it down."

"You have all my data? Everything I had to submit for admission to New Beijing U?"

"Yeah, and everything from our years there. Want to see? I'd have sent it to you, but the Victoria filters would have caught it."

Mia's chest tightened. The university had asked for an obscene amount of information—more than they required for students from Earth. She'd never been comfortable having so much of her history in one place. Like that joke about blindfolded people trying to decipher an elephant and assuming whatever bit they felt defined the whole, she trusted that anyone seeing a few of her records would assume she was a typical child of overeducated parents. Someone with access to all of it might figure out that she wasn't typical at all.

Claire, oblivious to Mia's anxiety, hunched over the screen, diving in and out of the data.

Much of what appeared on the screen—high school transcripts, GPA, work history—was banal and easily accessible, but other documents were extremely confidential. Intelligence scores, financial records, medical and psychiatric history. Had Claire read any of it?

Mia poked futilely on the red delete X's. "You've got to get rid of all this right now. If any of the Six find out you have this data you'll lose your permit."

"They won't. I know how to cover my tracks."

An image of someone walking down a dark hallway appeared on the screen, obliterating the pieces of Mia's life.

Claire leaned forward. "Lucas is coming." She whispered. "Hear him out. We can help you, and you can help us."

The office door opened and Lucas entered. He was taller than average, thin and muscular with short, dark brown hair. Probably somewhere between his mid-thirties and mid-fifties. No way to be sure. People from Earth tended to look older than they were. He'd adopted the Victoria's business dress style—short-sleeve shirt, vest, and loose dray-fiber pants. He was good-looking, in a distinctly worn and rough Earth way, and didn't appear to be modded. On Victoria, there was no social stigma against men getting mods, and everyone was loaded with credits, so the male population was surgically blessed with smooth wrinkle-free skin, straight noses, white teeth, strong chins, and thick hair. The thin, pale scar running down Lucas's cheek could be removed in five minutes. Mia wondered if he'd fall into the trap of easy perfection offered here.

"You must be Mia. I'm Lucas Dunn." He took off his glasses, revealing calm, disinterested, dark blue eyes, faint dark circles beneath. He took in everything from her shoes to her data glasses in one quick glance, then held out his hand. Handshakes weren't popular now on Victoria—not after the nanobot incident—but he wouldn't know that. His hand was cooler than it should have been given he'd just come inside.

"Mia *Julian*," she said. They weren't on a first-name basis.

He glanced at the screen with her personal data on it and gave Claire a sharp look. She shrugged and flicked off the screen.

"We'll talk in my office." He gestured to the cube in back.

His office was dark and gray like the rest of the place, but a faintly luminous glow ceiling gave the room the feel of dawn breaking over a steely sea, the black desk forlornly adrift. The ceiling brightened when Lucas crossed the threshold. No art adorned the stark walls, neither were there windows, just two chairs, the desk, and one tall black cabinet. He took the chair behind the desk and it whined and adjusted itself to his attentive posture.

Mia sat on the chill metal chair across from him. "I'm not sure what position I'm being interviewed for. Claire didn't give me many details."

"You aren't being interviewed. Claire has been hounding me to get someone to help out, but we've got things covered."

Mia had done some research of her own during the past few days. Summit Security was in limbo, their permit to operate ensnared in sector bureaucracy. "Why did Claire trick me into taking a veracity test and bring me in, if you weren't hiring?"

"She insisted on both. As you know, she's stubborn. Given your recent…*notoriety*…she wanted to prove you weren't a thief, or…" The corner of his mouth twitched. "A chicken farmer."

Mia leaned back heavily and the chair groaned. "I just found out about all that. I hadn't thought to search myself. Now I understand why I'm having trouble getting a job. None of it is true."

"I know," he said. "Jason's veracity detector is very good and Claire has documents supporting a less criminal version of you. Unfortunately, rumors aren't the problem. The official reason you were fired—breach of contract—has been leaked to the partners in every sector."

"Breach of contract? That's what the code means? How'd you find out?"

"That's what it means in your case. Claire tracked it down. Normally, they'd send the offending employee back to Earth, but they can't do that to you, can they?"

"No. I was born here."

Lucas nodded. "One of the first, and the first extraterrestrial I've met."

Mia winced. It was true, but not an advantage here or on Earth. She didn't have many peers. The six corporate owners of the planet made birth control more or less mandatory for its contract employees once the colony was established and stable. Her parents were pioneers, flying into the unknown and creating a city where nothing existed but sand and bugs. The children of the builders were anomalies, and getting rid of one of them had required a great deal of effort by Erika.

"Why you?" Lucas asked when Mia remained silent. "That's what I can't figure out. You were a rising star at Han. This wasn't a spontaneous act. It would have taken Ms. Brunhoff months to fabricate a case against you. At Itek, this would have been the setup for blackmail, not termination. If Ms. Brunhoff wanted to frame someone for crimes she committed, why not chose a poorly performing employee? Someone with motivation and who needed credits."

Mia checked the corners of the room for cameras and didn't see any, though that didn't mean anything. "May I speak privately?"

"Yes. The room and the building are shielded and I'm not recording this."

She believed him, though her instinct to trust made little sense after what Claire did. "Erika and I hadn't been getting along for a while. Once we were promoted to the executive floors, she started to give me projects that weren't aligned with the core principles of social engineering. My mandate was to create a positive and productive work environment and contribute to the long-term health of the company and employees. She and the partners had other goals, many of which weren't positive. We'd reached an impasse. I did what she wanted, but my success rate dropped." Mia thought of the sails that she'd replaced with poles. She'd intentionally caused suffering to hustle people into the building two minutes faster. Her professors at New Beijing U would have given her an F for that.

Lucas watched as she spoke, nodding slowly, a human veracity detector. Was she passing?

"Erika also wanted me to report on things I'd seen and heard on the executive floors, which would have been a breach of both of our contracts," Mia said. "Maybe she was planning to blackmail me, but something happened in regard to the Okafor patent, and she needed someone to blame quickly. I was already set up, if you're right that she'd been working on it for months."

"From what Claire can glean, she was." Lucas took a stylus from his vest pocket, drew a circle on the desk screen, and slashed it with three lines. The sectors?

"Claire can restore the documents Ms. Brunhoff falsified at New Beijing University, thanks to her backup. This should help your employment opportunities in other sectors. It certainly won't hurt. Six months from now, anyone doing a background check will be mystified as to why Han thought you sold secrets to Okafor."

"Why would you help me?"

Lucas met her curious gaze. He'd not put his glasses back on—odd and verging on improper, given the circumstances. Who was this strange man who'd come so far to start a business that would certainly fail? His expression held a mix of determination and resignation.

"We do need help getting this business up and running. Your bureaucracy is worse than any I've run across. I'm hesitant to trust this job to a stranger. However, a stranger whose future success is tied to the success of this firm is a different matter."

"Are you offering me a job?"

"It wouldn't be…" He grimaced, closing his eyes and holding his forehead as if overcome by a sudden, intense migraine.

"Mr. Dunn?"

"A moment," he said gruffly, his breathing slow and labored.

Mia froze. Should she text Claire?

Just as she was about to, Lucas removed his hand from his brow, the circles under his eyes darker, and the rest of his face paler.

"Ms. Julian, I'm offering you a contract job as…whatever you want to call yourself. The pay isn't good. We'll do our best to remediate your records, and you'll do your best to get this business off the ground." He gestured to the door. "Claire has the contract."

Mia left the office, taking one last look at Lucas. He leaned back in his chair, eyes again closed, motionless. She closed the door quietly.

"Thank god," Claire said as Mia joined her. "I hoped he'd change his mind if I got you in here. I told him I wasn't going to do any more admin work."

"Is Mr. Dunn okay? I think he's got a migraine."

Claire ignored the question, instead handing her a text-heavy screen. "Can you start Monday? I can't get business-grade connectivity until we're a business. It's been like wading through molasses this past month."

"I've never done anything like this."

"Oh, come on. You've got a master's degree in social engineering. Clearly some of those skills apply to our situation. If it was just filling out forms, Jason and I could figure it out, but there are people involved and they need to be…" She made her hands into fists and twisted them back and forth like she was wringing a customer service person's neck.

"I've done some of that," Mia said, smiling. "Metaphorically of course."

She read the generic employment contract. It was nowhere near as binding as what she'd had to sign at Han. She could quit anytime. The salary was low, less than she'd made in her work-study job in college, but it would cover rent. Though the situation was far from ideal, Mia had to do this. She *was* unemployable. Maybe Lucas and Claire could help. The records wouldn't fix themselves, and the longer they existed with false data, the worse the damage to her reputation. If she could save some credits, she could get back to Earth and start the interview process with another corporation. Triage was the best she could hope for right now.

She glanced around the dark room. She wouldn't enjoy spending time here, but on the other hand, her well-lit apartment was becoming another kind of prison.

A hot palm on cold glass marked the beginning of her new, temporary, career.

Chapter Four

The decrepit warehouse seemed less ominous when Mia arrived Monday. She wasn't proud to be working in a shack like this, but Han tower hadn't been looking so shiny the past few months either.

The front door opened at her approach, and Claire again waited at the end of the hall.

"Hi!" Mia's bright morning voice ricocheted down the dim corridor.

Claire mumbled something in response. Back in the day, she hadn't perked up until after noon.

Mia's anger at Claire for giving her a veracity test had faded. She'd spent half the weekend searching her name online, and the other half trying to forget all the nastiness with the help of some Baby Janes. The professionally altered photos were likely commissioned by Erika, as were anonymous posts implying she had a gambling problem, but her former coworkers had chimed in with alarming enthusiasm. Mia was aloof, secretive, unfriendly, and "definitely up to something" according to a "friend" who'd been "handed ridiculous excuses" as to why Mia wouldn't let her come up to her apartment.

I don't even think she lives in Equinox Towers. Whenever I met her, she was standing out in front. Could have come from anywhere. We caught a pod back from a work event, and I asked if I could pop in and freshen up before part two of the night, and she claimed she was having hardwood floors installed and everything was torn up. Another time, I didn't want to deal with my roommate and asked if I could stay over (after we'd been out drinking), and she said she was expecting someone. As if. She never dates anyone for more than a night. The idea that she is raising chickens is way more plausible than her having a secret boyfriend or girlfriend.

That was probably Leslie in Human Factors and loosely based on actual events. What surprised Mia was Leslie's simmering resentment over what seemed like a nonissue. Mia valued her private space and never had people over. What was the big deal?

What was worse were the outright lies. People who claimed to have seen her acting out the seven deadly sins both on and off headquarters property. People said they'd done things with her, and to her.

She'd stopped reading, knocked back a shot of bourbon, and acknowledged that Claire had gone to a lot of trouble to prove Mia wasn't an asshole. That Mia had a long and troubled history with veracity detectors was something no one needed to know.

Mia made her way down the corridor to the office. With the overhead lights off, the room hovered in a state of perpetual twilight. Desk lamps spilled cool white-blue circles onto tables and the floor, stepping stones of optimism in the gloom. Claire sat at her desk, scrubbing through a complex program.

"Can we please have some more light?" Mia asked.

"Don't start," Claire said.

"What?"

"Social engineering the office. This is my space, and this is how I like it." She pointed to a newly clean table across the room from hers. "There's your station. Cover it with glow balls if you want, but don't redecorate anything else. Now, go sit down. I need to get you set up."

Mia padded across the dingy carpet. She'd dressed appropriately today, in a long loose tan dress and flats. Something she'd wear to get coffee on a sleepy Sunday morning when she didn't want to attract attention.

The cheap metal chair creaked under her.

Claire, who'd followed her over, tapped the center of a wall-mounted screen. "Look here."

Mia did, and a blue laser flashed across her face.

"Hands on the desk," Claire said.

Mia pressed her palms flat, and the desk screen pulsed briefly with white light.

"Say your name and then keep talking."

Mia extolled the virtues of her favorite restaurant until Claire told her to stop. So far, all standard security procedures.

Claire pulled a black, gun-shaped thing from her pocket.

"What's that?" Mia asked.

"We need to chip you."

Mia balled her fists. "No way. That's not legal here."

"It doesn't matter. I have to do it. Our weapons and security systems look for this. If they don't find it, they lock up. Or worse."

"Why not just—"

"Whatever you're going to suggest, we already thought of it, and we still need the chip. It's completely passive and won't set off any alarms. We've all got them. You can't work here without it."

"Fine." Mia offered her left hand. Claire pressed the device against the fat part of her palm beneath her thumb and pulled the trigger.

"Ow!" Mia jerked away. "No anesthesia?"

"No," Claire said unapologetically. "We got the cheap model."

Mia licked away a tiny drop of blood. Claire put the gun away and came back with a small black cube.

"Put your hand near it. I want to make sure the chip works."

A small, faint green dot pulsed once, then faded.

"Again."

Mia waved her hand over it again, and a red light did the same.

"Good," Claire said. "You're set." She returned to her own desk, adjusted the large screen to block any view of Mia, and began to type.

Mia's own screen was blank.

"Do you have a checklist of what needs to be done? Can you give me access to the relevant files? Maybe let me see the business plan?"

"Lucas has all that. Ask him when he gets in."

It was already past ten and she couldn't count on headachy Lucas to arrive anytime soon.

"How about some background materials? Beginning security primers? I don't know much about this field."

"I'll send you what I've got from Itek."

An icon appeared on her screen. Mia clicked it and found a disorganized mélange of memos, training videos, textbooks, equipment inventory lists, and catalogues. Claire wasn't being very helpful considering she'd worked so hard to get her hired.

Mia picked a video with the promising title of "Physical Security for Beginners," then ran her hands back and forth on the arms of the chair, searching for the button that would reprogram it to fit her body, but there were no controls of any kind. She'd taken much for granted at Han; the transition to a low-budget office wasn't going to be easy.

A few hours later the door banged open and a man backed in, straining under the weight of a plastic bin full of what looked like bits of tech pulled from a recycler. He dropped it onto the table in the center of the room, then started when he noticed her.

"You're Mia? Claire's roommate?" he asked.

"Former roommate. You must be Jason."

Happy for a break, she joined him.

"I am. Jason Garza. Nice to meet you."

He gave her a quick, strong handshake, then drew back. He was tall, with short, dark hair. Large brown eyes, inquisitive but guarded, held her gaze for only a moment before he returned his attention to the table.

"You started today?" he asked. "Claire get you set up?"

Claire, wearing mirrored glasses and huge headphones appropriate for a shuttle landing site, didn't react to her name being mentioned.

"More or less. I'm not quite sure what I'm supposed to be doing."

"You and me both." Jason began to unpack the bin, which, judging from the dust on the wires and metal scraps, could have indeed been scavenged. He was around her age, mid-thirties, but had the physique and awkward movements of a high school freshman experiencing a major growth spurt.

Mia scanned the mess on the table, hoping to find a conversation topic. In the center, a hollow black rectangle rose slowly from inside the bottom of a clear, quarter-meter square chamber.

"A bio-plastic 0-prototyper. I've never seen one so compact."

Jason risked a quick glance in her direction and nodded.

She looked more carefully at everything else. The hardware catalogue she'd begun to study after finishing the security training video provided a new lens to view what she would have dismissed as junk a few hours ago. Many of the items matched the 3D product samples. This was the fun part of the job—learning something new and mapping it onto reality.

"Are these parts of a Peterson Sonic Stunner and an Axis portable laser room monitor?" she asked.

Jason stopped unpacking the bin. "Yes. That's right. How'd you know?"

"Claire sent me some catalogues. I've never worked in security before so I'm trying to catch up."

Jason held up a disk with a honeycomb pattern etched into the surface. "You knew this was from the stunner?"

Was it odd that she'd known? This was the un-fun part—trying to figure out what an average person would retain. Over-explaining usually caused more problems, so she opted for distraction. "Are you trying to fix them?"

"No. I'm using the parts to make a gun. The room monitor has a laser, which I need for targeting. And this," he pointed to the stunner, "has the power. I can't get bullets here, but I can buy diamond-edged, drill bit replacement teeth." He poked a small, triangular piece of metal. "Not ideal, but they'll do."

She took a deep breath and reminded herself where he'd been until last month. Earth was a dangerous place. Sheer dumb luck kept her from being mugged, or worse, during her first few months in New Beijing. She'd wandered, oblivious, through some of the most dangerous areas of the city. Jason was having the same experience, in reverse, expecting an attack that would never come.

"Projectile weapons are illegal here. That thing you're trying to make could get you deported and Summit Security closed down. Even CorSec only carries stunners," she said.

He smiled. "Don't worry. I know I wouldn't get this two meters out the door before one of those drone things that patrol the city knocked me flat. This'll never leave the building. Once I get it working, I'll disassemble it and use the parts for something else. I've got to keep up my skills. My job…" He shook his head. "Part of my former job, on Earth, was not only to keep up-to-date on technology, but investigate how technology could be repurposed."

"This is just an exercise?"

"Exactly." He picked up a long, slender rod and used it to pop open a compartment on the room monitor. "Weapons aren't my specialty, actually. The bigger challenge is detecting and disabling systems that control illegal weapons and surveillance."

"You made the veracity detector Claire used on me." Mia tried not to sound angry.

"What are you talking about?" Jason looked genuinely puzzled.

"Black box, this big, full of little boxes. Plus, a sensor she snuck onto my glasses."

Jason tossed down the rod. "She didn't." He strode over to one of the black cabinets and pulled the door open, revealing three empty shelves. "God damn it. I didn't think I'd have to lock these."

A jumble of equipment surrounded Claire's desk. From it, Jason extracted the familiar black box. He set it gently on the worktable and popped it open.

"Everything's dusty!" He looked at Mia accusingly. "This wasn't meant to be taken out of the building."

"I didn't agree to be tested. Claire told me it was a conversation shield."

Jason rubbed the equipment gently with a cleaning cloth. "I don't know what's wrong with her," he muttered. "She'd never have snuck into my lab at Itek and taken equipment. Ever since we got here, it's like everyone's forgotten the rules."

Once the device was clean, repacked, and shelved, Jason perched on a stool and began working on the room monitor. With a tool in hand, his awkwardness disappeared, his movements assured and precise. If implants hadn't been outlawed, Mia suspected he'd have screwdrivers for fingers.

"You were a social engineer?" he asked.

The "were" stung. "Yes, and hope to be again," she replied.

He tugged a circuit board free and disconnected the wires that tethered it to the interior. "How'd you end up here? I know you went to college with Claire, but that's about it."

Not everyone in the small office knew her story? What a relief. "I got on my boss's bad side, and she faked some evidence against me and got me fired." It was getting easier to say.

Jason nodded, seeming to take this as an ordinary chain of events. "Lucas and Claire should be able to help. Faking evidence is a tough job, especially on a planet like this."

He didn't need a veracity detector to believe her story. She liked Jason.

"Would you mind?" he nodded toward something that looked like big plastic tweezers. "Hold the board with those? I'm out of hands."

She wasn't particularly dexterous but did her best, suspecting this might be how a shy engineer made friends.

They both started when Lucas banged through the door a few minutes later. He gave Jason and her a look before he continued, without comment, to his office. Jason took a deep breath, and the smile that had begun to form as he worked faded.

She took the cue and stood. "If you ever need an extra pair of hands, I'd be happy to help."

Jason's face lit up again. "That would be great."

She hurried to catch Lucas. "Can we meet?" she asked.

A few heartbeats passed before he replied. "Yes. Come in."

He reclined in his chair, screens off, glow ceiling barely lit.

"I'm sorry to bother you Mr. Dunn, but Claire couldn't tell me what I'm supposed to be doing."

"Call me Lucas. I left Mr. Dunn on Earth."

This was a command, not an invitation.

"What do you need me to do?"

"Everything," he said. "We have a sponsor and a permit to operate and this office. That's it. There are dozens of forms we need to fill out and get approved before we can do any client work. We need insurance. We need…" He rubbed his temples with both hands. "I don't know what we need. You figure it out. I'll give you access to all the company files and a credits account. Make it happen, and as inexpensively as possible."

Mia knew nothing about Weber sector, but it couldn't be that different from Han.

"I'll do my best."

"Do it fast."

The folder Lucas sent to her desk screen held only a handful of documents. The business plan—which should have been groundbreaking to earn a sponsorship from Weber—was nothing more than a couple hundred words of generic text. Any security-related work that one or two people could easily do was listed as a service Summit would offer. Executive protection. Data protection. Asset protection. Intrusion detection. Access control. Privacy screens. Home monitoring. It read like the table of contents of the dull security primer Claire sent her.

Why had Weber sponsored this venture?

The scant information the team's VR 826 immigration forms contained—height, weight, birth date, palm prints—was more than she knew about her coworkers now. Lucas Dunn was born in 2103. That made him forty-two. She gauged he'd lost a couple kilos since he was weighed when he arrived. Jason Garza was thirty-seven. Claire was Mia's age, thirty-five. Mikey Chen, forty-three, wasn't tall, but weighed a hefty 110 kilos and was the only one who'd smiled for the arrival scan. The rest of them looked like they'd come for a funeral, not to start their dream business in the wealthiest city on any planet.

Mia leaned back in the squeaky chair and rubbed her eyes. She faced a conundrum. She could do a deep dive, right now, and find out everything about her new team. Where they grew up. Socio-economic status.

Parents. Siblings. Schooling. Employment history. Awards, patents, fines, partners, children.

Would that help the business succeed? No. Any information not freely given wouldn't help communications, trust, or team building. She'd only been at Summit Security four hours and needed to relax and let the facts diffuse naturally. Like dust, they'd fall through the cracks and eventually land on her desk.

Mia should have done the deep dive.

Forget team building and the gradual dissemination of information. A week into the maze of New Canberra's complicated forms, Mia hit a question that slapped her from her assumptions about Lucas and Summit security. What was the firm owner's former position and job title?

She'd assumed Lucas was a mid-level manager in a dead-end job who used family connections to finagle a permit from Weber and brought his direct reports with him. That couldn't have been further from the truth.

She dashed outside to intercept Claire when the cams showed her arriving—just past noon as usual.

"What are you doing out here?" Claire asked as she clambered out of a pod.

"Come," Mia said, indicating the thin sidewalk running along the shady side of the building. She didn't know if Summit had audio sensors out here but fuck it, she needed answers.

Claire examined the gray wall. "What's wrong? Did you find a device? I told Jason we needed more cameras out here."

"Nothing's wrong with the building. Look at this. The number one search result for Lucas Dunn." Mia held out a screen showing Lucas standing on the steps of a stately hotel on Earth, arm draped casually over the shoulders of stunning woman with silver hair, jet black skin, and a form-fitting magenta dress.

"Who's that?" Claire asked.

"Letitia Doherty? Famous singer?"

"Don't know her."

Claire could be maddening ignorant of pop culture.

"Yes, you do. She's had a dozen hits and won every award possible, and co-starred in *Rising Tide* last summer."

Claire shrugged. "So?"

"What is she doing with Lucas?"

"I have no idea. I don't know anything about Lucas's social life. He's my boss, that's it."

"Speaking of which, I assumed he was an ambitious manager who came here to make credits, but no. He was a partner at Itek and in charge of Internal Security for all of North America. He was earning a seven-figure salary and had the title everyone drools over. Or, at least the title my boss was obsessed with. Plus, according to numerous reputable publications, he's a minor celebrity. Not your average partner. Controversial. Intent on rooting out intra-company crime at the highest levels. After work, he found time to date actresses, models, artists, and other partners. Then suddenly, he resigned to, quote, pursue other interests. Really?"

Claire remained silent, arms folded, glasses on mirror.

"Then, there's this."

Mia zoomed in on the image of Lucas and Letitia. It had been taken just six months ago, but Lucas looked fifteen years younger, his face unlined and holo-star handsome. The man on Victoria was a two-dimensional shadow of that vibrant person. Whatever happened to him, it happened fast.

"He got space sick on the way here. I did too."

"Did you lose twenty kilos in three weeks? What's really wrong with him?"

"Nothing." Claire said it like a challenge, and Mia almost laughed.

"You want me to pull up more images? I'd swear he wasn't the same man if it weren't for the eyes. He's lost more weight since you arrived."

"Lucas's body mass index and personal life is none of our business. You're here to help get Summit up and running. Do that and don't worry about what any of us used to look like back on Earth." Claire pushed past her and disappeared around the corner.

Well, that confirmed it. Lucas was in a bad way and Claire knew why. Whatever caused him to lose weight, it *had* affected his job performance and still was. It may have driven him to quit or to be asked to leave. Despite centuries of research, there were still many incurable diseases. She didn't relish the idea of watching Lucas waste away before her eyes. Neither, apparently, did the upper management at Itek.

Stop. Correlation does not imply causation.

Lucas was a partner. He dated famous women. He left Itek. He is now very thin. These things may or may not be related. That said, something was clearly wrong, yet he managed to get past the medical screeners on Victoria. *He must have powerful friends, somewhere.*

Did this new information change things? No. Sure, she was curious about Lucas and what caused his fall from partner heights, and a little in awe of the man who'd escorted Letitia Doherty to an event, but that man was a world away from the owner of Summit Security here on Victoria. She needed this job, needed to get Summit up and running, and to do whatever she could to keep them all afloat while Claire fixed her records.

Everything else was a distraction.

Chapter Five

Getting Summit Security up and running turned out to be one of the more difficult projects Mia had ever undertaken. The terrible bureaucracy Lucas and Claire cited was real. Mia drowned in forms, not only from Weber, Summit's sponsor, but from Optima as well. She'd rarely interacted with the Optima Corporation. Named after the system's sun, and formed by the Six to manage shared assets like the MMARV drones, the streets between the sectors in New Canberra, and the strataport, Optima arbitrated disputes distant from the upper floors of Han.

The worst part of the process was discovering that any charisma she imagined she possessed had actually emanated from her executive-floor ID card. At Han, the answer to her questions had always been, *Yes, of course*. Now, low-level admins watched reality holos or picked over the remains of a seafood salad as they authorized her documents. It was painfully clear she wasn't interesting or funny or someone they'd like to get to know. She wasn't offered coffee or tea or a stim soda. She didn't go to the head of the line; her forms wouldn't be expedited. The sparkly burgundy and gold pass, not her sparkling personality, had generated the attentive service she'd come to expect from—

Underlings. That's what I am now.

No rank was lower in the New Canberran social hierarchy than hers. She gritted her teeth and reminded herself this job was temporary.

Near the end of week four, she sat on an intentionally uncomfortable metal bench in a Weber office far from Ring One, no longer sure what she was waiting for. On the far wall, a green light blinked, and five white cards slid from a slot and clattered into a metal bin beneath it. Curious, she went to examine them and discovered the culmination of her efforts: Summit's employee ID cards.

She was elated—until she saw they required activation by the business owner.

She'd been avoiding Lucas, which hadn't been hard. He wasn't in the office much and answered most questions via text. Knowing what he'd been discomfited her. Partners were a different species, with different motivations and expectations. Also, though she'd never admit it, she was uneasy around sick people.

Thanks to the pre-arrival screening and the custom daily pill everyone took to address any deficiencies, the population of Victoria was unusually healthy. College at New Beijing U on Earth was a time of many firsts—first cold and flu among them. She'd panicked when she'd gotten a fever in the dead of winter, convinced the thermostat was broken. Claire had to explain what was likely happening and shook her head as Mia admitted she'd never been ill. Having to sit shoulder to shoulder with hacking, wheezing people in every classroom and restaurant infuriated her. Why didn't the door scanners keep them out?

Proud as she was of picking her way across Victoria's spider web of regulations, Mia hesitated before knocking on his door. Was Lucas contagious? He couldn't be.

"Yes?" His impatience drilled through the hollow plasticrete.

"I've got our ID badges. You need to thumb them."

It took so long for him to answer she almost knocked again.

"Come in."

She kept her face impassive as she glanced at his. *Lucas Dunn. Itek partner. What happened to you?*

"You should have received the final versions of all the permits by now, and once you activate these badges, we can start taking clients."

Lucas held a thin arm out and took the envelope she offered.

"Sit."

Was she a dog? They didn't have dogs on Victoria, but she'd grown up with them anyway, thanks to holos.

"This didn't take as long as I expected," he said.

"Optima didn't expect me to show up in person. I don't think they've ever had anyone actually wait in their waiting room. Only one way to get rid of me."

The badges changed from white to light gray after Lucas thumbed them, and faces appeared, black dots slowly coalescing.

"I haven't met Mikey yet," Mia said as his beefy face resolved. Claire mentioned he was teaching martial arts somewhere in the sector as a way to keep in shape.

"He'll be in once we've got a job."

"Speaking of which, what next?" Most of the business plan, if it could even be called that, couldn't be implemented in New Canberra, seeing as it was taken verbatim from an Earth proposal and referenced organizations that didn't exist on Victoria.

"What next indeed, Ms. Julian. Put your social engineering brain to work on this. Find someone with a problem to which we are the solution."

"I'll need some help with that. I'm not sure people here need us." She'd put aside her doubts about whether or not this venture could succeed while wrestling with the bureaucracy, but here they were again, spreading in front of her like cracks in the desert floor.

Lucas rested his chin on his hands and stared at her intently. Why didn't he wear glasses when they met? That was standard protocol. Imagining the handsome man from the past transposed onto this wasted one made her uncomfortable. Handsome Lucas was still there, in those eyes. The rest of him urged her to run away.

"What motivates people to come to Victoria?" he asked.

The answer popped out before Mia could censor herself. "Greed."

Lucas nodded. "Good. What do greedy people want? More. Let's offer them more security. They're like you, brainwashed into thinking this planet is perfectly safe. They don't know more is possible. Let's tell them it is. We can't do much about the city infrastructure, so let's concentrate on personal security and privacy."

"I'm not brainwashed. It is safe. I've got data."

"It doesn't matter. You get my point. Offer them more."

Mia damped down her annoyance, same as she'd had to do every day she'd worked for Erika, and thought of all the things people bought that they didn't need. Was security that different than the insect wing scarves that had been so popular last fall? If Jason could encrust a conversation shield with emeralds or make a home security system with an impressive number of blinking lights, maybe people would be tempted.

"I'll think of places where we can advertise. What's my budget?"

"See what you can do without one."

She should have known. This whole thing was a joke, but as long as they paid her and helped get her records cleared up, she'd play along.

As Lucas slid her ID card back to her, she noticed a blue thistle pod stuck to his sleeve. Those would ruin a shirt if pulled off incorrectly. Without thinking, she reached across the desk, carefully twisted it, and after a successful extraction, set it in front of him.

He'd frozen during this brief exercise.

"I'm sorry," Mia said, standing, pocketing her badge. "You can only remove those by turning them counterclockwise. You wouldn't know that."

She moved to the door. "You've been walking out past Ring 20, based on the location of that thistle." The native plants within the sectors were trimmed. "Wear a MacAvoy coverall if you go off pavement. It's sunproof, bugproof, and nothing sticks to it. Where that thistle lives, so do deadly insects."

He picked up the thistle and examined it.

"How do you like Victoria?" she asked.

"I've always liked the desert."

He tossed the pod over his shoulder. A tiny sweeper emerged from the wall and vacuumed it up.

And with that, Summit Security was officially open for business.

Two long, quiet weeks later, Mia's screen flashed bright blue—a comm request from outside the building and the first she'd gotten. She slapped on the virtual office backdrop she'd constructed, then paused. What was she supposed to say? She hadn't prepared a script because a big part of her never believed a client would actually call.

With no credits to spend, she'd done what she could to spread the word for free, contacting small, chartered businesses in Weber sector and letting them know Summit existed and the services offered, and posting comments on discussions that strayed anywhere near the topic of security. She wasn't sure she was doing it right, but what she lacked in finesse she made up for in volume.

Ah well, she'd wing it. "Summit Security. Can I help you?"

A young man appeared on the screen. He was in his early twenties with an attractive, androgynous face, more cute than handsome. Large brown eyes, black hair shaved nearly to his skull, and skin so flawless she suspected he'd had his facial hair removed. His name and affiliation, which should have appeared on the bottom right, were conspicuously absent. He was in a pod, somewhere on Ring 7 near E, she guessed from the flashes of scenery.

His anxious expression didn't suit his youthful face. "I hope so. I read about Summit Security in a *Highrise 2250* discussion board."

Ah yes, the gamers. *Highrise* took place on Earth, and players tried to break into and secure as many apartments as possible. The perfect mind-set for a potential client.

"What can we help you with in particular?"

He darkened the pod windows and whispered, "I think my apartment is being bugged."

Mia had to do a quick frame-of-reference switch from Victoria's deadly bugs—always top of mind—to the small electronic kind.

"My friend was over the other night, and we were talking about the new add-ons available for *Highrise*. Real-life talking. No glasses. The next day, I got a sketchy ad offering a discounted version of all the new add-ons—even ones we wished for that didn't exist. Someone was listening."

Mia opened her mouth to explain all the ways this could have happened without bugs then shut it. This young man could be their first client. It wasn't her job to dissuade him.

"Here's what we offer as far as home security, and I'd be happy to schedule a free consultation." She slid a brochure to him. His head twitched left and right as he read.

"Yeah, one of these would work. Can we do the consultation tomorrow?"

His name finally appeared on her screen. Dezzie Adeyemi, Soils Research Associate, Han Corporation. Why did their first client have to be from Han? There were five other sectors. Odds were against Han. Ah well, bad luck.

"I'll check with the director and get back to you within the hour. I'm sure we can make space for you." Seeming busy was always more appealing than having too much free time.

"Lemme know," Dezzie said, and cut the connection.

Lucas, fortunately, had made one of his rare appearances and was locked in his office. She pinged him.

"What?" He answered, voice only.

"We've a potential client. He wants to schedule a consultation for tomorrow."

"I'll replay the call."

He could do that? Of course he could. Still, it was disconcerting.

A few minutes later, Lucas emerged from his office, brow furrowed. She couldn't tell if he was angry or tired; his beige shirt did not flatter his gaunt frame and wan complexion.

"What was that?"

"What do you mean?" Mia said.

He held out his glasses as if they'd fallen into something noxious. "That…room."

She'd built a virtual office for Summit, a penthouse on Ring 20 in an imagined building with high ceilings, limestone floors, real wood desks, large pots of lemonbush and snap grass, and a north-facing view of the mountains. In a dark alcove, she'd placed holos of the latest and greatest home security equipment—according to the Earth journals she was reading. Vendors provided the 3D models, and she painstakingly programmed tiny virtual spotlights to play over the pieces on the dark shelves, nearly invisible but for glints and shadows. She even threw in a couple of nonlethal weapons for Jason.

Why was Lucas disgusted? "It's so we can meet people in virtual. It's usually more reminiscent of the real office or store, but in our case…" She'd never want a client to see where they actually worked.

"It looks like a cross between a hair salon and the showroom of a third-world arms dealer. Get rid of it." Lucas said.

Jason pulled down his glasses and a moment later stifled a laugh. "You've never been to a security firm, have you?"

Mia shook her head. "Of course not—"

"Listen up everyone." Lucas cut her off. "We have a consultation with a potential client tomorrow. Claire, take off your glasses and pay attention!"

Claire pulled off her glasses, astonished. She always wore them and always multitasked. Jason hurried to remove his as well.

"His name is Dezzie Adeyemi, and he's a Soils Research Associate at Han Corporation. He believes someone is spying on him and wants his house made safe from unauthorized data access. Everyone will attend this meeting. In the future, Mia and Jason can handle consultations, but I want to get a feel for the clientele and see how his home network is set up."

"I can work from here," Claire said.

"No, you can't. You're coming with us."

"I'd rather not go into Han sector," Mia said. "Everyone knows—"

"I don't care. We take clients from any sector. Claire, gather whatever data you can find about Adeyemi, personal and professional, and send it to Mia." Lucas turned to her. "Send me a summary by this evening."

"Why are we investigating him?" Mia asked.

"We'll do background checks on all our clients. I don't want to find out I'm providing security for a drug dealer. We're not going to break any rules here."

He returned to his office. Claire started typing.

Mia faced her screen, not seeing the article she'd been reading. Aside from her apartment, which she was stuck with due to the lease, she was avoiding anything Han. She knew too many people there. Maybe in a few months a new scandal would distract everyone, but for now, she was likely still a topic of gossip.

An hour later, a file bundle appeared on Mia's screen, the results of Claire's digging into Dezzie Adeyemi, Soils Research Associate, Han Corporation. Thankfully, Mia had never worked with anyone in mining, so her disgrace would be unknown to him.

The bundle contained 476 files. "Claire, this is too much. I can't summarize all this by tonight."

"Sure you can," Claire said. "I remember in freshman year you had an art history class at 8 a.m. and never went. You read through the materials the night before the final and got ninety-eight percent. I think you can manage some bank statements and call logs in the next few hours."

Mia remembered the class, and cramming for it, but why had Claire? They both pulled all-nighters before finals.

"You bragged about it," Claire said in response to Mia's quizzical expression. "You complained about paying for a class that was nothing but memorization. You don't have to memorize this. Just read through it and call out anything unusual. You heard Lucas. He doesn't want to work for criminals."

Was Claire merely being thorough, or was there spite buried in this overwhelming volume? They'd never been competitive during university. They'd been on completely different tracks. Claire had complained continuously about the laziness of her lab partners and professors though, and Mia now understood. Claire wanted to be the top performer. How would that work when they were supposed to be partners?

Evening came and went, and it was close to 10 p.m. before Mia had looked through everything and picked out the salient info for Lucas. He hadn't left, and she imagined him tapping his fingers impatiently on his desk. She knocked tentatively on his door.

"What is it?"

"I have the summary and wanted to explain some things."

"Come in."

When she entered, he was behind his desk, screens blank, glow ceiling dim. Perhaps he set them to mimic the actual twilight outdoors. She waited for him to invite her to sit. He didn't, but he also didn't look angry.

Mia plucked the data from her screen and dropped it onto his desk. She'd color-coded the chunks either blue or orange based on whether it was professional or personal.

"If the data Claire got is accurate, Dezzie is a completely normal twenty-four-year-old. He graduated from the University of Colorado a year ago, got a four-year contract as a research assistant here, and spends his entire paycheck on gaming, legal drugs, alcohol, and shoes. His mom calls him a bit too often, and he doesn't have a partner. He has no access to classified data at work, nor do any of his friends. I can't imagine anyone wanting to spy on him."

"I asked for a summary of the background information Claire gathered, not conjecture."

He poked the squares. The orange and blue flashing across the screen left an afterimage in her eyes.

"She said you wanted to know if he was a criminal. He's not, and no one could spy on him even if they wanted to. We residents of Victoria are guaranteed privacy in our homes. Contractually and technically there is a barrier between the interior and the exterior. Any attempt to breach that barrier means huge fines. Demotion and thrown off the planet kinds of fines. It isn't tolerated."

"People that live here believe this?"

"Of course. We need a place to decompress. The Six did studies and determined it's not healthy to be under surveillance twenty-seven/seven. People become withdrawn and unproductive. It's the one thing everyone agrees on." She had proof. Her own childhood would have unfolded very differently if the Six had been watching her at home.

"You've been helping us set up a business that, in your mind, is completely unnecessary."

"I had doubts, but people here want more. None of our luxury goods are necessary, and that doesn't stop anyone from buying them. Extra home security is a novelty item. A conversation piece. But as far as Dezzie actually being spied upon…it's impossible, and it pains me to encourage his paranoia."

"I'm concerned with making credits, not the mental health of New Canberrans. I'd like to learn more about the mining research division. Send me five hundred words."

The order seemed to be a dismissal, so Mia returned to her desk. She knew little more than annual-report type information about Han's mining division. Those partners worked on a different floor, and she'd never been called upon to optimize any of the remote field offices where most of the work took place.

Han, like the rest of the Six, glossed over the fact that they'd wasted years and many robots combing over their territories, hoping to find concentrated deposits of the rare earth element scandium, a crucial component in spaceship burst drives, and nearly priceless due to its scarcity. Scandium turned out to be just as rare on Victoria as it was on Earth and none of the Six found much.

The mining of precious metals and gemstones, however, was a success and sent prices plummeting until the Six agreed to cut back production. The mining division, near as Mia could tell, was a tethered beast. It could chew through the planet and spit out emeralds, but no one wanted that, not if emeralds were worth less than sand. These days the division concentrated on digging up whatever Han needed for its domestic manufacturing and didn't bring in much profit.

She sent Lucas her brief report and hurried out the door before he could ask for more.

The office was almost lively the next day. Claire and Jason both got in early. Claire gestured a bit more energetically in VR than usual, and Jason cursed more loudly as he struggled with whatever he was welding. Lucas, locked in his office, was busy doing something intense, according to the network traffic data.

The inner door slammed open and a man in an electric blue suit paused, backlit, seeming to wait for applause. When none came, he stomped over and held out his hand. "Mia, right?"

This must be Mikey. A few inches taller than Lucas and twice as wide, he was a ball of showy muscle, with black hair cropped short and a clean-shaven face. He might have been handsome if he wasn't as puffed up as a frightened mota fish. Were steroids legal on Earth? And his tan… Tans that deep hadn't been popular in a decade.

Mia had a strong handshake but Mikey nearly crushed her fingers.

He laughed. "Good grip! You were born here, huh?"

She nodded, and he grabbed her wrist.

"I can see that. Thick bones."

She yanked her arm free. His light brown eyes were bloodshot. He'd either been drinking or spending time outside without glasses. Neither possibility recommended him.

He did a half squat, then patted his upper thigh in an approving manner. "Gravity here sucks. I'm getting a workout just by walking around."

He stripped off his jacket. His short-sleeve shirt and vest looked expensive, and were both a size too small.

He leaned over the desk. "It's true what they say about Victoria" he said, voice low. "All the women are beautiful."

His breath reeked of cheap, cane-cactus tequila.

"Mikey. Leave her alone." Lucas appeared behind Mikey, thin hand gripping the man's enormous shoulder.

Mikey straightened, his expression changing from vaguely lecherous to blankly professional in less than a heartbeat.

"In my office. Now," Lucas said.

Jason spoke up once the door closed. "Sorry about that, Mia. Mikey is…" He grimaced. "He's a lot of things. Loyal to Lucas and the team, but pretty much out of control when he's not working. He's stuck somewhere in the mid twentieth century when it comes to women. He thinks strutting around like a peacock on steroids will attract them."

"Unfortunately, it might. Women here crave novelty, and Mikey is definitely not a typical New Canberra man."

"What is?" Jason asked, suddenly attentive.

Mia drew a flat line in the air. "Homogenous. Screened and tested and vetted to above-average blandness. Attractive. Smart, competitive, but not overly aggressive. Good communication skills. Well-educated. Eager to please. Social. High self-esteem. Fit, but not obsessed like Mikey seems to be. Of course the partners are a whole different story, but the rank and file workers are hired because they have a lot in common and are likely to get along."

Most of these traits, it occurred to her, were sorely lacking at Summit Security. "That's for jobs at the Six. I don't know how the screening works for a private company like this. What did you have to do to get the contract?"

"Dunno." He turned back to the box of wires he was fiddling with. "Lucas handled all that."

That would have been impossible, but before she could follow up, Lucas and Mikey emerged.

"Time to go," Lucas said.

"You'd better get changed Jason," Mia said. "You can't go to a client meeting dressed like that." His usual outfit of t-shirt, stained pants, and worn canvas shoes looked especially shabby today.

"I left my good clothes on Earth." He gave Lucas a pointed glance. "I won't spend my miniscule salary on things I can't wear when I get home. Things like fancy vests."

Lucas grabbed a long-sleeved, button-down shirt from a hook behind his office door and handed it to Jason. "This will have to do for today."

Jason sniffed it, then shrugged it on. Though he was taller than Lucas, he was also thin, so the shirt more or less fit.

"You figure out a stunner for me?" Mikey asked Jason.

Jason tossed him what looked like a fat, blue pen. "It's low-power, but most scanners should interpret it as a game controller. I've carried it in pods and retail stores without any problem. I wouldn't bring it anywhere near a headquarters building though."

The device looked small in Mikey's hand. He pointed it at the wall and pressed his thumb on a button Mia couldn't see. Nothing happened as far as she could tell, but Mikey nodded and put the device in his front pocket.

"Thanks. I'll feel a lot more comfortable now. Being without a weapon is like," he turned to Mia, "being naked."

"Stop," Lucas said. "We're at work. Same rules as Itek."

"None of the rules are the same here," Mikey said. "This planet is bat-shit crazy. You don't want know what I did last night… And it was perfectly legal."

Lucas pressed his fingers to the bridge of his nose and shut his eyes, and for a moment Mia worried he was getting another migraine.

"Don't harass the staff," he said with exaggerated slowness.

Mikey, to her surprise, stood straighter and nodded. "Sorry, boss. I've been in vacation mode. That ends now."

Mia trailed behind as everyone exited, taking a moment after the black door hissed shut to reevaluate her coworkers. In the office they made a strange kind of sense, but out in the late morning sun, none at all. Claire, dressed for a funeral in a shapeless gray ensemble, Mikey, outfitted for a nightclub. Jason wearing borrowed clothes, and Lucas looking as if he were headed to a board meeting. They had nothing in common with each other and no interest in fitting in.

Lucas hailed the first pod that passed. It was a two-seater.

"We could call a bigger one and ride together if you want," Mia suggested.

He looked at her blankly.

"The pod icon, on your glasses? If you stare for a few seconds, you get options."

He turned away. "Right. Yes."

A larger pod arrived a minute later. Mikey and Lucas took the seat facing forward, and she, Claire, and Jason sat together across from them. Mikey positioned himself in front of her and lolled, open-legged, his hand resting on his thigh just shy of his crotch. Mia switched her glasses to mirror.

Jason leaned forward and broke through Mikey's leer, pointing out the window. "Who owns that? I see those everywhere."

A silver and blue MMARV drone flashed past the pod. "Optima," Mia replied. "Everything that flies within the 20 Rings belongs to them. The Six aren't allowed to fly any instruments in city limits."

"What is Optima?" Jason asked. "I saw that logo all over the strataport."

"Didn't you attend orientation on the trip over? It's compulsory."

Jason frowned. "We were compelled to stay in our cabins."

"Jason." Lucas said his name flatly, the menace implied.

Jason pressed his lips together and crossed his arms.

What the hell did Jason mean? Had they caused some kind of trouble on the way over and been locked up? Mikey didn't look the type to obey strict passenger ship rules.

No one spoke or met Mia's gaze. When the silence went from awkward to uncomfortable, she broke it.

"I'll try to get the Weber orientation materials for you. They give an overview of the planet's organization. Optima is the holding company the Six formed to find, then colonize, Victoria. Now it functions as a board of directors and arbitrates disputes. Each corporation has equal representation. It's become a fairly powerful entity." She pointed to a cluster of sensors on a pole in the center of the road. "Most things that are built-in—the cameras, IR and motion detectors, scanners, or anything hardwired into a network—belong to whichever corporation owns the sector. Optima owns the sensors on the streets that divide one sector from another in case there's a dispute. You'll see the Optima logo and color scheme."

Jason unfolded his arms. "Ring 9, Avenue B. Looks like engineers named the streets, huh?"

"Engineers did everything the first few years. Marketing and PR people came later and gave us all those ridiculous traditional Earth street names within the sectors. Elm, Oak, Chestnut; none of those can survive here. One of the sectors has a lake theme. We don't have lakes."

The pod crossed Avenue A into Han sector. Mia shrank into the seat. She tried not to, but knowing she was innocent didn't protect her from embarrassment. She'd run into a former coworker in the lobby of her apartment last week, and he'd stopped and stared as if she were an animal in an Earth zoo. He'd nudged his companion—a woman she didn't know—and whispered something.

"Why is she still here?" the woman had responded, not quietly enough.

The comment had been as unexpected and painful as a leafbug bite. They didn't know she'd been born on Victoria and couldn't be deported. She'd graduated from New Beijing U and ridden the ship to Victoria with everyone else who'd been hired. Only her close colleagues and personal friends knew she was one of the few native born. Now she was not only a criminal, but a mysterious criminal, overstaying her welcome and mucking up the otherwise perfect landscape.

She'd gone upstairs and cried, the first time she'd done so since she'd been fired. Crying was supposed to be cathartic, but her tears burned and left her tired and angry.

"Mia," Lucas said. "Mia…"

"Sorry. What?" He'd been speaking but she'd missed it. Her memories often took her away from the present. It was a flaw, but one that people usually forgave easily.

"Pay close attention during the meeting," Lucas said. "I'll do most of the talking, but I want you to jump in if Adeyemi asks specific questions about New Canberra or Victoria. You said it's not appropriate for us to wear glasses?"

"Correct. Dezzie might wear his because it's his house, but we shouldn't. We can use screens."

"I can't appear ignorant of things that are commonly known. If I offer Adeyemi a conversation shield and he asks, 'Can I use this at the annex?' I need to know if the annex is a bar, or club, or part of Han headquarters. If you don't know the answer, rephrase the question so that the rest of us can make sense of it."

"Got it."

The pod slowed when it entered the residential area. The plan was for the maximum height of buildings to decrease ring by ring until Ring

10, then to rise again, an inverted bell curve. Nothing much had been built past 10, so the enclaves of detached homes and low-rise apartment buildings scattered around Ring 8 were the frayed edges of the city, waiting to be woven into neighborhoods that didn't exist yet. The area wasn't popular so rents were cheap, attracting interns and junior employees like Dezzie.

The pod stopped in front of a modest, ten-story, apartment building. Mia thought she'd seen every building in New Canberra, but somehow, she'd missed the middle of this block. Easy to miss—the tan box had no distinguishing features.

The team tramped up to the lobby door, and Lucas pressed the button for unit 202. The screen flickered to life. Dezzie wasn't much better dressed than Jason. Mia relaxed.

"Summit Security?" Dezzie asked.

Lucas nodded.

"I'm on the second floor. Stairs are faster."

Stairs? Indeed, the modest lobby was dominated by a staircase that led to a second-floor mezzanine furnished with couches and an antique-style pool table. Nothing electronic, just colored balls scattered across faded green cloth. This building was older than she'd guessed. These kinds of communal spaces proved unpopular with residents who preferred to be home decompressing or out and about. This not-in-not-out space didn't make sense to them.

Mia ran a finger across a faux leather airchair. Dusty.

Dezzie's head poked out from a door down the hall. He glanced anxiously left and right and gestured. "Come in."

Lucas led the team into the sparsely furnished living room. A new but inexpensive brown couch ran the length of an unadorned wall, and a gaming chair—the prized possession of most single men—sat awkwardly in the center of the room. It, too, was low-end, armature exposed, seat and headrest worn. Research Associates made more on Victoria than they would on Earth, but the credits didn't go far, given the high cost of imported goods.

Dezzie was shorter than her—way under two meters—and thin. He'd paired a non-descript jumpsuit with trendy Black & Blue boots. The soles had built-in bug zappers and an animated kill score that twined around his ankles. 274 on the left, and 187 on the right. He must have gone off the sidewalk to get scores that high, and that was a bad idea. Any bug close enough to get zapped by the boots would be close enough to zap Dezzie.

"How do you find out if anyone is listening?" Dezzie whispered.

Jason smiled and whispered back. "We're going to walk around the apartment with a transmission detector and verify all outgoing signals. Anything that looks suspicious, I'll investigate."

Jason took out the transmission detector and, with Dezzie in tow, began to scan and eliminate legitimate signals from the home appliances. Mikey assumed an alert position by the front door, lacing his hands together and shifting his gaze lazily from left to right. Lucas disappeared into the kitchen.

"What are we supposed to do?" Mia asked Claire, who shrugged and sat on the far end of the couch. Mia joined her.

When Jason and Dezzie returned to the living room, Jason verified the team's glasses, screens, and PDSs. A smattering of red lights remained on the screen, some in the room. Jason knelt, detector in hand, and scanned the thick, none-too-clean carpet. Like a mother monkey grooming a baby, his fingers combed through the thick off-white tufts. A moment later he stood, a small black chunk of plastic held triumphantly between thumb and forefinger. He held it below the detector, and a number appeared. He showed this to Claire.

She fumbled through her bag, pulled out a square gray box—an Alphatronics model 267 transmission jammer—and set it on the floor in the center of the room. She adjusted a dial. A low note sounded from the device. The red lights on Jason's detector turned yellow.

He spoke. "Okay, that got all of them. Anything that isn't hardwired anyway."

Mia peered at the black square on Jason's palm. An actual bug? Was this possible?

Someone risked deportation and bankruptcy to attempt to spy on Dezzie. Was he involved in a secret project? Was the research associate job just a cover? At Han HQ, she'd noticed the elevator never stopped on floors twenty-five through thirty, and a number of employees had vague titles and no departments listed in their personnel files. Dezzie was not one of them. If he were, he wouldn't be hiring Summit—he'd have all the security he needed.

Dezzie fidgeted in the archway between the living and dining rooms, clasping and unclasping his hands like a cartoon mad scientist.

"I was right. Someone *is* spying on me. I've been getting invitations to join a Quest of Doom IV beta test, and no one knows I play Quest of Doom III. I brought that cartridge from Earth, and I only play it here. Can you leave that thing here?" He pointed to the transmission jammer.

"Wait a second," Mia said. "That bug won't be able to transmit to the outside. All the residential buildings in New Canberra have built-in privacy and data protection systems."

"They do?" Jason asked.

"Yes. This is called out in every rental agreement, and privacy in the home is guaranteed in employment contracts."

Jason gave the transmission jammer to Claire. "I'll check it out. Turn that off for a minute once I get outside."

He took the detector and quietly exited through the front door. Claire waited a bit, then flipped the switch. All the yellow lights turned red again. After thirty seconds or so, she turned it back on.

Jason returned a moment later and held the detector out to Mia as if she knew what the numbers meant. "The bugs were transmitting. I went all the way out to the street."

"Something must be wrong with his system. I'm surprised he didn't get an alert. When my window vibration dampener failed, my apartment let me know immediately."

"What exactly is this mysterious protection system? More importantly, where is it?" Lucas asked.

"It's part of the house. Built in. I don't know the details."

"There must be a control panel somewhere. How do you let your house know which transmissions are okay and which aren't?" Jason asked.

Mia held out her hands. "I'm not a tech person. I just know it works. My friends and I did some crazy things when we were young and trust me, if there'd been spyware in our homes, we'd definitely have been called out."

"I never read my lease," Dezzie interjected. "If there's something in there that says this shouldn't be happening, I'll talk to the property manager."

Lucas pinched the bridge of his nose. "That won't work. They'll promise to reset a circuit or update the firmware, then declare your apartment secure, but it won't be. We need to find and remove the bugs and install a home security system to keep an eye on things. Here's the information on our packages." He handed Dezzie a screen.

Dezzie blanched. "I can't afford this! It's more than my game subscription."

"You didn't check our prices before you called?"

Dezzie shook his head. "I assumed it'd be like a feed. Maybe fifty credits a month or something."

"You have no idea what the equipment to do this job costs. What's the price of this Alphatronics box?" Lucas asked Mia.

She recalled the data sheet. "Four thousand credits, and you can't buy them here on Victoria unless you're a registered security firm."

He snapped out a dozen more brand names of devices used in the home security packages Summit offered. "How about those?"

She froze, a buzz beetle in pod headlights. Was this information someone would know off the top of her head? "I don't remember all the details. Let me get my screen."

Lucas narrowed his eyes. "You don't remember? Never mind."

He turned to Dezzie. "You can't afford this equipment, and even if you could, who would monitor it twenty-seven hours a day? These bugs constantly change frequency, and they're cheap. You could be tracking them in on your shoes. You can't keep them out; you can only keep them from transmitting."

Lucas was angry, snapping his words out, and Mia realized he'd probably never had to woo a client. Sure, he'd had to negotiate, but it would have been over lunch with another partner, where the tab for wine alone would be more than the credits they'd get from Dezzie. The scale of this was too small for a former partner to comprehend, and these small jobs would be the core of the business.

Dezzie had backed away and stood against the living room wall, arms folded defensively. She had to intervene, though it was a lose-lose situation. If she did nothing, Dezzie might ask them to leave. If she interrupted and they got the contract, she'd have made Lucas look bad.

She touched Dezzie's arm and his attention shifted from Lucas to her. She circled until he faced away from Lucas.

"Dezzie, I get it. I'm on a limited budget too, and this shouldn't be happening, but it is. I've never seen so many bugs in a residence, and the only way to deal with tech is counter-tech. It might be worth spending some credits on security." She eyed his expensive boots. "You can play Quest of Doom III and talk to your friends and not worry someone is listening in. Either way, it's up to you. Think it over. You know where to find us."

She made a "go away" gesture to Claire, who turned off the transmission jammer and returned it to her bag.

"Don't take that!" Dezzie said. "I need it. Sign me up for the basic package for three months." He thumbed the screen Mia held. "Don't blame me for not knowing how much home security costs. I wasn't supposed to need it."

"We'll leave the jammer for now, and I'll come back tomorrow to figure out a more permanent solution," Jason said.

The team filed out. Lucas gave Dezzie a curt nod, and Jason instructed him not to mess with the equipment. Mia said to call if he had any questions.

Back out on the hot sidewalk, Mia kept away from Lucas. Contract or no contract, he'd be angry she hadn't answered his questions and had interrupted what he thought was a sales pitch. With luck she could delay the lecture until they were in private.

Fortunately, he was engrossed in his glasses.

Mikey clapped her on the shoulder. "Good work! I thought Lucas hired you to pretty up the office, but it looks like you might actually be useful."

She frowned. "I am actually useful. I'm the reason Summit can do business on this planet."

"I've been doing a lot of business."

Was he about to add, *in bed?* "This isn't a joke. We need credits. My paycheck has been late every week, and that's not a good sign."

Mikey nodded. "I've been getting by teaching at the gym, but I need more than that to really live. There's fun to be had on this planet. I'll be glad when credits start rolling in. Plus, Lucas needs to get out of that garage."

"What garage?"

Lucas was out of earshot, pacing and gesturing.

"The front half of the Summit office building. Someone ran a custom tool fab shop out of there before we moved in. Not a good place for entertaining, not the way Lucas is used to entertaining anyway."

She hadn't given much thought to where they all lived. Everyone but her listed the office as their official address, out of remnant paranoia she assumed. She'd wondered at the always-closed door on the left side of the long corridor. That explained Lucas's abrupt appearances and disappearances.

"I need this business to succeed. I'll be living in a garage if I don't get paid," she said.

Mikey lifted his glasses and gave her a salacious wink. "There's plenty of room for you at my place."

Mia set off down the sidewalk, away from Mikey and the team. She wouldn't suggest they share a pod again, and her next task would be to set up codes of conduct for the office, infractions punishable by fines. Mikey's next wisecrack might get her the advertising budget she needed.

Chapter Six

Fortunately, Mikey didn't return to the office with the rest of the team. Jason and Claire burst through the door, chatting excitedly about the bug. They'd never seen the model before. Jason had it disassembled and under the magnifier in minutes.

Lucas came straight to Mia's desk.

"This isn't working," he said.

Claire and Jason looked up.

Mia pulled off her glasses. "You're right. You can't be so aggressive with clients, and if Mikey makes one more rude comment—"

"In my office. Now."

Fine. She'd had time to collect her thoughts on the pod ride back. She wouldn't tolerate a lecture for doing her job, not for the meager pay she was getting, not even from a former partner.

She sat down hard in Lucas's guest chair and waited for him to begin.

"I asked you how much various home security equipment costs. Why didn't you answer?"

His question surprised her. "I didn't have a screen."

Lucas raised an eyebrow. "You read the equipment spec manuals Claire sent?"

"Of course." Where was he going with this?

He unbuttoned his vest, pulled a small stun gun from the inner pocket, and tossed it across the desk. "Tell me everything you know about that. In detail."

She didn't know her coworkers carried real guns. Why hadn't this one set off Dezzie's alarm? She picked it up tentatively, weighing it on her palm. It was heavier than expected. She examined it from different angles and noticed the chip Claire installed in her thumb didn't activate it.

She wasn't wearing glasses now, but sensed this wasn't the time to hold back. "It's an Essalin S-67 stun gun, short range, two meters or less. Shoots an electric bullet, briefly stops neural activity and is effective regardless of body weight. Causes unconsciousness. Manufactured on Earth, legal on Victoria but only to corporate security, costs about five hundred credits…" She took a breath to continue.

"Enough." He pulled open a drawer and took out a shiny, flat black box the size of an open hand and set it on the desk. A small green light flashed. He gestured to it, as if she should pick it up.

"Take a closer look."

"No thanks. That's a Delta Engineering adjustable force field generator. I'd guess you have it set to a quarter of a meter or so. It's not lethal, but if I tried to touch it, I'd be knocked out of this chair."

"I think you'd be thrown all the way out the front door." He waved his hand over the device. A small red light winked on, then off. "I need my staff to perform to the best of their abilities."

"What's wrong with my performance? I just signed our first client."

"How did you know this was a force field generator?" He held it up, glow ceiling flashing across the slick surface as he returned it to the drawer. "There are four or five other identical boxes on the equipment list."

"Not identical. That one has—" She stopped, suspicion belatedly flaring.

Lucas nodded. "Has what?"

"I don't know. I guessed."

"No, you didn't." He swiped his hand across the glossy black desk and plucked four documents from the chaos.

Expecting to see a spec sheet, she leaned in.

Instead, she was confronted by the official scores from her earliest childhood aptitude tests.

Fucking Claire and her fucking data hoarding.

She took a breath and fought the familiar tension forming in her chest. These test scores didn't matter much anymore, but her childhood anxieties had shaped her as surely as the wind shaped the stunted seaside trees of the north coast.

When she was a child, her mom told her not to get perfect scores on tests. To her, not perfect meant one wrong. So, she'd gotten exactly ninety-nine out of one hundred right on the aptitude tests every year from age four through age seven. Scores weren't normally shared with parents, but a well-meaning teacher called her mom to try to understand why Mia did well on tests but refused to participate in class. Her mom was furious. Not at her, she came to understand later, but at herself for not giving better instructions. She sat Mia down and told a story far more frightening than the ghost stories Mia liked at that age.

She told Mia about REA, the Registry of Exceptional Abilities.

If Mia continued to score highly in all subjects she would be "registered," and people from REA would come to the house and take her away. She'd be sent to Earth for school and wouldn't see Mom or Dad for years. After that, she'd have to work hard for Han until she died. Mia had pictured herself shriveled up in a corner of the Han lobby, the only part of the headquarters she'd seen.

REA testing started out innocently enough on Earth as a placement exam for students but evolved into an elaborate legal ranking system designed to spot and capture any child in the top one percent of various categories. Incentives to parents in the form of scholarships and "financial aid" meant that, by the time a gifted child was thirteen, a corporation or government owned them. Eminent domain on intelligence. People on Earth didn't mind their children being on the Registry; it guaranteed prestigious employment on a planet where most people couldn't find jobs.

Han took the REA tests in a different direction. Firstly, they had no affiliation with the non-profit that administered the tests on Earth—they merely paid a licensing fee and gave the tests themselves. The hundred or so children of Victoria were already on shaky ground as far as civil rights were concerned, and testing highly on the REA blew those rights out of the water. No corporation wanted to lose a bright star to a competing sector, so the Six agreed on a special clause for any geniuses that might happen to be born into the cold arms of a corporate embrace. The Education and Employment Contract wasn't that different than the REA contract on Earth, with one important exception. No retirement age. Han and the others had a right to work their luminaries to death.

Her mother's description of what would happen if REA got her spawned nightmares of chase and capture that she had to this day.

"After age seven, your scores dropped to below registry levels," Lucas said.

"The tests got harder."

Lucas tapped his desk and blackness returned. "Claire tells me you have a very good memory."

"Really?" Mia responded with practiced calm, but inside she cursed. She'd let her guard down during their years together as roommates. It was hard to maintain a façade at home, especially after finals when she'd had a few too many cheap Chinese whiskies. She'd slipped up dozens of times, but Claire was always on her glasses, absorbed in god knows what and not paying attention to Mia rattling off the details of a dim sum take-out menu she wasn't holding.

"I had an aptitude for social engineering and didn't need to study much. What does that have to do with anything?"

Lucas leaned back; the chair creaked. "It's my job to notice when things don't add up. When they don't, there's a problem. Usually one that lands in my lap. Let me clarify something. This building has better shielding than what you imagine you have at home. This is the most privacy you've had in your life. I guarantee it. You can speak freely."

"About what?" This conversation had taken so many turns she felt like a character in a badly designed driving game.

"I know registration here is different than on Earth. Specifically, that there is no fixed retirement age. I can see why you would want to avoid it, and I will never do anything to bring you to the attention of the REA board."

"If you have a photographic memory, I need to know." He spoke the words calmly, inviting her to respond.

Time slowed. No one had ever said it out loud. Not even Mom and Dad.

"You aren't the only one who doesn't want to be registered," Lucas said when it became clear Mia wasn't going to speak. He pointed toward the door. "You think they'd have let me keep Claire in my department as a mid-level tech if the partners at Itek realized she was Registration-level? I suspect Jason would score, too, but he refused to be tested."

Mia forced herself to look Lucas in the eye. He'd caught her off-guard, but she was good at hiding the truth. She'd had a lifetime of practice. "First, you know nothing about the REA. They stop testing after age eighteen on Earth and Victoria because the whole point is to give kids an elite education and form them while they're still malleable. No one is going to snatch Claire and Jason away from you, and there is no REA board on Victoria to pay attention to me. You aren't the first to notice my strange test scores, but I've never been accused of having a photographic memory for acing an exam when I was four, or for doing well in a major my roommate knew nothing about."

Lucas pushed back his sleeves and leaned toward her, hands open, almost imploring. "I don't expect you to prattle back facts like a trained parrot, but I'm trying to start a business on a planet that needs a new security firm like it needs another poisonous insect. I have to take advantage of all the resources I've got, or I'll fail."

She pulled her chair forward and met him on the battlefield of the desk, her own hands pressed flat against the cool surface. "Say someone on Victoria did have a photographic memory. How would that play out? The REA tests are administered by the corporation that owns the sector. You think they go public with what they discover? The child would become, as you said, a resource. An advantage. Something to bring to a tech-free meeting. Something to walk around a secure R&D facility. Something to collect and hold a secret—temporarily. Even after the REA testing years have passed, if someone was suspected of having this ability, a combination veracity detector and memory test would reveal it."

Lucas frowned.

"Tell me, former partner in Itek Internal Security, what you would do with the sole copy of a piece of information that could fatally damage your company?" Mia asked.

"Wipe it," he said without hesitation.

"Exactly. A person with a photographic memory wouldn't worry about having too long a career at one of the Six. They'd worry about being retired early."

The fingers of his right hand rippled against the desktop. "You're right. I wasn't thinking about the new tech-free regulations." He stared fixedly at the wall. "You're lucky you got fired from Han. You'll be safer here with us than stumbling around on the executive floors. I'm amazed they didn't figure you out."

"Stop right there. We aren't talking about me. I don't have a photographic memory. You say that one more time, and I quit."

"Fine." Lucas held up his hands as if to stop her, but she'd made no move to leave. "I don't care what you call it, but here in the office I want no pretenses. I won't be patronized."

"What do you mean?"

"Don't play dumb. Respond to my questions if you know the answer. Out in public, I understand that you'll have to plead ignorance if you aren't wearing glasses."

Mia considered her options. She could quit now, before Lucas had more evidence to support his theory. However, without his and Claire's help in clearing her record, she'd never be able to work in social engineering again.

"Fine. You don't ask me questions in public, and I'll perform to the best of my ability in the office," she said. "Now, please delete all my pre-college data from your archives."

"Erika might have—"

"I don't care. If Erika painted me a kleptomaniac teen, so be it." She dampened her temper, took a deep breath, and risked a truth. "I'm not safe if all my data is in one place. You drew a conclusion based on four test scores and a rumor. Someone with access to my entire childhood might do the same. Claire hacked New Beijing U. What if someone hacks her?"

She expected him to protest, to claim no one could access the data, but he nodded. "Your records are safe enough for now, but if I—"

He cut himself off with a swipe of his hand across the desk. Her records appeared first as tiny icons, then an ordered list. He sorted, typed, and a third of the lines changed to red then disappeared. He went through the added step of adding random data, then wiped that as well.

"What about backups?" she asked.

"In a few hours, the backups will reflect this. Delete means delete in this office."

He wasn't the powerful man he'd been at Itek, but his voice carried a gravelly authority, and she had to trust the files were gone. She sat straighter and loosened her shoulders. Lucas had given up a good deal of the leverage he held over her. She appreciated the gesture.

She offered something in return. "You should be careful what you leave on your screen when I'm around."

Lucas gave her a quizzical look.

"You had other documents on the desk when you pulled up my old test scores. I saw them. I thought you should know."

She'd only gotten a glimpse before the tests filled the space, but that was enough. She had a mental snapshot she could peruse at will. If they were going to work together, he needed to be more attentive. She'd seen more than she wanted to many times at Han, and sorting through what she officially knew and actually knew made conversations tricky.

His customary cockiness disappeared. "What did you see?"

She was as honest as prudence allowed. "A mail message from Sergeant M. Johnson, NYCPD, titled, 'Still no date set,' and the message said, 'Lucas, haven't heard back from the attorneys. They're stalling.' The rest of the note was covered by the tests. There was a brochure from Atlas Security, which I don't need to recite unless you want me to."

He frowned and shook his head.

"Finally, an alphabetical list of drugs, which I suspect is the over-the-counter medicines we can get here on Victoria. That's all. You can search and confirm."

He pulled on his data glasses and typed quickly, probably checking dates and documents to see if what she said matched his records. After a few minutes, he took his glasses off and rubbed his hands through his short hair, his face relaxed. "It was sloppy of me to leave those up."

"I'm observant. That was a big part of my job at Han."

"Your former job. That reminds me, I'm sending Jason to your apartment tomorrow morning to check for bugs."

"No. Give me the transmission detector, and I'll check it myself."

"There's more to it—"

"I don't care. My apartment is off-limits."

"We need to make sure it's off-limits to Erika Brunhoff. If an unremarkable person such as Mr. Adeyemi rates half a dozen bugs, what about you? What about any executive-floor employee?"

She couldn't argue.

Jason would arrive at 8:00 a.m. She hadn't had anyone over in years.

Back at her desk, she had only a moment to collect herself before Claire confronted her.

"Well?" she asked.

"Well what?"

Lucas came out of his office. "Let it be, Claire."

Claire looked from her to Lucas and back again. "She bullshitted you. I told you, I'm not working like this. I did it for five years, and I'm not doing it again. You promised."

"Mia is going to—"

Claire cut him off. "You don't know how it is. You want to spend hours a day coddling her? I don't."

Her cheeks had the same bright red blotches Mia had seen when Claire grew overheated on the rooftop café.

"Sure, it's fun at first. A mystery to solve. How did Mia learn to read Chinese in a week? How can she dictate a whole paper from memory? I assumed new technology from Victoria, but after months and months of it…"

Mia had never seen Claire so agitated.

Lucas tried again. "Mia understands how we work here."

"I won't be called a liar!" Claire burst out.

Several things suddenly made a lot more sense. The way Claire had been treating her since she'd been hired. Her constant low-level irritation when they lived together in college. Mia thought she'd been putting up with Claire—the way she put up with all normal people. The truth was, Claire had figured her out and decided to play along. She hadn't thought Claire capable of such…kindness.

Mia broke the silence. "I'm not calling you a liar."

Claire, clearly about to spout more damning evidence, was caught short.

"I've never been officially tested—so, I don't legally have a photographic memory." Mia picked up her glasses, did a quick search, and sent the results to all present. Jason desperately tried to look as if he were soldering, and failed.

"As you can see, the lawyers have weighed in on this—in court. No one is registry-level who hasn't been tested in an accredited facility. Not after every kid in Argentina turned out to be a genius and eligible for the best schools. Don't use any Registry terms to refer to me, or I will quit. And you need me."

"*We* need *you*? You'd have been caught within the first month of school if it hadn't been for me," Claire snapped. "I got us off the school data network and tweaked the safety cameras. Otherwise, someone would have noticed all you did without glasses."

Mia took a moment to collect herself. A bandage had just been ripped from a wound that desperately needed light and air to heal, but she'd expected that to happen sometime in the future, at a time and place of her choosing.

"You're right. You kept me safe at school, and I'd be homeless if you hadn't taken the time to convince Lucas I wasn't a thief. Thank you."

The red blotches on Claire's cheeks faded to pink. "You're lucky most people are idiots. You're terrible at hiding your ability."

Mia flinched. "I've gotten better since graduation." She had, though taking time to decide how to respond in conversations gave others the impression she was distracted, aloof, or uninterested. None of which won her friends.

"Don't bother with pretending here." Claire slapped the wall next to her desk. "You think we rented this place by accident? These walls are half a meter thick, and nothing goes in or out without my permission. You aren't the only one who doesn't want to be overheard."

"Enough." Lucas said. "We're all clear on this. No more discussion of anyone's memory or registry-level abilities or college habits. You've got work to do. Do it."

Mia's not-legally-perfect memories of what just happened sent her head reeling. She'd been outed to the Summit Security team. Her distress was tempered by facts she couldn't ignore. Lucas was right. It was lucky she'd been fired from Han. If Erika had discovered her talent, she'd have blackmailed Mia into helping her ruin her rivals, and Mia would be trapped.

This wasn't the worst-case scenario. Jason, Claire, and Lucas wouldn't intentionally reveal her secret, but…unintentionally? Even she couldn't keep it one hundred percent of the time—it had just been proved—and she was motivated.

Lucas shut his door, Claire returned to her desk, and Jason plucked and pulled at a holo floating above his work table.

The dark office wasn't the heaven of the upper floors, but it wasn't the hell she'd have been in if she'd made a mistake at Han. She needed time here in purgatory to rethink her strategy. Though the team knew what she could do, for the first time she'd be able to get feedback on her public persona—what worked, what didn't, how to improve. She needed this badly.

The next breath she took felt deeper than any she'd taken in a long time.

Chapter Seven

Mia was hesitant to allow Jason and his big black bag into her apartment. Not only had he overheard the discussion about her memory, but she never had people over. Her not-very-long-term relationships played out in bars, restaurants, and seaside hotels. Home was sanctuary. She was living proof that it was private. She'd done impossible things here without glasses or data screens. If Han had been watching, they'd have snatched her up long ago. She wouldn't change her worldview based on a few bugs in one man's house.

"Nice place." Jason paced the length of the main living area, stopping to examine the ugly sculpture on the coffee table. She smiled. A guy she'd dated briefly in college made it for her. She kept it not for sentimental reasons but because the lumps of clay, the black and gray glaze, the asymmetry, all of it so improbable and unpleasing, made it the only thing in her apartment that caught her eye every day.

"You just move in?" Jason asked.

The room was open and uncluttered, nothing but a couch and table to obscure the view from the floor to ceiling glass windows. People from Earth overdecorated their homes, perhaps in some unconscious effort to recreate the crowding they were used to. Her apartment was modeled on Victoria. Wide-open and spare. Plus, with her memory, she didn't need mementos.

"Nope. I've been here five years. You want something to drink? Coffee, tea, water?" She watched him carefully, but the revelation that she might have a very good memory hadn't changed his normal demeanor.

He set his bag on the floor. "Coffee. Thanks."

They took their mugs out to the balcony. The air was clear and the mountains so near and sharp she could almost touch them. Jason set a small conversation shield on the table between the two lounge chairs and activated it. She worried he might say something about the scene in the office yesterday, but he seemed content to admire the view.

She pointed out Han Tower, reflected in a building across the street. "I used to work there. The big thumb, people call it." It was one of the many puzzling architectural design decisions made by the Six. "My office was there, right where it starts to curve back out."

Jason's glasses darkened as he examined the gleaming tower. "The buildings here look so tall with nothing around them. In New York, everything is so close together we lose the sense of scale. It's nice to have open space."

This might be her chance to learn more about him and the team. She didn't initiate personal conversations in the office. Summit might be shielded from the external world but inside, everything was monitored. She'd had Lucas delete all data from yesterday's drama, and he hadn't protested, but that meant he kept data from other days.

She'd start with something easy. "What made you decide to come to Victoria?"

Jason searched the cloudless sky for too long, seeming to mull over what should have been an easy-to-answer question. "It was a chance to do something different. I've lived in New York for most of my life. We'd all reached…dead ends at our jobs, so when Lucas got the charter to start a firm here, it seemed like a good opportunity."

Mia supposed that Lucas achieving the title of partner was a dead end of sorts, though it was the dead end everyone drove toward at full speed.

"Seemed? How is it actually?"

He flopped down onto a lounge chair—not seeming to mind the cloud of dust ejected from the cushions—and stretched. "Well, much better since we hired you. We were having trouble getting started."

"Yes. I noticed a certain lack of preparation."

"We didn't have time. The contract was approved, and we had to jump on it. Besides, it was impossible to get anything going until we were here in person. You know that."

She shook out the cushion on the lounger next to him, dislodging some of the dirt, and sat.

"How did you like Earth?" Jason asked.

"I didn't while I was there. Poor Claire put up with a lot of bitching from me. Nothing was as good as what we had on Victoria. But when I got back here, there were things I missed."

"Like what?"

She thought back on her college years. "The people. To be honest, at first they frightened me. Everyone seemed like a caricature. So many shapes and sizes and ages. They were so loud and in my space. I didn't get most of the references or jokes. I felt like an outsider. But here…" She gestured to the gleaming buildings surrounding them. "The employment screening process means anyone the Six hires has a lot in common. Nearly everyone on the planet lives in this one city. We all eat at the same restaurants, shop in the same stores, see the same views. We understand each other and communicate well. We're very productive. But there's no variety." She glanced at Jason. "Except for the Summit Security team. You weren't screened, were you?"

"I'm not sure what you mean. We walked through a dozen scanners at the strataport."

"I mean months of interviews. Intelligence tests. Physicals."

He shook his head. "None of that."

He had no idea how hard it usually was to get onto this planet.

"Lucas has friends?" Mia asked. "Partners in Weber? I didn't know it was possible to get here without screening until Claire called. She'd never pass, not with her personality."

Jason ignored her question and stood. "We should get to work. You weren't kidding yesterday about all your apartments supposedly being impervious to bugs?"

"No. It's true. If we told Optima about Dezzie's apartment, they'd be all over that place."

"We aren't going to do that. You understand why?"

"Yes. We aren't allowed to discuss our clients. It's in the contract."

Jason smiled. "I was going to say we need the credits." He drained his cup. "Let's do the scan."

"You won't find anything. I'm sure of it."

"Let's hope not."

Back in the living room, Jason set the conversation shield on the coffee table, then took a harder look at the walls and the ceiling. "What is this?" He ran his hand across the image of a calm blue ocean on the living room wall. A fish darted through the clear water.

"Playa Placida, the view from the new hotel Avenir." Mia's cheeks grew warm as she confessed, "It's free. The image feed I mean. I used to get my views from a camera I leased out in the wastes, but I had to cancel that when I lost my job."

Jason stared at the scene that surrounded him, appalled. "This is live? All your walls and ceilings are interactive screens?"

Mia nodded. "Everything that was built in the last ten years has this."

"What about your comm system? Where is it?"

She waved a hand. "Wherever I am. The apartment brings up a window based on my location." She turned her head to the right. "House, display building front door camera." A meter wide and high box appeared near her in the blue of the ocean, showing the sidewalk in the front of the building.

Jason frowned. She thought, as a hardware nut, he'd be excited by her system. She upgraded it last year when she received a bonus.

"You have these on Earth, too."

"Actually, we don't. Not like this. Not built into every wall and ceiling. Not unless you're a billionaire. People install one wall in the living room or bedroom as their media center." He shook his head. "I wouldn't need a bug to spy on you. I could just tap into the building network."

Mia called up the section of her lease detailing the measures in place to protect her privacy, displaying it large on the wall. Maybe too large; Jason had to walk back and forth to read it. He turned to her with the same incredulous expression Claire often wore. The one that screamed, *are you a complete fucking idiot?*

She smacked her finger against the oversized text. "You know why I believe this?" Though it belied her point, she lowered her voice. "I'm myself at home. If someone was watching, they'd know about me."

"You lucked out. Your apartment can never be secure, not with all the amenities you have built in."

He launched into a deeply technical explanation as to why. Did he expect a switch to flip in her head and she'd announce, "You're right, I've been living in a glass box my whole life with the Six watching my every move"?

Jason gave up trying to convince her. "Where's the access panel?"

She opened the closet by the front door and pushed her hanging clothes to one side to reveal a matte gray door, flush with the wall.

"I assume that's it. I've never opened it."

"You weren't at all curious about a mysterious door in your own apartment?"

"There are mysterious doors everywhere. I don't need to open every one to know what's inside. Wires and pipes."

He sighed, squatted down in the closet and pulled the door open. Inside, a colorful umbilical cord of cables and wires rose from a fat hole in the bottom and disappeared into holes on the left, right, and top.

Jason glanced back at her, brow creased. "I've never seen so much cable in one apartment. This is more than we have at the office."

The panels she'd seen at Han held a couple dozen at most. At least sixty snaked through this box. "Strange. I thought all my appliances were wireless."

He hefted his black bag, and she followed him into the kitchen. He pried the front panel off her oven before she could protest, then wrestled the whole unit out and set it none too gently on the floor.

"Careful! I can't afford to replace that!"

A thin yellow wire trailed from the back.

"Power?" she suggested hopefully.

He scoffed. "No appliance uses wired power anymore. It's for data." He detached it, and the control panel lights stayed on. "What sector are we in? Han?"

"Of course."

"They own the building? This was all here when you rented it?" He gestured around the kitchen.

"Yes, everything but the furniture."

"I'd guess that wire leads straight down to a room in the basement, into a central processor, then straight to headquarters. Han can manipulate every appliance in every unit."

"I'm sure it doesn't go to headquarters." Mia recalled the sales brochure for her building. "But yes, the building can control the appliances—for safety and power balancing. This place is more energy efficient than anything on Earth. Everything goes on standby when I leave and comes back on when I return. If that oven overheats or the sink overflows, the apartment will turn them off for me."

He hoisted the oven back into place and snapped the front panel on. "You don't need a wire for that. No modern oven can overheat. This is about uninterruptable access and control. They can lock you in. Lock you out. Turn off the air. Anything."

"Maybe they can," she said. "Forty years ago, there was nothing on this planet but bugs. We don't have enough historical data to accurately predict anything. Are there flash floods once a century? How long do dust storms last? Is the dust ever toxic? Do the southern tsunamis ever make it this far north? Deadly insects outnumber humans a million to one. Most of them can fly. Imagine a swarm over the city. It might be nice to be able to remotely shut every door and window and prevent people from going outside to their deaths, don't you think?"

"Don't get mad at me. There are good reasons for central control, but there are other things you can do once you've got it. Imagine all the possible uses, not just official ones. I'm not talking about good and bad or right and wrong. If we're going to guarantee our clients' privacy, we need to consider every way it might be taken away and guard against that." He patted the front of the oven. "If this thing can transmit anything but temperature data, I need to know. I'm glad we have your apartment to practice on."

"What do you mean?"

"You want privacy? I'm going to give it to you," he said as he returned to the closet control panel.

The idea that her oven was watching her was preposterous.

Jason made an aha sound. "This isn't so bad. Look. Connectors. I can work with this." The wires he held all had square plastic bits somewhere on their length.

He shut the panel and stood. "Let's check for bugs." He followed the same procedure he had at Dezzie's, and as she expected, found nothing.

"I'll be back tomorrow morning with Claire, and we can figure out where the wires go and what kind of information is flowing."

"No. Absolutely not." Mia did not want to be one of his experiments, one of which would draw the attention of CorSec sooner or later. "Everything's fine here."

"Everything isn't fine. You've been lucky, and you already know you don't stay lucky forever. I'm certain that you are at least occasionally monitored by an AI. Fortunately, one that isn't programmed to flag your behavior as unusual. One day, a Han IT staffer is going to do an update, and the fact that you don't wear glasses will be noted. I can keep that from happening."

Jason didn't avoid eye contact. This time, it was her.

She didn't want to believe anything bad could enter her sanctuary, but the umbilical cord of wires might be nourishing a creature that would harm her. She needed this place to be safe, to be hers.

"You're right. Do whatever you need to do."

"One more thing. Claire mentioned your mom lives in town. Should we—"

"Absolutely not. She's retired and has no access to proprietary data. I never talk to her about work."

"Okay then." Jason said, raising an eyebrow. "We'll leave her alone. Want to catch a pod to the office?"

"Sure."

She locked the apartment, feeling for the first time it might be a futile gesture.

Jason and Claire spent the next week working ten to twelve hours a day at her apartment. They didn't find any bugs, but her appliances and walls were still suspect. When she got home from work, she'd find screens, wires, and boxes with blinking lights strewn about her living room floor and inevitably, something important wasn't working. One night, none of her lights would turn on. On another occasion, she discovered her fridge was off and her food spoiled. Without her live view of Playa Placida, the walls were nothing but ugly gray slabs. Jason disabled all audio input, forcing her to communicate with her house via text. He crippled the IR and motion sensors, so she had to get within fifteen centimeters of a wall for it to know she was there.

At last they finished.

"Everything back to normal at my place?" she asked when Claire returned to the office.

"Better than normal."

"What exactly did you do?"

"We're routing everything through here. We'll spend the next few weeks analyzing the traffic, learning what it looks like when you tell your house to close the blinds or turn on the air conditioning. We'll watch what the house does on its own and find out what triggers those actions. We'll use all that to build a predictive model. For instance, at sunrise, external building sensors send your windows a message and they darken forty percent. If something tries to talk to your windows at midnight, that's wrong. We won't let that command through."

It sounded fairly innocuous until she thought harder. "You and Jason will know every time I have a cup of coffee or take a shower." In her head, she said shit, not shower.

"Yes."

She grimaced. It was more disconcerting to have one person she knew monitor her than all the faceless technicians of Han.

"Don't worry. This is how your life looks to me." Claire brought up a screen filled with dozens of graphs, lines fluctuating, bars shrinking and growing. "You're a test case. That's it. In the future I'll never even see this. I'll only be alerted if there is unusual activity."

Why did getting more privacy feel like having less?

Chapter Eight

Claire and Jason learned all about interactive walls and appliances from the data they collected from Mia's apartment. She put up with annoying queries from Claire for weeks.

What did you just do? would appear in text across every wall and ceiling.

Mia would type back, *I turned on the mist system*, or, *got a glass of water*. This enabled them to learn what a normal conversation between her and the appliances and walls looked like.

Jason's theory of a mysterious central control unit turned out to be correct. The appliances received a signal every five minutes—via the yellow wire—telling them they were okay and should continue to work. If they didn't get that signal, they wouldn't function.

Jason installed his own control panel—which took up way too much of her closet—and routed the apartment's entire bundle of wires through it. First and foremost, his panel sent its own "okay" message so that nothing could be turned off remotely by anyone but her. Claire used the models they created to automatically grab unusual queries from the outside world and to respond with innocuous information. Thus, if her walls got a request to transmit visual data from her bedroom as she slept, beautifully flawed pixels the right size and shape would be returned instead of an image of her snoring.

The great thing about the box was that it didn't require everything to go through the Summit Security office. Mia finally had privacy for, if Jason was to be believed, the first time in her life. So far, no one had tried to spy on her. She checked in with Claire each day and was relieved to find everything was normal. Jason engineered a more compact version, and the Appliance Data Manager, ADM—their name for the control box—became the key component in the basic package Summit offered to clients.

Mia would be offering it to Anna Lee and Alex Newburg today. Anna worked with Dezzie, and Mia booked the initial meeting herself—no help needed from Lucas.

When she got to work, she expected to see Jason professionally dressed, but he was at the table in his usual, grubby, half-mechanic, half-college student outfit. An hour before they planned to leave for the meeting, she asked him to change.

"Change?" He seemed to have honestly forgotten that the meeting she'd been obsessing over was today. "Ah, right." He brushed at his pants. "I don't have better clothes. I worked in a basement at Itek. I never saw clients."

She hated to tap into the firm's credits, but he couldn't go out like this. "We're going shopping. Right now. Consider it a uniform."

He didn't argue.

She took him to a mid-priced men's store and forced him to try on a stylish vest, button-down shirt, and pants. He transformed from gawky to pleasingly slender, and from student to junior executive. The clerk, a handsome man in his early twenties, fawned over Jason. Though the laser needed no help to take Jason's measurements, the clerk found reasons to touch Jason's shoulder, straighten the vest, and brush non-existent lint from the back of the pants.

Mia watched, curious, expecting Jason to react like a taciturn child being forced to dress for a fancy party, but he didn't. He obeyed instructions to turn and raise his arms, all the while casting furtive glances at the clerk, who grew increasingly flirtatious.

It didn't take her long to realize what was going on. It was easy to meet people in New Canberra, but you had to leave the office, and she wasn't sure Jason ever did.

She moved away, ostensibly to look at the unisex t-shirts, but really to give them some space. The clerk asked Jason where he was from, and when Jason said New York, the clerk began an excited monologue. He was from Reno and had recently graduated from the Fashion Institute in Las Vegas. He'd never been to New York but was eager to visit as soon as his contract was up.

The bell rang on the alteration machine, and Jason's new clothes slid out, but he and the clerk kept talking. She saw an ease in Jason she never saw at the office—a loosening of the always straight posture, and fluid hand gestures illustrating a story that had nothing to do with repairing weapons. She checked the time on her glasses.

"We need to get going."

The clerk took the neatly folded garments from the metal tray and slid a card into the vest pocket. Not, she noted, one of the official, bright yellow store cards displayed on the counter.

"If there's any problem with the fit, these can be retailored. Be sure to come when I'm here, though. The other staff isn't very good at scanner calibration."

"He won't need these altered. They have to fit. He's going to wear them right now," Mia said.

The clerk glared at her. She hastened to reassure him, once Jason disappeared into the dressing room to change. "He'll be back. He just arrived and needs more clothes. You saw what he was wearing? His whole wardrobe looks like that."

The clerk smiled and leaned close. "Tell him I'll give him my discount."

She promised she would.

Once in the pod, Jason focused on a screen displaying basic facts about the clients.

"Are you going to call him?" she asked.

Jason scowled.

"Too young, maybe? I try not to go out with anyone under thirty, but mistakes have been made..." She trailed off as Jason flushed red and turned away.

What was wrong? If she'd misread the situation, he could simply tell her he didn't date men. No one in New Canberra was shy about their sexual preferences, or the fact they might shift depending on the situation. Though they'd spent a fair amount of time together at work, she actually knew very little about Jason, and nothing about what he did at night and on weekends. Was he in a monogamous relationship and annoyed she'd seen him flirting?

They were, she hoped, good enough friends now that she could be direct. "I offended you somehow, didn't I? I'm sorry. Your personal life is none of my business."

Jason drew in a deep breath, held it, let it out, and faced her.

"Not your fault. I assume you don't follow New York City politics."

"I don't. Earth has a lot of cities, and things don't make headlines here unless it's something huge."

"The economy isn't great in the city, and we've had a series of conservative mayors who've directed the collective angst toward minority groups. It's not a great time to be Hispanic and gay."

"It's not like that here."

"I know," he said sharply. "But it's going to take me more than a few months to get used to it." He took another deep breath. "Again, not your fault. I'm…" He smiled. "We're all complicated, aren't we? Maybe Summit isn't such a bad fit for you after all."

Mia returned the smile. "It's not a bad fit. You just can't afford me."

"You and me both."

Something in Jason relaxed. Not the same level of relaxation he'd had with the clerk, but it was something. No more time to bond, though. They were nearly at the apartment.

"Please," Mia said, "Don't tell the clients everything in their apartment is linked back to some central control unit. We don't know if all buildings do this. I don't want people quoting us. We could get in legal trouble."

"I won't say anything."

"This meeting has to go well, or we don't get paid."

"I understand and support getting paid."

It did go well, if finding a hidden holo camera was a good thing. The couple gave each other a knowing look, signed a six-month contract, and Jason got a new toy.

He grinned while examining the camera as they rolled back to the office in the pod. "Scanning these apartments might not be such a bad job. I can keep all the illegal tech I find." He twirled the camera between his fingers. "Anything I can't use, I'll disassemble for parts."

"I don't like this."

"What?" he asked. "Taking the tech?"

"No, not telling Optima what's going on. They're supposed to take care of things like this. The Six agreed on privacy in the home, so if it is being breached, it matters to all of them. What if an Earth company is behind this?"

Jason shrugged. "What if it's Newburg's ex-wife? What if it's the perverted building manager? What if Han's trying to track down a hardware thief? What if your Six scatter these around like confetti?" He tossed the camera in the air and caught it. "It doesn't matter. Our job is to secure the apartment. We can do that."

"It does matter. This isn't Earth. If someone has found a way to broadcast data from our apartments, Optima needs to know so they can fix it."

Jason grinned. "You're going to show me your apartment lease again, aren't you?"

She'd just put on her glasses and begun to gesture.

He hefted the bag onto his lap. "I'm not mocking you. I know things are different here. Let me drop off this equipment, and you can tell me more about it at The End."

The team frequented a crummy bar down the street called "The End of the Universe." Though it wasn't her kind of place, it bothered her that after two months at the company, no one had invited her to join them.

She waited outside while Jason disappeared into the office and emerged a minute later with Claire in tow. Claire groaned and shielded her eyes against the setting sun, despite the fact her glasses had already compensated for the brightness.

"It's still light."

Jason blocked her when she tried to go back inside. "Walk in my shadow. You need a break. You've been working too much."

Claire grumbled her way down the block, indeed staying in Jason's shadow. The pavement radiated heat, and the thick Earth fabrics she refused to abandon doubtless functioned as a greenhouse.

If there were an award for the ugliest structure in the Weber section, The End of the Universe would be in close competition with Summit's office for first place. The lonely, windowless structure squatted on a large undeveloped lot, sheet metal exterior coated in tan dust. The building looked more like a hazardous materials storage shed than a place to recreate.

Aggressive, retro rock music assaulted Mia as soon as the outer door slid open. She stepped into the darkness and waited for her eyes to adjust. A battered metal bar hugged the length of the left wall, a surprisingly eclectic and upscale selection of bottled alcohol on industrial shelving behind it. To the right, fake porthole windows displayed intentionally bad holos of twentieth century space views. Booths lined the back wall, and the battered tables and chairs scattered through the rest of the space were affixed to the floor as if on a low-grav ship. The clientele, mostly male, wore drab gray jumpsuits or inexpensive button-down shirts and pants and probably worked in low-level jobs in the nearby industrial buildings.

The original décor was probably meant to evoke an old freighter. The current owners didn't seem to have the stamina to maintain a consistent space theme. Figurines of porn stars and dusty shot glasses from Earth's national parks shared shelf space with the bottles. Faded, lighted signs advertising beers she'd never heard of blinked on and off.

She'd been to bars in the E districts that tried for a look of artful decay—placing fake broken windows in between sandstorm-proof glass, installing wallpaper in vintage patterns, then fading and distressing it, commissioning carefully wrecked furniture that would never actually collapse, and serving drinks in chipped, mismatched glasses.

The End sat in silent mockery of those set pieces. She'd forgotten that genuine decay was ugly, unsanitary, and uncomfortable.

The bartender, as tired and unkempt as the rest of the place, nodded at Jason and Claire and narrowed his eyes at Mia. The expensive ZBG suit she'd worn for the client meeting screamed she didn't belong there.

Claire pointed out subtle cameras in each corner of the room. "Those are ours. We did a complete overhaul of the security system. The bar gets free protection, and we get a safe place to hang out." She ran her hand down a thick, dark gray frame lining the inside of the front door.

"Weapons detector," she said, as if Mia had asked. "The booths are data shielded, and we've got conversation shields hidden in the light fixtures."

Jason led them through mismatched furniture. Mikey and Lucas slouched in a booth on the far left, an impressive collection of empty glasses between them. Lucas smoked what looked and smelled like an Earth cigarette. Tobacco was illegal on Victoria, but no alarms sounded. He nodded in their direction, but didn't invite them to join him and Mikey.

Jason slid into a high-backed booth on the right—the furthest from the other two men. Mia joined him, the cracked, fake red leather of the seat scratching the back of her legs as she made room for Claire. The table, thankfully, had a built-in menu. Mia wouldn't want to try to chitchat with that bartender. Jason ordered a beer, she, bourbon on the rocks, and Claire, her usual stim soda.

One night in college, Mia made it her mission to get Claire drunk. After six months of living together, she'd grown tired of Claire's jittery, precise energy. She wanted Claire to relax, get sloppy, stop fact-checking and meet some people in the flesh. Claire spent weekends pacing the living room, immersed in intense multiplayer games with an invisible group of friends, glasses on, fingers twitching. If Mia tried to talk to her, she'd get a one-word answer at best, more often a dismissive shake of the head. Did a fun, social Claire lurk beneath the surface, and would a strong drink free her?

No. When Mia finally managed to get Claire into a bar and infused with alcohol, the results were horrifying. Claire was a mean drunk. After a few cocktails, she slurred loud comments about the people around them—mostly related to their assumed majors. Asking her to quiet down amped the whispers to loud mutterings. *She's obviously in marketing. Maybe sociology. Look at her glasses. Useless.*

Claire's gesticulations had knocked Mia's nearly full drink out of her hand, splattering the woman next to them with a double bourbon and soda. Mia apologized profusely and tried to pull Claire out of the crowded space, but Claire could barely stand—and couldn't stand to be touched. It took two bouncers to get her onto the street and once there, she vomited profusely in front of the Sparrow on a Stick stand. The vendor, a wizened man of indeterminate age, berated her in Cantonese as she stood unsteadily and tried to push clotted hair from her face.

Mia abandoned any further attempts to socialize Claire and left her to the invisible gamer friends. She forgave herself for assuming Claire never noticed her extraordinary memory. Mia was nothing more than furniture to Claire back then, and badly behaved furniture at that. She'd worried Claire was obsessive compulsive because she kept the apartment so tidy, but eventually figured out Claire's glasses were set to one hundred percent opaque. She lived in worlds of data and fantasy and relied on muscle memory to move through their tiny, shared space. Mia learned to dance around her like an automated luggage cart at a busy strataport.

Though she wasn't much friendlier and her fashion sense hadn't improved, Claire seemed better now. Her current career had been good for her, tying her beloved data to real life objects.

The bartender brought the drinks, setting them down without a word. Mia used her napkin and the condensation from her glass to scrub away the sticky rings on the table in front of her.

"We can speak freely here?" Mia asked Jason after the bartender shuffled away.

"Yes. It isn't as secure as the office but it's close." He hunched over and examined the underside of the table. "Yep, conversation shield is on and working."

"Great." Mia took a small screen from her bag and began searching for information on how the privacy in New Canberra's apartments worked, technically. She was tired of her coworkers acting like she was crazy to believe true privacy was possible.

"Hey," Jason said when he saw what she was doing, "can we talk about that at work tomorrow? I need a break." He held up his beer in a salute and took a deep drink.

"Sure." She put her screen away, pleased that this had been a purely social invitation, especially given she'd strayed into touchy territory with him earlier.

"What was it like growing up here?" he asked.

Claire sighed heavily and shoved in her ear buds as if she'd heard this story a thousand times, but she hadn't. She'd never asked about Victoria, only given opinions.

Mia took a big sip of the bourbon. She'd worked with many new arrivals and either they didn't know she was a native or didn't care, seeing Victoria as nothing more than a tan smudge from a pod window as they rolled from work to club to home. As a result, she didn't have a polished story ready to recite. "You know the history of Victoria?" she asked.

He made a wishy-washy gesture with one hand. "In general. The Six discovered the world, colonized it, and started selling us fish."

She laughed. "That pretty much sums it up. My parents were engineers, part of the second wave, arriving right after the initial crews got habs set up and the desalination plants running. I was one of the first children born here. While my parents were busy building the city, I had all the undeveloped lots as a playground. When I wasn't in school, I ran wild."

"Wasn't it dangerous?" Jason asked.

"In retrospect, yes, but probably less dangerous than running around an Earth city."

"Good point. You had deadly insects. I had Eddie and Todd Antonelli and a park with more junkies than trees."

"We didn't have junkies or trees. We did have a few Eddie and Todd's but the MMARVs kept them in check, and I usually played on my own, anyway."

Her handful of truly happy memories were like gems, and she welcomed the opportunity to show them off. "My next-door neighbor was a visiting scientist at the university annex. I helped him collect bugs for his research." She smiled, even now amazed that he'd managed to make her feel like an adult, a coworker. "I wouldn't have understood what it meant to be on a newly-colonized planet if it wasn't for him. To me, all this was normal, but he taught me to be excited and curious."

Jason drained a quarter of his beer and echoed her grin. "I'd have loved to grow up here. No one to bother me."

"I found insects that no one had seen before. Some of my samples are in the Natural History Museum." As a social engineer, she'd done projects that saved Han millions of credits, but nothing compared to the pride she felt knowing she'd brought in the only sample of the glass wing spinner beetle.

She was going to tell him more about the beetle, but stopped, suddenly embarrassed. Guys she'd slept with knew less about her than what she'd just shared with him. Jason didn't seem to notice her discomfort. He held his beer mug up to the light, trying to decipher the faded printing. She saw mountains and a waterfall, but the text was nothing but curves and lines.

"You have a natural history museum? I'll have to visit. New York's natural history ended a couple hundred years ago."

Claire pulled out her ear buds. "You said you found a holo cam. Do you have it?"

Jason nodded and took it from his pocket. Mia relaxed as they began to argue about its likely origin. The focus was off her and her history. They'd stayed on firm ground, but if the conversation had gone on much longer, Jason might have asked questions she didn't want to answer.

She leaned to the left until a thin slice of Lucas and Mikey came into view. She'd never seen Lucas at play. In the darkness of the bar, gesturing and animated, he almost looked like the handsome man in the holo. He caught her eye and frowned. She leaned back, picked up her drink and finished it, thumbing the table for another as soon as she set it down.

Jason tapped her arm. "We're boring you. We can talk about other things."

"Don't worry about it. I'm happy to be out. I haven't gotten many invitations lately. My former coworkers…"

"Won't contact you because of the code," Claire said, matter-of-factly.

"Right," Mia agreed, then had a thought. "Speaking of coworkers, did you all work as a team at Itek? Given your titles and jobs, it wouldn't have made much sense."

Jason shook his head. "Not like this. Lucas was the partner in charge of all of North America, meaning he was technically my boss and Claire's, but he didn't manage either of us. Mikey was his private security detail."

"How did he pick you to come with him to start Summit?" *How did he even know your names?* Jason would have been so far below Lucas on the org chart it would have taken magnification to even trace the line.

"I worked with Lucas at NYCPD," Jason said.

Mia took a moment to process the acronym. "You and Lucas were police officers?"

"No, Lucas was a detective, and I was a tech."

"Is that a normal career path? I thought the public sector—"

She caught herself before the faux pas. She'd heard that government employees had little more status than people receiving food and housing vouchers.

"Itek hires good talent from anywhere. Not that I was good talent, but Lucas was recruited and brought me with him. Our first posting was in Venezuela. Mikey was already there. The three of us worked together for a couple years."

He seemed to be viewing a memory now, not the ancient pint glass he encircled with his hands.

"Once we were back at Headquarters and Lucas got promoted, we rarely interacted. I definitely never saw him socially. He ran with a different crowd."

Claire chimed in. "I worked with Lucas on investigations he didn't want going through official channels. He trusted me."

"Did you like your job?" Mia asked her.

Claire nodded. "Very much. We had a big budget. You should have seen my office. I had a full holo data…" Her eyes narrowed. "Why do you ask?"

The bartender set Mia's new drink on the table with a clunk.

"Thanks," she said reflexively, but he was already on his way back to the bar.

This glass was in better shape than her first. Would her third order arrive in cut crystal? She took a sip, the bourbon floating her toward honesty.

"I don't know what you are all doing on Victoria or how you got a permit. No offense, but this isn't the team anyone would pick to start a business, and none of you but Mikey seems excited to be here. And Lucas…" She shook her head. "Partners don't leave unless it's for a better opportunity. Certainly not for this." She gestured to the shabby surroundings.

Claire's brow creased beneath her glasses. Jason held up a warning finger.

"Claire, relax. Mia isn't stupid. It's obvious we don't belong here, and every day you make some crack about 'this ridiculous shopping mall of a planet' and how pretty much everything is better on Earth." He turned to Mia. "We all signed a mountain of confidentiality agreements so I can't say much, but the short and sweet is that we pissed off a whole bunch of Itek executives in the course of doing our jobs, and it was suggested we'd best find employment somewhere far from Itek HQ. This is about as far as we could get."

"Jason," Claire hissed. "We can't talk about this."

"You were all fired?" Mia asked. "That doesn't make any sense. You didn't even work together."

"Not fired exactly—"

"Shut up!" Claire sounded more frightened than angry.

Jason banged down his pint. "I won't shut up. This isn't fair to Mia, or us. She thinks we're idiots, and I'm tired of lying to her. We weren't prepared for this move, or for starting this business, but trust me, we're here now and committed and we need Summit to succeed."

No one spoke, but the would-be silence filled by the wail of an electric guitar and pounding drums.

Mia stripped off old facts and pasted on the new, and the collage that was Summit Security became a lot less surreal. Lucas was in charge of policing intracompany crime. The opportunities to piss off partners while in that role were as numerous as the grains of sand in an empty lot. She'd seen the popular Earth holos—she knew what kind of trouble powerful people there got into.

Jason watched warily, waiting for Mia's reaction.

She smiled, only now realizing how hard she'd been working to ignore the reality of what was in front of her.

"Thanks for letting me know. This all makes so much more sense. Don't worry, I won't pry."

"You aren't mad?" Jason asked.

"No. I'm in the same situation. I can't defend myself from Erika's bullshit because of everything I signed."

Jason grinned and ordered another pint. "I didn't want to come here, but now that I'm getting acclimated, I'm beginning to like it. There's so much space. I can swing my arms without hitting anyone. And it's quiet. When I stand outside the building at noon it's like I'm wearing earplugs. I didn't realize how much the din of New York was stressing me."

"I'm surprised you didn't go to Novus instead. It would suit you better, and you wouldn't have had to pull any strings."

Novus, a good deal further from the sun than Victoria, had temperatures below zero in most latitudes, was barely populated, and an Earth protectorate. After the Six made it to Victoria and began efforts to set up a human colony, they didn't have the time, budget, or inclination to deal with the other planets in the solar system. The Associated Governments of Earth, in a fight against irrelevance, sent a slow ship to Novus and claimed it. Any citizen of Earth could homestead five acres and own them outright after a year. No corporations allowed. So far, upward of four thousand people had taken the offer.

"We need to make credits. No one lives on Novus but retirees and anarchists, and none of them need our services." Jason slid his hands back and forth like he was loading an old-fashioned shotgun. "Weapons are legal there."

"There's a ski resort in the north catering to partners, and they'd be happy to have more security. Plus, it's so beautiful," Mia countered.

"You've been?" Jason asked.

"Not yet. I hope to visit someday. It has everything we don't—volcanoes, rivers, waterfalls, geysers. I was obsessed with it when I was a kid. Dad promised to take me after I graduated from high school."

The last fact slipped loose thanks to lubrication from the second drink, and she cursed her sloppiness.

Jason waited for her to continue. When she didn't, Claire spoke up. "He died. She doesn't want to talk about it."

"Oh. Sorry."

"It's okay," Mia said. "It was a long time ago, but not so long for me." She slipped a hand into her purse, felt for a Baby Jane, and took it surreptitiously with her next sip of bourbon.

"Novus does look amazing," Jason said, "but we need to make credits, and we wouldn't have been as safe there."

"Safe?" Mia asked.

It was Jason's turn to look uncomfortable. "I meant secure. We wouldn't have been able to get the equipment we needed."

"True. There're no gadget stores in Crater City. Hardly any stores at all, according to what I last read."

"I think I'd like it there," Claire said, "if people like gaming and staying indoors."

Mia wasn't sure if the offhand comment broke the tension or her Baby Jane was kicking in.

"I bet they like both. Maybe we can do a teambuilding exercise there after the credits start pouring in," Mia said.

"I don't want to get on another spaceship unless it's back to Earth," Claire said.

"Hey, Mia," Jason said, "Don't mention what I told you to anyone. Stick with the official story. We're eager entrepreneurs, here to squeeze credits from Victoria." He glanced over his shoulder. "That includes Lucas and Mikey, okay? I don't want to get in a debate with them about what I legally can and can't disclose."

"Of course."

Mia ordered another drink and Claire, who'd managed to break into the camera while they'd been talking, shared the data with Jason.

Once attention shifted away from her, Mia leaned back into the red plastic and let out a deep breath. It was no secret her dad had died when she was young, but it stung every time it came up. For once she was grateful for Claire's bluntness in shutting down the conversation.

Jason and Claire argued but neither displayed any of their characteristic social awkwardness, Claire even going so far as to put her glasses on clear when Jason began sketching a diagram on the table.

Maybe this will work out. They had something in common—all of them professionals, derailed from dream careers and forced to start over. It had been a long time since she worked as part of a real team, and though she professed to love working alone, something about this felt right.

Chapter Nine

Mia's foot slipped, and she nearly fell from the climbing wall. Secured by ropes and a harness, she couldn't really fall—but the jolt of primal fear sent her heart pounding. She hung for a moment, arms straining until her foot found a wide shelf, allowing her to relax.

Mikey had offered her a discounted membership at the upscale gym in Weber sector where he taught mixed martial arts. He'd done this with no winks, no pelvic thrusts, no thigh rubbing. An offer of a truce or an apology? Mia would have taken it even with a wink. She missed Han's gym almost as much as she missed her job. Working out cleared her mind.

The gym, brand new, was practically a resort, with indoor and outdoor pools, a reconfigurable climbing wall, weight rooms, immersive mountain bikes, classes in dance, yoga, and martial arts, onsite massage therapists, wet and dry steam rooms, eight-jet showers, Japanese soaking tubs, and a rooftop cafe. Mia wanted to live there, and more or less had for the last month, given the dismal state of her social life.

Tonight, fatigued from the difficult climb and dizzy from too long in the sauna, she was on her way to shower when she caught sight of Lucas and Mikey sparring in one of the martial arts practice rooms. The window running the length of it resembled a huge screen stuck on a fighting channel. She paused, captivated by their disparate physiques. Mikey, a chemically enhanced muscle man, Lucas, an engraving from a nineteenth century anatomy textbook. She tried not to worry about his weight loss. He hid it well at work, covering himself in loose, long-sleeved shirts, padded vests, and crisp tailored pants. With that outfit and a pair of large glasses he could pass for fashionably gaunt, but at the gym he was exposed. She drifted to a stop, screened by a potted palm, and watched from between the fronds.

Lucas was fast, but whatever was wrong left him with little stamina. He and Mikey would exchange a flurry of punches and kicks, then Lucas would step away, panting. Mikey was clearly holding back. She'd seen him enthusiastically wallop defenseless beginning students during his Monday night class. With Lucas he had a wariness that was less about self-defense and more about preserving Lucas's body and dignity—a tricky balancing act. She guessed that, in the past, they'd been evenly matched.

Lucas paced, damp shirt clinging to his gaunt frame, ribcage clearly visible. Abruptly he stumbled, fell to his knees, then to the ground, rolling to his side, face strained, teeth clenched.

Mia dashed through the door, concerned. "What happened?"

Mikey was at Lucas's side in a heartbeat. No one walking by the big window paid attention. It wasn't unusual for someone to be on the ground—even unconscious—in the martial arts room.

Mikey pressed two fingers to Lucas's neck. "He'll be fine. I hit too hard."

"You didn't hit him. You weren't anywhere near him."

Mikey kept his hand on Lucas's shuddering shoulder. The vacant and vaguely lecherous gaze she'd come to expect from him was absent.

"I need his bag," he growled. "Get it."

Mia ran to the side of the room and grabbed the gym bag from atop a spectator bench. Mikey sorted through the contents purposefully. He knew what was happening.

"Is he epileptic?"

She'd never seen anyone have a seizure, but it was all she could come up with to explain the collapse and Mikey's practiced response.

"We should call the medic," she urged. The gym had an onsite clinic.

Mikey shook his head. She couldn't tell if it was in response to her proposal or in frustration. He dumped the contents of the bag onto the floor.

"Get out of here." He searched through the pockets of Lucas's work clothes. When she didn't move, he grabbed her wrist, hard. "You hear me?"

She tried to pull away, but he held tight.

"Yes, I hear you! Let go!" The buffoonish muscleman had been replaced by a stranger—someone smart and dangerous.

He released her and pointed to the door. "Now. And don't mention this to anyone. I'll find out if you do."

She hurried out of the room, rubbing her sore wrist, then lingered on the far side of the wide corridor, watching them. Mikey found what he was looking for—a hypo. He ripped it open and pressed it to Lucas's bare arm. Half a minute later, Lucas's shuddering subsided, and he loosened from a tight ball to a limp circle. Mikey rolled him onto his back and pillowed his head with a sweatshirt. The gray cast gradually left Lucas's face, his eyes fluttered open, and Mikey helped him to a sitting position.

What would cause him to collapse like that? She'd seen people pass out from drinking or drugs, faint from heat or sunstroke, but this was different. Lucas seemed fine the moment before.

She lingered in the corridor until Lucas stood, drank most of a bottle of water, and began to pack up his gear.

As soon as she was home, she curled up on the couch, screen in hand, ready to do a search. With this new data point she might be able to figure out what was wrong with Lucas.

No. She set the screen down. *I should let it be.*

Throughout her career she'd been plagued by too much information, not too little, and was tired of lying about what and how much she knew. Images that flashed before other's eyes were still frames in hers. She knew passwords, confidential text quickly deleted from screens, return addresses on packages, and a thousand other details she had to remember to forget, especially when the data points formed a stippled portrait different than the ones people sported on their ID badges.

The day would come, soon she expected, when a client asked her what was wrong with Lucas, and she wanted to be able to look them in the eye and say she had no idea.

Chapter Ten

"Dezzie!"

Mia greeted Summit's first client enthusiastically. He'd been nothing but trouble since he signed on, blaming Summit for slow feed speeds, overloading Mia's mailbox with dozens of messages that were "proof" someone was still listening in, and demanding Jason come out and tune the transmission jammer nearly every week.

He was also recommending Summit to anyone in the mining division who stood still for more than five minutes, as far as Mia could tell. All potential clients who called mentioned him. Security was a game he'd won, and he was eager to share the news.

"How can I help you? You want Jason to stop by?"

"No, everything's good. Do you do security for meetings? I'm having lunch with someone at Antonio's. I'd rather not talk in public, but I don't want to be alone with this guy…"

A common problem. With no truly private places but the home—she held her finger up to silence Jason in her head—and all land owned by one of the Six corporations, finding a place to bitch about your boss or discuss an idea or breakup was tough. Of course, everyone still did it, assuming the AIs parsing text out of the babble of a bar weren't going to flag every drunk who complained that Emile was an asshole. However, you also had to assume it *might* end up in your record. A small conference center able to handle confidential discussions was under construction in

Center Park—Optima property, and thus technically owned by all—but that wouldn't be open for months.

"Yes. We have several varieties, both clandestine and overt, and if you're worried about physical security, we can work with the restaurant as well."

He shook his head vehemently. "No, no one can know. Not the restaurant or other patrons, and especially not the person I'm meeting."

"Of course. Here's a list of options and prices. I'll give you a ten percent discount as a referral bonus."

She sent the info to him.

"Um, I'll take the data protection pack. We need to hurry. The meeting is in a few hours."

Lucas wouldn't like it, but Summit's calendar was completely empty today. They might have to scramble. So be it.

"What time's the meeting?" Mia asked.

"Noon, at Antonio's in Andaman sector. You know that restaurant?"

"Yes." She and her coworkers used to go there when they wanted out of Han sector. "I'll discuss logistics with the team and get back to you in a few minutes."

"Thanks, Mia."

She disconnected and grinned. These credits put them in the black for the month. Finally. She typed a quick summary of the job and sent it to Lucas.

He emerged from his office moments later, brandishing a screen as if it were a stunner. "We can't do it. There isn't time to prepare."

"The contract is signed and credits are in our account. We need them. If there are any restrictions on the services we offer to clients, put it in writing. Otherwise, I'll say yes to everything."

"Show me the contract."

She slid it to his screen.

He took off his glasses. His face was bones and sinew, blue eyes sunken. She must have flinched or gasped because his mouth twitched up at the corner.

"Tell Adeyemi to meet us at The End in half an hour. Claire, get into Antonio's reservation system and make three reservations. One for Mia and me at 11 a.m., another for noon, and one for Mr. Adeyemi at noon that will result in him being seated at our recently vacated table." He stalked off.

Claire grinned. "I haven't tried to break into any restaurants here yet. If they're anything like places on Earth, this shouldn't be too hard." Her lazily drifting hands flew into motion.

"Shouldn't you take Jason or Mikey instead of me?" Mia asked. "I'm not qualified for this job."

"You're the expert on what's normal here. I'll need you to keep an eye on things and tell me if anything unusual is going on."

"Indigo," Claire said a few seconds later, triumphant.

"What?" Mia asked.

"An artificially not-very-intelligent restaurant seating system. This won't be a problem."

"Won't it be strange when we switch tables?"

"People are strange. I doubt they'll think much about it," Claire said.

Fifteen minutes later Lucas loomed over her desk, his casual fiber vest replaced by one of burgundy silk. The strap of the heavy black bag he toted wrinkled the fabric. "Let's go."

"What should I bring?" she asked.

"Your eyes and your glasses."

Lucas called a pod to take them to The End. Odd, given it was only a block away, but the bag seemed a burden to him, dragging down his right shoulder.

Dezzie was already there when they arrived, seated in one of the back booths as she'd instructed. He looked anxious, more anxious than he had when they found a bug in his apartment.

"Tell me what you need today," Lucas asked.

"I don't want to be recorded," Dezzie said. "And I don't want him to be able to get into my PDS," he brandished a battered, low-end model, "or follow me when I leave."

Though everyone hired by the Six was screened for mental and physical health, something strange happened when the best of the best ended up in the same city. They grew competitive. Even the most mild-mannered math prodigy was stunned to find she or he was not the highest common denominator.

The Six didn't mind. Mia suspected they encouraged it.

Dezzie was probably embroiled in an elaborate multiplayer AR game, and the first to utilize Summit as a secret weapon.

Lucas outfitted him with a PDS shield, a decoy PDS, and a conversation shield.

As Mia watched, she detected in Dezzie not the excitement of someone about to score one hundred extra points on a game, but the twitchy unease of someone who'd walked by a conference room and heard something not intended for his ears. Something worth credits. He kept glancing at the front door, scrolling through his glasses, and shifting from left to right on the worn plastic booth bench seat.

"One more thing," Lucas said. "I've set up a direct channel from my glasses to yours. The text will appear in light green letters in the lower left. Do you see?"

Lucas typed. Dezzie nodded.

"If I tell you to do something, do it. Don't ask why, don't think, just do it, quickly."

"What would you ask me to do?" Dezzie asked.

"Stand up, sit down, call the waiter, leave the restaurant. I have no idea, but I expect you to obey."

"I will," he said.

"Also, don't acknowledge us. We've never met." Lucas stood. "Mia and I are going to the restaurant now. You should arrive a few minutes before noon. Wait here until then."

Lucas was out the door before she'd picked up her purse.

Lucas and Mia sat across from each other in a four-person pod. She'd called a large one to give them extra breathing room.

"What's the plan?" she asked.

"I'll do a baseline scan of the restaurant, check out their security, and prepare the table for Adeyemi. Have you been to Antonio's before?"

"Many times." She worried she might see her old friends, but they had short attention spans and would be likely be frequenting another place by now.

"Good. Let me know if you see anything strange. Anything that doesn't belong. Staff or clientele behaving oddly."

They merged onto busy Ring 3 and slowed to match the speed of the other pods.

"I'm not sure what to point out. There are new things in this city every day, and not all of them make a lot of sense." She pointed to a bench in the park-like center median. "That's strange. There's no way to get to it, and if you did, you'd get sunstroke sitting out there."

Lucas pinched the bridge of his nose. He was either annoyed or having another migraine.

"Use your brain and common sense and think in terms of our client's safety and privacy. Take stunners as an example. You've seen Jason, Mikey, and me carrying them. What do I have in my vest pocket now?" He leaned back. The heavy silk pulled tight against the familiar shape of an SSR stunner.

"You always carry that."

He nodded. "You should be able to recognize this shape in anyone's pocket."

"In someone else's, it could be anything."

"Don't deny evidence from your own eyes because you believe no one carries illegal weapons. All businessmen wear these vests. A stunner in the inner pocket will look like this. The cloth will fall like this, the shape even more pronounced on someone heavier. I don't expect you to tell me definitively what's in a pocket, I want you to tell me what's *likely*. I can't be everywhere at once, and I can't watch everyone."

Lucas assumed she was consciously avoiding facts that didn't align with her worldview, when actually, he'd hit on one of the flaws of her memory. She could list a hundred objects—alone or paired—that would look exactly like a stunner in a pocket. More importantly, she could see them. The infinity of images she carried were like the contents of an overstuffed closet. She had to open the door carefully or the whole mess would cascade over her, a deluge of details that could drown out the present moment.

Should she try to explain? No one in the office had mentioned her memory since the day of her blowup with Claire. The team knowing her secret joined the pile of everything else she was in denial about—her side-tracked career, her family history, her inability to sustain relationships. The list was long, but things that troubled her could also be crushed by the cascade. Even now she was tempted to dive into a perfect bouquet of tulips she'd had on her desk at work six months ago. Sunny yellow with feathery petals, they'd—

"Mia. Are you listening?"

Lucas leaned forward, dark eyes quizzical.

"Yes, sorry. I'll let you know if I see anything strange."

"Send me as many texts as you want. I'll decide what's important."

The pod slid to a stop in front of Antonio's, a blocky, burnt umber structure with mirrored windows and a black and white, striped awning.

Lucas slid his hand over the door button as she reached for it. "Keep your glasses on mirror. You need to look around without being obvious."

"I can't. Only senior execs wear mirrored glasses in a restaurant. I'm clearly not." She gestured to her outfit—professional but not exec level. Lucas gave her the same quick once-over he'd given her when they first met, but it was clear he didn't understand and wouldn't ask for an explanation.

He pressed the door button, clambered out, then held his hand against the door as if he were holding it open. This wasn't something men on Victoria did, nor did pod doors shut unexpectedly when a passenger was exiting.

When she hesitated, he ordered, "Come on, we don't have much time."

She scrambled out and hurried across the hot sidewalk and into the awning's shade. The first set of double doors opened, and she waited for Lucas to join her before waving her hand over the laser for the inner doors.

The large room was half empty. She glanced around to see if she knew any of the diners and didn't recognize anyone. The host, a small man in a vest more elaborately embellished than those of the waiters, welcomed them with practiced enthusiasm.

"We have a reservation for 11 a.m. Dunn," Lucas said.

The host pressed the "2" square on the screen, and one of the tables on schematic of the restaurant glowed green. The one Claire promised them.

After they were seated and the host had scuttled away, Lucas took two devices from his black bag and attached them to the underside of the table, the long, white cloth cloaking his actions. The hiss of the conversation shield was masked by the irritating screech of violins in the classical piece playing over the dozens of speakers throughout the restaurant. The transmission jammer made a satisfying click as it stuck to a metal bracket.

Mia checked the restaurant's interior for any major changes. Sadly, there were few. This was her least favorite happy hour venue. She felt like an extra on the set of a nineteenth century Earth historical drama, a role her giggly female coworkers seemed to enjoy. The large room was paneled in darkly stained fake wood. Bookcases held artifacts an ill-informed and time travelling naturalist might have collected from junk shops. A bird skeleton. A 3D printed human skull. A wildly inaccurate map of South America. Artificial palms bracketed thin, tall windows hung with red velvet drapes. Colored film on the glass cut the intense sun to a late-afternoon-on-Earth ambiance. The overly plush burgundy carpet muffled voices and stripped them of passion.

A bar, set in an alcove to the left of the front door, was sparsely populated. The ceiling held the usual 360-degree holo cams. The clientele was well-dressed senior management types. No partners and nothing to report to Lucas.

A waiter arrived and handed out menus. "Welcome back," he said to Mia. "It's been awhile."

"Hi Xander." He wore no nametag but had served her at a couple of the more raucous birthday lunches back in the day, and had written his name on the check with an exaggerated X. He was handsome—and way too young for her.

He set a basket of bread on the table and poured a dollop of olive oil onto a small plate with a flourish.

"We have two specials," he began, when Lucas interrupted.

"We're just having drinks and appetizers."

Xander nodded and without missing a beat, exchanged the large menus with two smaller ones. "I'll give you a moment." He headed back toward the kitchen, white apron tied tight around his waist. She admired a man who could glide through Victoria's gravity like a fish in water. Tough as it was to remain standing all day, he'd acclimated better than most and it showed.

"You know him?" Lucas asked.

"He used to serve me and my friends."

"How about the rest of the waiters?"

"I recognize about half of them."

"Anything different than the last time you came?"

"They've replaced the ceiling fans. They used to be fake palm fronds. Some of the chairs have been recovered."

Lucas frowned. Anything new related to security, she reminded herself.

"I don't know what that is," she said, nodding toward a locked metal box on the wall by the front door. "And the camera above the bar is new. There was a smaller one before."

"Pay attention to the waiters. See where they come from, where they go, where they pick up water and food. The patterns should remain the same when our client arrives."

She reexamined the room with the critical eye of a social engineer. The flow was terrible. It wouldn't be a good place to try to steal anything physical. There was no quick way to the door. Her gaze strayed back to the appetizer menu in front of her. Baked, steamed, fried, sautéed. She hadn't eaten out since she'd been fired, and the prospect of professionally prepared food had her giddy.

"Can I order something?" she asked.

"Of course."

When Xander returned she asked for butterfish rings and iced tea. Lucas asked for a glass of water. Mia realized she'd never seen him eat.

Lucas remained immersed in his glasses, typing and swiping. The behavior wasn't uncommon; half the people at the restaurant were doing the same.

Mia was only halfway through the rings—god, they were good, perfectly fried—when Lucas signaled for the check. She hurried through the last of them then wiped her mouth. Now came the embarrassing part. He paid, they rose, and went back to the host station.

"I have a reservation for Mia Julian—at noon," she said.

The host looked from her to the recently vacated table. She shrugged.

"Right this way," he said, irritated but unable to decide how or why to protest. They were seated a few tables away from where they'd been before. Lucas took the seat facing their former spot.

Xander was amused to see them again, but Lucas had left a good tip on the small bill, so he merely nodded. "May I tell you about the specials—this time?"

"Yes, please," Mia said.

She chose a hydroponically farmed green salad, seafood ravioli, and iced coffee. She shouldn't order so much given the company finances, but the butterfish rings had stoked her appetite. Lucas had plain grilled longfish, no oil.

Would he eat it, she wondered?

"Can I go to the restroom?" she asked, feeling ridiculous but not sure if she was allowed to leave the table.

"Yes, go now before Dezzie arrives."

Xander was in the corridor when she emerged.

"What was that all about?" he asked, more teasing than curious.

She took off her glasses. "I screwed up our reservation and couldn't figure out how to change it, so I made another."

Xander raised an eyebrow but didn't inquire further. "Where's your posse?"

"I don't work with them anymore."

"Different department?"

"No. I quit Han." She hadn't intended the lie, but it slipped out like a rebellious teenager now that she was here in Andaman sector where no one knew of her disgrace. "I work for a small business now in Weber sector."

Though this was clearly a demotion, Xander smiled broadly. "That's great. I want to open my own place someday. It's tough here in the Andaman sector. Maybe Weber is more open to private businesses?"

"I came on after they had the permit, so I'm not sure."

Her glasses, held loosely in her right hand, vibrated. "Sorry, I've got to get back to work."

"Right. Me too."

He moved aside so she could pass, just not quite far enough, and she had to sidle by to avoid the prickly fake tree to her right. For a moment they were chest to chest. Dating outside the sector where you were employed was frowned upon, and more or less forbidden for anyone working on the executive floors.

I can date people from any sector now, Mia realized. She glanced back to see Xander grinning at her.

"I told you to keep your glasses on," Lucas said as she sat down. "I need to be able to communicate with you at all times. And do put them on mirror. I don't care if it's not socially appropriate. It's appropriate for the job."

She nodded and reluctantly changed the setting.

A few minutes later, Dezzie came through the doors. Whatever Claire did to the reservation system worked; the host brought him to the correct table. Dezzie took Lucas's admonition to act as if he didn't know them seriously, stalking by stiffly, glasses down. Once seated, he pulled a conversation shield out of his pocket, set it on the table and turned it on.

Lucas, to her surprise, allowed her to view from his glasses. She could see Dezzie and the rest of the restaurant without craning around. Though this made sense given the job, it simply wasn't done—a superior never allowed an underling that kind of access. Friends shared views, and bosses demanded them from employees but never reciprocated.

Mia reduced Lucas's view to a small square and watched the lunch crowd arrive. Five minutes later a man toting a suspiciously large black case—thanks to Claire, she was now suspicious of all black cases—pushed his way through the small crowd in front of the host's stand and scanned the restaurant. He was in his early forties with an averagely handsome face and bushy brown hair. Mod for sure. Men who couldn't afford much always did the hair first. His age and clothing said he was a mid-level manager with enough credits to buy a decent suit, but not the accessories to go with it.

He was clearly annoyed to find Dezzie already seated. He argued quietly with the host, pointing repeatedly at a table near the bar, but to no avail.

Why that table? Mia wondered. Most barstools were occupied by people having a casual lunch, but one patron faced out, half sitting, half standing, holding a beer he wasn't drinking. He and the brown-haired man exchanged a quick nod. Were they colleagues meeting by chance, or something more?

The man at the bar was expensively dressed. The suit said exec, but he was too fit, his pecs straining the front buttons of his fitted shirt. Execs carefully sculpted their bodies to show they had enough credits for a human trainer but were too busy to work out more than a few times a week. This guy might be corporate security, CorSec, though he wasn't wearing a logo pin. Mia called up a virtual keyboard overlay onto a clear area on the table, typed her observations and speculations, and sent them to Lucas.

The man meeting Dezzie walked past their table, and Mia caught a whiff of last year's popular cologne. His shoes—heavy black leather clunkers made for wet winter weather—were from Earth. As was he, though not a recent arrival. He moved easily in the gravity. Why keep those hideous shoes? Only a lack of credits could explain it.

The man noticed the conversation shield and frowned. Dezzie rose to greet him, and the man's expression changed from irritation to a benevolent blandness with astonishing speed.

Stop playing with your necklace. You look tense. Lucas typed onto her glasses.

She unfastened her fingers from the heavy, rough-hewn silver links. More than once they'd brought her back when she drifted into a daydream—her finger would hit a rough spot and jolt her back to present time.

She took a sip of water and watched the man at the bar. His glasses were on mirror. If he were looking in the direction he was facing, he was fascinated by a gold-framed antique map of Africa. If he were viewing data, he wasn't making any of the telltale head twitches or hand gestures. He brought the beer bottle to his lips, tilted it, yet the amount of liquid inside was the same when he returned it to the counter. As he turned, his vest pulled tight, and she saw something outlined in the interior chest pocket that looked very much like a gun—not just a stunner. She recalled the weapons sheet Claire sent her when she started. Portland laser pistol. Legal only for corporate security.

So, he was CorSec. She texted Lucas.

I saw him when we came in, Lucas replied. *He isn't the only CorSec here. There are two others. One woman, off duty, is having lunch alone back by the kitchen. The other, a man, is on executive protection duty at that big table of ten by the center island. CorSec are everywhere. You don't usually need to worry about them, but the nod was a good catch. I'll see if Claire can get facial recognition on him.*

Mia glanced around. The woman was obvious. She wore an Andaman logo pin on her vest, and wires trailed from her glasses. She couldn't see the face of the man at the big table, but his neck was thick and his back, broad.

Xander set a hot plate in front of her, and she jumped.

"Parmesan?" he asked.

"Yes please."

She forgot about the dramas around her as he grated a snowstorm of cheese onto her steaming ravioli, covering the pillows of pasta and the bits of fried sage.

"Tell me when," he said.

"Oh, sorry, when!"

She hurried to eat a few bites before Lucas could admonish her to get back to work—though not eating would have drawn attention, so, in a way, she was doing her job. His grilled longfish looked good, if plain. He didn't touch it.

She watched the feed from Lucas's glasses as she ate. The man with Dezzie was oilier than her butterfish rings had been, oozing fake friendliness and forcing a greasy smile. No way he worked for one of the Six.

He's trying to get into the decoy PDS, Lucas wrote. *He's in, but the transmission jammer is working. He can't transfer any data. Dezzie's PDS is safe behind the shield.*

Who was this creep and who did he work for?

Lucas worked hard on an invisible math problem on the white tablecloth, the fingers of his right hand sliding back and forth, circling and tapping.

Dezzie and the man traded terse words over an untouched plate of rockfish appetizers. The man abandoned his friendly façade and leaned close, spearing out talking points with a small, sharp fork. Dezzie shook his head.

After ten minutes of back and forth, the man threw down the fork, exasperated, and poked the air three times with his index finger. Dezzie smiled, then, to her surprise, pulled out his real PDS, not the dummy unit with the fake data. He took it out of its shield and slid it across the table like he was piloting a small boat around appetizer island. The man thrust it into his vest pocket, struggled out of his chair, and left with no goodbye other than a sour frown. The CorSec guy at the bar followed.

Lucas waited a moment, then made his way out to the busy sidewalk. Mia saw from his glasses that both men were gone.

Dezzie was by her side a second later. So much for the rules.

"Thanks!" he whispered loudly.

"Go," she said. "Pay and get out of here. Lucas is waiting for you out front."

Xander approached once Dezzie scurried away. "Everything okay?" he asked, eyeing Lucas's untouched food.

"Yes, very good. He had to take a call," she said. "I'll have the fish to go."

"I was wondering," he said, crouching so that they were eye level, "if you'd be up for meeting sometime and telling me what it's like to work for a small business."

Gold flecked his brown eyes. His very *young* brown eyes.

"I got my MBA last year from Oregon State University, but OSU isn't top tier. I'll need to work my way up to management before I can even think of trying to open my own place."

He dug in his front pocket and handed her a vid card showing a band playing out in the desert. Xander, if she recognized him amidst the tiny figures, played bass. On the back was contact information for each of the musicians.

"My band plays around town a lot. You should come to a show sometime. That card is good for free admission. I'll buy you a drink afterwards and you can tell me what it's like to get out from under the thumb of the Six."

Lucas strode toward the table, eyeing her, Xander, and the card. Mia dropped it into her bag.

"Yes, sometime," she said.

Xander followed her gaze to Lucas and stood, refolded Lucas's napkin, and turned smoothly to the couple behind her, asking if they needed anything.

Lucas sat down at Dezzie's vacant table, and retrieved the devices he'd put underneath with a casual stretch.

"What was that about?" he asked when he rejoined her, their tech safely stowed.

"Xander wanted to know if everything was okay with the food." She indicated the untouched fish. "Dezzie get away okay?"

"He did."

Lucas signaled for the check. Xander produced it, packaged the fish, and had the good sense to ignore her as he waited for Lucas to thumb and add the tip.

"Let's go," Lucas said.

Mia grabbed the bag, smiled at Xander's wink, and followed Lucas out the door. He hailed a pod and again held the door open for her. How this one, antiquated habit survived the long trip to Victoria was a mystery. When he slid into the seat next to her, she realized he didn't like to ride backwards. Shit. She inched left.

"What went on back there?" she asked after Lucas activated the conversation shield. She'd grown accustomed to the hiss, thinking of it as the oxygen that sustained conversation.

"Dezzie had something he wanted to sell, and that man was trying to get it for free."

"Did Dezzie tell you that?"

"No, but the man attempted to break into Dezzie's PDS—the real one, not the decoy. After he failed, Claire logged a large credits transfer into Dezzie's account." Lucas frowned. "The PDS shield we gave him wasn't strong enough. Claire had to use the conversation shield to disrupt the data link. Jason will need to develop something beefier. The off-the-shelf models here are flawed. Maybe deliberately so."

Mia flashed through memories. "Things like this happen all the time, don't they? I see the evidence." She hadn't meant to use present tense but it was too late to take it back. "Large bags, strangers dining together, arguments, packages changing hands, abrupt departures." The interiors of a hundred restaurants in the Han sector filled her vision.

"It's understandable you didn't notice," Lucas said. "Architects notice the building, doctors hear everyone cough, chefs pay attention to the food. Change your lens, and you'll be surprised what you see."

She was fine with her current lenses.

"Do you think Dezzie did something illegal?" she asked.

"It's possible, but if so, this is the first time. Claire's gone through his accounts. Nothing out of the ordinary."

"You said you don't want us to work for criminals."

"I don't. I do background checks so we can avoid it. We didn't have time to do one today." He held up a hand before Mia could protest. "We wouldn't have found anything, but please don't book same-day meetings. We need at least three days lead time for any job."

"I'll add that info to the sales sheet." It was better sitting next to Lucas than across from him; he couldn't see her fuming. She'd tried hard to get his input on the generic sales sheet she put together and he'd approved it without reading—that was clear.

"Next time we do this, order only finger food. You spent more time fiddling with that ravioli than you did watching the waiters, and wear something more subdued," Lucas said.

Mia stared down at her dress, then up at him, perplexed, given he was the one getting the curious stares back at the restaurant. His expensive outfit couldn't cloak his unusually low body weight.

"This is how everyone dresses. Didn't you notice? Look out the window."

They were still in the heart of the restaurant district on Ring 3. The shaded walkways, crowded with workers strolling to lunch, held a florist shop's worth of roses, daisies, and sunflowers printed on cotton and silk. What the planet lacked in colorful native vegetation, the inhabitants made up for with multihued clothes and hair. One big perk of losing her job was being able to wear the patterns Erika deemed "lower-floor style" and had forbidden.

He glanced out, seeming to see the spectacle for the first time. "Everyone dresses this garishly?"

What was meant as an insult merely revealed his ignorance. "All the non-execs. Partners dress more conservatively, and senior executives mimic them. I'm okay in this dress. Antonio's isn't partner territory."

The pod turned right, away from the traffic but also away from the office. Lucas raised a hand as if to grab a lever, then let it drop.

"I don't like these pods. I'm used to choosing my own route."

"You drove your own vehicle?" A shocking occurrence, even for chaotic Earth.

Lucas shook his head. "I had a driver. After the Gupta incident, all the partners got waivers and human drivers."

"What's the Gupta incident?"

"The president of ATX was riding in an autonomous vehicle that got hacked, and he ended up splattered against an embankment near the Brooklyn Bridge."

Mia wasn't sure how the partners on Victoria got around, but she doubted they used human drivers.

"I've never driven. There's an off-road recreation area down south, but it seems so dangerous," she said.

"Trusting an autonomous vehicle can be just as dangerous."

Only on Earth, Mia reassured herself as the pod came to a gentle stop in front of the office.

Mikey was just leaving. He gave Mia a nod when they passed on the narrow path. They'd settled into a guarded truce after that day at the gym. When she didn't say anything about what happened to the rest of the team, he stopped his demeaning comments and ogling. She, grudgingly, respected him a bit more. He wasn't the dumb oaf he liked to portray—he was Lucas's trusted right-hand man and knew exactly what was going on.

She left him and Lucas chatting and hurried inside.

"How'd it go?" Jason pulled off his safety goggles and rubbed his forehead with a sooty hand.

"Fine, I guess. The guy meeting Dezzie did try to steal his data, but then after all that, Dezzie handed over the drive."

"Yeah, Claire told me. Sounds like we need to take a look at the PDS shield we used. It wasn't strong enough."

Mia pulled up a stool and tried to catch Jason's eye. He'd gotten much more comfortable around her the last few months, but still grew nervous when she got serious. "I'd rather not work these kinds of meetings. It's one thing to stand around in an apartment chatting with people while you scan for bugs, and something completely different to be out there trying to protect someone. The way Lucas talks, I'm supposed to be looking out for guns and suspicious waiters. What if that guy tried to grab the PDS? That's physical security. And that's Mikey's job."

Jason did look her in the eye, and grinned. "Look at you, all paranoid. This isn't Earth, you know. No physical crime happens here. Who told me that?" He furrowed his brow dramatically. "I can't quite remember, but let me show you the stats."

Mia swung her bag at him, and he swatted it away.

"Seriously, Lucas would never put you in a dangerous situation. No one is going to start shooting in…whatever the name of that restaurant is. And truthfully, he won't be expecting much from you other than simple common sense and camouflage. He's busy and needs someone to keep an eye on the room, handle inquiries from the waiter, chat a bit, make things look normal."

"It's more than that. He wants me to tell him if I see anything unusual." Mia threw up her hands. "What does that mean? I thought it was unusual that the host was so short. These places usually put a two-meter-tall model up front. Is that important to Lucas? I doubt it."

Jason glanced at Claire, who wore glasses and earbuds and moved her hands as if conducting a tiny orchestra. "I know we all promised not to talk about it, but he's probably hoping you'll use your…"

He twirled his forefingers around his eyes and despite herself, Mia laughed. Her excellent visual memory—her deepest, darkest secret—depicted as crazy eyes. Pretty apt, actually. She was surprised it had taken this long for the subject to resurface, even though she'd sworn she'd quit if anyone mentioned the topic again.

Jason, technically, hadn't mentioned it.

"Use it to do what?" she asked in a non-defensive tone.

He opened a drawer and took out a fat black rod, a dozen buttons running down its length and a pair of thin metal tines at the end. It looked like a beefy tuning fork.

"Do you know what this is?" he asked.

"No."

"It's a tool," he said. "Do you know what it does?"

"Of course not," she said.

"That's probably how Lucas feels about your memory. He has to beat around the bush, telling you to pay attention, things like that, because he can't ask you what you can actually do."

"My memory isn't part of the Summit Security tool chest."

"I get it. Just be aware, this is what your memory looks like to the rest of us." He held up the black rod before throwing it back in the drawer.

She was on the road to making the same mistake she'd made with Claire so many years ago. Refusing to talk about her memory was tantamount to saying she didn't trust Jason. She wanted to be friends, but he didn't realize what he was asking. That said, one of the many things she'd lost thanks to being on guard about her memory might have been her sense of humor. It felt good to laugh when Jason did the googly-eye thing.

"I get what you're saying. I don't want to be a weird thing with a bunch of buttons, but dealing with this issue is complicated."

"Dealing with this is complicated, too," Jason said, indicating the office, or maybe all of Victoria. "Go to lunch meetings with Lucas, eat food, do your best."

"I will," Mia said, and she meant it.

On Monday, Mia met Dezzie at The End to get Summit's equipment back. He was a different Dezzie. Excited, almost cocky. Lucas made her promise not to ask what happened Friday, but his theory that Dezzie sold something appeared to be correct. He wore new data glasses, same brand as hers, but the higher-end model. Not something a research associate should be able to afford. There were many things Dezzie could have legitimately sold to get those credits, but the smug smile told a different story. He'd done something at best inadvisable, and at worst, illegal.

He didn't notice her grim mood. "You want a drink?"

"It's a little early. I just had breakfast."

He laughed. "My treat."

She wasn't supposed to ask any questions, but if she got a few drinks in him, maybe he'd tell her on his own. She poked the table and ordered two shots of tequila.

Dezzie pulled out the conversation shield and turned it on. "I like this thing. Can I keep it?"

"If you sign up for a basic privacy package you can. It's two hundred credits a month—"

"Sure, sure. Sign me up. You've got all my info. I'm so glad I hired you for the meeting. Did you see how Mr.—" He tapped a finger to his lips. "Did you see his expression when he saw this on the table?" He patted the black dome. "He thought he could rip me off. He tried to steal my data, didn't he?"

"Yes."

Dezzie laughed. "Well, fuck him."

The bartender, John, set the tequila shots down hard on the table. Mia wasn't exactly unwelcome at the bar—given Summit set up their entire security system for free—but he didn't like *her kind*. That he'd mistaken her for an executive had given her ego a boost. Months in, though, he had to know this place was all she could afford, and she wasn't faking it.

Dezzie drank his shot in one gulp.

"Cheers!" he said, clinking his empty glass to hers.

Mia sipped, and Dezzie ordered another round.

He was young, thin, and quickly drunk. He painted an exuberant but abstract picture of the lunch meeting and his associated emotions. He wasn't stupid enough to admit he'd done anything wrong, but he used terms from multiplayer games that painted Mr. X as his opponent and the payment as a score.

"What do your friends think of this?" Mia asked.

Dezzie's eyes widened. "Nothing! I didn't tell anyone. You can't talk about it, right? That's what it said in the contract."

"All our client interactions are completely confidential." She set down the mostly full shot glass, suddenly tired of his youthful idiocy. "I gotta go. This is a workday for me."

He hoisted a black bag onto the table.

"Here's the rest of your stuff. Tell Lucas thanks for everything."

"I will." She didn't dislike him—she'd done things in her early twenties she regretted, some of them quasi-legal. She'd try to take Jason's advice and not speculate about the clients. *Fulfill the contractual obligations and stay professional.*

Back at work, she set the bag of equipment on Jason's table.

"You were gone awhile," Lucas called from his office.

"We had a drink. He was wearing new DV glasses—the newest Lucida model. You know how much those cost?"

"It doesn't matter. If you believe people have the right to attend a meeting and not have their data stolen, then you support what we do. The nature of the data is none of our business."

"Can't you take Mikey to these meetings? You'll look like an exec with a CorSec guy."

"No. I need you. Mikey doesn't take direction well and won't notice anything other than what types of tequila the bar stocks. It was helpful having you with me."

She'd done much for the company and received scant praise from Lucas. Come to think of it, she hadn't heard him say anything nice to anyone. Perhaps this was his version of a standing ovation. He *was* standing, arms folded, eyes invisible behind glasses, cheekbones too pronounced.

Jason once described her as a strange tool no one knew how to use. Though she'd initially taken offense, it now felt like a compliment. She may be strange, but least she wasn't broken.

Chapter Eleven

Mia usually arrived at work before Jason and Claire. They'd come in early during the first month of her employment, perhaps forced by Lucas, but day by day pushed back their start times. Now, she rarely saw them until after lunch. She was glad to have the hours to herself. She'd installed small, intense, full-spectrum lights throughout the large room, and when Claire was out, she banished the gloom.

This morning the office was silent as usual. She was about to instruct her glasses to turn on the lights when she noticed a sliver of silver spilling from Lucas's open office door. He was never here at this hour and kept his door locked when he was out.

"Good morning," she called and heard no response. "Lucas?" She walked over to peer into the small room.

Lucas was slumped forward in his chair in damp workout clothes, arms wrapped around himself, breath quick and shallow. One of the desk drawers lay upside down on the floor, its contents scattered.

Oh, fuck. Her mind flashed back to the gym. Lucas on the ground. *It's happening again.*

She froze in the doorway, her breakfast suddenly a leaden lump in her stomach. She was nervous around sick people—an unease bordering on phobia. She fought the urge to back away. *I can do this.* Lucas needed help.

She stepped into the room. "Are you okay?"

He raised his head slowly. His forehead was furrowed and his eyes shut tight, skin pale and sweaty. "The hypo—on the floor."

She dropped to her knees and rifled through the mess. In the midst of the batteries and stunner chargers and business cards, she spotted a lone unopened hypo. The large red letters spelled SIONALL. She knew this drug, a heavy-duty painkiller used post-surgery and by stressed out execs after a bad week at work. Definitely not something you could get over the counter.

She tried to rip open the thick foil and failed. This was meant to be used by a coolheaded medical professional, not a frantic social engineer with trembling fingers. She pawed through the contents of the drawer again, found a small, sharp screwdriver, and dug it in to the edge of the package.

She finally worried the metal canister free and twisted the dosage dial. "How much?"

"Four…units."

Five was the maximum, and that was for someone Mikey's size—if he'd just fallen off a building. She recalled the lethal dose charts she and her friends pored over in high school. They all had access to prescription drugs, thanks to inattentive parents. They weren't worried about dying, only about getting caught, so they dosed judiciously. She needed to know Lucas's body weight. He was so thin now. Sixty-five kilos?

"Four is too much for you," she said and set the dial at two.

"It's not." He drew in a short, ragged breath. "Give me four, now. Hurry."

Shit. Her common sense screamed this was wrong, but he was rigid with pain, and she was no doctor. Lucas seemed very sure of the number. She turned the dial to four, pressed the can against the bare skin of his forearm, and held her breath as it hissed.

She watched his face. After a minute, his forehead smoothed. His arms unfolded and dropped to his lap. He listed toward her, and she grabbed him by a clammy shoulder and pressed him back into the chair. His breathing slowed, each long inhale and exhale followed by lengthening silence until, for a time, it seemed he didn't breathe at all. His head lolled to one side. A chill ran through her.

Is this the part where his heart stops because I just overdosed him?

A medic wouldn't be able to get there fast enough to help. She laid a hand on his cool neck and felt his pulse, each beat seconds apart and slowing. Hers speeded in panic. What should she do? Would a stim help? She had some in her desk but was afraid to leave him.

Abruptly, Lucas took a deep shuddering breath, then another. After a few minutes, his white cheeks showed a hint of color. He straightened his head and half opened his eyes. They beheld a distant landscape visible only to those under the influence of heavy narcotics. She kept hold of him until she found the controls to his chair and reclined it to forty-five degrees. Once he was settled, she pulled his extra shirts, vests, and pants from the hook behind the door and covered him in a makeshift blanket.

He blinked slowly and tried to focus on her. "Why are you crying?"

She touched her cheek, surprised to find it wet. Somewhere in her head a fire alarm was ringing. "I almost killed you. Why are you taking Sionall? What's wrong with you?"

She didn't expect an answer. He was swimming in a sea of absolute relaxation. She knew. She'd taken Sionall before—just one unit had kicked her ass, reducing her to a dreamy heap for hours. She was amazed he was conscious.

He pulled his hand from the clothes she'd piled on him and reached for her. She stepped away.

"S'okay. Getting something out of my system." He let his hand drop to his lap, closed his eyes, and surrendered to the drug.

When she was sure he wasn't going to fall out of the chair, she dialed Mikey. Her terror that Lucas might die drained away and an unreasonable anger poured into its place.

Mikey picked up immediately. She focused the camera in her DV glasses on Lucas.

"That *thing* happened to Lucas, the same thing that happened at the gym the other day."

"What did you do?" Mikey asked.

Her voice caught. "I gave him the dose of Sionall he asked for, and it almost stopped his heart." She paced out into the main room. "What the fuck is wrong with all of you? Lucas is dead on his fucking feet, and everyone is pretending nothing is wrong. What would have happened if I wasn't here? Should I call a medic?"

"Don't call a medic. Keep an eye on him. I'll be right there." He disconnected.

She hovered over Lucas. She'd never had the chance to do what she was doing now—blatantly stare. He rested peacefully, if being drugged into oblivion was peace. She pulled back the shirt she'd used to cover his torso. She could almost reach right around his collarbone, the muscles and flesh were so far retreated from it. He needed real help, not the temporary fix Sionall provided. She covered him again, then rested her hand lightly on his forehead. He was warming up. Good. He twitched, and she pulled her hand back.

Mikey better get there soon. She could treat hundreds of different insect bites and deal with sunstroke and dehydration. Her memory was deep and wide, but only in the oceans she'd chosen to swim in. This one rose and fell off the coast of New York.

Lucas stirred. He opened his eyes and tried to focus on her but his gaze wandered. "I'm alright now. You can go," he slurred. His pupils were huge.

"I will as soon as Mikey gets here, believe me."

"Am I on boat?" Lucas asked.

"No, you're on drugs. Relax and enjoy it."

Mikey arrived, all business. He scanned Lucas with a medical device, nodded at the result, then hefted him over one shoulder and carried him out of the office to the front apartment.

Mia followed at a distance. She'd never seen where Lucas lived. Mikey slapped his palm against the lock and the door opened inward. Light flooded the normally dark hallway.

The room—it appeared to be only one room—was much brighter than the back office, thanks to sun pouring in from the high, round, front windows. Mikey dumped Lucas on the unmade bed centered beneath them. A black cabinet—identical to the ones in office—held neatly folded clothes. A quartet of wall-mounted screens showed north, east, south, and west views from the exterior of the building. No attempt had been made to decorate. More hotel room than home.

Mikey strode to the portable kitchen unit and made coffee. For himself or Lucas?

"Can I help with anything?" she asked, thinking Lucas should be straightened out and covered. He was still in his wet running clothes.

Mikey wheeled around. "Get out of here." He pointed the cup he held toward the street, not in the direction of her desk.

He should be thanking her, not threatening her, but she didn't have the energy to protest. Now that the adrenaline had left her system, she was woozy, and her hands shook. She stumbled down the hall and out the front door and hailed a pod. Luckily, one was close. It pulled to a stop in front of the office as Mikey called to her. She was in no mood for a lecture on how she was not to mention this incident to anyone.

He jogged down the path and put a meaty hand on the pod door before she could open it.

"Hang on a second." He took off his glasses. The anger was gone. "I didn't mean get out of the building. Lucas doesn't want anyone in his apartment. Thanks for what you did. It would have been really bad if that happened when he was alone."

There was nothing threatening about his stance, other than the fact that he was blocking the door. "What's wrong with him?"

He had the decency to look pained. "Lucas decides who knows, not me."

"Is he dying? Can you at least tell me that?"

"No. He isn't dying. He'll recover."

She could see he believed this, but she wondered what a partner would tell his staff if he had a terminal disease. Lucas was probably a very good liar.

Mikey removed his hand so she could open the door, and she collapsed gratefully into the pod's cool interior.

"Lucas can't work if this is going to keep happening, Mikey. He could hurt himself. And I can't work with him. We have a client lunch next week. What if he collapses in the restaurant? Not only would we lose the client, but Lucas would be carted off to a hospital in whatever sector we were in, and this illness he is trying to hide would be discovered. If it's serious enough, we could lose our charter. You and the team better figure out what to do with him, and don't ask his advice. He's not fit to give it."

Lucas didn't come to work the next day, and neither did Mikey. She didn't see either of them at the gym. Days passed. Mikey didn't answer her messages. Mia pressed her ear against Lucas's office and apartment door each morning and heard nothing.

She gave up and asked Jason if he knew where they were.

He hesitated before he answered. "South Shore. At a clinic."

"Desert Springs," she guessed.

"Yes, that's the place. How did you know?"

"There aren't many clinics down there."

It wasn't good news. Desert Springs was where people went if they didn't want to be seen in the hospital. The terminally ill, the bruised and swollen recipients of full-body mods, and people undergoing treatment for drug addiction. No habit-forming recreational drugs were allowed on Victoria, but occasionally someone did have a problem. The Six called it a "psychological incompatibility."

"How long will they be gone?" she asked.

Jason replied with a noncommittal, "A few days."

"You know what's wrong with him. Everyone does but me."

"I don't know. I suspect. Lucas is a very private person. When you work closely with a team like this, you establish boundaries. If someone doesn't offer, I don't pry."

Was Lucas sick or was it drugs? He had a suspiciously high tolerance to Sionall. She was still traumatized by the fact she'd nearly killed him. Mikey didn't have to warn her to be silent. She was ashamed. She'd ignored her common sense to take orders from a man half out of his mind in pain. When she'd returned to her apartment that morning, it had taken two Baby Janes and a drink before her hands stopped shaking and she could take a deep breath.

Lucas and Mikey's absence stretched from days to over a week. Mia checked the schedule. One lunch meeting and two new client visits were coming up. She and Jason could do the lunch and new client consultations, but the stress level in the office was rising.

She thought they'd been running the business with little help from Lucas for the past few months, but she was wrong. Many clients weren't satisfied speaking to her, and her feeble excuses as to why "the boss" wouldn't be available for a few weeks were unconvincing. No one was unavailable for weeks in this day and age. Even passengers on ships to and from Earth experienced only brief communications interruptions.

Also, it turned out Lucas had been arbitrating technical disputes between Jason and Claire, wading through the often incompatible hardware and software solutions they proposed and hammering out a plan. Now the two of them bickered constantly. "Lucas said…" and "Last time, Lucas told me to…" or "We didn't do it that way in the Martinez apartment." Mia jammed in her earpieces and turned up the music.

She was sure the worry about Lucas and the future of the business was the fuel for many of their heated exchanges, though neither would admit it.

Jason received occasional updates from Mikey, but all he passed on was, "Lucas is fine," or, "He'll be there a few more days."

Midway into week two, Jason received a call from Mikey that propelled him up and out of his seat. She and Claire pulled off their glasses and watched Jason pace, his hands pressing his earbuds tight to his head. He was so agitated he didn't bother to type and shouted his half of the conversation.

"What do you mean? Why, what's going on?" He paused. "Yesterday? Where were you? Oh, that's just great, Mikey." He listened. "Should I come down? No, I have no idea. How would I know that?" He shook his head. "Just in case. Great. Well, call Mitch. He'll know, maybe." He strode out into the hall. As the door shut, she heard, "Don't leave there again until he is conscious. If you can't manage that, I'll catch the next shuttle down."

She and Claire exchanged anxious looks.

Jason came back in, jaw tight.

"What happened?" Claire asked.

"What happened is that Mikey is an irresponsible drunk. We shouldn't have let him do this alone."

"Lucas didn't want us to come. He said it would be a circus."

"Well, it looks like Mikey is a circus all on his own. He was supposed to be on call for the clinic but he was at a bar, glasses off, and didn't get their messages," Jason said.

Mia broke in. "Is Lucas okay? You said he wasn't conscious."

"He isn't supposed to be conscious. He's fine…now. The nurse at the clinic had a question about the treatment, and no one to answer it. Fortunately, she made the right decision on her own. Mikey swears he won't go away again."

"Mikey is an idiot," Claire said.

Jason let out a long breath and sagged onto a stool. "I do have good news. The treatment was a success. Lucas is in recovery. Nothing should go wrong now." He pointed a rusty pair of pliers accusingly at Claire. "This was supposed to be easy. Come to Victoria and do contract work for a few months. Lucas is supposed to be running the business. He hasn't done a fucking thing since we got here and now he's flat on his back. If it wasn't for Mia we'd be out of credits, all because of yet another one of Lucas's problems."

Claire bristled. "Shut up, Jason."

"I'll shut up in the privacy of my apartment. I'm not working until he does." He tossed the pliers onto the table and stormed out.

What was that all about? Mia had never seen Jason so angry. His usual response to conflict was a retreat to sullen silence. Which, now that she thought about it, was how he often reacted to Lucas. And what did he mean about only being here for a few months?

"Claire?"

Claire pulled on her glasses and stuck in her earbuds. The tiny sounds of beating drums and a wailing synth meant the volume was all the way up. Mia would get no answers from her. She didn't need them, though. It was obvious. Drugs. Lucas had just completed a nasty withdrawal from some horrible designer drug. Earth authorities didn't give a shit about the illegal substances killing hundreds every day. A dead body was cause for celebration on a planet overloaded with human cargo.

None of those substances made it onto Victoria, nor were they fabricated here. Drugs were safe, tested, and legal. Lucas must have been going without his drug of choice for months, and grudgingly, she sympathized. After she checked into her dorm at New Beijing University, she hurried to a pharmacy only to learn they didn't sell Baby Janes on Earth. She struggled through the next five years using alcohol, marijuana, and muscle relaxants when she needed mental down time.

Did Lucas leave Earth to escape his addiction? A harsh but effective tactic. Did Jason and Claire know about his plan when they signed up? Jason implied they'd been forced out of their jobs, but perhaps he'd been referring to Lucas alone. A dependent partner was a vulnerable partner, and if he'd been unable to stop using, the board might have politely suggested it was time to leave Itek.

She might never find out whether any of her speculations were correct. The team didn't want to talk about what happened and frankly, it didn't matter. Lucas was recovering. Everything was going to be fine. They wouldn't go out of business. Claire would have the time she needed to repair Mia's records without attracting the notice of an AI security agent, get those bullshit pictures of chickens taken down, and eventually Mia might be able to get back into social engineering.

Chapter Twelve

Ten more days passed before Lucas returned. Though Mia had been anticipating the moment, she was still startled when she came in Friday morning to find him in his office, door open, glow ceiling on bright. She crept quietly to her desk and didn't turn on any lights.

How was she supposed to react to his absence? Ignore it? She had many things that needed to be dealt with but was hesitant to bother him.

Mikey, who must have set up an alert tied to her arrival, sent a message. *Don't mention that day Lucas passed out at the office. He doesn't remember what happened. He thinks I found him.*

She quickly wrote back. *Good and don't worry, I won't.* That much Sionall would cloud any memory and she was relieved it had. Mikey might remember this incident as the time she helped Lucas, but to her it was the time she almost killed him.

She'd treat this as a normal day—not that there'd been many normal days here. She compiled her questions, tacked on the things Lucas needed to do, and sent him the document. She fervently hoped he wouldn't want to talk to her.

He did.

She went to his office and stood just inside the threshold, trying to banish the memory of his heart slowing nearly to a stop. She glanced down at the floor, half expecting to see the used hypo she'd dropped, but the carpet was clean.

"Have a seat. Let's go over this." His voice was quiet and flat, not the crisp commanding tone she'd grown used to.

She sat reluctantly and gazed at the small screen on her lap. "First off, we have a lunch meeting next Wednesday, and the client is insisting it be at Sage, which is going to be a total nightmare."

She went over all the items, avoiding looking at Lucas until he asked, "What about this? I don't understand."

She raised her head. His glasses were off. He looked tired, but much, much better. Thin, but not verge-of-death thin.

There was something different in his expression. He held her gaze for only a moment before he looked away, uncharacteristically reserved. It took a moment for her to put her finger on what had changed. His eyes had always been as heavily shielded as the building—irony, sarcasm, and scorn creating a barrier as impenetrable as the plasticrete surrounding them. The barriers were gone, replaced by an open, weary calm.

Something clicked about the Lucas she'd known before his time at the clinic. While Jason and Claire had the detachment of people who didn't expect to be in New Canberra long-term, Lucas hadn't expected to be anywhere. He hadn't expected to *be*. He didn't think the treatment would succeed. From what she'd overheard on Jason's call from Mikey the other day, it almost hadn't.

Memories of Lucas's expressions and reactions flew across her vision. She'd interpreted many as disapproval of her and her city. Now she could see them as the irritation of an intelligent man forced to undertake what he considered a completely futile task—preparing for the future.

She emerged from her musings to find Lucas waving a stylus in front of her face. "Mia? Are you alright?"

"Sorry. What were you asking?"

"I have interior photos of Sage, and I don't understand the layout." He put his glasses back on and addressed the screen, not her.

Mia struggled to concentrate and give appropriate answers. She couldn't understand why someone expecting to die would drag a team all the way to Victoria and go to the trouble of setting up a business that couldn't operate without him.

They finished going through the items, and she stood. She wanted to pretend nothing had happened, but couldn't. She hesitated until he looked up, his mirrored glasses reflecting her anxious face. She tried to relax it into polite interest.

"You are...better?"

He nodded. "Yes. Thank you for asking."

She needed more. "One hundred percent totally…" How to phrase it? Cured, detoxed, disease-free?

"I have a clean bill of health." He smiled—a rare occurrence. "I might even pass the physical everyone has to take before they can come to this planet."

How *did* they all bypass the screening?

"I need to get back to work," he prompted.

"Right. Sorry." She left, closing the door behind her.

The situation was strange, yet oddly familiar. The high-ceilinged executive offices of Han held more than just priceless art. She'd navigated her way around whispers, pointed looks, strange packages, odd requests, intriguing flashes of text on casually held screens—things she wasn't meant to see or remember or piece together…not if she wanted to stay safe. A veracity test was never more than a heartbeat away, so she'd learned to slam down walls around her curiosity. It was time to build a new wall.

The mystery of Lucas's past would soon be subsumed by the pressing concerns of today. She'd make sure of it.

Lucas remained subdued for the next week. He had the air of someone who'd just returned from a long space journey in zero gravity and struggled to readjust to harsh sunlight, hot air, and crippling gravity. He spent a lot of time outside, leaning against whichever wall was in shade, smoking and staring out at the surrounding empty lots. She was glad he'd given up the illegal tobacco and switched to Cyclones, a smokeless, herbal cigarette laced with stimulants.

He showed up to work early every day and kept his office door open—a big change from his former aggressive solitude. He never rebuked anyone for bothering him the way he had before. Claire was in and out a dozen times a day. She seemed eager for approval—a side of her Mia had never seen before.

Jason returned to work, his sullen anger gradually fading as the new Lucas proved to be calm, focused, and reliable.

Mikey rarely came in. He'd fucked up badly at the clinic. Jason and Claire avoided speaking to him and even Lucas was oddly formal, treating him like a colleague from another department, not a friend. She almost felt sorry for him as he passed her desk, heading to the bar alone.

Lucas quickly made up for the time he'd missed. He read the client files and questioned Mia, Jason, and Claire on the details. He even asked about meetings he'd attended, and Mia wondered how much Sionall he'd been taking these past months. He seemed genuinely puzzled by some of the decisions he'd made and had Jason and Claire reconfigure much of the hardware and software.

By the end of the third week back, he no longer looked sick. It wasn't so much the weight gain—which filled the valleys between jagged bones and sinew—but his carriage. The brittle weariness vanished. He moved like a person in expensive new clothes—pleased, cautious, and a bit self-conscious. She'd felt the same way the first time she tried on the exorbitantly priced suit Erika got her from Garcia DuBois. Was there any chance he wouldn't move beyond this phase? She liked this version of him. The next might be an overly handsome man holding up his hand to fend off paparazzi drones. He wasn't famous here though, so that wouldn't happen…would it?

Monday morning, Lucas approached the worktable where she and Jason prepared for an initial client meeting.

"I'll go to this one. Jason, you can stay here and finish that ADM," Lucas said.

Jason smiled. Mia frowned. The two of them had developed a solid routine for initial home security meetings. By now, she understood the technical aspects of the software and hardware and the emotions she was likely to encounter in their nervous, arrogant clients. While she reassured, Jason raised doubts. Not intentionally, but his thorough sweep of walls, floors, ceilings, and appliances made it clear nearly anything in the apartment could be used to spy on its occupants. Even when he didn't find any bugs, many people signed up "just in case." When she was first hired, she'd have said they were playing on fears, but her experience at Summit convinced her everyone should have an ADM—just in case. What harm was there in ensuring rights that were supposed to be guaranteed?

"You don't have to come. It's a waste of your time. Jason and I have it down," Mia said.

Jason, more quickly than she'd ever seen him move, stripped off the nice vest and shirt and threw on a dirty t-shirt.

Lucas shook his head. "Jason's time is more valuable than mine. I can't build hardware, and if we get more new clients, we'll need more appliance data managers. It's been a while, but I still remember how to scan a room."

The circles were gone from under his eyes, and the barriers were back up. Not impermeable as they'd been before—more like the temporary fences put up to hide messy construction sites. A courtesy, to mask something unfinished.

She couldn't argue with Lucas's logic. "We'd better get going."

The meeting wasn't the disaster she feared it might be. Lucas stayed in the background, genuinely absorbed in scanning the apartment. Nothing was amiss and the man, a manager from Han, nodded gruffly and didn't sign up. Didn't matter—she was so relieved to discover Lucas could interact with a client without blustering and posturing, she considered the meeting a success.

Lucas insisted on walking to Ring 3 afterwards. To get a feel for the place, he said. She suspected he was trying to get his legs back in shape. She didn't mind. It was a beautiful morning, and at this early hour, the mid-rise apartment buildings cast long, cool shadows across the wide sidewalk. Lucas paused frequently to take a closer look at streetlights, access panels, and other parts of the city infrastructure. And, she came to realize, to rest.

A few weeks later, Mia was the one who couldn't keep up. Lucas was back at the gym sparring with Mikey, lifting weights, and swimming. When

they walked the long halls of the more sprawling apartment complexes, he'd stride ahead, arriving at the client's door minutes before her. She
blamed her shoes, relics from her executive floor days.

Mia and Lucas now handled all initial client meetings, though her
presence was becoming superfluous. Lucas did the scanning and the
talking, and she hovered uselessly, holding a screen in case he had a
question. He insisted he needed her expertise since politeness dictated
they not wear glasses, but out of a dozen meetings she'd jumped in only
a handful of times.

The truth was, he was good at this. Much better than her and Jason.
Lucas was attentive, shrewd, and intuitive. He asked open-ended questions, circled and tested until he found the right button to press. It was
such a change from the awkward, aggressive way he'd handled Dezzie, she
couldn't believe he was the same person. Most unexpected was his charisma. Yes, she'd seen this trait in many of the partners at Han, and even in
Erika when she chose to deploy it, but given Lucas's abrasive manner up
until now, she assumed he'd intimidated his way to the top.

Maybe not…

Bradford Patel nodded agreement as Lucas suggested he sign up for
the most expensive package, as if he and Lucas were in this together.

The client list grew slowly and steadily—all Han employees from the
mining division.

Today, they were on route to a lunch meeting at Antonio's. Dezzie
must have made good on his promise to recommend Summit—they'd be
providing security for his supervisor. Dr. Andrew Lerner was a senior scientist at Han, working on technology for single-stage extraction of rare
earth elements.

Mia rode backwards, facing Lucas. Now that his arms had filled out,
he could wear short-sleeved shirts. Admiring glances had replaced quizzical when he walked into a meeting. He stared out the half-open window
and began the now familiar interrogation.

"Which corporation installed the pod system? Who controls it now?"

Before his visit to the clinic, Lucas stayed glasses down on pod trips,
ignoring the jewel-like city. Now, he asked penetrating questions about

everything. Why did they choose this location for the original colony? How are the desalination plants powered? How many people stay on after an initial ten-year contract? What happens when someone breaks a rule?

He listened to her answers with such intensity it made her nervous. Their formerly awkward times alone together were now nonstop New Canberra history and sociology lessons.

She worried he was playing her like he played the clients, trying to make her feel comfortable and knowledgeable, but there was nothing to be gained by it. She was an employee, and spewing back facts certainly didn't make her feel smart. It would be like being proud of having fingers.

After a query about one of the local slang words, she finally understood. She was the only New Canberran he could question like this without being mocked. Slipping in under the radar meant he and the team hadn't attended the official training sessions. Had they been trained, they'd know how to hail a pod, why it was a good idea to stay on the pavement, what "burn," "bit," and "dry" meant here, and hundreds of other facts. In short, how to fit in and get along.

Though it was more an inquisition than a conversation, she happily pulled off her glasses when Lucas took out the conversation shield. She could speak freely and not worry she was saying too much or giving details no normal person would remember. At first, she was afraid she was "showing off," as her mom used to put it, but she found, with amusement and relief, that Lucas would often fact-check and correct her. The population of the city? It changed every day so her number was out of date. The members of Optima's board? She didn't know three of them had been replaced in the last election. She could have cited the date she learned what she knew, but why bother? Her "mistakes" put Lucas at ease. She had a good memory and to him, that meant the high end of a normal range. This misperception suited her fine.

"Anything special I should look out for today?" she asked as they approached Antonio's. She'd read up on the client, but it never hurt to ask.

Lucas glanced down at the screen. "Dr. Lerner has the standard privacy package. Conversation shield, transmission blocker, scrambler."

"Who's he meeting?"

"He didn't say."

The pod door opened and Lucas gestured. "After you."

She'd gotten used to the exiting the pod routine—it was the rest of it that bothered her. As he'd gained weight, he'd added layers of civility that coated and buffered his formerly caustic personality. She should have been happy about it, but every time he tossed out a lackluster "please," she cringed. There was something visceral and real about Lucas when he'd been at his worst. Even though he'd been difficult, she was glad she'd gotten to know him when he had no spare energy for politeness or small talk. He'd been harsh, but not unfair. Now he was developing the slick outer coating of partner. *Redeveloping it,* she thought, remembering the photos of him with holo stars on his arm.

She slid across the seat and out into hot, noonday sun, shielded her eyes, and examined Han tower. A small dust storm had swept through a few days ago, and the scrubber bots hadn't fully cleaned the building. Spirals of sparkling orange glass swirled around the big thumb-shaped building; the rest was matte tan.

"Are you planning to join me?" Lucas stood inside the restaurant, a touch of his old irritation surfacing.

Mia hurried in. The host today was the tall woman with the wheat-blonde hair. Mia still didn't understand how the other host—short and angry—kept his job. Son of a partner was the only plausible explanation.

"Mr. Dunn!" The hostess beamed. "Your table is almost ready."

The Lucas from images in Earth gossip pages was back. The handsome one who wore barely dressed female partners as accessories. The hostess wasn't the only one affected by his transformation. Everyone from executives to waiters interacted with him differently now that he wasn't sick. The last client Lucas saw before his visit to the clinic recoiled when he sat next to her to explain how the conversation shield worked. Now, people leaned in, and the accidental touching that Mia told Lucas never happened here—because there was so much space—began to happen to him.

Mia tried to remain unaffected by the change, but Lucas reminded her of what she missed about the men on Earth. Specifically, those who couldn't pass the tests needed to get a contract on Victoria, or those that didn't bother trying. They were odd, unpredictable, and intriguing.

Her junior-year boyfriend, blissfully blinded by a haze of pot smoke, hadn't noticed Mia's frequent slips into omniscience. He'd poke a clay-covered finger onto the plasticrete table in the art studio and declare he'd never sell out. She loved his crooked teeth and strange impulses. It never occurred to her to take the long way to a restaurant, or to sit on a bench and giggle at people trying to get a beverage from a machine with a bad UI. Eventually, she'd gotten bored with him, but not until after he opened her eyes to the joys of imperfection.

That was the thing with Lucas. His kind of handsome was impossible to order from a mod catalogue. The men of New Canberra would never have the guts to go to a surgeon and ask for asymmetry, a small scar buried in one eyebrow and another cutting straight across the right cheekbone. A few random freckles. Permanent creases from worry or concentration. A scattering of gray hairs amidst the dark brown. Teeth slightly askew, one chipped. They might ask for his amazing dark blue eyes, but they'd want the green flecks in the left one removed. In short, they'd try to fix all the imperfections that added up to something unique and beautiful, and end up with yet another horribly perfect, characterless visage.

On top of all that, the man was giving off pheromones like a flat bush gave off seed pods. At least, that was what Mia guessed was happening. Most men opted for suppressors in their daily pill, and Lucas clearly hadn't. She'd have to up her own dose or risk unprofessional thoughts. Sexual relations between coworkers could destroy a firm as small as theirs. She'd seen it happen in departments at Han. The moment things went wrong, invoices weren't processed, meetings ended in shouting matches, and overall productivity dropped until one of the two parties was transferred.

No one at Summit could be transferred. All of them were stuck at the firm. Jason was gay, so he'd not hook up with hetero Lucas or Mikey unless huge amounts of drugs were involved, and Mia could not picture that scenario happening—ever. Claire was Claire, making her unavailable to nearly everyone on two planets. That left relations between her and

Mikey and Lucas. She had zero attraction to Mikey, and he knew it. The ground beneath her and Lucas was shakier. Not because of anything he'd done—he'd been nothing but professional—but Mia did miss men too imperfect to end up on this planet. Still, quirky guys might be out there, maybe in another sector. She'd not be so lazy and destructive as to look for it in the plasticrete shell of the Summit office building.

"Your table is ready, Mr. Dunn," the hostess said. She bent to retrieve menus from a much lower location than they were normally stored, angling her ample cleavage toward Lucas.

Mia sighed. *Another past-her-prime but still beautiful model here on a short-term contract.* The Six waived higher-education requirement for these art objects; no master's degree needed to greet patrons.

What did Lucas think of the sudden attention? His expression was neutral. Until recently he'd gotten nothing but cold stares at Antonio's. He must be painfully aware, maybe for the first time, that his face and body were components in his past successes. Mia had worked with enough beautiful people to know they denied—even as they smiled their way to the best table in the restaurant—that looks were as important as skills and intelligence.

The hostess took them to the usual table and leaned in, her honey hair forming a silky curtain that excluded Mia.

"Can I tell you about the specials?"

"Not now," Lucas said, and something in his face must have warned her off. She straightened abruptly and left.

"Anything I need to know?" he asked.

Mia inspected the restaurant as if she were a partner displeased to be brought to such a pedestrian establishment. "Nothing important has changed."

"The clientele?"

"The usuals."

She watched the front door over the top of the menu. Lucas never let her face the client's table. She was a hopeless gawker, and even with glasses on, it was evident she was staring.

She'd barely had time to orient herself before the hostess brought a young woman to Dr. Lerner's table. Dezzie's boss had not yet arrived.

The woman was early and also way too early for the late-night dance club she appeared to be dressed for, a wisp of a top barely covering her breasts. No one on Victoria was prudish, but the corporate and social hierarchy dictated a time and a place for everything—and everyone—and she didn't belong there now. Lucas sent a message to Claire to make sure the restaurant hadn't given the table to the wrong person.

No, she was Dr. Lerner's lunch date. In her early twenties, she had a moonlike face, large, innocent brown eyes, a tiny nub of a nose, and a small full-lipped mouth that begged a pacifier rather than a kiss. Her inexpensive clothing suggested she might be a research associate from Earth, on a two-year contract to Victoria. Her purse said otherwise. Mia knew that purse. She couldn't have afforded it even when she worked on the exec floors.

A gift from an affluent lover? If so, it wasn't from Dr. Lerner. Not because he was married—he was, to a system administrator in Andaman's finance division—but because senior research scientists didn't make enough credits to buy a girlfriend a purse like that. He and his wife were firmly middle class, their extra credits going to their young daughter's college fund and back to Earth to support his wife's aging parents. Mia knew way too much about them, thanks to Lucas's research requirement.

A message from Lucas popped onto Mia's glasses. *Lerner's lunch date is capturing high-quality audio and visual data. Not from her glasses though.*

Claire responded. *Signal is coming from her necklace. I'm adding interference. She'll get garbage data.*

Recording a meeting was not unusual. Glasses had a protocol for this. One pair would ask another for permission, and a set of rules determined whether it was given or if the request was bumped up to the wearer for confirmation. At Han, anyone of higher rank was allowed to record interactions with anyone of a lower rank, but not vice-versa.

Did this young woman work for Dr. Lerner? That would explain the secondary recording device, as her glasses wouldn't be able to record without alerting him.

The woman rummaged through the expensive purse and pulled out a lip kit. The latest model and also not cheap. She made an elaborate show of running the laser across her pout, and, once her lips were irritated to plumpness, applied bright red varnish.

She was getting frank stares from the other diners, and the hostess conferred with the manager. The issue would likely be "ambiance." Every restaurant aspired to attract partners, and Antionio's would not do so with off-brand clientele.

Dr. Lerner arrived in time to avert a crisis. He was in his mid-forties, tall, with salt and pepper hair and a professorial air. Everyone relaxed, re-casting the woman as a newly arrived intern or visiting niece. He stopped a few meters away from the table and examined the young woman skeptically.

She leapt to greet him. Her shriek would have echoed throughout the room if not for the sound-dampening tiles on the ceiling. Mr. Lerner politely fended off her attempted hug.

"Mia." Lucas had a hundred different ways of saying her name, and this meant *stop staring*, but staring was practically required; the woman again had the attention of most of the patrons. Dr. Lerner sat quickly and encouraged the woman to do so as well. She obeyed after giving him a squeeze on the shoulder.

"Fried ringfish for a starter?" Lucas asked.

Now that Lucas was better, the food he ordered wasn't a prop. He ate abundantly, relishing the planet's seafood; many varieties were not exported to Earth. He was distracted by his returning health. As was Mia... usually. At the moment, she was utterly absorbed in the strange drama.

By the time the main course arrived, it was clear Dr. Lerner was under siege. He ceded all territory north of his plate of butterfish, abandoning his water glass and forgoing salt and pepper. He slid his chair back until it knocked into that of the man behind him. Even so, his lunch date's flashing red nails darted ceaselessly forward, sliding down the back of his hand, picking nonexistent lint from his sleeve, spearing a bit of his fish, tracing wavy lines down the condensation of his glass, and bringing the drop of liquid she collected to her cherry lips.

If it were an attempt at seduction, it was the worst Mia had ever seen. Dr. Lerner called for the check when the woman began to slowly lick butter from a slim piece of imported asparagus.

He paid and hurried out the front door. The woman followed, as did Lucas. Mia watched their goodbye through his glasses. Dr. Lerner hailed a pod and gestured for the woman to enter. She hopped in and patted the seat next to her. When he declined to join her, she leapt back out and grabbed his hand, her coquettishness verging on desperation. Dr. Lerner pulled free and leaned close to her for the first time. Whatever he said caused her to back away. He got into the pod alone, locked the doors, and departed.

The young woman stomped like a spoiled child, pulled down her glasses, and began an animated, angry conversation.

"What was that about?" Mia asked, when Lucas returned, hoping he'd heard the tirade.

Lucas ignored the question. "We're done. Get the shield from Dr. Lerner's table. Subtly please. Pay the bill. I'll meet you outside."

She did both and was nearly out the door when the blonde hostess blocked her exit. Mia hadn't realized how tall the woman was until she faced clavicles as sharp as knives.

The hostess waved a shiny black card. "Your coworker dropped this."

Mia turned it over and saw the hostess's contact info.

The hostess arched a penciled-in eyebrow when Mia looked at her quizzically.

"You'll give it to him or be seated by the restrooms from now on."

Mia suppressed a smile. "I'll give it to him, but I can't guarantee he won't drop it. Again."

"And I can't guarantee your reservations."

Mia knew all about Nadia Korotkov. Not her personally, but about former models hired to be beautiful for six months and then go away.

"How long is your shift?" Mia asked. "Not today. On the planet."

Nadia scowled. She wanted to stay longer. They all did. They hadn't the credentials to get a real contract. They were seasonal décor and treated as such, but they also made more credits in half a year than they'd make in a decade on Earth.

She muttered something in Russian and stalked away on twig-thin heels. Mia wouldn't normally have antagonized her, but Nadia would be fired if the manager found out what she'd said to a customer. The short-term staff's eagerness to find a "patron" was tolerated as long as it didn't interfere with their assigned duties—in this case pleasing Mia now, not Lucas in bed later.

She dropped the card into her purse and exited, squinting against the glare and searching for Lucas. He was half in a pod, right leg extended so the door couldn't close.

"Hey," she said when he didn't move, absorbed as he was in typing.

He retracted his leg without looking up.

She turned on the conversation shield once they were in motion. "You made a friend at Antonio's." She handed him Nadia's card. "She threatened to seat us by the bathroom from now on if you don't call."

Lucas caught the shiny slab, read the back, then threw it out the window.

"Hey! We can get fined for that."

She glanced at the pod's screen but Lucas must have blocked the cameras because no warnings displayed.

"What was that about? Not the hostess—Dr. Lerner."

"Mia."

Meaning, *Mia, be quiet. We fulfilled the contract.*

"Someone made his lunch date do that—whatever that was. But why? And why did Dr. Lerner hire us? How did he know she'd try to record the meeting? Who did she call after he left?"

Lucas, surprisingly, didn't rebuff her.

"The young woman was a summer research associate for Dr. Lerner two years ago. Claire found messages suggesting the woman had a crush on Dr. Lerner."

"I didn't see those."

"No, you didn't. I'm sparing you the excesses of Claire's research. I doubt anyone made the young woman do anything. Dr. Lerner's marriage contract, since the birth of his daughter, requires monogamy. Whatever the woman tried, failed."

It made sense. A last-ditch effort to force Dr. Lerner into bed. The presumed success would be recorded and sent to the wife, breaking up the marriage. Mia had never seen anything like that happen in real life, but it was a familiar plot in the holos she watched to relax.

When she looked at Lucas, he was almost smiling. "No argument?"

"There isn't any logic when it comes to relationships."

He didn't argue.

Chapter Thirteen

Relationships became more and less logical the next weekend.

Friday evening, Jason dragged Mia to The End for a drink after work. To their surprise, they found a small group of young, expensively dressed men and women hovering just inside the front door, whispering to each other conspiratorially.

Mia's heart sank. The End had been discovered.

She knew the cycle. A few adventurous young partners would scope out an unpopular bar and, if it was bad enough to be good, they'd quietly invite friends. For a few weeks, it would be *the* underground hot spot. As soon as the support staff found out about it, the partners would flee. When the glow left by the partners faded, the support staff would drift away, and the bar would return to peaceful obscurity once again. Could she do anything to stop it? Probably not. The décor was too dismal, dirty, and tasteless, and the patrons hopelessly out of fashion.

She followed Jason to a booth in the back. Though she knew about the phenomenon, she was never connected enough to learn an address until it was too late. She worried this group might be from Han until she saw a glittering A logo on one woman's purse. Andaman. Small mercy.

The interlopers surveyed the old space holos, the dinged up chairs and tables, and more subtly, the clientele. One brave woman approached the bar, careful not to let her draping sleeves touch the filthy counter as she reached for a drink screen. What she read made her laugh, and her cohorts swarmed around her.

John, the bartender, brought Mia a bourbon on the rocks she hadn't ordered.

"What are they?" he asked, eyeing the young partners as if they were scarra beetles.

She was apparently the resident expert on the overdressed. John had likely never set foot in a headquarters building. "Partners from Andaman. Legacy, I'd guess. Their fathers or mothers are partners, so they get promoted young. It takes them a few years to settle down after college on Earth."

"What are they doing here?"

"Being ironic. Double the drink prices. You are going to make a lot of credits in the next few weeks."

He gave a sour smile. "My regulars won't like them, but if I can make enough to close for the summer, it'll be worth it." He plodded back to his post.

By the next Friday, the group had swelled to a small crowd. She and Jason claimed a small table in the shadows near the broken jukebox and stared, morbidly fascinated at the spectacle. Mia had never seen partners at play. They twined themselves around the bar like barbed wire, scaring away the regulars. They didn't actually drink the cheap, strong drinks John served but used them as props, gesturing and spilling as they pressed hypos to each other's arms, their tinny laughter cutting through the deep bass of the music.

Mikey and Lucas, who'd arrived early and secured a back booth, also watched—but with intent. Time had healed their clinic-related riff, and they were bar buddies again. Mikey drank exuberantly. Tequila, she knew, from smelling it on his breath too often. Lucas sipped the best scotch the bar had, which was better than it should have been. His drinking looked forced, almost medicinal. Mikey's side of the table held skyscrapers of piled glasses; Lucas formed his empties into a neat, short row. Mikey leered; Lucas methodically evaluated each woman as if she were going to steal data from one of Summit's clients.

She was about to learn what type of woman Lucas preferred. The idea that he'd be attracted to one of the spoiled junior partners nauseated her. Harsh and stylized, the young women flaunted numerous mods. Identical cheek implants. Bone scraped away or added to create small but strong chins. Flawless skin. Various sizes of artificially perky breasts peeked from shirts that were little more than shredded silk. They all wore the long, platinum, *clicky-clacky* nails popular now with women with too much money. Expensive purses, expensive clothes, expensive bodies—The End's shabby environment set off their wealth better than any luxurious room ever could.

Once drug wrappers began falling to the floor, Lucas and Mikey moved in. Lucas walked purposefully to the bar, inserting himself between two women. Mia couldn't hear what he was saying but didn't need to. She saw him as they did—a stark contrast to the clean, domesticated executive boys around them. Tough, disheveled, dangerous. Exotic. Just what these women came for.

Lucas decided on the brunette.

Mia suspected the woman had spent at least a year's worth of her trust fund on beautification mods—with great success. She was stunning. While she'd have to tone her looks way, way down for work, tonight she'd let loose and packaged herself as a product from a sexual fantasy vending machine. High heels, skirt just this side of inappropriately short, jacket and shirt both open and loose. Lips shiny red, face flushed, pupils wide from god knew what drug. She knew just how far to lean forward, how to swing her hair, and when to touch Lucas's arm or hand as she told a story.

Lucas seemed to know this dance as well. He held her with his gaze—intense, unmodded dark blue eyes perfectly set in his worn, handsome face. Once she was drawn in, he slid his hand around her waist, under her shirt, and yanked her close. His look and stance were predatory, almost angry. Did it look like ordinary lust to the woman?

Mia forced her eyes down to the glass she was trying to crush. She wasn't jealous. Any attraction she had to Lucas was due to his proximity and maddening lack of hormone suppressants. She needed to attend to her own needs—no more stalling. She finished her drink in one swallow, mumbled a quick excuse to Jason and worked her way to the door, sticking to the wall farthest from the bar.

Outside, it was cool and calm. She dug through the front pocket of her purse and found the waiter's card from Antonio's. Xander, the one in the band. She'd never called him but she did now, quickly, before she could change her mind. Her glasses directed her to a camera embedded in the wall of The End. She walked to it.

Xander's voice was nearly drowned out by the noise of a crowd. "Mia?"

"Yes. We met at Antonio's," she added, in case he'd forgotten.

"Hang on." A moment later, he switched on his camera. He stood in the back of what looked like a packed bar. He'd pushed his wavy hair away from his face—which sported a day's worth of stubbly beard growth. He looked older out of uniform.

"What are you up to?"

"I'm at Speck's. My friend's band is playing. You should come by. They're good." His smile turned shy and that sold her.

She nodded. "I will. See you in a few." She disconnected and rummaged in her purse for a Baby Jane as she hailed a pod. As she got in, she caught an unfortunate glimpse of Lucas and the expensive woman stumbling out the front door of the bar. He pushed her up against the dirty wall. Her nails flashed on the dark back of his shirt as she pulled him hard to her.

The drink Mia had downed too quickly gurgled in her stomach. "Speck's bar," she instructed the pod, "and hurry."

Mia woke the next morning unsure where she was. She lay on what felt like a pile of balled up socks. Her head ached, and her mouth was as dry as Victoria's empty riverbeds. She opened her eyes tentatively. It took a few moments to focus on Xander sleeping peacefully, face half buried in a pillow. She closed her eyes again.

Fragments from the night before reassembled themselves into a jerky timeline. She met Xander at the bar. Once the Baby Jane kicked in, her doubts about him dissolved like the sugar in an absinthe cocktail. They drank and danced and made out by the stim cigarette machine. He was a good kisser. They took a pod back to his place and had, as far as Mia could recall, brief and underwhelming sex. Once her head cleared, she'd remember the rest, albeit flatly, due to the Baby Jane.

Why had she stayed over? She must have been too drunk to make it back out to the street. *Ugh.*

She blinked the dawn-lit room into focus. Band holos on the walls, no furniture but the lumpy futon they rested on, and a bookshelf holding game controllers and folded t-shirts. A guitar leaning against the wall served as a coat rack. The room of an overgrown teen. She hoped the lights had been out when she made the decision to sleep with him.

Mia worked her arm out from under Xander's torso and grimaced from the pins and needles of returning sensation. Given it was on the floor, the futon didn't shift when she rolled off. She stood unsteadily and searched for her clothes. They'd landed in improbable locations, implying they'd had a more acrobatic time than she remembered. Did Xander play guitar for her? Had she danced? She vaguely recalled a strip tease to the thrum of a bass line.

It'd been a while since she'd overdone it like this. Hangovers were a luxury she couldn't afford when she worked on the executive floors at Han. Not only because of the workload, but due to the risk she might say something inappropriate. Even now she struggled to organize the snapshots of last night, scanning the slightly out-of-focus images for odd looks from Xander, but he'd been stumbling drunk as well, and they hadn't spent much time conversing.

Mia dressed carefully, working around the obstacles of empty hypo packs on the floor and her seasick dizziness, then paused before opening the door. What if Xander had roommates? Would they be used to seeing disheveled strangers emerging from his room? He *was* in a band.

The front room was unoccupied. She made it out of the apartment and into a pod without incident, dimmed the windows, and closed her eyes. She'd probably spent all her credits for the weekend on drinks and hypos and would have to face Xander the next time Summit had a job at Antonio's.

A less hungover part of her smiled. Why did she think of it as *facing* him? The beginning of the evening was fun. He might not be long-term relationship material, but with fewer drinks and drugs, maybe the sex would be better. After all, she'd been half the problem.

The specter of dating, with all its complications, was too much to contemplate right now. She needed a shower, a greasy breakfast, and a long nap.

Chapter Fourteen

Mia and Lucas sat knee to knee at a tiny table at The Drift. She disliked evening meetings, especially on Friday nights. They cut into her personal time and raised the likelihood she'd run into an ex-colleague.

Plus there was the problem of the knees. She held hers together and pressed uncomfortably against the metal railing. Lucas straddled the pole holding the table, seemingly oblivious to the fact his left leg strayed into her territory far too often.

It'd been a few weeks since the junior partners started showing up at The End. While she'd avoided the place, Lucas and Mikey went there every night. Lucas might be growing a little too comfortable in his own skin, now that he fully inhabited it.

Though credits were at stake, Mia had argued against taking the job at The Drift. The aisle between their table and the client's was crowded with overflow from the bar, everyone cheering a sports game being shown live on holo a meter below the ceiling, the tiny translucent players throwing a silver disk and running headlong through bottles of tequila and ceiling fans. An exuberant fan's high five went wide and he lurched into their table, spilling Mia's iced tea onto the nigiri sushi she'd been about to eat.

She swore and mopped up the mess before it could drip into her lap.

"Why are we here?" she asked Lucas, immersed in data on his glasses. "We can't get to our client if someone tries to steal his PDS. I told you popular bars on weekend nights will be impossible, especially during happy hour. I can't keep track of changes. Customers drag tables and chairs around. I've never seen half the servers before, and god knows what *that* is." She pointed to the misshapen lump in the pants pocket of a rear end situated much too close to her face.

Lucas chuckled. He never used to laugh. He'd been too brittle, too easily broken to crack a smile.

"Calm down," he shouted, leaning toward her to be heard above the din. "All he wants is to not to be recorded. The jammer under the table is taking care of that."

He picked a damp sushi roll from her plate and popped it into his mouth. Mia pressed her knees harder against the railing and switched her glasses view to one of the restaurant's many cameras. Their client, another employee of Han's mining division, was an anomaly. He'd had no concerns about safety or data theft—he was breaking up with his boyfriend and wanted to do it in a public place and not have the scene recorded and rebroadcast. Louis, the soon-to-be ex, might just do that once he saw the way things were going.

They weren't going well. Louis, furious, poked their client repeatedly in the chest and seemingly speaking loudly, though his words were trampled by the hoots and shouts of the sports enthusiasts.

Mia kept an eye on them and the nearby drunks, though none of the latter paid any attention to the drama happening below the game.

Finally, the game, happy hour, and breakup ended. The music morphed from frantic beats to a mellow, head-nodding groove. Lucas saw the client safely to a pod, and Mia retrieved the scrambler from under his table. She stretched, trying to loosen the cramp in her leg. Did she need to wait for Lucas? Probably not. She could bring the equipment back to work on Monday.

Lucas caught her as she wound her way through the thinning crowd.

"I'm going to get a drink. Do you want anything? Something to eat? Your food was ruined."

She had no plans—other than a vague idea of going to the gym—and her stomach rumbled. She could eat on Summit's tab if Lucas was buying.

"Sure. Bourbon and soda and fish fries, please."

Lucas caught the bartender's eye immediately. That's what happened now, wherever they went. Lucas had something that was in short supply on screened-into-blandness Victoria, but Mia tired of seeing educated people react to him like a pack of dogs to a dangled bone.

He returned a few minutes later, plate and drinks held aloft like he was leading a tour group. He nodded toward an empty spot against the wall. She took the glasses and set them down on the waist-high rail, then seized the plate, too famished to care the hot grease burned her mouth. The fish was delicious, the coating, perfect. She wolfed every piece down before realizing, embarrassed, that Lucas was watching, and she hadn't offered him any.

"I'm so sorry. Did you want some? I'll get another order."

He shook his head, smiling faintly. "No. I've got what I need." He lifted his scotch and inhaled what to her smelled like old socks.

She took one soothing sip of her own drink before noticing a cotton-candy swirl of blonde hair a few meters away.

Was it Erika? She'd mistakenly mapped her former boss onto a hundred different women on the streets of New Canberra during the past months and imagined how an encounter would play out. Her first instinct had been to hide. That'd morphed into a kind of fearful curiosity. How was Erika doing? Was she fine without Mia? After that came the self-righteous phase where Mia told her off, regardless of what sector they were in.

Erika laughed her weird one-note laugh that sounded like she'd been punched in the stomach. Mia clenched her drink tight.

What was Erika doing here?

This was a lower-floors hangout. Now that the moment was upon her, the animal part of her said to run. She envisioned the floor plan of the restaurant. Erika was blocking the quickest way to the exit, but Mia could work her way around the back of the bar and out the front door.

Before she could offer an explanation to Lucas and flee, boney fingers clasped her arm.

"Mia!" Erika spoke too loudly. Wisps of her normally perfectly contained hair had escaped the bun and made their way toward the ceiling.

Her eyes were bloodshot and too wide. She held a nearly empty martini glass in one hand, and the other returned to grip the railing in what she tried to portray as a casual stance but was clearly necessary to keep her upright.

Mia had never known Erika to get messy drunk. Her modus operandi was to get others tipsy and attempt to pry secrets from them. She recognized the man beside Erika as a senior manager from Han IT. He looked at Mia blankly.

Erika leaned forward and instead of a snide or cruel remark, she was gin-flavored honey.

"Where have you been hiding? I've been looking all over for you. I was sure I'd run into you at Aster or Pinnacle, but you've been laying low. We need to catch up!"

She spoke in a sing-song, friendly manner like she was from Georgia instead of Pasadena. None of the scenarios Mia imagined played out like this. Was Erika on a hallucinogen? Did she forget she'd fired Mia?

Lucas, perhaps noting Mia's distress, moved closer. Erika eyed him, not as a delicious appetizer, but as the possible answer to a troublesome math problem. She set down the martini and held out her hand.

"I'm Erika Brunhoff, Director, Han Corporation."

Lucas glanced at Mia, then shook Erika's hand. "I'm Lucas."

That he'd not given his title and affiliation would rouse Erika's curiosity.

Erika smiled conspiratorially and gripped Mia's arm again.

"Can I steal her for a minute?" She winked at Lucas. "We need to chat."

The part of Mia that wanted to escape was overruled by curiosity. Running into Erika was an inevitability. This bar was a safe place. They weren't in Han sector, and she could call Lucas if things got strange. She slid a hand into her purse and turned the jammer on. Whatever Erika was up to, she wouldn't be able to record it. She caught Lucas's eye. He frowned, but nodded, and reached for the stunner he wasn't carrying tonight.

Erika led her to a recently vacated booth and sat, trying to take a swig of the martini that she'd spilled on the way over. She punched in an order for another on the table. Mia heard the hiss of a conversation shield coming from Erika's purse.

"I can see why you never dated Han men if that's your taste." She nodded toward Lucas. "Rough, no mods. It works on him. If I were—"

"I'm not dating him. He's my boss."

"Right. I heard you got a contract job." Her falsely friendly demeanor dissolved into sober desperation. "Listen. I never wanted to fire you. Yes, you're irritating, and everyone who works under you complains you're overbearing, and you never had my back, but you were a good social engineer. The department is struggling without you. More than struggling. This might be the first time I don't meet my numbers in a decade."

Never did Mia imagine those words coming out of Erika's mouth. For a moment they stared at each other, Erika doing nothing to hide her stress.

"Why did you fire me then?"

"My hand was forced."

Mia thought for a moment. "You had to find someone to take the blame for the IP leaks. Were you covering for a partner? He or she promised to support your promotion if you made their problem go away?"

Erika made a dismissive gesture, nearly knocking over the martini the server was about to set down. After he scurried away, she took it in both hands and drank deeply.

"It doesn't matter what happened," she said after nearly finishing the glass. "There's nothing I could have done differently. I serve the partners."

"You serve yourself. I've been watching you for ten years. You're no pawn."

Erika laughed, and Mia leaned away from the sprayed gin.

"That might be the nicest thing you've ever said to me. I am no pawn, but I had to fire you. Move on. We can help each other now."

Erika fished a large, rumpled envelope from her purse and set it beside her drink.

"You have got to be kidding. You think I'm going to look at anything you show me? Put that away or I'm leaving," Mia snapped, the shock of running into her former boss dissipating, replaced by anger. "I'm glad you're failing. It won't undo the damage you've done to my reputation, but it will prove I was responsible for the success of our department." She stood. "I look forward to your demotion."

"Wait." Erika grabbed her wrist. "In here is a list of theoretical problems a social engineer might be asked to solve. Nothing to do with Han. It's just an exercise. If you write up what'd you'd do, in detail," she pulled Mia closer, "I'll give you a list of every file of yours that was altered. It's too risky for me to fix them, but maybe you can."

Lucas appeared. Erika let go and smiled up at him. "I hope to see you both again, next week, this same time." She slid out of the booth and weaved her way back to the bar.

"What's in there?" Lucas asked, indicating the envelope.

"All the work that's not getting done by my replacement," Mia said, sniffing her wrist, which smelled of the nauseating gardenia perfume Erika wore.

"And?"

"If I tell her what to do, Erika will give us a list of all my files that were altered."

He inclined his head toward the battered envelope, tapped his glasses, and stood quietly for a moment.

"It's not explosive or toxic." He slipped it into his bag. "Let's go."

"I don't care what your glasses say—everything Erika touches is toxic."

"It's not appropriate to discuss this here."

He was right.

Once they were ensconced in a pod, conversation shields activated, Lucas opened the envelope and leafed through the fifty or so sheets of paper.

"These appear to be what she said they are. Detailed reports of failed projects."

"I'm not going to look at those. That's exactly how she trapped me last time—showing me data I couldn't unsee."

"I'll read through them. If she's done a good job of anonymizing, you might consider taking this on. Claire is doing her best to figure out what happened to your records, but some of the changes are pretty obscure. If Erika gives us that list—"

"It will be bullshit, or worse. Links to viruses that will kill our system."

Lucas held up a hand. "What else did she say? You had quite a long conversation before she brought out the envelope."

Mia took off her glasses, leaned back into the plush pod seat, and listened to the comforting hiss of the conversation shield. "She said she didn't want to fire me, but her hand was forced. It might be true," she admitted after a pause. "I didn't sell that IP, but someone did. Maybe it was a partner who needed someone to blame, and they asked Erika for help." Mia stared out the window at the crush of pods heading to the inner rings for Friday night fun. "I was everywhere on the executive floors. I'd be the perfect scapegoat for just about anything."

"True. You know what I did at Itek?"

"Investigated intracompany crime."

He leaned forward, elbows on knees, face serious. "I tried to stop things like this from happening. IP theft, partners finding scapegoats for their own crimes. Why would Erika willingly fire you? It makes no sense."

He was right. She and Erika had butted heads throughout the years, almost concussively at times, but there'd been an undercurrent of respect. Erika's harsh words in that conference room hurt because they were unexpected. There were places they'd agreed not to go. Erika's crass ambition and Mia's poor leadership skills never came up in performance reviews.

"If I read through these and they don't seem to be the negative sorts of projects you objected to, is there any harm in providing guidance? You told me that social engineering was about creating a positive work environment and contributing to the long-term health of the employees."

Mia closed her eyes. "This isn't fair. I help myself, I help her."

"You don't have to decide now. I'm meeting Mikey at The End. Join us for a drink. I don't think you got to finish yours."

She never sat with Lucas and Mikey. They would acknowledge her with a nod or wave but never invite her over. By now it was unwritten law. She couldn't imagine Jason walking in and seeing her sitting with them.

"It's Friday night," she reminded Lucas.

He frowned, puzzled.

"Mikey won't want me hanging around. The women will be there." She'd not meant to be so blunt, but there was no other way to phrase it.

"The women? There are an equal number of men."

"I didn't like them on the upper floors of Han, and I don't like them any better when they're drunk and high at The End. Drop me at the office."

The pod rolled to a stop in front of the shabby building.

"Thanks for your help tonight," Mia said. "I might have slapped Erika when she grabbed me, if you hadn't come over. I wouldn't want that on my record."

"Not a problem. You're going to the gym?"

Mia got out. "Maybe."

He handed her his black bag. "Can you put this in my office?"

"Sure." That meant he wasn't planning to return to his apartment.

The pod rolled away, flashing from white to black as it passed beneath streetlights. She heard bursts of faint laughter and music whenever the door to The End opened, and nearby, the clacks and snaps of insects emerging from their daytime hideaways.

She sat on the curb, suddenly overwhelmed. Erika had been a specter hanging just out of view in every venue she'd visited in the last months. Mia might have a great memory, but she'd used it to focus on the most disturbing aspects of her last day at Han. The stiff formality of the guard herding her into the conference room, the disapproving looks on the faces of the employees around her, Erika's menacing stance and violent gestures, and the final humiliation of being handed her belongings in a dirty plastic bin in front of everyone.

Now Erika said her hand was forced? What wasn't forced was Erika's glee as she told Mia how annoying she was, how the junior SEs didn't like working for her, and that ninety percent of the job was politics, not picking flooring.

Fuck her and fuck Han.

Mia jumped up and paced the still hot sidewalk. She'd fantasized about convincing a partner she'd been set up, getting Erika fired, and returning to work with a promotion and an office with windows. But why? The place was toxic. Partners ordered directors to cover up crimes. Co-workers spread horrible rumors. "Friends" disowned her.

She didn't want to go back.

The decision warmed her like a sunrise on Playa Placida. She was in control of her life, employed, and would never again work for Han. Summit Security opened her eyes to opportunities she never imagined existed on the planet. Perhaps she'd start an independent social engineering firm and be her own boss.

She liked the sound of that.

She picked up Lucas's bulky equipment sack and gazed at The End, a spot of color in the dark desert. Should she go for just one drink? Not tonight. Tonight, she'd climb.

If Lucas was surprised when, on Monday morning, Mia handed him the envelope and a PDS with plans for dealing with most of the projects Erika needed help with, it didn't show. Despite being done with Han, Mia wasn't done with social engineering. Friday night, she'd dropped the bag on his desk—the envelope sticking from the top like the card a bad magician wanted his mark to pick—and started to wonder what happened with the DSC.

The Data Storage Center at Han HQ was five stories below ground, air-gapped from the rest of the building, so data had to be delivered by hand. Security screening for the elevator was none-too-gently handled by armored CorSec guards, and the chilly, dark, underground reception area was commonly known as the tomb.

Delivery of physical objects to floor -5 took four hundred percent longer than to anywhere else at HQ. Mia was assigned the project to fix the issue and had come up with an inspired idea right before she'd been fired: a fish pond in the reception area featuring nocturnal, bioluminescent creatures from the equatorial zone. New Canberra had no public aquarium, so the only time residents saw a fish was when it was fried, poached, or grilled.

Given the security restrictions, the only way to see these exotic creatures would be to be tasked with delivering data. She'd get the delivery time to above average, and no one would mind the gloom when a *Loligo opalescensa* went swimming by, leaving a glowing trail in its wake.

Lucas hadn't given her his bag to drop off at the office because he was off for a wild night—he'd given it to her because he knew she wouldn't be able to resist looking in the envelope. He was right.

"You did it?" He picked up the PDS, seeming to weigh it.

"Most of it. I live in this city and would like to be surrounded by happy, healthy residents. I ignored the projects that would cause more drug use."

"Which you oppose," Lucas said, face neutral.

That he had a sense of humor still surprised her.

"The wrong kinds of drugs. I won't go to the meeting with Erika. You can handle it. She'll probably rip up half the records she was going to trade when she finds out I didn't do everything. Get what you can from her."

Lucas put the envelope in a drawer. "I'll get everything. She doesn't realize who I am."

His dark expression threatened an avalanche, and Mia realized she hadn't seen him angry since he returned from the south shore clinic. He hadn't needed to employ force once he'd regained his striking looks.

"She probably did a background check on you the moment we left the bar."

"I hope so. She won't be eager to intimidate any Summit employees after she reads my bio. We had real crime at Itek, not the bickering over lunch that goes on here. Erika has been away from Earth for too long."

Mia—having tried and failed to get work done during the past two hours—spun her chair around the moment the interior office door opened late the next Friday evening.

"You were gone so long. What happened?"

Lucas held up a PDS. "I've no idea if Erika gave me all the files she altered, but there are over one hundred on here."

"What did she say?"

"About?"

"Everything!"

Lucas smiled. "She definitely didn't want to fire you. I have weapons-grade biometric software in my glasses, and while it's not as good as the skin-contact version, it's pretty good. Someone is leaning on her. She knew the department would suffer without you. Even though you're arrogant and tone deaf and terrible at delegating."

"I'm not—"

"Calm down. I'm sorry this happened, but partners have thousands of people depending on them for employment, and to keep those people employed, they have to keep the shareholders and board happy. A partner committed a crime, got caught, and the shareholders and board needed to be told a junior employee was responsible so they could keep trusting the captains of the ship. Erika made you the likely culprit, showed the evidence, explained why you couldn't be questioned, and fired you. Problem solved. Status quo maintained."

"Not my status quo. I'm a social engineer that can't get a job."

"This isn't a job?"

"You know what I mean. I want to do what I'm best at, and it's not this." Mia waved a hand over her desk, which unfortunately held a lamp she'd been trying to reprogram—something she might actually have done as a social engineer.

Lucas looked at the lamp for a few too many seconds, then grimaced and double tapped his temple with one finger. It was a gesture Mia had become familiar with in the months since he'd returned from the clinic. It seemed to mean he'd overlooked something in the days when he was unwell.

"We should be offering your skills as a service here at Summit."

Mia tried to imagine how what she'd done at Han could translate to her current job. She'd had the budget to literally move mountains, if it would make a partner more productive or get employees to work a few minutes more each day.

Lucas noticed the skeptical look. "What do you do when we arrive at a restaurant? Complain about how badly optimized everything is, how we can't protect our client, how we should have chosen a different table." He pulled Claire's chair over and sat. "We've been missing a huge opportunity. We can offer meeting planning and strategy. I don't know why we've been letting our clients pick the venues."

Mia did. It was because former Lucas had done a terrible job setting up the business.

"Write something up," he said. "I want to offer this right away. It could make our lives easier and bring in more revenue."

He stood, straightened his vest, and returned to his office, the partner in him confident what he'd ordered would be done.

Mia couldn't blame former Lucas for not marketing her social engineering skills. She'd been too unfamiliar with the security industry when she started the job to do anything more than imitate their competitors. Since then, she'd read hundreds of journals and should have seen that social engineering was a natural fit. Too much data sometimes equaled not enough creativity—but no one needed to know that.

Something that might have been excitement compelled her to begin to type. She wouldn't move mountains at Summit, but a table here or a potted plant there could make a difference for their clients—and she'd be doing a version of the job she loved.

Chapter Fifteen

Sticking to the principle of using social engineering only for good became a bit awkward when a new client called two weeks later.

The screen showed a woman with chin-length, glossy black hair, long bangs, and dark glasses sitting in a pod stopped in front of the Outdoor Adventure store in Andaman sector. Her clothes said she was an executive, maybe even a partner, and a tightness in her jaw said she was worried.

"Mia Julian?"

How did she know her name? No one but Lucas was listed on the literature.

The woman's look was so generic it was difficult for Mia to be sure they'd never met, but she was fairly certain they hadn't. One of Summit's clients might have used Mia's name in a referral to a friend, but that would have been odd. Everyone remembered Lucas.

"Yes?"

"Is this a secure connection?" She held something in her lap, possibly a conversation shield.

"It is on our end."

The woman darkened the pod windows and gestured, and her contact info appeared in the corner of Mia's screen. Yvette Tanaka, Partner, Asteroid Mining Division, Han Corporation. Mia definitely knew her name. Ms. Tanaka had come grudgingly to Victoria when Han acquired her successful mining company and remained vocal about the lack of innovation in slow-moving megacorps like Han. She was a bit of an embarrassment but purported to be a brilliant engineer, so Han tolerated her critiques.

"This conversation is confidential?" Ms. Tanaka asked.

"Of course. All our client interactions are. Here's our privacy policy." Mia sent the file over and Tanaka took her time, probably the first client to actually read the document. While the woman perused the file, Mia studied her. She wasn't wearing any of the status jewelry partners used in their attempts to outdo each other. Interesting.

"I need a social engineer, and you might be the only freelancer on the planet. You worked at Han for ten years?"

Mia nodded, though admitting it felt like she was incriminating herself.

"I hear you're a firecracker."

"Excuse me?"

The corner of Tanaka's mouth twitched upward. "That's what we partners call it when a junior employee is blown up to distract from something an executive did wrong. There's no way you went from being Han's best social engineer to selling IP to a competitor for a few hundred thousand credits. Given your career arc, you'd have been a director in five years and making that and more in bonuses. Erika Brunhoff is an idiot for choosing you to go down for whatever happened, but," she held up an open palm, "it's none of my business. I don't have the time or authority to police everything that goes on here."

Lucas's theory about what happened was correct.

"Does this firecracker thing happen often?"

Tanaka smiled wide, revealing slightly crooked teeth. "All kinds of things happen often at Han. One of them is happening to me, and I'd rather it didn't. Your firm offers meeting optimization. I need you to optimize a meeting I'm holding next week at The Center."

The new conference facility in Center Park had recently opened with a gala event that Mia wouldn't have been invited to even if she'd still been working on the upper levels of Han. The venue claimed to be the most secure, most private event and meeting space on the planet, situated as it was on neutral ground in the center of the city and run by Optima.

"We haven't done any work there. Do they allow private security?"

"They allow just about anything—if you pay for it. I need you to optimize my meeting for failure. Make it unproductive. I don't want to hold it at all, but I can't put it off any longer. I must appear cooperative, but the less that gets done in there, the better. I know you social engineers can make things go wrong as well as right."

Mia scowled, and Tanaka hurried to explain. "I mean no disrespect to your profession. You spent ten years studying all the things that go wrong in a space. I'd like to tap into that knowledge. I'm looking for subtle. No ceiling tiles falling down or fire alarms. Merely a series of minor inconveniences that nibble away at the time. You and your team can work with The Center on the physical environment and, though I can't show you the agenda, I'd like your input on how to structure a meeting so that nothing gets done."

Mia had vowed not to use her skills for negative assignments. "I'm not sure about this. I'll have to talk to Mr. Dunn—our firm's owner."

Ms. Tanaka took off her glasses. She was younger than Mia expected. Young to be a partner. "I'm not hiring Mr. Dunn. I'm hiring you. We've only got a week to prepare, so I need an answer now."

She raised her chin and in the set of her mouth, Mia saw the entitled attitude she'd come to expect from partners. Tanaka gestured, and a bank transfer appeared in the bottom of Mia's screen. It was for ten thousand credits. "Ten thousand more if the meeting goes badly, plus expenses."

Mia's eyes widened. 20K was as much as they'd make in two years for a top-tier home-monitoring contract. They'd get all the credits now. Summit had the potential to be a successful business, but until there were credits for advertising and spare parts for Jason, they couldn't grow.

Tanaka smiled. "You'll do it."

Mia took a deep breath. "Maybe. I do need to talk to my boss."

"I'll keep that bank draft active. You accept it and I'll know you've accepted the job. I'll call tomorrow to discuss the details." She cut the feed.

Mia sat for a moment, staring at the blank screen, then went over and tapped on Lucas's half-open door.

"Yes?"

He was engrossed in the streaming squiggles running across his big screen. The output from one of the Appliance Data Managers.

"We got a call from a potential client."

When she didn't say more, he looked up. "Was there a problem?"

"You record all the calls. Play it."

She pulled up the extra chair and sat across from him. He didn't keep the office as dark as he used to when he was sick, but it always took some time for her eyes to adjust to the pale gray light. He brought up the log and watched the call, glancing up at Mia when Tanaka described what a firecracker was. He paused the recording when the flashing *10,000 credits* draft appeared.

"Do you know her?" he asked.

"I know of her. She's a partner in the mining division who came to Han by way of an acquisition. She's very critical of the company."

"What do you think of this job?"

"It's odd, but I'm not opposed to doing it."

"It sounds uncomfortably similar to the assignments Erika tried to force you to do at Han."

She gave him a sharp look. Nothing about his face or tone betrayed sarcasm, so she relaxed. "It does, but this is Ms. Tanaka's meeting, and if she wants it to be unproductive, that's her prerogative. And, truthfully, it feels good to mess with Han."

"I'm afraid your time here has eroded your ethics."

Was he joking? "The fear of being forced to move back in with my mother has eroded my ethics. We can't turn this down. The credits will cover a couple of months' salary for everyone plus the rent—and Jason can buy a bigger bio-printer."

"Do partners on Victoria often hire third-party security firms?"

"Rarely. Partners can use CorSec whenever they want. That said, I've heard that for small, private events, they do sometimes use one of the spin-off security firms from within the sector. For Han, that would be First Line."

"Itek Partners always hired private contractors for personal events. In New York, hundreds of firms offered executive protection. You have under a dozen here in New Canberra, and only one of them has a staff of more than ten people. Based on that, I'd say this is unusual."

"It is," Mia agreed. "As is Yvette Tanaka and The Center. It's the city's first truly neutral, private meeting space. If a partner wants privacy, the last thing she'd do is bring corporate security."

"Good point. I'd like to be in on the call tomorrow," Lucas said.

"Why wouldn't you be?"

"Ms. Tanaka made it clear she wasn't hiring Mr. Dunn."

Mia smiled, glad he noticed. This job was getting better and better. All those credits, the chance to fuck with Han, and someone valued her skills. Lucas was being facetious, but she answered him seriously. "She's hiring the firm. We're a team."

Once back at her desk, Mia pressed *Accept* on the credits.

Ms. Tanaka called early the next morning. Despite the fact that Mia had accepted the credits and thus the job, Tanaka seemed relieved to see her. She was in a pod again, this time circling Ring 20, desert scrub visible through the back window.

Lucas asked Claire to do a client background check but to stick to publicly available data. Partners—a class of client they hadn't expected to attract—likely had extra data protection.

Mia read the bio with interest. Born and raised on Earth, Yvette Tanaka grew the family business from a small-time drill bit manufacturer to one of the largest makers of automated asteroid mining machines. She hadn't wanted to sell the company to Han, but her father was the majority stockholder. Tanaka, in a bizarre, almost medieval twist, was also sold— and required to run what would become a division of Han for five years. She was six months shy of fulfilling her obligation. Her husband and two kids were vocally eager to return to Earth.

Lucas introduced himself in the way that usually commanded attention, but Tanaka addressed Mia. "I'm so glad you took the job. What do you need to get started?"

Mia glanced at Lucas. He nodded, so she went through the list. "I'd like bios of all the meeting attendees. I want to meet with your contact at The Center and I'll also need an open line of credits for the meeting room and other expenses."

Tanaka shook her head. "No on the bios, sorry. Five people will attend." She typed on a screen on her lap. "I'm opening the line of credits… should be on your screen now." A blinking blue square appeared. "I don't have a contact at The Center. My assistant reserved the room. Talk to anyone. Also, I'll need security staff from your firm onsite. Have them check for prohibited devices at the door to the meeting room. It would be best if your people appeared to be in-house security. I don't want anyone to know I hired you." She hesitated. "The others will bring guards. I don't want them in the room. I'm not sure there's any way to keep them out, but if you can…"

"I'll talk to the staff at The Center and see if they can suggest anything," Mia said. "I'm sure you aren't the first person who didn't want eavesdroppers in a confidential meeting."

"Any suggestions on how to slow things down?"

"I've got a list I'll send you, but I've observed one no-fail tactic. Ask the others to clarify. Whatever they say, ask how long, how tall, how deep, what they mean by daylight hours or project completion. You get what I mean? People love to talk. It won't come across as stalling; it will seem like you're interested."

Tanaka nodded, face serious. "It will indeed. I can do that." She directed the pod back to the city center. "Let's touch base again tomorrow afternoon." She disconnected.

Mia stood. "I'm going to check out The Center."

"I'd like to come along, if you don't mind."

She did mind. Handsome Lucas drew unwanted attention, and when they worked jobs together, he took charge. She was used to having a disengaged boss, not one that was less than a meter away. She worked better alone and intended to do this job her way.

"You don't have to come. I just want to learn more about the services The Center offers."

He trailed her back to her desk. "So do I. If we like it, we can encourage our clients to hold lunch meetings there instead of out in public."

Mia closed her eyes, took a deep breath, tried to picture herself lucky it was Lucas and not Erika following her around and failed. Erika would have found whatever passed for a bar at The Center and let Mia do the work. Lucas would ask penetrating but Earth-based questions and screw everything up.

"Let me do the talking. Whatever we've been experiencing in restaurants, it won't be like that at The Center. It's an Optima project, and that means all the Six were involved. It will be secure, and the only variables will be human."

"You may recall from my resume that I have some experience with corporate security."

She held her frustration in check. "Let me run this job. I don't want to explain myself."

Lucas inclined his head like a benevolent dictator. "Of course. Ms. Tanaka did hire you."

She bit off her reply and headed to the door.

In the pod, Lucas sat across from her, facing forward as usual.

"You got new clothes." She hadn't noticed in the dim office, but in the sunlight his vest glimmered, a luxurious thick silk with a subtle diamond pattern woven into it. The shirt was long-sleeved, white, Earth linen with bamboo buttons. Definitely by Legassian, an up-and-coming designer from the Faroe Islands. His pants had a small split cuff, and the shoes, a distressed open-weave leather. She shook her head.

Lucas frowned. "Are they inappropriate? I got the impression—from you—that clothes are an important measure of status here."

"Here and everywhere. They're fine. You look successful." He'd picked an outfit a partner would wear on a day off. Trendy and expensive but not flashy. Because, she had to remind herself, he'd been a partner.

He persisted. "Are they appropriate for my job title?"

She shrugged. "I don't know what the owner of a security firm is supposed to wear."

He examined his shirt-sleeve critically, and she relented.

"They're perfect. You look professional but not staid. Those clothes say your business is a success, you've got plenty of credits, good taste, and probably eight more pairs of those John Jacob shoes."

It wasn't the designer names, it was how carelessly comfortable he was in the ensemble. She'd worn the upper-floor outfits Erika had purchased for her—when Erika had realized Mia had been promoted as well and might reflect badly on her—with a giddy self-consciousness. The clothes from Garcia DuBois made her feel smarter, taller, more capable, but also slightly uncomfortable—as if someone might realize she was an impostor.

Today, she wore a nine months out-of-date Amelia Corsica dress. It was okay for now, but would soon whisper that she was a junior employee with a low salary who shopped at sales or was oblivious to trends. Some of that would be accurate.

She pushed those thoughts aside and pulled up information about The Center. Construction had taken half a year—a long time for New Canberra—and she was curious to see the result. It was the latest work from Naomi Habib, a young architect who'd designed the award-winning Cape Town Contemporary Art Museum right after graduation from New Beijing U. Mia found the seashell inspirations of her work heavy-handed and literal, but the Six were more interested in novelty than critical acclaim. Much as she loved New Canberra, it glittered like gaudy costume jewelry thrown haphazardly on the sand. The rare, tasteful building only accentuated that. The Center was on trend—an oversized and half-buried nautilus shell dropped into the park, probably by the spoiled child of a partner.

The pod exited Ring One and headed into the park on a below-grade, tree-lined track. Half a kilometer in, a grassy berm appeared, the gleaming pearly roof of The Center barely visible above.

They came to a stop at the foot of a long set of white marble stairs leading, presumably, to the entrance. Mia waited for Lucas to perform his ritual of holding open the pod door for her, then slid out, intrigued despite herself. The building was no longer visible, and it would be impossible to get a malicious pod anywhere near the front doors. Smart way to do a big reveal and prevent access to anyone with a vehicle loaded with explosives. Lucas switched his glasses to mirror and looked around, nodding in approval, then gestured for her to precede him.

When she reached the top of the stairway—steeper than usual for New Canberra—she caught her breath. The Center was lovely. At ground level, the seashell design was muted. The pearly roof morphed into a wall that flowed into a reflecting pool encircling the building. *Not a pool, a moat,* Mia thought, shifting perspective from a passerby to a security professional. Round, randomly placed mirrored windows of all sizes, set seamlessly into the wall, reflected the sky or trees, making the building look transparent, a stylized sea urchin missing its quills.

Lucas lagged a few steps behind as she crossed a solid slab of marble serving as a bridge to the front door. She paused, gazing down into the water. The dark blue tiles lining the pool slid down into infinity. The pool might be as deep as an ocean. Only when Lucas grabbed her arm did she realize how far she'd leaned over, trying to see the bottom.

"Be careful," he said.

"I can swim."

"I don't doubt it, but now might not be the best time."

He kept hold of her, grip tight, until she stepped away. The moment might have been awkward, but she was saved by the bell. A chime, actually, from the entrance door. A screen to the left of it popped to life, and a facsimile of a human—brown-haired and brown-eyed and lacking discernible gender or race—smiled. "Welcome to The Center. We are proud to provide a weapons- and toxin-free environment. Prescription medicines are welcome with proper documentation. Recreational drugs are prohibited. Please check all restricted items at the station to your right."

A large, metal drawer slid out from the wall. The person on the screen spoke again. "Lay your items in the bin, then place your palm on the sensor. You can retrieve your items when you leave by again placing your palm on the sensor."

"You have anything?" Lucas asked.

Mia hesitated, then pulled out a pack of Baby Janes and placed them in the drawer. They were legal but not prescription. Lucas glanced down, and she cursed herself for not leaving them at the office. He'd seen her take these pills before but hadn't seen the label. She slapped her hand on the sensor to shut the drawer—too late. The foil backing had logos all over it.

The drawer retracted and the main door to The Center, narrow and thick like an old-fashioned bank vault, opened outwards. The voice instructed them to enter one at a time and check in at the front desk.

Mia went first, walking only a few meters before a wall blocked her path. The front door shut behind her, and a moment later the wall slid aside to reveal a narrow hallway, lighted arrows on the floor urging her forward. Bursts of warm air buffeted her, and dim lasers played across her body. Standard security for strataports but not used much in public buildings.

At the far end of the hall, another door opened, and she emerged into the reception area, disoriented by the brightness of the cavernous space. The floor was white marble and the walls the same pearlescent material as the exterior. Sunlight lanced in through the round windows, seeming to burn circles of gleaming iridescence on the shining floor. Two large, sunken conversation pits, to the right and left, held couches and small tables.

Lucas joined her a moment later. He still wore his glasses on mirror, and she couldn't tell what he thought of this room. Was it stunning or pedestrian compared to the interiors of New York?

They click-clacked their way across the wide expanse of slick marble to the reception desk. The young woman sitting behind it had been hired, Mia was quite certain, because of her literal resemblance to the room itself. Alabaster skin, pale blonde hair, eyes as blue as the bits of sky above. Lucas took off his glasses and moved ahead. The young woman gazed up at him, and her polite smile shifted to genuine pleasure as she took him in. He leaned onto the counter and relaxed into the slight slouch he assumed when he planned to charm. Mia frowned and joined him.

"Welcome to The Center. How can I help you?" the woman asked Lucas.

Mia could tell she was an underling from her sing-song cadence.

Lucas started to speak, and Mia held up her hand. He stopped.

"May I speak to the facilities manager? I'm planning a meeting, and I have special needs. *Very special.*"

The receptionist moved her hands across a screen hidden by the countertop. She glanced at Mia but replied to Lucas. "Sergei will be right out."

"Great," Mia said. "Could you take my colleague on a tour? This is our first time here."

The woman jumped up. "Of course! We have a state-of-the-art facility, and most of the features aren't obvious. I can go over everything with you." She came out from behind the counter, screen in hand, and gestured to one of the conversation pits.

"Keep your glasses on. Claire might call," Mia said.

The receptionist chimed in. "You won't be able to receive outside calls unless you sign in to our network. All communications are routed through us, and we do scan them for malicious activity."

Lucas gave Mia a cool look as the woman led him to one of the couches.

A minute later, a door to the left of the reception desk opened and Sergei emerged. He wore what must be a uniform because the receptionist wore the same thing: stone gray pants, white shirt, and light blue vest. On her, it was form fitting and attractive; on Sergei, it was silly. He was a big man, not particularly fit, and the vest strained to contain his stomach. Mia could tell he'd had his sleeves rolled up until a moment ago because they were heavily wrinkled to the elbow and unbuttoned. He reached over the counter to shake her hand. His was rough. He was a technician, not just a manager.

"Hello Miss Julian. How can I help you?" he asked in a heavy Russian accent.

He was in his mid-fifties, face heavily lined and amiable. A peculiar scar marred the side of his head. She'd seen this before. Implant removal. Implants were illegal on Earth too, but if you never rode public transportation and worked for a company willing to look the other way, people sometimes had them for years before they were caught. Of course, it was impossible to get on a passenger ship to Victoria with one, so anyone who landed a contract had them taken out right away. He wasn't afraid to break the rules and must be skilled and intelligent to win a contract, given his looks and dubious past. Exactly what she needed for Tanaka.

"I'm planning a meeting here, and I have some very specific needs. Is there somewhere private we can talk?"

"Yes, sure. Follow me."

He lumbered out from behind the counter and led her to a room to the right of the reception desk. Lucas watched, clearly not happy to be excluded. The young woman touched his arm to bring his attention back to the diagram on her screen.

The room was small and windowless, and when Sergei shut the door, completely silent but for the hiss of the air conditioning. Mia took a seat at the compact conference table. Sergei sat across from her, activated the table screen, and pulled a stylus from his front pocket.

She took a conversation shield from her purse and activated it. "Do you mind?"

Sergei waved a hand. "It is not needed. This room is a box. A sealed box. But you can leave it on."

"You work for Optima?"

"Of course."

"Whatever we discuss, whatever you do for my meeting, is confidential?"

He sat up, looking less tired and more interested. "Of course. That is the whole point of this center, no? I come especially from Earth for this job. I am confidential. I never worked for any of your Six."

"Excellent. My client, Ms. Tanaka, has a room here next week."

Sergei slid his stylus across the table. "Ah yes, I see that. Three p.m. next Thursday."

How to word this? She'd never had to involve anyone else in a social engineering project. "I can request any kind of lighting, temperature, and room configuration?"

He nodded.

"Can I request extra security screening at the front door if I'm concerned that some of the attendees might try to bring in restricted items?"

He nodded again. "It is impossible to bring in those items, but yes. We have the rules of The Center but some meetings have their own special rules. You can forbid glasses, screens, paper and pen even, if that is what you want. Anything. We will enforce." He smiled and winked, not salaciously like Mikey, more like they were friends planning a practical joke.

Mia handed him her screen. "I have an open line of credit that includes petty cash. It doesn't matter to my client how much it costs to run the meeting. That said, I don't want any special instructions to appear on the invoice. Do you understand?"

His smile broadened. "I do understand Miss Julian. I am very happy to add extra services, and there is no rule that says I must itemize them."

They were going to get on well together. Mia pulled her chair closer and explained the plan.

Ms. Tanaka called the morning of the meeting to get final instructions. Mia put her on one of the big screens so the entire team could see, given everyone had a role to play. Tanaka looked like a real partner today, wearing the expected understated makeup and oversized jewelry.

"Everything is set?"

"Yes," Mia said, praying Lucas wouldn't jump in.

"You still won't tell me what you have planned?"

"No, Ms. Tanaka. I assume you don't usually handle the logistics of your own meetings. You have an assistant do that?"

"Of course."

"Well then, this is just another normal meeting. Prepare your materials and show up. Your reactions to anything that happens need to be genuine. I don't want anyone suspecting you of anything."

She frowned. "I gave you ten thousand credits and won't even know what you did."

"Trust me, you'll know," Mia said.

Tanaka smiled, the first genuine smile Mia had seen from her. "Fair enough. I hope you're as good at this as you think you are. I'll see you at The Center? I'll be there early."

"You won't see me. I'm not going."

Tanaka, Lucas, and Mikey looked at her quizzically.

"Why would I be there?" Mia said. "Lucas and Mikey are posing as Center guards. They'll do the meeting room screening and keep an eye on things. I'll work remotely."

"How can you? The Center isn't connected," Tanaka said.

"Sergei, the facilities manager, will keep me posted. Don't worry. Everything will go perfectly wrong. Your job now is to forget you hired us. Clear your head and react honestly to whatever happens. I'll make sure nothing gets done."

"I trust you." Tanaka gave a small nod and disconnected.

"You two, time to get dressed." Mia tossed Lucas and Mikey each a flat box. Sergei wouldn't let her borrow real uniforms but was kind enough to share the brand names of the pieces, and she found them easily in a catalogue.

When the men emerged from Lucas's apartment minutes later, she and Jason couldn't contain their laughter. Claire, lacking a fashion sense, didn't know what was wrong.

Mikey looked ridiculous. The cut of the vest wasn't suited to men with a large chest. He'd managed to secure one of the six buttons. Sergei had the same problem with his belly.

Lucas tugged at his own vest and tried to smooth the pants. The cheap cloth hung stiffly, pleats in all the wrong places, stitching unintentionally visible. He probably hadn't worn anything so badly made in decades, maybe ever.

Mia took a breath, glad for a moment of levity, but the job was serious. "Keep your glasses on mirror and remember…you are ordinary security guards, underpaid and merely following orders."

"Got it, boss," Mikey said with a wink. He'd been calling her boss all week and relishing how it irritated Lucas.

"Sergei will help if you need anything," she said.

"We know," Lucas said as he headed to the door. "See you in a few hours."

Mia tried to start meeting planning for next week, but couldn't concentrate. She tried to sit, but found herself pacing. Would it work? Would Sergei deliver on her long list of requests? Lucas would record what he could, but would not send any data back to Summit, even when he was outside The Center. Claire said that was the equivalent of pointing a big red arrow straight at the office. She wouldn't know what happened until this evening.

"Enough!" Jason commanded after Mia had crossed and recrossed his field of view a dozen times.

"Sorry. Claire, could you…?"

Claire shook her head. "I can't and won't do anything related to Lucas, Mikey, The Center, the roads leading into The Center, the bakery you ordered the food from. Nothing. And stop asking."

Mia forced herself down into her uncomfortable office chair. If Tanaka paid the other 10K, forget a bioprinter for Jason; the first thing she'd buy would be a new chair.

Tanaka. How did this young partner fit in with the rest of their clients? She didn't. Mia pulled up an org chart of the mining division—all Summit's clients highlighted in bright green—looking for a pattern that never emerged. They all worked in the same division but not on the same projects, and many performed routine jobs and had no access to classified data.

What they did share was a cafeteria. Not Tanaka of course—her bright green square hovered levels of hierarchy above the common workers—but the rest of them would likely dine on the thirty-second floor. Since nearly all their clients were referrals, if their first client had by chance been from finance, perhaps all their clients would be from that division instead, Summit's name shared during early morning coffee or a long Friday lunch on a different level in a different cafeteria.

Tanaka was an outlier. She heard Mia's name at a party—a party none of their other clients would have been invited to. A disgraced social engineer might have been exactly what she was looking for. She wasn't a piece of the puzzle.

Mia turned off her screens and leaned back in the squeaky chair, irritated not to have access to the data she needed to get to the heart of a problem, or to even know if there was one. Han might be allowed to spy on its own employees if there was an investigation underway. If it wasn't Han, if it were espionage by one of the other Six or an Earth corp, she still couldn't do much about it thanks to the contracts and confidentiality agreements they'd signed with their clients.

She took a deep breath and willed her nervous, jangling leg to be still. Whatever was happening, Summit was on the right side of things, giving the residents of New Canberra the privacy their contracts guaranteed. She had to be content with that for now.

Mikey and Lucas didn't return until after 7 p.m., a good two hours after the meeting let out. The inner door banged open, and they entered, both throwing off their cheap vests and unbuttoning their shirts as if they were the entertainment at a bachelorette party.

"Where have you been? Why didn't you call me when you got out? How did it go?" Mia rushed to meet them.

Lucas stepped around her. "One moment. I've got to change." He disappeared into his office.

Mikey, wearing nothing but gray slacks and a deep tan, held his hand up for a high five.

"What happened?" Mia demanded.

"Calm down. The job was a success. Didn't you check the bank account?"

She hadn't. She tapped a screen and there it was—ten thousand more credits. She sagged into a chair, worry leaving her before elation had a chance to prop her up.

Lucas emerged in a fresh shirt and pants.

"Tell me everything," Mia said.

Lucas settled into Claire's chair, distractedly stroking the sleeve of the charcoal-colored shirt he'd thrown on.

"I don't know what you did and didn't do, but I'm impressed. We got there early. Ms. Tanaka arrived just after we did, but there was a group of people ahead of her trying to get into The Center, and they were having trouble. They all seemed to forget they had just one more contraband item. Were they yours?"

"Mikey's actually. Students from his class. Thanks, Mikey. I'm glad it worked."

He grinned. "They love causing trouble. Not much opportunity to do that here."

Lucas's quick, sidelong glance revealed Mikey hadn't told him. She'd asked him not to, but assumed he would. Their "understanding" was developing into professional respect.

Lucas continued. "The other attendees from Han arrived and had to wait outside until that group got things sorted out."

"Who were they?"

"All junior partners. Two from mining, one from finance, one from HR, and one from corporate communications. I'll send you files from my glasses later."

That configuration was typical for a newly funded project. Why not meet at Han HQ? Perhaps it was something controversial, or a project that had been shot down by senior partners, and the juniors were secretly reworking it before they submitted it again.

"We finally got in, but one of the partners set off the toxin alert in the hallway," Lucas said.

"Those things can be very sensitive. I hear even cold medicine can trigger them."

"You?" he asked.

"Yes," Mia answered.

"The receptionist had to wand him and take a blood sample in front of everyone. He was furious, and she was mortified. I got the impression that wasn't a normal part of her job. She wasn't very good at it."

Ah, Sergei. She wanted to hug him. "Then?"

"Mikey and I led them to the room. There was a CorSec guard waiting outside."

"He didn't get into the meeting, did he?"

"No." Lucas said. "He tried, but the door wouldn't close. The Center concierge came onscreen and explained there was a six-person limit for the room. The other partners were annoyed, but Tanaka pulled up the attendee list. No one mentioned they'd be bringing other staff. This was not her assistant's fault."

"There isn't actually a limit," Mia volunteered, worried that Lucas wouldn't realize this was part of the plan.

"Obviously. They went in and got started. Sergei let me know they complained the west-facing room was too warm and bright. He offered to move them, but the only available space was in the other wing. Tanaka left the decision up to the other partners, and they decided to stay. They were busy eating. Was there something special about the pastries?"

"Yes. They're a fad. Honey cream puffs with a mousse center, made by hand. Only one shop sells them, and it doesn't matter whether you are a partner or a peon; you have to queue up to get them. Thanks again to Mikey. He got some of his students to line up at 4 a.m. Bonus meeting stopper—each cream puff is about fifteen hundred calories. Pure sugar." Mia made a diving motion with her hand. "Brief high and then crash. You probably didn't see the drinks I stocked in the room, but there were no stims. Just water, fruit juice, herbal tea."

"At this point you'd shaved almost half the time from the meeting, and no one noticed. The Center let them know they had to be out of there by 6 p.m. because the room was booked. Also," Lucas added, "There wasn't a bathroom in there."

"The really secure rooms don't have them."

"What else did you do?" Lucas asked.

"Little things. I set the chairs at a lower-than-normal height and locked them so the attendees would have to wrestle with them. The main screen was dim. The window glass wouldn't darken past fifty percent. If they'd decided to change rooms, I had another ready with opposite problems. I gave them options so they'd feel in control. As long as I could get the meeting down to under an hour, I was sure they wouldn't get any-thing done. That's barely enough time to go over an agenda. Ms. Tanaka could handle them for that short of a time."

Mia ran her finger across the ten thousand credits figure on the screen. "It worked. She did it. This will get us through the next few months even if we don't get any new clients."

 "Tanaka seemed genuinely angry about the quality of service. She yelled at Sergei in front of everyone." Lucas said.

"I told her it was important to be herself. No one will suspect she had anything to do with the problems. That was part of the assignment. She shouldn't hire us again, anyway. You can't do that twice to the same people."

Mikey hefted himself out of the chair. "Well, good work. I'm gonna get a drink. After I get dressed of course." He grinned but didn't wink. "Join me, Lucas?"

Lucas gave Mia an appraising look. "That was well done."

"Give me an open line of credit, and I can make anything happen," Mia replied.

"I don't think the money had anything to do with it."

"It had everything to do with it. I bought two hours of time and space. No matter what they chose to do in there today, as long as they didn't leave The Center, I had control of their experience. It wasn't cheap. Our fee wasn't the half of it."

She was good at her job, but doing things right required an infra-structure, and infrastructure required credits.

"Come on Lucas, I'm thirsty," Mikey said.

"Have a drink with us," Lucas said. "We won."

Jason, at the worktable, noticed Lucas addressed only Mia.

She shook her head. Former partner Lucas Dunn could be insensi-tive. "No thanks, I'm going to the gym. I've got a day's worth of adrenaline to work off."

She buzzed with the feeling of success, something she hadn't felt in too long. She wouldn't waste it on a pointless evening at The End. She'd try a new level on the climbing wall.

Lucas shrugged, and he and Mikey left.

She joined Jason at the table. "That was rude."

Jason kept working. "What are you talking about?"

"You know what I'm talking about."

He snapped a panel shut on the ADM he was repairing. "I don't want to have drinks with Lucas and Mikey. We have nothing in common."

"It's rude of them not to invite you. We're a team."

Jason snorted. "We're people working next to each other, not with each other."

"That's not true. Without all of us this falls apart."

"We aren't a team. Have we ever had a team meeting? One where we discuss how the business is run? What projects or clients we should take? I heard you trying to convince Lucas not to do meetings at bars on weekend nights and I agree. We're setting ourselves up for failure if we take jobs like that, but Lucas is in charge so we do whatever he tells us to do. That isn't teamwork."

Maybe not, but it was the only structure she'd ever known. Businesses in New Canberra were extremely hierarchical. Summit was as flat an organization as she'd ever seen.

"Come to the gym with me."

"I'm not a member."

"I have guest passes."

"I'm busy."

"Fine." Jason wasn't going to ruin her fine mood. "See you tomorrow."

Chapter Sixteen

Thursday night was the unofficial start of weekend social events, so the gym was quiet. Two men finished a climb on the wall, rappelled down, and left the cavernous room. Once they were out the door, Mia went to the control panel and set it for *Random Configuration, Difficulty Level 12.* She'd only made it to the top of a twelve once, but tonight she felt confident. She pressed the *Set* button, and heard the scratching and grinding of each of the centimeter-square rods sliding into a new position. She never watched it reset, so as not to ruin the surprise, but the sound and the slight shaking of the floor always gave her a shiver.

She half loved, half hated climbing. It cleared her mind, terrifying her into clarity on some irrational, biological level. Every meter of the wall exposed her fear of falling and of the unknown. When she laid a hand on the simulated sandstone, she dropped into her body, memory forced away more thoroughly than Baby Janes could ever do.

She darkened her glasses and began. The face was difficult. She slipped again and again, unable to find solid footing, her strength giving out as she hung and flailed. She started from the bottom each time, learning the route slowly. It took almost three hours, but when she finally pulled herself onto the ledge at the top, arms and legs shaking with fatigue, she felt good. Not the giddy pride of seeing ten thousand credits on the screen for a group effort, but the quiet satisfaction of having completed something difficult purely for herself.

She switched her glasses to transparent and willed herself to look down. She wasn't great with heights. They didn't bother her if she had a solid railing to lean against or a glass wall between her and a sheer drop, but when she leaned over this edge with her climbing rope slack, something in her always screamed.

Tonight, her panic was supplanted by surprise. Lucas sat on the bench by the control panel, his face tilted upward. She was the only one on the wall. Had she forgotten something related to the job? She'd taken her glasses offline for the climb. She switched them on, but there were no waiting messages. Well, she'd know what he wanted soon enough. She turned to face the wall, leaned back, and instructed the belay machine to lower her slowly to the ground.

Lucas walked over unhurriedly as she unhooked her harness and shimmied out of it. She bent to examine her right knee, which had gotten badly banged when she fell on her first attempt.

"Is everything okay? Does Tanaka need something?"

Lucas appeared to be sober, which was strange given he'd been at the bar. He wore workout clothes—a white tank top and loose black pants.

"No, everything is fine. Were you climbing blind? It looked like your glasses were blacked out."

She nodded, surprised he noticed. She kept the exterior of the glasses on mirror so people would think she was looking at a 3D representation of whatever mountain the climbing wall was imitating. "It's the only way I can keep from cheating. If I see the configuration before I start..."

She let the sentence trail off and hoped he'd be careful with what he said in public.

"It's still good exercise, but there are no surprises. I can only do this when no one else is here, or I'd end up bumping into someone. I can usually get the wall to myself on weekend nights or early any morning."

The wall wasn't very popular; only people who'd been on Victoria for more than a few years and were completely acclimated were any good. New arrivals didn't bother. They still struggled with stairs.

Lucas gestured at the rough vertical surface towering above them. "I'd like to try it."

He was wearing perfectly clean climbing shoes, not a scuff mark on them.

"Do you climb...much?" Mia asked.

He shook his head. "I've never tried. There was no wall like this at my gym in New York."

So, Lucas was interested in climbing but didn't want to try something new and fail in front of Mikey and the rest of the snobby gym patrons.

Her adrenaline was long gone and she was ready to go home, curl up on the couch with a drink, and watch bad holos until she fell asleep, but she hated to discourage anyone interested in the sport.

"I can help you get started."

"I'd appreciate it."

She retrieved the harness, still attached to the belay machine, and told him how to put it on. Helping him tighten it was awkward, given the straps encircling his groin. Flustered, she hurried and got away from him as quickly as she could.

"This is how to set up the wall," she said as he followed her to the control panel.

"First, set the level, then you can pick from real mountains." She slid her hand over the images. "An Earth company made this, so there aren't many from Victoria. Alternatively, the system can make something up. Either way, synch your glasses and you'll see a 3D representation of the climbing face."

She punched *Random Configuration, Level 1.*

"I want to do the one you did."

She shook her head. "That's no way to learn. You'd get frustrated. Get a feel for the wall first." Her discomfort at interacting with Lucas in a non-work setting diminished as the wall slid into place, and she focused on the task at hand: helping a beginner have a good first experience. The wall sported numerous easy routes, practically a ladder.

"In level one, you can always count on a good hold being within reach, for both your hands and feet. It's not a question of if, just where. You'll be afraid of falling at first, or constantly if you're me, but don't worry. The belay system is foolproof." She led him to the left side where he couldn't go wrong. "Start here, okay?"

He faced the wall and turned his glasses to black.

"Don't do that."

He grinned. "It looks like fun. Plus, it doesn't matter if I fall, right? You said the system is foolproof." He fumbled for the wall with one hand. "How do I start?"

No point in arguing. He'd do what he wanted regardless. She took his right wrist and guided his hand to a good hold, then hefted his left ankle up so his foot was on a flat, wide shelf.

"Okay, knock yourself out. Remember, on this setting, you don't have to reach far. Yell if you need a hint."

He got three meters without trouble, then stalled. Climbing blind was a stupid idea. He didn't ask for help, and after a bit of fumbling, found his way again. Mia gave him a couple of pointers but for the most part stayed quiet. He only fell once; pretty impressive for a first-timer. In half an hour, he made it to the top. He leaned over, turned off his glasses, and grinned down at her. It was a boyish grin, without irony. His smiles usually said, *this is amusing but I've seen better.*

He lowered himself to the ground.

"You did great. Did you enjoy it?" she asked.

His grin persisted. "Very much. More interesting than lifting weights. I'll try another."

Mia stifled a yawn. She liked this version of Lucas and wanted to get to know it better, but she'd worked too many hours this week and was, after her own climb, nearly dead on her feet.

"I'll leave you to it then. Stick with easy routes tonight. Don't black out your glasses until you get a few meters off the ground."

He took a step toward the control panel, then stopped. "Once is enough. I expect I'll be sore if I do another."

"You'll be sore regardless. You used different muscles than you normally do."

He picked up his bag but made no move to leave. "Is there anywhere to get a drink around here?"

Did he hope to find some of the superfit women who worked out at the gym having a cocktail afterwards? None of the bars around there were trendy enough for the clientele, who wouldn't be caught dead in workout gear or rumpled clothes from their day jobs.

"Yes, but…nowhere popular."

He looked at her quizzically. "I don't need a crowd. I just want a drink and maybe something to eat. Did you have dinner?"

She hadn't. Lucas and she sometimes grabbed a quick drink in whatever restaurant they happened to be in after a job, though that was more medicinal then recreational. They'd never gone anywhere together that wasn't work-related. *What is this about?*

Lucas seemed to read her thoughts. "You did an excellent job today. Summit owes you a good meal. I suspect you haven't eaten all day."

He'd noticed her appetite vanished when her nerves surfaced.

Why not? She'd done a good job today, and when he'd said the word *dinner,* her stomach had growled.

"I haven't, and I'm starving. There's a place near here. I need to shower first." Her arms were streaked white from the dust the wall generated. "I'll meet you in the lobby in fifteen."

She showered and put her rumpled work clothes back on, sorry she'd chosen a short dress today; her knee was beginning to bruise, and there was no way to hide it.

Lucas waited by the front doors. He wore his work shirt but no vest and clearly hadn't showered. His forearms and face were smudged with dust, and he smelled faintly, and not unpleasantly, of sweat.

Outside, the streets thrummed with pods heading to the inner rings. None stopped on Ring 7. The gym was so big they'd had to build further away from the center than was ideal but there were no empty lots of this size any closer. A handful of restaurants and shops, hoping to capture the credits of the wealthy members, had sprung up nearby. Mia chose a restaurant she'd seen from the weight-lifting room, a rooftop place called Stars. It wasn't trendy but had a great sky view and so many plants it could have doubled as a nursery.

The waiter led them to a table overlooking the street. MMARVs passed at eye level and Lucas watched them, fascinated. He'd probably never been so close to one. Unless they were responding to a call, they stayed a minimum of fifteen meters above the ground. The flat, pearlescent exterior of the ovoids looked smooth from the street, but from here, they could see the glassy eyes of cameras, the tiny sensor grids, and the thin lines of panels concealing stunners, bug zappers, and hypos for medical emergencies.

"A rep from IVS, the company that makes those," Mia pointed to the nearest MMARV, "brought one in to my third-grade class and took it apart. I was horrified. I always assumed they were angels like in Earth fiction, above us and protecting us."

"And after you found out it was a machine?"

"I decided all angels were robots, and the ones on Earth were designed to look like humans with wings."

"That makes more sense than most explanations. Drink?"

He handed her the menu, and she was pleased to see signature cocktails made with accents from native plants. She ordered a blue cactus martini, and that and Lucas's scotch appeared what felt like only moments later.

She finished hers too quickly and just as quickly regretted it. The liquor hit her like a slap. Lucas did his usual swirl, sniff, and sip, silently evaluating the scotch. The flickering light of the artificial candle on the table exaggerated his asymmetry and imperfections—his foreignness. That, and the lush plants behind him dripping from a recent watering, transported her back to summer nights in New Beijing.

A MMARV whizzed by, and the illusion of being on Earth vanished. Lucas set a conversation shield on the table.

"The job went well. All of it, from the planning to the execution. It's the first time I've seen the person on your resume," Lucas said.

His words tossed them back on familiar ground and Mia's world steadied. "You didn't hire the person on my resume. You hired an admin. Claire won't even let me update the office."

"I'd like to hear your ideas."

"It isn't worth it. I'd rather have Claire happy than proper lighting and flow."

"I mean, your ideas in general. We added meeting strategy to our offerings and immediately landed a client. What other social engineering skills can we apply to security?"

"Can I write something up for you when I'm sober and not ravenous?"

"Yes, of course. This is supposed to be a celebration, not more work."

Lucas poked at the screen, and a few minutes later the waiter brought fresh bread, garlic fish cakes, savory meat balls in a red sauce, and several other appetizers, as well as another round of drinks.

They ate in companionable silence for a time, Mia taking a bit more than her fair share but unable to stop. She really was hungry.

"What made you decide to be a social engineer?" Lucas asked.

Mia leaned back in the chair, fatigue and alcohol threatening to relax her right down onto the fake wood floor. "If this was a job interview, I'd say I like to fix things that are broken, which is true, but it's more true that I'd be bored doing anything else. I got to study everything in college, and I use all that in every project. Used to use all that, I mean."

"Are you bored at Summit?"

"Sometimes, but if I can find a way to slip more social engineering into our jobs and keep up my skills…" she stared up at the stars, missing Earth's moon. Victoria didn't have one. "How about you? Are you bored?" The two strong drinks made it a logical and not impertinent question.

Lucas snorted what might have been a laugh. "Not yet. There are some perks to living in this city. I'm very much enjoying being anonymous and being able to get some actual work done."

"I don't understand."

"My last promotion was meant to ensure I didn't have time to handle the day-to-day operation of my division."

"You investigated intracompany crime, right?"

"Too well, apparently."

"How could they shut out a partner?"

"By roping me into high-profile events. Keynotes at conferences. Representing Itek at charity events and fundraisers. Media appearances. Liaising with governments. It took me a year to realize what was going on."

Lucas never talked about the past and what happened at Itek. Mia was afraid he'd realize who he was talking to and clamp shut the flow of information.

"You couldn't do your real job."

The ice clinked in Lucas's glass as he swirled it. "I tried. I had a good second-in-command, but investigating internal affairs is a tricky business, and I didn't want to launch any major operations until I could be there to lead them. And I never did find the time."

He leaned back, receding into the shadows, holding his scotch in both hands and looking so intently into it, she wondered if something were written on the bottom of the glass.

"Another drink?" he asked, after draining the last of his.

"Not for me. I'll barely be able to make it to a pod as it is."

"Dessert then." He poked the table before she could say anything.

Lucas never ate dessert.

A trio of sorbets arrived with another scotch. Lucas pushed the dessert toward her and took the drink.

"Listen," he said. "I didn't do much to earn your trust when you started with us."

That was an understatement. Mia picked up the tiny spoon and tasted the green ball. Pistachio.

"I hope you're more comfortable with the team now."

"I am. We've been doing good work."

"You don't seem…completely…comfortable. In the office."

"Is this because of what I said about Claire not wanting me to fix the lighting? That's not a big deal."

"No. You don't seem to be able to *be yourself.*"

Mia finally understood what he was getting at. Jason had made a few tentative forays into the territory of her memory but never pushed. Claire ignored it, and until now, Lucas had kept his promise that it wouldn't be discussed.

"We should talk about this at the office," she said as another MMARV drifted by.

"The conversation shield is functioning, and I'm not going to be specific."

This was exactly what she feared—coworkers discussing her memory in public.

She glanced around. She and Lucas were alone on the roof-deck now—the other couples had left. Safe enough for a casual conversation and public enough that Lucas wouldn't push.

"Hang on a sec." She rummaged clumsily through her purse. All she wanted was to go home and lie in a sleepy daze on the couch and celebrate her success. Instead, she pulled two hypos from the mess. She hated doing this but…

Step one. The green. She ripped it open, pressed the cold cannister to her arm, and unleashed ten thousand alcohol-hating nanos into her system. Gentle inebriation was ripped from her like a bandage from a half-healed wound.

Step two. The yellow. This one hurt. She sucked in a breath before what felt like a thousand pins pricked her and jolted her into wakefulness.

"What did you do?" Lucas picked up the spent hypos and read the labels. "Spark? Sober-ite? What are these?"

The icy pain receded and left her alert and irritated. "They're what I need to have a serious conversation. You have these on Earth. Different brand names, I guess." She drank an entire glass of ice water in steady, forced gulps. "Okay. Now, how exactly should I be more *myself* at work in a way that will improve my performance and deliver results?" Spark always made her a little grumpy.

"You're holding back. You censor yourself constantly. In work, speech, actions, everything. It slows you down."

She'd just brought in the most credits Summit had ever made for a job, and instead of congratulating her, he was prodding for more.

"I'm not working too slowly. I've never missed a deadline."

He shook his head. "You haven't, and your work is good, but I want you to relax. You don't have to put on a bland façade."

She smiled. "I was shooting for average, but I'll take bland." His attempt to goad was actually a compliment. Bland had been a goal that seemed unreachable when she was a kid.

What did an average person expect from someone with a photographic memory? Despite knowing the conversation shield protected them, she leaned forward and spoke softly. "What do you want, some tricks? You want me to describe every outfit you've worn? Recite the menus from the restaurants we go to?"

He leaned forward as well, and the uplight from the candle carved his face into something more horror movie than handsome. "If it's relevant, yes. Last week Claire asked Jason about the setup at that apartment off Ring 3. You know the one?"

She nodded.

"Jason lost track of what model controller he'd installed there. It'd gone offline so he had to go back and check."

"Yeah?"

"Do you know what model it was?"

She now knew where this was going. "Yes."

"Couldn't you have told him and saved him two hours?"

"I could have if he'd asked."

Lucas shook his head. "You can't be so literal."

"I can and I will. First off, I'd never get my own job done if I sat around acting as a search engine just to save everyone else time. Second, everyone would hate me." Lucas started to interrupt, and she held up a hand. "Let me finish. I've spent a lifetime figuring out how to interact with average people. You help them with some obscure tidbit once, and they're grateful. Twice, and they start wondering why you remember, and they don't. Keep doing it, and they get uncomfortable. Finally, they don't like being around you. Everyone finds a different reason, but it's a visceral human reaction. Jason might have been glad if I yelled that out last week, but if I did that every day, he'd get irritated."

Lucas retreated from her admonishing finger. "Give us a chance. We aren't average."

"That's an understatement."

"Don't patronize us. Be yourself, and don't worry about being liked."

"I'm not expecting to be liked. I'm hoping not to get slapped when you find out I know more about your favorite subject than you do. You want me to tell you about that scotch you're drinking? The county it's from? How many bottles are sent to Victoria? The name of the cooper who makes the barrels? You think I'm kidding but I'm not." No documentary was wasted on her.

Lucas didn't reply.

She pushed her chair back from the table. "I really have to go. When this Spark wears off, I'll be dead on my feet." She had an hour, tops, before she crashed hard.

"I'll walk you out." He thumbed the table in payment and stood, gesturing for her to precede him.

Once they were down on street level, he hailed a pod and opened the door for her. "Thank you for all your hard work on the Tanaka job."

"You're welcome."

He continued to hold the door open after she was inside and eager to leave. "It isn't appropriate for me to tell you how to do your job, and I certainly don't expect you to do everyone else's. Jason needs to keep better track of his equipment."

Another near apology.

"I'll try to be more helpful, but it's a slippery slope. I should have told Jason the model of the controller. He wasted two hours, and his time is worth credits. You all need to meet me halfway, though. You think I might know something? Ask."

"That's fair. See you tomorrow." Lucas let go of the door, and it hissed shut.

All in all, she was glad they had that chat. The time for denial was over; she needed to strategize. Lucas was right. Her new coworkers weren't average people. They were people who knew about her memory and would have expectations about it, and failing to meet some of those expectations could mean trouble.

So, yes, time for some tricks.

Chapter Seventeen

Ms. Tanaka called the next morning. Mia—fighting off a Spark headache from the night before—wasn't sure if she was imagining that Tanaka looked tired too.

"Thanks Mia. Everything went perfectly. We didn't get anything done. Of course, they want to reschedule, but it's next to impossible to find a time when we're all free, and I'm going on vacation soon." Tanaka was again in a pod, again circling Ring 20. "Does your firm do home security?"

"Yes, that's the majority of our work."

"Good. I need to know if my apartment is being bugged."

"Do you want to see our offering sheet? We have several diff—"

"Bring it all and bring it now," she said. "Whatever you need to secure my house. I've got kids. If it was just me, I could put up with this bullshit, but I won't have them spied on."

Tanaka didn't need to sign a contract, not after all the credits she'd dumped on Summit already.

"I'll send Jason over right away," Mia said.

Jason—elbows-deep in something on the worktable—looked up quizzically when he heard his name.

Mia thought Tanaka was going to sign off. Instead, she gestured, and her personal contact number appeared on Mia's screen.

"Use this if you need to get in touch, Mia. Not just today. Anytime. I'm afraid…" She took a moment to gather her thoughts. She was once again plainly dressed, no status jewelry, no makeup. "I'm afraid that someone will figure out I've hired you. That might mean trouble for Summit. You know how things are on the upper floors."

"I do," Mia said. "Can I transfer you to Mr. Dunn? He's the expert on this sort of thing."

Tanaka shook her head. "No. Just do what you can to keep our interactions discreet, and call if you need me." She disconnected.

That was odd. Firstly, because a partner wouldn't give her personal number to anyone but close friends and family, and secondly, she'd said "anytime."

"What's up?" Jason asked.

"Tanaka wants total privacy, and she wants it now. Would you mind scanning her place today and figure out what she needs? Don't make her sign a contract—she'll pay us."

"Fine by me." Jason was already wiping his hands and heading to the cupboard where he kept his nice shirt. "If someone is spying on a partner, I'll bet they are using really good equipment. She'd better let me take it."

"She'll want you to."

Mia knocked on Lucas's half open door.

"Yes."

She went in, surprised to see a map of New Canberra printed and posted a bit crookedly on the wall. It wasn't a decoration per se, but the first hint of personality the room had seen.

"I had a strange conversation with Ms. Tanaka. She said that if anyone finds out she hired Summit, it could be bad for us."

Lucas twirled a stylus between his fingers like he was a conjurer at a carnival. "We've been making enemies ever since we got our first client." He raised a brow. "You didn't realize? Unknown entities want data. We cut them off. They aren't happy. Every client we add frustrates someone somewhere. Claire's been dealing with virtual attacks since we set foot on this planet."

Mia hadn't realized. The devices Jason found week after week were an intellectual problem—not something that could affect the business.

"We have enemies?" she asked.

"And friends. People like Ms. Tanaka who appreciate what we do. Don't worry. We're on the right side of things. Anyone we annoy is in the wrong and can't do much to bother us in a city like this."

Mia didn't want to worry. She also didn't want enemies.

Jason returned that evening, having spent hours at Tanaka's. Claire had left and Lucas and Mikey were at The End.

"Well?" Mia asked, as Jason dropped a heavy bag on the table.

He smiled, eyes bright. "So many bugs. Big ones, small ones, all state of the art." He stroked the black bag. "I can't believe I get to keep them. At Itek I'd have to submit them as evidence. Now I get to play."

"Did you set up an ADM?"

"I did, and it lit up like a Christmas tree the moment I connected it." He swept his hand around the room. "Any appliance with a microphone got a listen request for a few seconds, one after another sequentially. The oven, then the drink dispenser, then the game console, then the medicine cabinet, all around the apartment. Whoever was listening would have seamless audio coverage. Anyone trying to use an appliance might notice a glitch from time to time, but the interruptions would be of short duration."

"Shit."

"Yep. Ms. Tanaka was really angry, mostly at herself for not checking for this sooner."

"The ADM worked? It sent all the requests to our server?"

Jason shook his head. "Not exactly. Tanaka doesn't want the listeners to know she knows what's going on, so we can't block all the requests. I set up a monitoring station in a walk-in closet so she can keep track of what the appliances are doing, see what data is flowing out, and created a privacy mode she can use in one room at a time. It isn't ideal but it gives her some control."

"This is the most invasive surveillance we've seen."

"Tanaka seemed to know who was responsible. Every time I found a bug, she nodded like it explained something. This might be partner infighting."

Mia's surprise at the scope of the surveillance faded. Partners existed on a different plane, one she didn't understand and would never be a part of. Infighting was certainly a possibility. She'd been an unwitting weapon in an ongoing war when she worked on the upper floors of Han, and her job had been a casualty of it.

"What was her apartment like? Did she have nice art? Anything you recognized?"

Jason laughed. "What? No lecture on how we have to report this to Optima?"

"I can't feel too sorry for partners."

"Finally, you talk sense. Her place was big and messy. Toys everywhere. I warned her those things can transmit audio as well. She ordered some locking cases that block signals. If I go back there, I expect the place will be a lot neater."

Jason began to put his tools and equipment away. "She said thanks again for your help with the meeting."

"I hope you told her it was a team effort."

Jason waved that away. "Take the compliment. It was your project."

Speaking of which, she needed a cocktail. She'd felt shitty all day thanks to the Spark, and alcohol would take the edge off.

"Want a drink? My treat," she said. "I miss The End. Fuck the directors or whoever is invading this week. It's our bar."

Jason nodded. "Sure. Give me half an hour. I'll meet you there."

Perfect. If she took a Baby Jane now, she'd be relaxed and able to have a normal conversation by the time Jason got off work.

She swallowed a pill and headed to The End.

The sidewalk radiated its collected heat through the soles of her sandals, and stars glistened from horizon to horizon. Mia wished for the hundredth time that Victoria had a moon. Granted, when she was in college, the light pollution in New Beijing was so bad and the skyscrapers so densely packed she rarely saw it, but it was always a thrill when she did.

Still, she wouldn't trade Victoria for Earth. She paused and took a deep breath of the baked-clean air, and listened to the chirps and clicks of the emerging insects. This was her planet and she loved it—because of, or in spite of, its deficiencies.

The street was deserted but for one pod rolling toward her, slowly. Even with the Baby Jane kicking in and her judgment impaired, Mia registered that as strange. *Pods don't go slow.* You get in, they calculate the fastest route to the destination, then zip to it.

Other than its speed, it was ordinary—bubblegum pink under a thin coating of tan dust. Earth immigrants liked to "brighten up" what they considered the too-neutral palette of Victoria, which translated into a full spectrum of garish colors on the city's thousands of pods.

It stuttered to a stop a dozen meters in front of her. You couldn't direct a pod to stop at a nonexistent address, which was what this empty space between The End and the office would be.

It must be broken. She'd seen surprisingly few out-of-service pods in her lifetime. She approached; someone inside might need help getting out if the power failed. There was no New CaTS logo on the door. Was this a prototype?

The back window slid down as she came abreast of the vehicle. The interior lights were out, but the faint glow of the streetlight revealed a man in the back seat. He turned to face her, huge glasses covering a third of his face. His hair was short, dark gray, and his vest buttoned to the neck with brushed titanium X's—the logo of the upscale XYZ brand of men's clothing.

And, she realized with a start, he was almost certainly the same man she'd seen get out of the elevator with Erika and Ms. Mills all those months ago. She took a step back.

"Mia Julian?"

He raised his right hand and thrust it out the window. For a moment she thought he was only pretending to hold a gun, then she saw the dull gleam of the metal and plastic composite material Jason used in his prototype machine.

She half turned toward the office as he pulled the trigger. A wave of nausea hit her. She stumbled then fell as the world spun madly. Her glasses bounced away and she gripped the sidewalk desperately, feeling as if she were about to slide off it.

The pod door slammed.

"Works well, doesn't it? Brand new. Inner ear disrupter." His voice was conversational.

Mia retched.

"Was that too much? I'm still getting a feel for it." Strong hands gripped her wrists and wrenched her off the sidewalk, down the embankment, and into the brush. Rocks and thorns tore through her dress and into the skin on the back of her legs. The stars careened crazily above. He dropped her arms. She wrapped them around her stomach and fought the urge to throw up.

Calloused fingers took her chin in a tight grip and forced her head back. She tried to focus on his face but couldn't. He was a dark smudge against streaks of white.

"Summit Security should not take any clients from Han. Do you understand?"

She couldn't speak. She could barely breathe.

He realized this. "You can hear me. Tell your Earth friends they can do business with the other five. Stay away from Han."

He let go of her head, and his shoes crunched on gravel as he hiked back up the slope.

"Don't leave me out here!" she gasped. The sidewalk was charged to repel the bugs but that charge extended only a few meters into the brush. How far had he dragged her?

The pod departed with a quiet hum.

"Help..." She tried to yell, but couldn't draw in a full breath, and her voice didn't carry. Where were the MMARVs? They circled this ring continuously on a normal day. Killing bugs and providing medical assistance was as important as their security duties. One would surely fly by soon and register her location and distress.

She closed her eyes tight against the twirling star field and listened for the whir of a MMARV. She couldn't believe that after a lifetime on this planet and a thousand stupid juvenile stunts out in the wastes, she was in the most danger she'd even been in on the side of one of the ring roads, meters from her office.

It's not like it used to be, she reassured herself.

Twenty five years ago, there were only a handful of barely trained MMARVs. Today there were thousands, and years of eradication efforts meant the inhabited rings had far fewer bugs. Fewer than millions, which wasn't few enough. She was glad for the Baby Jane now. She couldn't recall the names of all the insect venoms and how they killed.

The scratch of a hard exoskeleton dragging across a harder rock brought her to her senses. The longer she lay here, the worse her odds. Part of her said it was an appropriate way to die—following in her father's footsteps—almost literally.

Most of her said, *Fuck this.* She'd lived on the planet longer than most of the brainless creatures around her. They had no right to end her tenure. Time to get off the bare ground. She forced herself onto her hands and knees, swaying like a tent in a strong wind. She shouldn't crawl. Many of the bugs weren't aggressive but if crushed they would sting.

Crawling was, unfortunately, the only option. She raised her head and tried to orient.

Darkness and stars. *Wrong way.*

She shuffled in a slow circle until the dirt of the embankment filled her view. Moving made the spinning worse, and she shut her eyes. A series of loud clicks startled her back into motion. She fumbled forward, head down, blinking, trying to focus and failing. She set her hands down gently, but the ground was a jumble of things hard and prickly. Rocks and serpentine beetles would feel very much alike to a calloused palm.

At length, rough dirt gave way to smooth plasticrete. The sidewalk. She swept her arms in long arcs until she found her glasses—undamaged from their fall—fumbled them on and lay flat.

"Office four," she said, her voice stronger. She'd programmed this command to contact everyone at Summit—though she never imagined having to use it.

Lucas's tiny voice emerged from the earpiece. "What's happening?"

He saw what she saw—stars.

"Someone stunned me. I'm between the office and The End."

"Mia?" Jason was online as well.

"Are you alright?" Lucas asked. His breath quickened, and the sounds of the bar faded. Moments later, she heard multiple footsteps. She suspected the chip they put in her was for more than just activating weapons, and she was glad of that now.

In less than a minute, Lucas was on his knees beside her, Jason and Mikey arriving moments later. Lucas ran his hands over her body, trying to determine if she was injured.

She pressed her hands hard against the bucking concrete. "He said it was an inner ear disrupter. Everything is tipping."

"Who did this?"

"I can't say." She wanted to say he looked familiar, but it wasn't the time or place.

"Mikey, get her back to the office."

Mikey scooped her up and ran. His pounding steps worsened her nausea, and she retched. She couldn't throw up on his suit. He'd never forgive her. She repeated the mantra until they reached the office.

"Put me on the floor," Mia said, once they were inside.

Mikey complied, and she focused on the ceiling and took deep breaths, waiting for the sea to calm.

Lucas appeared with a black suitcase, one she'd never seen. Something from the locked cabinet? He crouched beside her and opened it to reveal a tiny pharmacy—hundreds of small hypo cans, each one numbered, and a palm-sized device. He pressed that one to her shoulder.

"You weren't poisoned," he stated. "Good."

He ran his finger down the rows of little cans, pulled one out, set the dial, and pressed it to her shoulder. Tiny needles pierced her skin, then retracted.

"That was for motion sickness. It should help."

Indeed, after a minute, the room settled. She took a deep breath. "Yes, better."

"I've never heard of an inner ear disrupter," Mikey said. "No pun intended, Mia. I thought I was up to date on all the stunners."

Lucas put away his kit. "IEDs aren't legal. The manufacturer wants them classified nonlethal, but the mortality rate is above five percent."

Mia struggled to sit, panicked at Lucas's mention of mortality rate. "I've got to get out of these clothes. Now."

All three men stared.

"Jason, I need help. He dragged me off the sidewalk. I could be crawling with insects."

"I can—" Lucas offered.

"Absolutely not," Mia said.

Jason helped her up and into the bathroom/supply closet, shutting the door with his foot.

"What should I do?"

"Find something airtight to hold my clothes and bring my gym bag. And put on gloves."

As soon as he left, Mia stripped off her dress and threw it into the corner. Underwear followed. The bathroom, clearly an afterthought, held a toilet, a large industrial sink stained dark from whatever the last tenant had poured down it, and open metal shelving. Mia had hung a small mirror above the sink, and she grabbed it, holding it over her shoulder and anxiously searching for small gray ticks or the long thin stick bugs that were content to ride a host for hours before they bit.

Jason returned with a plastic bin and the gym bag, eyebrows raising when he saw she was nude.

She set aside the mirror and covered herself as best she could with her hands, but modesty took a backseat to mortal peril.

"Put those," she pointed to the rumpled garments, "in there, and shut the lid."

Jason did. She checked the floor where they'd lain. Nothing but dust.

"I need you to check me for bugs. I can't see all my skin."

Jason was all business. "Not a problem. What am I looking for?"

"Anything. I shouldn't have anything on me. If you find something, don't touch it. Describe it, and I'll tell you what to do."

He turned on a small LED light and set to work examining her with the same patient thoroughness he used when working on a complex circuit board. He held out her arms, went up and down her back methodically, and crouched to examine her legs.

"I've got an antivenom kit in my bag," she said.

"What's that?" Jason asked.

"You don't know?" That he didn't know was nearly as horrifying as being stunned. "You need one within a few meters of you at all times."

"I thought the drones took care of the bugs within the rings."

"They do their best but they can't get them all. Some of the deadliest are the smallest, and the MMARVs can't spot them from the air."

"I've been taking breaks out behind the building. So has Lucas."

She hadn't the patience to explain. "You got lucky. Read the *Welcome to Victoria* primer I sent you. Am I clean?"

Jason stood, knees cracking. "I think so."

"One more thing. Can you look through my hair? It dragged in the dirt."

She shut the lid on the toilet, sat, and Jason began picking through her hair like she was a baby monkey in a documentary.

"I'm so sorry to make you do this."

"I don't mind."

After a few minutes, he declared her hair clear, and left. She took a sponge bath in the industrial sink, scrubbing every inch of herself with hot water and a rag, and washing her hair with the harsh hand soap. When convinced she was really, truly bug free, she patted herself dry, rubbed antiseptic into the scrapes on the backs of her legs, and dressed in the dusty shorts and tank top she climbed in.

The last of the adrenaline trickled away, and she made her way back to her desk on shaky legs. The Baby Jane, still in her system, took the edge off the rocks she'd been dragged over and gave the incident a holographic feel, as if she'd observed rather than lived it.

Lucas handed her a glass of water and a pill.

"What's this?"

"Anti-shock. Helps neutralize stress chemicals. You're probably still feeling dizzy and nauseous."

He was right. She took the pill and drank most of the water.

"Tell me what happened. In detail."

She did, and as the story progressed, her heart began to beat as hard as it had when the man pointed the gun to her chest. Lucas listened attentively without interrupting—until she got to the part where the man told her Summit shouldn't take any Han clients. Lucas looked to Mikey, who nodded and tapped the side of his head.

"You were right," Lucas said. "We shouldn't have taken the Tanaka job."

"It was a risk," Mikey said. "No one cares if we do security for Joe Nobody in accounting, but if we get involved in partner infighting, we're asking for trouble. We don't know how things work around here. That was a warning—"

"It was a warning that could have killed me," Mia said, irritated the two of them were being so clinical about this. "And him as well. We were off the sidewalk and he wasn't wearing protective clothing. None of you new arrivals understand how venomous the insects are here."

"What do you mean by none of you? He was a new arrival from Earth?" asked Mikey.

Mia struggled to organize her thoughts through the shock and Baby Jane fog.

"He must have been…and…he looked familiar. Someone I might have seen at Han HQ right before I got fired."

"Someone you *might* have seen? I didn't think there was a might with you."

"Give her a break," Jason said. "She could have died out there." He shot Mikey an unkind smile. "You *might* want to change clothes. You carried her back. The MMARVs don't get the tiny bugs, and those are the most deadly."

Mikey looked down at his suit.

"Tell the cleaner to sanitize it," Mia said.

"I'll be right back," he said, and strode out.

"Sorry," Mia said. "I'm not following procedure. We should scan the whole office. Jason, check online. It'll tell you what to do."

"Got it."

Lucas shook his head, brow furrowed. "I'm not following procedure either. Please finish the story. He delivered the warning, then what?"

"He left me out there, got in the pod, drove off—then there was nothing. No MMARVs, no pods, no people. You know how often MMARVs pass our building. I've never in my life been out of sight of one for more than a few minutes. I can't walk to the bar without seeing at least four. From when I left the office until you found me, there were none."

Claire banged through the door in a surprisingly colorful outfit—yellow cotton pants and a moss green shirt with *2087* written across the chest in a black scrawl.

"What's the emergency?" she demanded, face flushed. "Do we have to go?"

She wore a backpack and carried two bags, both stuffed to the point of bursting.

Lucas frowned and shook his head. "No. We're fine. I didn't mean to scare you. Mia was attacked, and someone hacked the drones and pods in this sector. I didn't want to discuss any of this while you were remote. Our network might be compromised."

Claire dropped the bags. "You did scare me. Why did you use the panic code? You could have just asked me to come in."

"I wanted you to come quickly."

"I did, and wiped every device in my apartment before I left. That's the panic code protocol. You shouldn't have used it for something like this." She gave Mia a once-over and seemed bothered that she appeared unharmed.

"We can refine our alert codes later. Get me images in all bands from our cameras, those at The End, and any on the street you can access on the stretch of road between here and The End from forty-five minutes ago until now. I want to identify Mia's attacker. Also, tell me when MMARVs or pods passed by during that period."

Claire gave an exaggerated sigh and got to work. Mia leaned back and shut her eyes, glad for a moment of peace. Tonight, their windowless room felt safe, not oppressive. Was that why the rest of the team liked it? Were they always afraid?

"I've been monitoring the MMARVs that patrol our ring, and the longest interval without one was four minutes," Claire said. "Tonight it was twenty."

Squares resolved on the wall screen. Camera data. Mia forced herself out of the chair to get a better look.

The images were time-stamped an hour ago. In the top right, the four views from Summit's security cameras, top left, those from The End, and on the bottom, data from Optima's street cameras.

Claire pointed to the screen with data from the office sensors. "Mia was out of range of visible, but we did get thermal and bio detection." She displayed the weird, false color images that turned everything rainbow-colored and ringed objects with spectral auras.

The north and east facing cameras showed Mia walking toward The End. The white-hot pod rolled slowly past her, then stopped. Mia approached, drew back, then crumpled. A human shape emerged from the pod and dragged her out into the brush. The Baby Jane in her was fascinated by the swirling river of green trailing in her wake, fading to match the cooler blue of the surrounding desert seconds after she passed. The man loomed over her, bright orange, and when he grabbed her chin, it left behind a handprint on her face.

He trudged green footprints as he hiked back to the pod and fled in a blur of white.

There she lay, cooling from red to pink. She tried to calculate the distance from her body to the road. Four meters? Not as far in as she feared. Out of range of the safe zone, but only just.

It was a long fifteen minutes before she began her uncertain crawl back to the sidewalk. The length of time surprised her—she thought she'd only been dazed for a few minutes.

The quality of images from the cameras at The End was better, but not good enough to identify her or her attacker.

The street cam data, which Claire shouldn't have been able to access, was by far the highest resolution. Pods and MMARVs glided by. Lucas and Mikey walked to The End. More pods passed, then the landscape stilled. Specifically, to a still frame. Claire fast-forwarded. The frame stayed the same for twenty-five minutes, then abruptly jumped. A pod appeared mid road, and normal, real-time motion resumed.

"Rewind that last part." Lucas said.

Mia's heart sank. "Optima owns the MMARVs and cameras. They can't be hacked. Optima did this." *Another enemy and this one is in every sector.*

"Everything can be hacked," Claire retorted.

"Have you hacked a MMARV?" she asked.

"I haven't tried."

"Stop!" Lucas said. "Of course the MMARVs and cameras can be hacked, and it wasn't Optima that did this. If they didn't want us working for Han, they'd revoke our operating permit. I was surprised they allowed us to work in all Six sectors in the first place."

"Well, that's one player off the board," Jason said.

Mikey returned in gym clothes, his fancy suit crumpled in a plastic bag.

"I'm not convinced Tanaka has any connection to the rest of our clients," Lucas said.

"Me either," Jason said. "What's going on in her apartment is magnitudes above what's happening to anyone else who's hired us. I agree, this warning is about her."

"But from who?" Lucas asked. "Mia, you said the man looked familiar. Maybe someone you'd seen at Han?"

The Baby Jane receded like the tide, leaving her heavy on the shoreline of memory. She returned to her desk chair. "Maybe. The day Erika fired me, she asked if I'd seen who she was with a few days earlier. I thought she was testing my boundaries. She always wanted a little more than I was authorized to share. Everything that happens on the upper floors is confidential—including interactions with coworkers. I was working late, and she got off an elevator with a partner and a man I assumed was a guard."

"Was he the man that attacked you tonight?" Lucas crouched in front of her. "Can you sketch him? I've got a program that can help." He held out a tablet.

"Tomorrow," Mia said, pushing the tablet away. "I was far from the elevator, and it was dark tonight. I can't be sure it was the same man. I've got a good memory but average vision. Whoever it was, there's a bigger issue. This isn't how we do business on Victoria. People don't get stunned and dragged off roads."

"How would you know? Victoria doesn't have a free press," Lucas said.

Maybe he didn't intend to sound condescending. Mia could have recited a list of Earth's news sites and the organizations that controlled them, but resisted, as she did a hundred times every day when people recited fallacious "facts."

"Gossip," Mia said. "I've heard about everything from kleptomaniac au pairs to sex parties gone wrong. No one has ever been assaulted by a stranger."

"She's right," Claire said. "I've been doing key word monitoring of Weber-sector communications, and once I remove references to games and holos, there's almost no mention of violence. If assaults were happening, people would be talking, and they aren't."

Lucas rubbed his chin. "Are we witness to the birth of crime in paradise? Or have references been erased like they were tonight? Send me all the image data, Claire. I might be able to find something." He retreated to his office.

Mia looked to Jason, who shrugged.

"You can't have a zero crime forever," he said.

No one on the team seemed particularly surprised by tonight's events. Concerned, yes. But not surprised. They couldn't understand what it meant, not after living in one of the most dangerous cities in North America. The idea of violence on this peaceful planet sickened Mia and not just metaphorically; she really wasn't feeling well. Now that the Baby Jane was wearing off, vivid images of other bug encounters from her life filled her field of view, staccato still frames in a ghastly documentary. When she was emotional or fatigued, it was hard to keep her memories in check.

"Jason, can you ride home with me?" She wasn't eager to get into a pod alone, now that she knew they could be controlled by something other than the AI.

"Of course."

"Wait a second," Lucas called from his office. "Let me see how you're feeling."

Let me *see* how you're *feeling*? Only a man could make a statement like that.

He knelt beside her and clasped her wrist. She flinched.

"Calm down. I'm taking your pulse."

"With your fingers?"

"You're cold. You have a jacket?"

"No."

"Wait a moment."

He rummaged in his office and returned with a sweatshirt she'd seen him wearing at the gym and a flat black box. A force-field generator. The same one he'd used to test her months ago.

"You remember this. You have a front door and a sliding door onto the balcony. Those are the only ways to get into your apartment, correct?"

"Yes."

"Put this on the ground outside your bedroom door, the perforated part facing forward. Set it to 180 degrees, ten-meter depth when you go to bed. That will cover both entrances and the kitchen window. I'll have Jason beef up the security at your apartment tomorrow."

"Thanks." She slipped the heavy slab into her purse.

He held out the sweatshirt like he was a waiter at a nice restaurant bringing back an item from coat check. Was he going to help her put it on?

Apparently, yes. The musky citrus smell of him enveloped her, and she flushed. It was as if he were hugging her in front of everyone.

"Tell Weber what happened. They might be able to track that pod," she said.

Lucas shook his head. "Weber sector ends a kilometer down the road. They'll have less data than we do, which means they'll want what we got from our cameras, and I'm not inviting corporate security into our office." He glanced at Jason's worktable, the black cabinets, and Claire's screens populated with data from ill-gotten feeds.

Mia understood. What went on here was twenty percent legal at best. "We aren't going to take clients from Han, are we?"

A tendon in Lucas's cheek flexed. "I'm not making any decisions until I have more data. This might turn out to be an isolated incident."

"You said—"

"Go home, hydrate, and sleep. We'll have more information tomorrow. Jason, check out her apartment and make sure she knows how to operate the FFG."

Once she and Jason were in a pod with the conversation shield on, she asked, "Why does Lucas have to think about this? We can't work for Han clients."

"We can't shut down our business because an asshole threatened us."

"He didn't threaten us. He threatened me."

"I know. I'm so sorry this happened to you. We can take steps to be sure it never happens again, but all our clients are from Han. We have signed contracts. This kind of thing might be rare here, but it happened all the time at Itek when we tried to get rid of intracompany crime. If we investigated missing funds, our discretionary spending budget would come under review. If weapons disappeared from the CorSec arsenal and we tried to track them down, we'd get a bad batch of ammo, or our laser sights would be off by a few degrees. That might not sound like a big deal, but it could mean the wrong person got stunned, and then our department would be in legal trouble."

Mia got a sudden, clear vision of what it would have been like to be the social engineer tasked with derailing Lucas's team. That could have been her if she'd been willing to go along with Erika's schemes.

"This is about Tanaka. Instructing us not to work for all of Han solves the problem without giving anything away," Jason said.

Crude Earth tactics. Her attacker was from Earth. He wasn't trying to kill her. He didn't know about the bugs. To him, the empty lot next to the road was a convenient place to chat. A messenger dead on the side of the road accomplished nothing.

Did that make her feel better? A bit.

Actually, more than a bit. She took a deep breath and leaned into the not-quite-comfortable seat.

The man was stupid, not murderous. She'd known many stupid recent arrivals. Agnar, a guy from Iceland she'd dated a year after college, wooed her with a romantic pavilion set up in an unpopulated area in Ring 18, complete with a tent, firepit, and him sprawled naked on a blanket. She hadn't been sure what to do first—giggle or call a drone to safeguard him. She managed to do both.

When they arrived at her building, Jason followed her out of the pod.

"You don't have to come up." Mia pointed out the security features like a flight attendant on a stratoshuttle. "MMARVs," as two obediently flew by. "Cameras." The light poles lining the wide path to the front doors all had silver globes atop them. "People." A group stood on the sidewalk nearby, happily chatting, and a pod pulled up to drop off two more. "They can't hack all this. Plus, the nearest empty lot is kilometers away, and I know how to use the FFG."

Jason leaned forward and gave her an unexpected and sincere hug. "I'm sorry about tonight. We won't let it happen again."

"Thanks," she managed, once he let go and she could breathe.

"I mean it. We'll monitor pods and MMARVs and foot traffic, and no one will be able to bother us anywhere near the office. I can install—"

"Tell me the plan tomorrow. I'm tired."

"Right. Sorry. Call if you need anything."

Her purse strained under the weight of the black slab. Screw the other clients. She'd keep it as long as she worked for Summit.

Her apartment appeared to be undisturbed, and the daily summary from the ADM showed no attempts to control the appliances. Why did it feel so chilly? The temperature was the usual twenty-three degrees.

She set the force-field generator outside her bedroom and activated it. No hum or other comforting noise or visuals indicated her new pro-tected state. She balled up a tissue and tossed it at the door. It bounced back. She picked up a shoe—a strappy pink number she'd never been allowed to wear on the executive floors—and pitched it underhand. It shot back, almost hitting her, and the heel knocked a centimeter chunk out of the wall.

Shit! She was going to have to fix that, and her sandal.

After a long shower—complete with a good scrub of her hair with lavender-scented bug killing shampoo—she felt pretty good, but still cold.

She closed the blinds—so seldom used they rained dust upon her—then took a blanket from a high shelf in the closet, threw it on her bed, and crawled beneath it, still shivering. How would she get to work from now on, that was the question. Not by herself in a pod, not if they could be controlled by anything other than Optima, unless…

She put on her glasses. Within a few minutes she found official pod repair manuals as well as technical papers on the software and algorithms used to control the system. Her fear receded, pushed back by a treasure trove of data.

Working for a security company meant being faced with new problems. She could solve them. She would solve them.

Sometime before dawn she pulled off her glasses and slept.

Chapter Eighteen

After a weekend spent completing a suite of pod diagnostic and repair certification courses, Mia felt confident enough to take one to work on Monday. The man who'd attacked her had clearly hacked *a* pod not *all* pods. It wasn't hard to take one offline. Screwing with the system as a whole would be orders of magnitude more difficult.

What remained worrisome was the dead zone around the office. Redirecting MMARVs required more skill and more risk. As Lucas pointed out, if Optima didn't want Summit working in Han sector, all they needed to do was withdraw the charter. Someone had messed with Optima equipment, and neither Optima nor any of the Six would be happy about that. The wedges that made up New Canberra fit snugly together to make a whole—despite the fact that each corporation competed ferociously with its neighbors—because everyone agreed on the ground rules.

To her surprise, Claire and Jason were already in and hard at work. Neither of them showed up until noon on days without client meetings.

"Find out anything?" Mia asked Claire.

"About what?"

"Twenty minutes with no MMARVs on Friday?"

"I'm working on it."

That meant *no.*

"Mia." Lucas waved her into his office. "How are you?"

He glanced at her legs. The scratches, hidden by loose pants, had scabbed over and now itched more than hurt.

"I'm fine. I'm also a certified pod technician. In theory. I've never actually worked on a pod, and I'm no good with tools, but I took the classes this weekend."

Lucas scrubbed his chin. "You were trying to figure out how your attacker got the pod to stop."

"I did figure it out. It's easy to do an override."

Mia was prepared to explain, but Lucas ignored her, staring intently at his screen. After a few moments of silence, he swiveled it to face her.

"Have you ever used SusSketch?"

"What's that?"

"I know you didn't get a good look at the man, but you said he resembled someone you'd seen before."

Lucas poked his desk keyboard, and a genderless mannequin head appeared, slowly rotating.

"All you have to do is talk," he said. "Describe the man you saw in the pod or the man you remember from Han HQ."

Mia's memories of the event should have been perfect, but were watered down by the Baby Jane. Still, better than an ordinary person's. "I'll start with the man in the pod. He was lit only by one streetlight, which was probably fifty meters away."

The light on the mannequin changed and dimmed, the background faded to black.

"Yes! That's good. Can you make him more...manly? Heavier features?"

The head morphed to an apish visage.

"What was his age and race, approximately?" Lucas asked.

"Caucasian, somewhere between thirty and fifty."

"Hair color?"

"Blond or gray. Maybe both. I couldn't tell if it was natural or dyed."

Lucas continued to question her, and the man took shape. She'd remembered more than she gave herself credit for, and within twenty minutes they had a decent sketch of the man who'd stunned her.

Lucas regarded it contemplatively. "Too bad about the lighting." Half the face was in shadow. "Could be anyone in CorSec. They like this type.

Square chin, generic features. A citizen can't lodge a complaint if they can't identify the person who abused them."

She knew there was a CorSec type but never thought this might be a deliberate technique.

"Let's sketch the man you saw at Han HQ."

Mia, getting a sense of how the program worked, stated how far she was from him, the lighting conditions, and what he wore, whereupon the head morphed into a full figure.

She stood and pulled the screen closer, amazed at seeing her memories come to life. "I had no idea anything like this existed." She added more details. "There were two women as well." She described Erika and Ms. Mills, the corridor, the elevator. Lucas came around and watched as Mia fired off facts and the scene solidified.

She was delighted with the results, though distance and limits of her vision meant the man still could have been nearly anyone.

Lucas took more of an interest than she expected. "The relative heights are accurate? How tall is Erika?"

"One point six-five meters."

He slid in front of her and typed on the desk. A grid appeared and overlaid the scene. "That would make him just about two meters." He stared at the screen, arms folded.

"You recognize him?" Mia asked.

"When did you see this?"

"The Friday before I was fired. In fact, Erika asked me about it. She didn't see me, but I filed a report that night about the lights I was adjusting, so she knew where I was."

Lucas turned his head sharply toward her. "Why didn't you mention this?"

"I did, in general. Erika always tried to get me to tell her what I'd seen on the exec floors. I didn't know why she asked about that night since she'd been there herself, but I figured it was a test to see if I'd bend the rules. When I wouldn't, she decided to make me the scapegoat for the data leaked to Okafor Industries."

Lucas pulled down his glasses. "Mikey, take a look at this." He drew a square around the screen with his finger and flung it to the right. "Yeah. I know. Impossible."

He took his glasses off. "Is this the same man that was in the pod?"

"I don't know." She hated admitting it. If she hadn't been on Baby Janes, she'd have a crystal clear image to compare with the man at Han HQ.

"He spoke to you. Would you recognize his voice?"

"Maybe." Her memory was visual, not auditory. "He sounded like a newscaster from North America after a hard night out."

He sat back behind his desk and pulled the screen to face him. "Listen."

"Do you know—"

"Sit down and listen."

She did. Lucas held his hand up, one finger raised dramatically. "Shut your eyes. It was dark the night you were attacked."

Mia settled into the cold chair and remembered the starkly lit face in the pod.

Lucas, presumably, pressed *play*.

A mélange of voices. Pod doors slamming shut. Indistinct advertisements for a hydrofoil tour of the Statue of Liberty. The whir of Earth drones. A brief, loud hiss. The crowd quieted.

"I'm here to address concerns about the safety and security of the Emerald Tower bridge."

Mia opened her eyes. "That could be him." The gravelly voice sent a chill down her spine. "Who is it?"

Lucas faced her, hands flat on the desk. "Someone who couldn't have been here a few days before you got fired. I'll make some calls to be sure, but…" He pulled in a deep breath, leaned back, let it go. "It's impossible. I'm projecting. As I said, all CorSec guards look the same."

"Who did you think it was?"

Lucas waved the question away. "It doesn't matter. You aren't sure the two men are the same, and the sketch of the man that stunned you is a partial match to over eleven thousand residents. I did the search as soon as you finished. We aren't going to figure this out based on looks. Even if Claire tracks the pod on cameras in another sector…" Lucas trailed off. "We aren't going to solve this crime. Claire's been at it for twelve hours, and it'll raise flags if she continues."

"But—"

"We won't take any more partners as clients. No one above senior manager, just to be safe, regardless of which of the Six they work for. Anything higher and we risk annoying CorSec."

"They were more than annoyed. I might have been killed."

Lucas slammed his open palm down hard on the desk. "I realize that. I'm not taking this lightly. Back at Itek…" He got the same look in his eye she'd seen at the bar—a predator anticipating the hunt. "No one touched my staff."

He dropped his hand to his right hip. Reaching for a weapon that wasn't there?

"This won't happen again. We'll beef up security here and at your apartment. If you follow your usual routine, you won't be bothered."

He stood and marched into the main room. Mia followed.

Claire took off her glasses as they approached her desk. "I'm not having any luck—"

"I know. Let it go for now. Concentrate on securing our block. Jason, install chip detectors on the edges of the sidewalk between here and The End. Any Summit Security staff crosses those, and we all get the alert. Install a screen here," he pointed to a blank swath of wall, "showing the passage of all MMARVs and pods in the area. Any of them deviate from normal operation, and I want it called out. We need better cameras on this building and on The End. I want full spectrum and audio in every direction. We won't be blindsided again."

"You," Lucas pointed to Mia. "Will not go to introductory client meetings alone. Jason or Mikey or I can go with you from now on. As a matter of fact, no one does any client work alone," Lucas said.

He opened one of Jason's black cabinets, grabbed a stunner, and tossed it to Mia. "You know how to use that?"

She caught it reflexively. "No, and I don't want to."

"Yes, you do. Keep it in your purse. Or better yet, your pocket. This model will get by any scanner but those at the headquarters of any of the Six."

She held the gun out on a flattened palm, skin taut as if she were trying to keep a tarra beetle from latching on. "I won't use this." It wasn't just illegal, it was an affront to everything she believed about her planet.

Lucas took her wrist in one hand and with the other, closed her resisting fingers over the small weapon and held them there. His hand was strong and warm, a far cry from the weak, damp grip of the man she'd interviewed with.

"I don't want you defenseless. I'll do everything I can to keep you safe but you have to help."

She tugged away when the moment stretched on too long.

"Jason, show her how it works. I've got to make a call."

"Let me see that," Jason said once Lucas was locked back in his office.

She handed him the stunner. "Keep it. With my luck someone would use it to shoot me."

Jason laid the weapon on the programming pad and typed onto the table. "They can't. It only works with your chip now. I'll send the control panel to your glasses. Come out into the hall, and I'll show you how it works."

"No way. I take that thing, and I'm betraying the values of my planet. Zero violence. No one but CorSec has weapons, and theirs are all non-lethal. I'm not going to perpetuate whatever Earth-based bullshit is happening here now."

"Even though—"

"Especially because! There's a rogue asshole loose on my planet. I'm not going to model my behavior on him or any of you. It's not right that you found a way to get weapons past the scanners. It galls me every time Lucas strolls through the front door of a restaurant. Victoria is not like Earth, and I don't want it to be."

Jason made a placating motion, and Mia realized she'd nearly shouted the last phrase.

"I get your point. I know you aren't comfortable with us carrying these, but we've always needed to protect ourselves, and you can't blame us for wanting to protect you."

"It wouldn't have helped last Friday."

"Probably not, and I'm thinking you've already got a better weapon than this. With your memory and social engineering expertise, you should be able to spot a dangerous situation from a kilometer away and avoid it."

"It isn't like that. I'm not an AI. I can't filter through all my memories in a split second."

He twirled the setting dial on the gun with his thumb and avoided her gaze. "I've been reading about photographic memory. What type are you?"

Of course, he'd done research. He was Jason. She tried to stay relaxed. Talking about it would never be easy.

"I tested myself a long time ago. I'm closest to what they call a *visual generalist*. I'm good at remembering anything I see for more than a second or two. The information isn't time and date stamped, though I can usually figure that out if I can string things together."

"Would you take a test now?" He stopped fiddling with the stunner and gave her a big, bright, New-York-City-kid-getting-a-present smile. He loved charts.

"No tests. I don't want the data out there."

"It'll be on here." He patted his PDS. "Completely off the network. I can delete the results afterwards."

She scrambled for another excuse. "I'm not going to waste my whole night on this."

"There's a new version developed by New Beijing U. and Harvard, and it only takes two hours. I swear there's zero risk. I'll laser the PDS into a thousand pieces afterwards."

She examined the matte gray device he offered. She *was* curious. She'd taken the other test twenty years ago. A lot more research had been done since then, thanks to all the so-called geniuses that REA had captured and studied. The number she'd had floating in her head for so long—that she'd imagined was the sum of her—might be wrong.

"I'll do it…if you don't make me learn how to use the stunner."

"It's a deal." He handed her the PDS and a screen.

She went back to her desk and began. Surprisingly, the test was fun, better than the one she'd taken so long ago. Not as much of the unsubtle, "memorize this thousand-digit number" stuff, though there was some of that. When she hit the two-hour mark, the timer dinged and the screen locked. She hadn't finished but suspected there was no real end. How far a person got would be part of the metrics.

She beckoned Jason back into the hall, out of Claire's view, and handed him the PDS and screen so he could tabulate the results.

"Was it as bad as you thought it would be?"

"No. It was interesting."

He brought up the administrator screen, poked at it, then frowned.

"What's wrong? Didn't it save my results?"

"It did." He tapped and swiped then gave her a skeptical look. "According to this you're a ninety-eight percent accurate Visual Generalist."

Her heart sank. The same score as before. Freak territory.

"What does it mean?" he asked. "You remember everything?"

"Ninety-eight percent of everything, in theory. But the two percent I miss is the really important stuff," she tried to joke.

"Why aren't you on this scatter plot of everyone they've tested? I don't see any dots past ninety percent."

No way to avoid this now. "You're looking in the wrong place." She pointed out the smattering of tiny dots hugging the x-axis past ninety. She knew this chart well. The x-axis, functional ability, and the y-axis, the score on the memory test. The dots started out a sparsely at *0,0*, swooped up and right to form a loose flock as they crossed into the "normal" zone, then continued a slow rise, until, at eighty percent, they thinned and flew apart, some of the dots falling. At eighty-five percent, most of the dots were below normal functional ability; at ninety, nearing idiot levels. Ninety-eight percent, her score, was as good as being brain dead.

"I don't understand," Jason said.

Before she could distract him, he'd done a search on the score, and the dreaded reference to "Occipital/Temporal Lobe Parity" topped the results. He clicked on a summary. Phrases jumped out such as "reality perception deficit," "abnormal internal orientation," and "sensory dissonance reaction disorder."

"Almost everyone who scores as high as you did on this test has a syndrome. OTLP." He spoke the unfamiliar acronym slowly.

She hadn't thought about it in so long. It reminded her of being fourteen again and not in a good way. "They obviously didn't study everyone. Corporations aren't going to give up proprietary data."

He paged through more documents, more charts and graphs, then looked at her questioningly. "How is it that you are perfectly fine?"

She longed to take a Baby Jane, but held off. "I'm not fine."

"What do you mean?"

"The problem with my memories is that they're processed by the same part of my brain that processes what I'm seeing now. They compete with present time reality. Does that make sense?"

Jason nodded. "When you think back on something, you literally see it."

This wasn't an unusual concept, given everyone's glasses recorded in stereovision. In high school, Mia and her friends shared live views and piggybacked onto whoever was seeing the most gossip-worthy events. At Han, all the conference rooms had stereo cams, and it was common to attend less important meetings remotely, flipping back and forth between the meeting and real work.

In all those cases, switching was a voluntary decision. In her case, it wasn't. Did she trust Jason enough to tell him her great flaw? He'd been a solid, reliable coworker over the past months and… Why hesitate? He'd seen her naked and searched her for poisonous insects just days ago. She did trust him, and he was a real friend.

"I'm no different from the people who have OTLP. I was just lucky. I had the chance to sort out the different types of real, and no one locked me up or medicated me during the process. My parents figured out what was going on and helped as much as they could. Touch and smell usually worked." Mia ran her fingers down the uneven plasticrete wall. "I'd wake up crying about a centipede, and my dad would stroke my face with my favorite furry blanket and say, 'You aren't in the desert, you're home in bed,' and I'd snap out of the memory. They made sure my life was simple and routine. I woke up, went to school, played out in the bush, came home, ate dinner, and went to bed. We never changed apartments. I wasn't overstimulated. I didn't have too much new data to assimilate. If I had, I might have been overwhelmed."

"You have immediate access to full resolution, full-frame imagery of everything you've ever seen." He shook his head. "When you see the past, the present disappears?"

"For a moment, yes. Let me show you." She had an urge to make Jason understand what it meant to be her and see through her eyes. She pulled down her glasses and brought up the raw recording of a recent client meeting.

She selected a two-minute segment—her and Lucas in a restaurant. The client had left and they waited for the bill. Lucas leaned forward, hands folded in front of him, in the midst of what she termed the post-meeting training session. Even now, the images his words brought to mind flashed before her eyes. She searched for similar pictures on library and news sites and used them to recreate her experience of those minutes.

She finished, surprised that she'd never thought of trying to recreate her reality like that before, but there had been no one to show it to. She sent the file to Jason.

"Okay, there you have it. First, two minutes, the actual footage. Then, the two minutes as seen through my eyes."

He viewed the montage through his glasses. When the file ended, he took them off and pulled at the top of his head like he was trying to loosen it. He blinked, repeatedly, before focusing on her. "That's what you deal with all day, every day?"

Despite her discomfort with this subject matter, his woebegone expression made her smile.

"Yes." She'd pulled over one hundred images for those one hundred and twenty seconds. Whereas most people had the luxury of calling up stereo images of whatever they chose to research, it was no option for her.

"That was intense. Lucas said the crab was good and then you saw the crab, then crabs at a market, then a table with people, then a park, then an apartment…" He trailed off. "So much, so fast."

"Those were bits of my life…not exactly what I saw, but similar. Some was from that day, some from when I was a kid. You understand? It's all equally clear. Did you notice anything strange at one minute twenty-seven seconds mark?"

He shook his head.

"Check it out. That was Lucas from another client meeting. We always sit at the same table, and he doesn't have that many different vests, but you'll notice the background change. It's hard to tell the difference between the past and present at that moment. See?"

Jason slid his hands back and forth. "I missed that completely. I thought you looked away and back again. I didn't know that was a memory. Very confusing."

"It can be confusing. I'm lucky I don't remember senses other than sight perfectly, or I could literally go into my own world of the past without even knowing it."

"The others like you can't distinguish between past and present as well as you can."

"I assume not. I've never met anyone like me, but I'm guessing they didn't have the chance to figure things out by trial and error." She gestured toward the undeveloped rings. "When I was a kid, the city was only half the size it is now. I ran wild in the empty lots. I figured out that *now* had physical consequences and *before* played out the same every time. If I tried that experiment in New York City, I'd have been run over by a car before I was eight. Plus, there were rules. My parents taught me to keep quiet and to act like the other kids. That helped me to focus on what everyone else saw."

"You have to concentrate all the time to stay in the present."

"Well, usually, but not when I take this." She dug the Baby Jane out of her pocket.

He took it and examined the logo. "What is this?"

"Baby Jane. A neural inhibitor with some muscle relaxant thrown in. My savior. It feels like it was designed for me. When I take one, my memories go flat and stay put. I can see the present with no competition from the past. I spent most of high school on these. I didn't want the perfect recall that made my friends seem stupid and forgetful, and the schoolwork idiotic. Once I got over my teen angst, I started researching careers and found out about social engineering. I could apply myself and use my ability for something useful."

She wasn't used to talking about herself. Anything she said was one more secret out in the open. Was this how friends interacted? Did she sound pompous? She'd just insulted all her high school friends. "That was more than you wanted to know."

"No, I'm interested." Jason was back to his usual techie self, concerns about her possible insanity forgotten. "I'd like to do my own recall tests sometime, if you'd let me. Compare footage from your glasses to what you remember."

"I'd rather not. That one test was it. Okay?"

He frowned. "I'm curious—"

"I know, but I don't want to be a lab rat, not even for you."

"Fair enough. You won't mind if I ask about our clients, though? We don't record when we're in their apartments, and I don't always get everything in my notes."

"Of course not."

"Great. Last week—"

"Not right now. I need a break after the test." And the soul baring.

He gave an exaggerated grimace. "Sorry. I don't like tests, either. Or being assigned a number. Or being told something's wrong with me."

He met her eyes briefly, flashing a look of pain, anger, and shame before he found something on the stunner that needed his attention.

"Please don't repeat anything we talked about," Mia said. "This is between you and me."

"Agreed." He offered her the small gun. "You need this. I was wrong about your memory being a weapon. All that," he made a swirling motion around his head, "isn't going to help if you're in an uncomfortable situation and whatever the person says triggers a memory and you lose seconds. Flip the switch, point, shoot."

Mia, to her surprise, almost accepted. Her digressions into the past had never been a problem, not in a city with no crime.

New Canberra wasn't that city anymore.

Chapter Nineteen

Taylor Rodriguez looked exactly like he had in high school, minus some hair. Mia gave him credit for not getting implants and instead opting for a super short crop that begged to be touched.

He stood when she entered his office at Optima HQ.

"Mia. It's been a while."

She'd always admired the delicacy of his birdlike frame. They'd lost their virginity to each other in freshman year—before she'd gotten tall, and he hadn't. The few native-born children were an incestuous group, full of drama and heartbreak and betrayal, and when they realized they could get the hell off the planet for university, they'd run in different directions as fast as they could.

She wasn't sure whether to hug or shake hands, but he made no move to come out from behind his desk, so she did neither.

He raised an eyebrow when she took out a conversation shield and activated it. "What's this about?"

"May I?" She indicated the chair.

"I've got a meeting at two-thirty."

She didn't sit. "Something impossible happened. I was assaulted last week. A man stopped a pod next to me as I was walking to a bar in Weber sector. He shot me with something called an inner ear disrupter. It causes nausea and dizziness. Then he dragged me into the brush in an undeveloped lot and left me there. No MMARVs flew the area during the course of all this."

Taylor's expression morphed from confusion to incredulity. "Is this some kind of joke? I haven't seen or heard from you in over fifteen years, then out of the blue you appear at my workplace and recite what sounds like the plot of an episode of *Dark Times*."

"I would have thought this was fiction a few months ago, but strange things have been going on. You work in compliance. You have access to MMARV flight records? Check out my story."

She gave him the latitude and longitude, date and time, and he swiped and typed. A few minutes later a map of Weber sector appeared on the desktop overlaid by a dense fabric of bright green lines—the paths of the MMARVs. The fabric had a rip in it—right over Summit Security.

"Huh. That's strange." He zoomed in. "I've not seen that before, but MMARVs aren't my specialty. I work in airborne pollutants."

"Can you play an animation of the paths of the MMARVs on another day?"

He did and the green line fabric was seamless. "You know we don't control them. They're a web of autonomous AIs."

"I do know, but Optima owns them, and they're everywhere all the time. I didn't see one for twenty minutes. You remember how we tried to get away from them in Center Park?" They'd spent most of high school trying to elude the silver spheres and their uncanny ability to detect and confiscate whatever recreational drugs the teens had managed to pilfer from their parent's medicine cabinets. "Isn't it odd they all decided not to go to that one spot? You got hacked."

Taylor shook his head. "I'm sure if I looked at more days, I'd see holes like that from time to time. What were you doing out in the middle of nowhere in Weber sector anyway? Don't you work at Han HQ?"

"Not anymore. I'm at a small security firm."

His eyes narrowed the way they had when he was doing crossword puzzles, an archaic pastime of his she'd found charming when she was fifteen. Now she worried she was the blank set of boxes in front of him.

Indeed, he wiped the map from his desk and did another search.

"Code 88? Really? What did you do?" He typed more without waiting for an answer, then began to giggle. "Chickens? Oh my god. Who thought that up? Anyone who knows you would know you have a feather phobia. What did you call them? Avian dandruff? Remember when we surprised you with a pillow fight and feathers were *everywhere* and you practically had a heart attack?"

He laughed so hard tears streamed from his eyes, and Mia remembered how he could switch from stone-cold analytical to a giggling mess in a breath. God, it was nice to have someone know her—and know it was impossible she'd do anything with birds.

"This is too ridiculous." He enlarged the picture of her holding a frightened hen. "I'm sending this to Sabrina."

"You're still in touch with her?"

"We hang out sometimes. We all do. You're the only one who completely cut ties."

The thought of being faced with the high school gang made her stomach flip.

"Why did you get fired from Han? I heard you were doing well there."

"I was. Perfect record, steady promotions, in charge of a team, trusted to work on the upper floors. Then, they needed a scapegoat to explain some leaked IP. It wasn't me, but I had the right accesses. I miss my job but I wouldn't go back to Han."

"That explains your assault. It was Han CorSec. They're the only ones with stunners. You're involved in some upper-floors bullshit and couldn't have been in real danger because no one dies here. He'd probably cleared the area with lasers beforehand and just wanted to scare you."

The man wasn't CorSec and the ground was crawling with bugs. She'd heard them.

She took a deep breath, reminding herself why she was here.

"You love Victoria," she said.

He nodded slowly.

"I do too," Mia said. "I want to keep it safe. I'm in a difficult situation. My security firm is coming across things that shouldn't be happening, but we have confidentiality agreements with our clients, and they don't want us to report what we're discovering to anyone."

"What are you discovering…*in theory*?" Taylor made air quotes.

"Appliances collecting unusual data. Hidden bugs and holocams that can broadcast to outside an apartment. All in Han sector."

"What does that tell you? It's Han HQ. They're trying to root something out. Yes, we're guaranteed privacy in our homes, but it's a wiggly line. There's language in every lease that allows collection of personal data in extraordinary cases, which can mean almost anything. I've got a law degree, and it pains me that we don't have overarching laws to protect the residents, but none of the corporations want that. We're lucky Optima even exists. We're the gun each of the Six holds to each other's heads to keep things running smoothly here, but if they decide we aren't needed, we vanish. I'm allowed to help safeguard the planet from pollutants and I'm proud of my work, but I can't help with this."

"Someone here will care if the MMARVs are being manipulated. Can you at least pass the information on to them?"

She took a breath and stepped into uncomfortable territory—honesty.

"My boss doesn't know I'm here and wouldn't want me to tell you any of this. The man who dragged me off the sidewalk wasn't CorSec. He was a recent arrival and had no fucking idea the empty lots are crawling with bugs. I'd know if the ground was clear, and it wasn't. He said my company shouldn't take any more clients from Han. I don't know who he works for, but he was causing trouble in Weber sector, able to divert Optima's MMARVs, and clearly isn't an official contractor or he'd have gotten the safety training. He could have been bitten as well. This might be the first violent crime on Victoria, and I don't want to sit by and do nothing about it."

Taylor nodded. "I believe you. You're a lot of things, but dishonest isn't one of them. I agree Weber wouldn't tolerate this in their sector, and Optima has a responsibility to secure the MMARVs. As to the first violent crime—I suspect intimidation tactics like this have been happening here for years. The HQ towers are tall and the partners untouchable. The lack of laws and accountability galls me, and I hope someday Optima has real power to protect people and the planet…but that day isn't today."

He glanced at the desk. "I've got to go. I'll let IT know about the MMARV anomaly. I can't tell anyone about you being stunned if you don't have proof, and there's no official proof without the MMARVs."

"Hopefully the *anomaly* will be a thread that unravels something."

"I hope so, too." He tucked a small screen under his arm and stood. "I'll walk you out."

Heads swiveled as they made their way to the lobby. Taylor was possibly single, and Mia had dressed well for this meeting.

Once outside, Taylor turned his face to the sun and shut his eyes. "I hate being indoors all day. I wish we had national parks here. I'd be a park ranger."

Mia laughed. "You hated being outside when we were in high school. When we went camping you refused to leave the tent."

"I've changed. We all have. You should give us another chance."

Mia didn't answer.

He opened his eyes. "I wasn't kind to you after we were together, and I regret that."

Mia puzzled over the meaning of his words, then guessed that "together" meant sex and "after" was when he'd hooked up with her friend Tara the week after they'd done the deed.

"Oh, no…I wasn't…" She didn't want to say she hadn't been interested in him—only curious about sex—and hadn't minded that he'd wanted to do it with other people. "I wasn't mad. There aren't many of us native-born. I'm not sure our parents knew what to do with us or had the time to figure it out. We raised ourselves. Of course, we got some things wrong."

"More than a few. Still, the unkindness is something I'd like to take back. I only recently thought about what your life must have been like when your dad died and your mom pulled you out of fourth grade for home schooling. You must have been lonely, and it wouldn't have been easy to acclimate when you rejoined us for high school. We'd established social groups, a pecking order…" He blushed and the rest came out in a rush. "None of them would have slept with me if you hadn't done it first. They called me 'the rat.'" He gestured to his long nose and large, upturned olive-shaped eyes. "They'd never seen a real one, but I was small, and someone had to be the thing everyone tried to stomp on."

Mia had been so grateful to have a social group after years of isolation with her mom that she hadn't minded the petty bickering and casual betrayals. She, too, hadn't been very kind to anyone—herself included.

"I'm glad I could help. And don't worry, you didn't hurt my feelings. Like I said, we were all making it up as we went along."

"We meet every third Thursday of the month at the Tiki Room for happy hour. Join us sometime."

"I might. I'll see."

Taylor's screen buzzed. "Gotta go. Hopefully see you at the bar one of these nights."

He wouldn't. High school had been a rough and wobbly stepping stone to get to New Beijing U where her real life began. Nostalgia was fiction that people with poor memories used to create a rosy past that didn't exist. She carried the past like a bag of rocks and didn't need any more shaped like Taylor and Sabrina.

Chapter Twenty

This job is a huge mistake.

The entire Summit team, laden with heavy boxes of equipment, stood on the stone steps leading to Dr. Lerner's house as he and his wife argued in the piercing morning sunlight. He'd opened the door half a meter, held up a finger, then turned to her. She was tall and thin with a dancer's grace and honey-blonde hair pulled into a loose chignon. Not the type of woman Mia would have imagined being attracted to professorial Dr. Lerner.

"This party is a mistake," Dr. Lerner said.

"We aren't taking Stella off this planet without letting her see her friends one last time."

"But—"

"You don't think I'm taking this seriously? I want to kill the bastard that cut Stella's hair. I know it could have been her throat. That's why we've got this…" She gestured to the crowd on the porch. "And why we're only inviting people over that we've known for years. After this we can lock ourselves in until the pod comes to take us to the strataport."

They faced off for a moment, then Dr. Lerner shrugged. "Fine. Siobhan, this is Lucas Dunn and the Summit Security team."

"Nice to meet you all. I've got to finish the cake. No caterers for this party." She turned and padded out of view.

When Dr. Lerner had called a week earlier, it had taken Mia a heartbeat to place him. He'd hired them to secure that odd lunch date with the too-pretty, too-young woman with the expensive purse. Dezzie Adeyemi, one of their first clients, worked for him.

"Dr. Lerner. It's good to see you again."

She'd not interacted with him much during the last job, but had liked him because he reminded her of one of her favorite professors at New Beijing U. Both were prematurely grey with sparkling blue eyes and took thoughtful, deliberate pauses before speaking. Dr. Lerner had been gracious to the aggressive young woman who'd crudely tried to seduce him, and Mia admired his forbearance. Patience was a trait she'd had to develop to deal with normal people spouting inaccuracies and contradicting themselves and knew it took effort.

"How can we help you?"

He leaned back in a large, eel-leather chair in what looked like a home office. The windows behind him revealed sand, a row of agave plants, and a putty-colored wall.

"Mia Julian. You helped derail that awful meeting at Antonio's."

"I did."

He shook his head, scowled as if he'd taken a bite of bad bluefish.

"The first of many," he began, then held up a hand as if to silence himself. "You do event security?"

"What kind of event?"

"A small party at my house in Andaman sector."

Summit offered this service but had never been hired to provide it. "We do. I'll have to transfer you to Mr. Dunn. Events are on a case-by-case basis. We don't have a large staff."

"You shouldn't need more than four or five people."

"Okay, one moment."

She pulled off her glasses and called to Lucas. It was analog and the best way to get his attention when he was deep in data—as he'd been the past few weeks.

"It's Dr. Lerner," she said when he'd stopped dogpaddling through who knew what. "He wants us to secure a party at his house."

Lucas made a beckoning gesture, and she transferred the call.

He emerged from his office fifteen minutes later.

"Well?" Mia asked. "What's the event?"

He held out a screen.

She took it and scrolled through twenty or so images of gap-toothed, pigtailed, grinning six-year-olds. "This must be all the children on Victoria! It's a kid's party?"

Mia wondered about the origin of these children. Pregnancy while under contract was forbidden. The customized one pill everyone took to protect against skin cancer and other Victoria hazards included birth control. Despite the best efforts of the Six, accidents did happen. Since it was next to impossible for anyone born on Victoria to immigrate to Earth, pregnant women were granted a six-month leave of absence to give birth in their hometowns, after which they dragged their newborns back to Victoria where they'd develop the same enviable bone mass Mia had. Other new hires signed a contract stipulating they'd be allowed to bring existing minor children to Victoria. Lerner was far enough into his contract that Mia suspected Lerner's daughter had been an accident.

"Are we doing it?" Mia asked.

"Ordinarily I wouldn't, but this isn't an ordinary birthday party. Dr. Lerner and his family have been riding out the last few weeks of his contract at home. He's being pressured to sign up for another ten years." Lucas took back the screen and pulled up an image of a scraggly, blonde braid—detached from the six-year-old it likely belonged to.

"Stella, his daughter, was assaulted after school last week. Cam data is, not surprisingly, missing. She told Lerner a man with very big glasses pulled her hair when she was waiting for the pod home. She didn't know what happened until her friends laughed at her haircut."

"What?" Mia stared at the braid. "A man with big glasses? Is it the same guy?"

She tried to control the volume of her voice and failed.

"I don't know. I sent Lerner the illustration of the man that attacked you, but he doesn't want to upset his daughter by asking more questions. His wife told her it was an accident, that the man had been wearing a fancy coat with big buttons that caught on her hair when he walked by."

"Back up," Mia said. "Children are being attacked on Victoria. Tell me they reported this to Andaman or Optima."

Lucas shook his head. "If there were an investigation, Lerner and his family would have to stay until it was concluded. All they want to do is go home."

"Are any of our other Han clients nearing the end of their contracts? Could all the spying and bugging have something to do with contract extensions? It costs a lot to send workers back and forth from Earth, but very few want to sign a twenty-year."

Lucas touched his glasses then airtyped. "We've got clients in all phases of contract, and none have recently signed up to stay longer. Claire, get me stats on the number of ten-year extension contracts in all sectors and whether Han has seen an uptick recently."

Claire made short work of his request. "It's about twelve percent on average, all sectors, and nothing unusual happening in Han."

"It's about his specialty, then," Mia said. "He's a senior scientist working on technology for single-stage extraction of rare earth elements. Why would they want to keep him longer? Han scoured their sector when they arrived. There are no concentrations of rare earth elements here."

"If he works on hardware, the tech he's developing could have alternative uses, but it doesn't matter. We aren't detectives. We provide security and we're going to provide it for Lerner. I promised female screeners, so you and Claire will have to help onsite."

Claire spun around in her chair, telltale pink blotches already forming on her cheeks. "No. I don't do physical security. I'm not required to do anything outside of this office. You promised."

Mia was put off as well. She didn't want to be near anyone who'd drawn the attention of men in oversized glasses and—truth be told—she was nervous about the children. She hadn't interacted with anyone under the age of twenty-one for a decade, and prior to that, only a handful of times. What did it even mean to screen six-year-olds?

Lucas clenched his teeth and sucked air in through them. "I did promise you wouldn't have to work outside this office, Claire, and I won't make you do it, but I want you there because I trust you."

Mia heard, in the last phrase, the cadence he used when charming reluctant customers. He took a few steps toward Claire's desk.

"Children's toys are so sophisticated these days. I don't want anything dangerous getting into the house. This is a job for an expert. I need you."

Claire, to Mia's surprise, straightened and nodded, her cheeks returning to pale. Was she actually falling for his flattery?

"I just read an article about an exploit to the TrailRunner," Claire said. "It's a glasses-controlled car, and there's a way to get it to run at full speed with the brakes on until it overheats and catches fire."

Lucas snapped his fingers and pointed at Claire. "That's what I mean. You're up-to-date on all this."

"I'll do it if I don't have to touch any of them. The children," she clarified.

"Agreed. Mia can deal with any…" He flapped his hands to simulate, what, Mia didn't know, but it probably meant she'd be digging around in grubby backpacks.

"What kind of security will we be providing? Is Lerner worried one of the kids will attack his daughter?" Jason asked.

"No. He wants his home locked down, invited guests only, and no electronic devices brought in. We'll let the guests know in advance and collect and store everything they're carrying, but we're going to meet with resistance from both the kids and their parents. Kids like their toys, and parents are used to monitoring their children twenty-seven hours a day. Also, there'll be adult nannies in attendance, and we'll do background checks on them in advance."

Jason, scanning through data, nodded. "Lerner lives in a detached house. That presents challenges, but I'd rather be on the ground than in a high-rise. We can do this."

"If you haven't already noticed," Lucas said, "this is in Andaman sector and our first non-Han job. I had Lerner's wife sign the contract and pay the fee. We're going to aggressively pursue business in the other sectors. Mia, I'm giving you the advertising budget you requested."

That was good news.

"The party is next Saturday. Jason, you and I will go check out the space tomorrow. I'm guessing we'll have to hire some of Mikey's students to guard the side and rear entrances."

"We'll need locking boxes to store the glasses and tech we confiscate," Mia said. "No one is going to want to throw their two-thousand-credit Lucida glasses into a bin."

"I need to be…" Claire put both hands in front of her as if holding shut a door, "away from…them. Find a place for me."

Lucas nodded. "Will do. I'll write up a project brief with Lerner's requests and send it around to everyone, with the contract. I know this is an unusual job, but children can't be any worse than the happy-hour drunks at *The Drift*."

He looked pointedly at Mia, and she nodded back. Children couldn't be as disgusting as legacy partners letting loose after a stressful week.

It would be fine.

Mia watched Dr. Lerner's wife stomp away to finish the cake, and waited as he took a few deep breaths before finally pulling the front door open the rest of the way and gesturing for the team to enter.

"Sorry about that. We've been a bit stressed lately. I won't be able to relax until we're on the ship and heading home."

"Not a problem," Lucas said. "We'll get started securing the house. Once we set up the data shields and cut over to the temporary network, no data will enter or leave these walls, so some of your usual home functionality will be disabled. Jason will be manually authorizing all requests from appliances, but he can't handle more than a dozen or so per minute."

"That means?" Lerner asked.

"It means your smart toilet won't flush until Jason says it's okay."

Lerner smiled. "Understood. What about glasses?"

"We'll authorize you, Siobhan, and our team to use the temporary network so we can communicate, but again, there will be no contact with the outside world."

"Perfect. Let me know if I can help."

Mikey, who'd hired two of his most competent martial arts students to assist, installed Annabelle outside the front door and Joshua by the back—the only entrances to the home. Lerner, despite fearing for his family's safety, would not allow the team to carry weapons of any sort, though Lucas assured him they couldn't be used by anyone but the owner.

Mia helped Claire set up the scanner—two upright poles a meter apart—just inside the front door in the generously sized circular foyer. An archway on the right opened onto the living room, the latter a blizzard of pink streamers and balloons. Straight ahead, a dark hallway led to bedrooms and offices.

"Where am I supposed to sit?" Claire asked.

Mia dragged a side table over and positioned it by the scanner, adding a small stool she found under a coat rack. "That work?"

Claire frowned. "I'm not very protected."

She'd been in a foul mood the whole ride over, seemingly regretting her decision to help yet unwilling to go back on her word to Lucas.

"The bins will keep the kids away from you, see?" Mia formed a wall out of the empty storage bins, buffering Claire from the doorway.

"Can I have the plant too?"

Mia sighed, and dragged a leafy potted palm, nearly as tall as the scanning poles, to the other side of the table. Claire sat down, bracketed by bins and vegetation, and nodded.

"This will do. Let's test the scanner. Walk through it."

Claire pulled down her glasses, and Mia obliged.

"I see your glasses, and three things in your bag. You've got a PDS, a data shield, and…" Claire's eyebrows rose. "A stunner? Since when, Miss *No-guns-on-my-plane*t? You better get rid of that, or we're in breach of contract. Plus, you've got Baby Janes. Dr. Lerner said no drugs."

Mia, blushing red, hurried out the front door. Annabelle, already sweating, stepped out of the thin band of shade she'd been hiding in. "Need something?"

"Yes," Mia said, handing over her bag. "Can you stash this out here? I brought some recreationals, and they aren't allowed in the house."

"Sure."

Annabelle put the bag behind a large terra cotta planter where her own gear was stowed. "Don't worry," she said. "It's all charged. The whole yard. No bugs."

Lucas met Mia as she came inside. "We have a potential problem. The invitation specified no gifts." He paused as Stella careened out of the dark hallway in a pink tutu and unicorn horn headband, skidded across the tiles, and disappeared into the living room.

"My guess is that no one read the fine print. We can't confiscate the presents." He glanced toward the back of the house, where Siobhan was presumably frosting a pink cake. "I need you to disable anything that triggers the scanner." He held out a heavy silver cylinder. "Think of this as a flashlight that—"

Mia shook her head. "Have Annabelle do it. I'm going to have my hands full tagging and stowing all the other gear everyone will try to bring in. She can zap every present and that should take care of it." She'd have felt bad about destroying toys, but the Lerners weren't going to be bringing all that crap back anyway. Contractors got to ship a hundred kilos to Earth for free; anything above that cost serious credits.

"Good idea. One more thing. After the guests are in and the front door secured, can you help keep an eye on things?"

"What do you mean by *things*? The bins?"

"No. The party in general. Some of the nannies didn't come to Victoria intending to care for children. We've got a former hostess, a musician with tendonitis, an architect whose project was defunded… You get the picture. This is not their dream job. People like that can be compromised."

If Lucas honestly believed there was a threat, he wouldn't allow the nannies to enter. He had that look in his eye, though. The serious one he'd had the night she'd been stunned. He was worried something might happen today but couldn't figure out what it might be. It was 11 a.m., sunny, and the street outside was busy with pods. She'd talked herself into feeling comfortable with this job, but now tendrils of unease crept in like dust from a winter storm.

"Of course. I'll keep an eye out."

He opened the front door and called Annabelle over to explain how to use the toy zapping cylinder. Before he could finish, a pod pulled to a stop and redheaded twins jumped out.

"It's not time," Annabelle said. "They're fifteen minutes early."

Mia smiled. She'd never seen real, live twins.

The boys were freckled and racing each other to the door. The nanny, a pale young man with dark brown eyes, chased after them. Was he a failed architect or musician? Mia guessed the latter. He grabbed them by the shirt collars with strong hands and turned them to face him, perhaps repeating an admonition they'd heard from their mother or father before they left, because they calmed down.

"Should I let them in?" Annabelle asked.

"Sure, after you deactivate any presents they brought."

The twins weren't much trouble. Annabelle shined the "flashlight" on the polka dot-covered boxes they held. They passed through the scanner, and Claire told Mia what they had and where it was. Mia asked the nanny to remove the offending items, relieved she'd found a way to not have to touch the kids herself.

Once everything was stowed, she locked the bin and gave the nanny a claim token, assuring him that no one else could unlock it.

Then…

All hell broke loose.

Annabelle opened the door for the next guests, and eight kids ran in. Mia flung out her arms.

"Stop," she yelled, belatedly wondering if it was okay to yell at children. "No one gets into the party until you go through the scanner, and I check your pockets! It's just like…going to a museum. Line up over here."

The kids settled into a queue that wriggled like a brightly colored, angry centipede. Mia looked them over. "Where are your nannies?"

All pointed at the closed door.

"Great."

Mia plucked the glasses off the head of the first boy in line, Josh Spencer, and put them in the bin she'd prelabeled with his name. His bulging pocket yielded the crusty remains of a peanut butter sandwich. What was she supposed to do with that? It wasn't tech, so she handed it back. He ran through the scanner again, and it glowed green.

"Go, be free," she told him.

Most of the kids went through the scanner a dozen times each. Claire couldn't rattle off the names and locations of the tech she spotted fast enough, so Mia grabbed what she could on each pass then sent them through again.

The most disturbing trend in toys—if it could be called a trend, given the small sample size—were the ultrarealistic robotic animals and insects. Mia nearly smashed a perfect replica of a jumping spider before realizing what it was. Why make a plaything of something so deadly? Why make kids comfortable with something that could kill them? People from Earth were so odd. She threw the thing into the bin with a little more force than necessary, and it clawed at the lid after she snapped it shut. *Creepy.*

The thirty minutes during which the mob arrived felt like several hours. Mia was exhausted and dirty by the time she'd checked the last of them in and affixed a palm-coded physical lock to the interior of the door. All the guests would have to be scanned and searched on the way out as well to ensure they hadn't pocked Stella's favorite toy. Mia wasn't looking forward to that, especially given the kids would be high on sugar, but Lucas was right. It was still better than The Drift at happy hour.

She settled onto the cool tiles on the floor, leaned against the wall and gave herself a moment to relax.

"What did you think of all that?" she asked Claire, who was fussily straightening the full bins. The spider robot paced its cage restlessly.

"I remember being six," Claire said. "I didn't behave, either. I wasn't so loud, though."

As sounds of shrill laughter ricocheted into the foyer, Mia realized this was the first children's party she'd ever attended. She didn't have close friends when she was young. Even her parents had trouble carrying on conversations with her, given all the non sequiturs. When she was four, they told other adults she had a great imagination; by the time she was six, the excuses were wearing thin. They kept her away from birthday parties, fearing that what children interpreted as silly, parents might recognize as something else. When Mia was older, she learned to hold her tongue, but by then her reputation was firmly established as *strange* and her classmates didn't invite her to anything.

Her one real friend, for a brief time, was a research scientist who'd lived next door when she was nine years old. He had no experience with kids and thus no expectations about how she was supposed to act. He'd been kind enough to give her a job as a junior lab assistant for a few months—until he was called back to Earth to take on a new position at his university. It was one of the happiest periods of her childhood.

Dr. Derek Singh had been a lifeline when her mom shut down—and shut them both into the apartment—after her dad died. During long calls from Victoria to Earth, he counseled her and even offered to bring her to Texas to live with his family. He could have gotten her an educational visa thanks to his university connections. She'd been tempted but couldn't leave Mom. They'd never gotten along, but Mom, always so coldly analytical, broke down completely when Dad died. She'd have starved, or lain out in the wastes at noon, or pressed too many Nightshade hypos while she was in the bath… Mia couldn't lose both parents.

Still, the expensive calls to Derek—that she now wondered how he could have afforded—kept her sane and anchored, and she'd fallen asleep every night dreaming of a small backyard in Austin with apple and peach and plum trees.

A few minutes later, Lucas stomped into the foyer, towering above her and Claire.

"Everyone in? Door locked?"

Mia nodded.

"It's time to open presents."

She'd never heard that phrase uttered so glumly. None of the electronic toys would work, thanks to Annabelle zapping everything. How would Stella react?

"I need your help," Lucas said. "Things might get complicated."

Mia smiled as she hoisted herself to her feet. Complicated was putting it lightly. These kids weren't dumb. If Stella ripped open a box and the deadly scorpion robot didn't immediately raise its tail, what happened next?

She followed Lucas and the din to the oversized dining room. The table, a four-meter-long slab of Earth wood, had been pushed to one wall and sported dozens of brightly wrapped squares. Siobhan had loosed her long hair from the tight bun and sat cross-legged on the floor. Stella danced in front of her, a spinning blur of blonde hair and pink tutu. Lerner stood a few meters away, a glowering cloud in an otherwise sunshiny room. He took a glittery box from the top of the pile, handed it to Siobhan, who tried to get Stella to read the card before tearing into the wrapping—to no avail. The rest of the children crowded close, eager to see what was inside.

Stella pulled a tiny zebra from its packaging.

"Walk," she said, and set it on the floor. The tiny articulated legs folded, and it collapsed onto its side.

"Make it gallop," another child said. "Mine gallops."

The zebra lay still.

Siobhan reached forward and plucked it up. "It probably needs to be charged. Let's open another one!"

After half a dozen more toys failed to fly, play holos, blow bubbles, or 3D print jewelry, Siobhan glared at Andrew and indicated he should accompany her into the other room. She clearly hadn't been told about the deactivating wand.

Stella, unsupervised, tore open the last of the presents and the kids, getting restless, began to throw the empty boxes and wadded up wrapping paper at each other. Others picked through the pile of dead toys, determined to make them work.

"That's mine!" Stella yelled, and tried to grab the zebra from a serious boy who'd produced a tiny screwdriver and was attempting to pry open the animal.

"This is mine," a tiny girl with a long black braid declared, holding up a dead gray cube. "My momma and I bought it at Zeno's. It makes fairies. I'm going to bring it home."

An ear-piercing shriek nearly deafened Mia. How did kids hit such high notes?

The nannies, sensing trouble, waded into the sea of fast-moving bodies and tried to catch their respective minnows. Andrew and Siobhan, in the midst of a heated argument and probably used to this volume, stood in the far side of the room pointing fingers and slicing flattened palms through the air.

Mia wasn't sure what she was supposed to be doing. She had no normal to compare this scene to. She searched for Lucas, who'd retreated to a corner and was holding both hands over his ears, clearly trying to hear something on his ear buds. A little boy—Tad Lee, she knew from the guest list—tugged at her skirt and said he had to go to the potty. Where was his nanny?

She bent to tell him where the bathroom was when a small red dart resembling a fishing lure flew past her face and lodged in the wall. Who the hell gives a six-year-old real darts as a present? She had no time to locate the culprit before a similar dart bit into her shoulder. She gasped in surprise and pain. Before she could pluck it out, it dissolved.

What the hell?

Tad Lee yelped. A dart quivered in his cheek before dissolving as hers had. Was this a toy or something else? Hot air pushed through the air-conditioned coolness of the room. The large, sliding glass window above the dining room table was open.

That isn't right. The house is supposed to be sealed.

Mikey must have seen it at the same time because he pounded into the room and slid the window shut with a bang. Nothing in or out of the house included no open windows or doors.

Tad's hold on her skirt loosened, and he wobbled and fell to the floor. She knelt beside him and saw a classic red ring forming around a purpling bull's-eye on his cheek where the dart had struck. He'd been bitten or stung. It didn't make sense, but a lifetime of training told her it was true. This is what it looked like when the deadliest insects on Victoria struck.

The darts held venom.

She tried to pick him up, belatedly realizing her right arm had gone numb and that her shoulder displayed the same red ring.

Fuck.

She wouldn't panic. She had an antivenom kit in her bag, which was, double fuck, outside the house. The numbness spread down her right side, and her pounding heart slowed.

This is bad.

She didn't have much time. Tad had less. No one in the chaotic room noticed things had gone very wrong.

She hoisted Tad with her good arm and stumbled to the foyer. By now her right arm was completely numb. Tad hung limp in her grasp.

Not again, she thought. *Please. Not again.*

Lucas caught up with her. "What's wrong with him?"

"Antivenom kit," she croaked. "My purse. Outside."

He fumbled with the physical lock, but couldn't open it, coded as it was to Mia's palm.

"Take him," she said, and Lucas gingerly lifted Tad from her. She grasped her limp right wrist, pressed her hand to the lock, and it unlatched. Lucas pulled the door open. Mia stumbled into the rock garden to the right of the door, sitting heavily on the rounded stones. They should have burned but felt only warm.

"Annabelle, give me Mia's bag."

He dumped it out and thankfully, seemed to have learned how to use the kit. He pressed the device to Tad's arm. The lights on the face of it flashed and danced a pattern she'd never seen, not in any of the training holos. She heard the hiss of multiple hypos. Was the kit malfunctioning? A green light meant the toxin had been identified, the orange light below, that the antidote had been administered. They both flashed over and over again.

"Multiple toxins," he said under his breath. "Paramedic drones are on the way. What happened?" he asked Mia. "Did a swarm of insects fly in?"

"It wasn't a bug," Mia whispered. "Someone shot darts in through the window. There's one stuck in the wall. The ones that hit us disappeared."

"Us? You're hit too? Why didn't you tell me? Annabelle, do you have a kit?"

She did. Lucas handed Tad to her. "Take him into the shade."

He knelt beside Mia and held the antivenom kit against her arm. It flashed the same staccato pattern. Mia blinked. It was getting harder to focus. Was she going to die? This wasn't what she'd expected. Whatever had bitten her dad caused pain and convulsions, not this sluggish sedation. Even so, he might have been saved if she'd been able to get him outside where a MMARV could have treated him. She was outside. That was good. She relaxed and leaned back, the stones a welcome support to her sagging body.

Lucas shifted, put something soft under her head. "Hang on, Mia," he whispered.

He might have been holding her hand. His expression reminded her of how he'd looked when he returned from the clinic. Raw. Her peripheral vision shrank like an iris stopping down until all she saw was him.

Abruptly he pulled away and a MMARV descended, a fuzzy white angel of salvation. The next minutes played like an art student's experimental film. The MMARV was far away, viewed as if through a dark tunnel, lights flashing, metal arms extending and retracting. For a while there was no soundtrack, then a hiss, like distant waves, then a more bass note which resolved into Lucas's voice. He spoke confidently, though she wasn't sure to whom.

Like a slap, sensation returned. She gasped and sat up. Lucas and a man in a white uniform, kneeling on either side of her, pulled back in surprise.

"It worked," the man said. "Ms. Julian, I'm John Miller. How are you feeling?"

"I'm not sure," she rasped.

He examined a screen. "I've got the report from the MMARV. Whatever bit you was nothing we've encountered before, but the MMARV synthesized an antidote based on an analysis of your blood. All the toxins were removed from your system, so what you are feeling now is probably shock. I'll double-check and make sure you're clean."

"We weren't bitten," she said. "We were hit by darts. Red darts."

The medic nodded. "I've not seen many red insects here, but this is definitely something new. Looked like a dart, huh? I'll pass that on."

"It didn't look like a dart, it was—"

Lucas put a hand on her forearm and squeezed hard. "Some of those toxins could have caused hallucinations." He looked pointedly at the Andaman CorSec staff swarming the front yard. Not ordinary security guards, these were executive-level, their black suits a harsh contrast to the bright sunny day.

"True," said Miller. "It's never a good day when we find an aggressive diurnal species. I'm not sure why CorSec is here, though. I'd expect a university contingent. Maybe because of the boy?"

"Where's Tad? Is he okay?" Mia asked.

"We need to get you inside," Lucas said. "You're overheating. Can you help?" he asked Miller.

"Of course." They each took one arm and helped her up. On the street a discreet white pod sat, doors open. Something small, covered with a blue sheet, lay still on the bench seat within.

Mia craned around to see more as the two men dragged her toward the house.

"Keep it together," Lucas hissed, squeezing her arm tighter than necessary. They led her down the dark hallway to a room on the left that was Lerner's office—she recognized it from when he'd first called—and sat her down on a stiff espresso-colored sofa.

"You've had a shock," Miller said. "You need rest." He turned to Lucas. "Can you get her home? A light sedative might help her sleep."

"Of course."

"On behalf of Andaman sector, I apologize Ms. Julian. I've been a paramedic here for seven years and never seen an insect bite happen in a home."

Part of her laughed. *Trust me, it happens.*

Lucas shut the door after him and set a conversation shield on the desk.

"Stop talking about darts. You didn't see anything. You and Tad were bitten by an unidentified insect." His voice dropped. "There will be an investigation. It won't be public. You don't want to be part of it. Lerner and his family don't want to be part of it. They just want to get back to Earth."

"What happened to Tad?"

"He was allergic to one of the venoms. They got him into a freezer and took him to the hospital."

Mia's stomach did another flip. "You're lying. He's dead, isn't he?"

"Calm down. You just got a blood transfusion from that drone, and as fine as Mr. Miller thinks you are, you aren't."

She struggled to rise. "I need to use the bathroom."

Lucas helped her up. She'd been given a clean bill of health, but her legs wobbled, and her head swam. Across the hall, the limestone-covered cell of a bathroom was, thankfully, unoccupied.

"Will you be okay on your own for a few minutes?" Lucas asked. "I've got to talk to the Andaman reps."

"Yes," Mia said, transferring her grip from his arm to a towel rack.

"I'll be right back," he promised.

She shut the door and leaned against it, taking deep breaths until her stomach settled. The coolness of the stone floor soaked up through the soles of her bare feet and chilled her. She looked down. Where were her shoes?

She'd been so hot out in the front yard—now she was cold. Freezing cold. She held out her left hand. It shook violently.

The shower beckoned. She stepped in, turned the tap on full and sat, letting the steam hide her from the world. Was Tad dead or alive? Whatever she'd seen in the back of the white pod was exactly Tad's shape. She should have taken him outside sooner—the moment she saw the red bull's-eye. She'd hesitated, puzzling over the vanishing darts. Those seconds might have meant the difference between life and death. She closed her eyes, feeling the weight of Tad in her arms and remembering a heavier weight—one she couldn't lift—and running down a corridor, pounding on doors that wouldn't open.

Chapter Twenty One

One moment she was immersed in hot water, the next Lucas leaned over her, awkwardly wrapping a towel around her like she was a small child just out of a swimming pool. She panicked for a moment, fearing she was naked, then remembered she'd gone into the shower fully clothed.

"Can you hear me?" he asked.

"Yes."

"Finally." He grabbed another towel and began to rub her hair dry.

"I can do that."

"We need to get you home." Lucas dropped the wet towels to the floor, then took off his jacket, draped it over her shoulders, and led her back to Lerner's office. "Wait here. I'll be right back."

The office, she hadn't noticed before, was largely packed up, walls and desk bare and belongings neatly arranged in plastic crates.

Lucas returned and pressed two pills into her unresisting palm.

"The medic left these for you. They'll help with shock and the processing of any residual toxins."

"He said the MMARV got everything."

"Just take them. Claire is in a pod out front. She'll get you home and stay with you until I can get out of here." He wore his glasses on mirror yet still seemed to avoid her eyes. "You'll have to palm a nondisclosure agreement before you leave. Do it. We'll sort everything out later."

She stared down at the pills. The red one was definitely a sedative but the yellow one, imprinted with an infinity sign, was a mystery. She knew all pills legal and illegal on Victoria and it wasn't one of them.

"I need water."

"Of course."

As soon as he left, she dropped the pills in the pocket of the jacket.

When Lucas returned, she pretended to toss the pills into her mouth, did a fake swallow, and reached for the glass he held out.

Lucas relaxed with every gulp she took.

What is that yellow pill?

Andaman CorSec paid surprisingly little attention to her when she left the house. She palmed the screen they offered without reading it and stepped out into a deceptively sunny and calm afternoon. Lucas helped her down the stairs, past the rock garden where she'd lain earlier.

"I'll check in on you as soon as I finish here. Don't leave your apartment."

Claire sat glumly in a waiting pod. When Mia tried to get in, her foot ended up in the gutter, and she missed the handhold and nearly fell. Lucas caught her. She was toxin-free. Why did she feel so weak?

"That was a massive fuckup," Claire said, once the pod was en route.

Mia stared out the window and willed herself to see the scenery and not the images in her head.

"We should never have been there," Claire continued. "Neither of us are trained for physical security, and Lucas promised I'd never have to leave the office if I came to this shopping mall planet."

Mia didn't reply.

"At least *you'll* feel better tomorrow." Claire said that with an odd certainty.

"What do you mean?"

Claire shrugged.

"What were those pills Lucas gave me?" Mia asked. "I've never seen anything like that yellow one, but I'll figure out what it is."

"No," Claire said. "You won't."

"Why not?"

"You don't have it here. It's Levotrum."

Mia knew this name from the list of drugs banned on Victoria, but it took a moment to recall the details. It was a memory-erasing compound used—with a patient's consent—on people who'd experienced a traumatic event. It blocked hormones that assisted in memory formation and caused an extreme migraine that overwrote all sensory input for a period of eight hours—the four hours before the patient took the pill until about four hours after.

It was also called the *get-out-of-jail-free* card, given that criminals used it to erase knowledge of crimes they committed. A special class of Schedule II rules governed its manufacture and distribution. Optima evaluated the many cases of its misuse on Earth and outlawed it here.

The pill in her pocket burned.

"You let him give that to me?"

"I didn't *let* him do anything. He asked us what was wrong with you."

"What was wrong? I was poisoned."

"No. Later. In the shower. Lucas turned off the water, and you sat there like a zombie. Eyes open. Kinda creepy. He shook you, splashed cold water on your face, and you didn't react. He asked me if that ever happened in college. He brought in Jason because he'd read all about your…you know." She did the irritating, finger twirling around temple gesture the team had adopted as a workaround to not talking about her memory.

They were all in the bathroom? Mia was equal parts embarrassed, angry, and horrified.

"I was about to tell him no, but I did see you like that once. You were at the kitchen table and wouldn't answer me. Your eyes were open, and you were muttering and moving your hands around like you were cooking something. I assumed you were on drugs. Later I asked what kind, and you looked at me like I was crazy. Jason told us about the syndrome people like you get, and Lucas worried that what happened might cause you to retreat into an endless loop of memory."

They'd made an armchair diagnosis and drugged her? Claire's complicity in this extinguished something Mia had been nurturing—and the sudden empty spot where trust had been hurt as much as the growing bruise on her arm.

They finished the ride in silence. Mia opened the door the moment the pod stopped. Claire slid forward as if to accompany her. She held up a hand, and Claire recoiled from the near touch.

"Stay," Mia commanded.

"I told Lucas I'd watch you."

"I don't need watching. I'm not about to have a blackout migraine. I didn't take the pill."

Claire opened and closed her mouth several times, a fish in a dirty tank gasping for air. She'd been speaking freely under the assumption that Mia would forget everything she said.

Mia tried to slam the pod door, but the vehicle buffered the gesture, and the door slid quietly back into place. Still, Claire flinched.

"Don't try to enter my building. I'm deauthorizing you now, and if I see you on any camera, I'll call security."

Mia walked quickly across the hot pavement, still barefoot, still unclear what had happened to her shoes.

Her apartment was clean, cool, and silent. She padded into the bathroom, took two Baby Janes from the drawer and swallowed them with tap water. She was surprised to see the woman in the mirror wore Lucas's tasteful gray and black jacket. She took it off and dropped it to the ground, then remembered the pills were still in the pocket.

She fished them out and set the sedative on the counter for later. She twirled the yellow pill between thumb and forefinger. Round like a small marble, an infinity symbol stamped across the surface.

Take it, a crazy part of her brain screamed, *and forget this day happened and that a child might be dead or dying because you didn't act fast enough.*

She nearly tossed it down the toilet before pragmatism replaced panic. Someone might need this someday. Not her, but someone unused to living with perfectly preserved pain. Someone who'd take it willingly. She pressed the pill into the empty Baby Jane pack and stowed it in the back of the drawer.

The Baby Janes weren't kicking in fast enough—she needed a drink.

Tad's brown eyes replaced the white tiles in stuttering bursts. Was he okay? Could she call the hospital and find out? Which hospital would they have taken him to? They wouldn't tell a stranger, regardless. Right now, she wanted to hope, not hear of tragedy. She pulled off her damp dress and put on loose pants and a tank top. In the kitchen she retrieved a bottle of whiskey—mostly full—and a tumbler from the cabinet, then rifled through the junk drawer to retrieve a few more Baby Janes, some pain hypos, and a muscle relaxant. She arranged this parade of numbness in a line on the coffee table and settled herself on the couch for a long, long rest.

"House," she called, "display all walls and ceiling pattern number five."

She was suddenly underwater in a shallow tropical sea. Sunbeams snaked crazily through the glass-clear water, blue going to infinity, sky above her a round aperture.

"Later in the day," she commanded, and the blue darkened, sunbeams dimmed. Good. She fumbled open a painkiller and held it to her throbbing arm. Relief rolled through her like a warm liquid. Finally, her thoughts slowed. Emotions and anxieties slid away. She relaxed and stared up at the underside of the water.

Outside, the real sun set and the room dimmed. The swoosh of rush hour traffic came and went. From time to time, she flopped a heavy arm onto the table and took a drink or pressed another hypo.

Later, stars filled the windows. Her comm beeped.

"Comm off," she mumbled to her apartment. "No calls, no chime, no light, no messages." She stared at nothing, body slack. Time splayed out…

A persistent knocking interrupted the stillness. Was that her door?

"Show front door camera." The sea parted, and a portion of the ceiling lit up with a view of the hall—and Lucas. She activated the door speaker. "Go away."

He looked up at the camera. "Let me in."

She'd worked hard to get away from him and the day. "Fuck off."

She didn't feel the guilt and anger, but they were there, swimming deep down below the heavy weight of the drugs.

"Claire wasn't supposed to leave you."

"Claire didn't have a choice."

"I'm coming in." Clicks and beeps emanated from the front door, Lucas doing a brute force attack on her lock. A few minutes later, the door whooshed open. Why hadn't she set up the force field generator?

He walked slowly into the room, pulled off his glasses, and examined her watery world.

"Turn on the lights," he said.

"Leave."

"Claire told me you didn't take the Levotrum. Is that true?"

"Yes, it's true." She struggled to recall the word that would summon her building's security guards. "Sedona."

"I disabled that before I came in. I'll go once I'm sure you're okay, so turn on the lights and let me see you."

"I was just beginning to trust all of you."

"Turn on the lights."

If it was the only way to get him out of there, she'd comply. "Pattern five, twilight," she told the house, and the sea brightened.

Lucas looked from her to the spent hypos on the table, then back to her, then to the half-empty bottle of whiskey on the floor.

He knelt, took her chin in his hand, and tilted her face toward the light.

He didn't seem to like what he saw. "What did you take?"

She tried to pull away. "Some Baby Janes and a pain pill, and…this." Her fingers brushed the glass.

Lucas arranged the spent hypos and empty metal foils on the table. "You took all these today? Anything else?" He reached under the table and found the empty pack of muscle relaxants. "How many of these did you take? How long ago?"

She had no idea.

He pressed two fingers to her neck, then pulled on his glasses and airtyped quickly, holding up each empty container briefly, probably to scan. A moment later, he swept his arm across the table, knocking the empties to the floor, and set a black suitcase in their place—the same mini-pharmacy the motion sickness medicine came from the night she was stunned.

Locks clicked, and he pressed something cold against her arm. A calm, low tone was followed by a series of high-pitched beeps.

Lucas swore, muttering something about Claire. After consulting the device, he took out five hypos and pressed them one after another to her skin.

The tiny needles threatened to pop the fragile bubble she'd built to protect herself.

"Stop," she said. "I don't want to be sober."

Lucas's eyes were black in the dim light. "You won't be anything if I don't fix this."

The last canister hissed out its contents. He waited a moment, then pressed the cold thing against her arm again and studied the screen like it held the answer to a critical question on a final exam. One reassuring beep issued from the device. Lucas released a breath he'd been holding, then placed the device into its bed in the suitcase and clicked the locks shut.

He picked the bottle of bourbon up, briefly consulted the label, uncorked it, and took a swig. He went to the kitchen and came back with an empty glass for himself and a carton of water for her.

Whatever Lucas did with the hypos didn't bring reality crashing down as she feared but seemed to clear the passageways between her mind and body—and her body was thirsty. Had been for some time, based on the dryness in her mouth. She accepted the carton of water and drank.

Lucas searched the room and found the only other piece of furniture he could sit on—a plush square she sometimes used as a footrest—and dragged it over to the couch.

"The boy is okay."

"Really?" Why had he waited so long to tell her?

"Yes. Thanks to you."

She laughed, relief and disgust mixed with exhaustion. The possibility that the child wasn't had fueled what might have been one of her biggest drug binges to date. "Cheers to us for providing such great security at a birthday party that two people were nearly killed."

Lucas winced. "We weren't—"

"Who opened the window?"

"I don't know, yet. There are no visual records, and I didn't get a chance to speak to any of the nannies before CorSec arrived. I'll pursue it after this all dies down."

"Great. Now please get out of my apartment."

He didn't move. "You want to know why I tried to give you the Levotrum."

A chill fog crept out from beneath the remnants of the Baby Janes. "I assume it was to assuage your guilt for putting me in a situation I should never have been in and almost getting me killed. Again. You blow up part of my brain so you can sleep easy."

"No. That wouldn't have worked. Any guilt I feel for putting you in danger, again, won't vanish if you forget." Lucas poured the remains of the bottle of whiskey into his glass. "I don't often get a good night's sleep, and I don't remember with perfect clarity." He took a long drink. "I didn't want you to have to live with what happened today, not with your memory."

The stars outside flared. "So, you get to trim me like I'm a human topiary? Cut out the parts you think I don't want?" She'd have slapped him if he were closer and she could move. Despite her inaction, he still winced. "It doesn't work like that Lucas. I'm made of memories. You take out the bad ones and everything comes tumbling down. No more Mia."

"When I found you in the shower there was no Mia either. Jason told me—"

"Oh, for god's sake, are you talking about the syndrome? What did Jason tell you? It doesn't work that way. I don't suddenly *get it* because something awful happens. Thank god this bullshit drug didn't exist twenty-five years ago." She clamped her mouth shut.

Whatever hypo cocktail Lucas had given her had her in a strange state. No longer underwater, but floating far from her usual restraint. She needed to stop talking. *Now.*

Lucas stood, glass in hand. "I need ice."

She watched his reflection in the kitchen window. He put on his glasses and began typing the moment he thought he was out of view. *Damn it.* Lucas was a detective, and she'd pointed a big red arrow at a significant event. He'd deleted her precollege data, but what happened twenty-five years ago was in the public record.

Indistinct memories leached through the drug haze. Her parents, belatedly noticing that elementary-school-aged Mia spent too much time alone, made an effort to spend more time with her in the afternoons. Mom interpreted that to mean she'd work at home. Their *together time* consisted of Mia watching Mom construct invisible buildings and give orders to people Mia couldn't see.

Dad, on the other hand, threw himself into playtime with relish, peeling off his dusty coveralls and glasses only long enough to wash his face and get something to drink, then they were out in the wilds, hiking and searching for bugs.

Mia arrived home from fourth grade one Friday—anticipating the promised hike—to find Dad on the floor, retching and delirious, first aid kit scattered around him. *Bug bite*, she'd thought. She was only ten at the time, but she'd been well trained. Beta version anti-venom kits had just been distributed to the population, and she kept hers at the ready. Anyone sneezing too hard in her general vicinity was in danger of being stabbed with a hypo.

She'd taken the kit from her school bag and pressed the machine onto his arm, confident that the green light would flash, the antidote would be delivered, and Dad would be up and hugging her a moment later. Maybe she'd even get ice cream as a reward for helping him.

The small screen displayed the ## symbol of no match.

She'd stared, puzzled. That hadn't happened in the promotional holo they'd watched.

Dad constricted into a tight ball and had grabbed her arm so hard it hurt.

"Take care of your mom," he'd said.

A moment later, he'd relaxed. His hand slid to the floor, and he'd looked skyward with the questioning look he often wore. She saw the question leave him, unanswered, and he'd drifted away, looking so blank it had scared her.

Someone in the building would have a better anti-venom kit. She'd run from door to door, pounding and yelling, but everyone had been at work. Would the MMARVs come up to their apartment? She'd never seen one at their level.

The first generation MMARVs were bigger and though Mia had managed to call one, it bumped helplessly against the too-small exterior entrance to the apartment. Mia hadn't been strong enough to drag Dad closer to the door.

When the human paramedics had arrived, it was too late. It had been too late for quite some time, but they'd gone through the motions of trying to resuscitate him. Mia had huddled in the corner of the room, holding a pillow from the couch in front of her as protection against Dad's blank stare and Mom's hysteria. She'd rushed in just after the paramedics. They'd had to sedate her before they could take the body away—she wouldn't let go.

They weren't sure which bug killed him. Mia supposed that now she could ask for a reanalysis of his blood and the culprit would be named, but it didn't matter. It wasn't the bugs' fault. Humans had invaded their territory. Many people died in the early days, before the rings of relative safety had been carved into the desert and defended.

She wiped her eyes and discovered Lucas standing in front of her with the expensive bourbon she'd stashed in a cupboard above the fridge.

"You probably shouldn't have this." He picked her glass off the floor and filled it halfway, dropping in a cube of ice.

She'd splurged on a clear ice machine. The cube was nearly invisible.

"May I?" Lucas gestured to the end of the couch furthest from her.

She nodded.

"You're right. You and Claire shouldn't have been there today." He spoke to the flickering sunlit water on the wall, not to her. "I told her she'd never have to leave the office, and neither of you have physical security training. I also made a bad call about the Levotrum. I don't understand what it's like to live in your head, but I do know that something triggered you today, and that leaving you with those memories means it could happen again… And next time, someone from the team might not be around to run interference."

Mia opened her mouth to argue then stopped. He'd been in the bathroom, trying to rouse her. Claire said she'd been like that once before, in college. Mia had zero memory of either incident. That scared her. Had these unresponsive states happened other times, when she was home alone, daydreaming? If it happened in public, and she were taken to a hospital, might a doctor discover her secret?

Lucas drained his glass and leaned back, massaging his temples with one hand. His jaw clenched and relaxed. Flickers of anger and annoyance crossed his face, echoes of an unpleasant inner dialogue. He let out a long sigh and…deflated. No other word for it. He was no longer the boss. Just a man. Rumpled. Imperfect. Exhausted.

She asked the house to turn the seascape to night again. Lucas didn't complain. They sat in silence in the flickering light.

The stars shifted and the level of bourbon in the bottle sank. Her anger at Lucas faded. Whether he'd tried to drug her to save her from psychic damage, or lessen his own feelings of guilt and responsibility, probably not even he could say with certainty. And to be fair to Jason, there were zero documented people with her level of ability who were able to function in the real world—and she didn't know if the syndrome could be triggered. What had she been remembering when she was in the shower? As far as she knew, she'd just been watching the steam. Had she gotten caught in a loop? Might she have stayed in that steamy shower forever to avoid thinking that it was Tad lying under the blue sheet in the white pod?

"I'm tired," she said.

Lucas rose, weaving slightly. The light from the ocean played across his face, dim and pale blue. "Let's get you into bed."

"I don't need help." But she did. She was exhausted and her head swam when she stood.

Lucas steadied her. They shuffled into the bedroom. She hadn't realized she was cold but Lucas, pressed against her side, felt like late afternoon sunlight. He pulled back the covers and settled her in so efficiently she wondered if he'd been a nurse at some point in his life.

"Where's the Levotrum?"

Thinking fast was not an option, but she knew what she would have done if she hadn't stashed it.

"Sanitized. In the washing machine. I didn't want to flush it. The toilet would have alerted someone."

"It would have indeed." He swept clothes off the bench at the foot of the bed and sat heavily.

"You can go. I'll be okay."

"I'll keep an eye on you for a while. You've had more than the usual amounts of drugs in your system today."

Was he teasing? She shut her eyes, too tired to retort.

"Was that you, that day at the office?" Lucas asked a few minutes later.

The non sequitur pulled her out of a doze. "What are you talking about?"

"When I was…ill in my office at Summit. When I needed the painkiller."

She fumbled through the deck of playing cards that featured images of Lucas. The sedative wasn't as crippling as a Baby Jane but did slow her recall.

"The day you collapsed at your desk? I didn't think you remembered."

"Mikey told me he brought me back to my room."

"He did, after I called him."

"I remember you crying."

"I gave you the amount of Sionall you asked for, and you stopped breathing. I was pretty sure I'd killed you."

Lucas chuckled. "I guess we're both experts at self-medicating. I was monitoring my body weight and the dosage. It was fine."

"It wasn't. You were losing weight faster than you realized. You could have died."

The mattress shifted, and she opened her eyes. Lucas sat beside her, silhouetted against the faint blue light emanating from the bathroom appliances. His laughter vanished.

"You're right. I wasn't myself then, and I have no idea what I weighed that day. I shouldn't have asked you to inject me. I put you and the business at risk."

He straightened and the mattress squeaked.

"I was addicted to Plex. I stopped taking it right before we caught the ship over here." He looked away. Maybe out the bedroom window, maybe back to a windowless cabin en route to Victoria.

"I thought it was impossible to quit Plex. Physically, I mean. Once you start, you have to take it forever," Mia said.

"More or less true. There's only one treatment, and it has a rather high mortality rate. Part of the Plex is stored in fat cells. To get clean, you have to get rid of the fat. You can only get rid of so much fat without killing yourself, but if you get down to under ten percent, there's a treatment. Toxic, but as long as your body fat is that low, not lethal."

So that was it. Mia had wondered for so long what had been wrong with Lucas, but after today, there was no thrill of a mystery solved.

"I'm glad you don't have a brain tumor. I figured it was that, Plex, or organ transplant failure."

Lucas barked a short laugh. "Why would I have exercised so much if I had a brain tumor?"

Exhaustion pressed her eyes shut. "I dunno, Lucas. Raging against the dying of the light? That seems like you."

His voice came from very nearby. "It does, doesn't it?"

Exhaustion rolled over her like a tidal wave, and she drowned in it, grateful for the oblivion.

Chapter Twenty Two

Mia didn't so much wake as crawl out from under an eight-hour nightmare. While her body lay passive, her mind wrestled with misshapen memories. None of the children's party, but good memories twisted into worst-case scenarios. A spring hike with Dad, but he'd fallen into a crevasse and lay at the bottom of the crack, leg broken, screaming in agony. Show and tell day at school, but the beetle she'd brought in escaped the cage and bit all her classmates, causing their faces to swell and ooze pus from every orifice. College graduation, and the ground began to shake violently as she tried to make her way up the long aisle to get her diploma.

I need a Baby Jane, she thought, shielding her eyes from the late morning light. And a moment later, *Lucas.* Was he still there?

She opened the bedroom door tentatively. The living room was clean. No bottles, no spent hypos, no sticky rings on the coffee table, and thankfully, no Lucas.

The drug drawer in the bathroom held everything it had yesterday—except the promise of relief. The candy-colored wrappers might as well have contained actual candy. Had Baby Jane packaging always been so garish? Mia rotated the silver foil, watching the unicorn's horn shift from left to right.

What was wrong? Why didn't she take one and make the bad dreams go away?

It might be possible a Baby Jane couldn't fix things this time. She set the pill on the bathroom counter and wandered into the living room. Tad didn't die, but he may have if that other dart had hit him—and the official response would have been the same.

Nothing.

She lay down on the couch and began to rethink all the so-called aberrations she'd witnessed, catalogued, and willfully ignored since she came back from college and started working at Han. New Canberra hung outside the windows, the shiny buildings and bright blue-green sky nothing more than a thin façade she could poke through with one finger.

This city is rotten.

A few hours later, the comm buzzed, and Lucas's face appeared in a small square on the living room wall.

"Sorry to bother you," he said.

"You shouldn't be able to do that."

"Do what?"

"Connect to the wall without my permission."

He was unshaven with dark circles under his eyes. "Andaman needs a statement from you. I can't put them off any longer."

"A statement? You mean a lie."

"Take a Baby Jane, now. I don't want you tangled up in this. You didn't see any darts. You felt a sting and realized you and Tad had both been bitten by something. Everything after that happened as it did."

"I don't—"

"You can do it remotely, or Andaman security will come to your apartment. With a veracity detector."

That got her attention. She levered herself upright. "We can do it on the wall?"

"Yes," Lucas said. "I've scheduled the call for noon. Promise me you won't say anything. Andaman will never admit a murder nearly occurred in their sector, and I'm not sure what they'd do to someone who insists that one did."

Mia looked from him to the ocean rippling on her ceiling and considered her options. She'd never been a traditionally ethical person, not with having to hide how much she knew about just about everything.

Plus, she'd never know what Andaman would do with any information she gave them, truthful or not.

"I won't say anything if we investigate this. I need to know if the man that cut off Dr. Lerner's daughter's braid is the same man that assaulted me, and if he's the one that fired the darts."

Lucas nodded, a deep frown making him look even more exhausted. "I'm already on it, but I'm running into the same problems as when I tried to find out who dragged you off the sidewalk. Each sector functions as a separate country, and security is tight. We're good, but there are only five of us with limited resources."

"We'll try?"

"We will."

"Move the meeting to right now. I'm ready. I don't need a Baby Jane. I'm sure I look harmless." Her hair unwashed, tear tracks through yesterday's makeup, eyes red from a troubled sleep—harmless or just plain pathetic. She was no threat to the flimsy fiction Andaman and Optima were constructing.

"Let me see if they're available." Lucas airtyped, and a minute later announced, "Yes. They can do it. I'll stay here, right beside the window they'll open. Don't look at me but pay attention to my cues. We need to get through this and divert attention from Summit Security. If they decide we were at fault, we could lose the business."

Mia pulled the throw blanket from the back of the couch and wrapped it tightly around herself until she was more pupa than human.

A gleaming white dot appeared on the wall next to Lucas.

"Susan Hodge, Senior Vice President, Andaman, calling. Do you accept?" the apartment asked politely.

Senior Vice President? A mid-level security grunt should be the one calling her—if they believed it was really an accident. They knew it wasn't. *Good.* "Yes."

A mature woman appeared on the wall, around Erika's age, but with fewer mods.

"Mia Julian? Sorry to bother you. I'm interviewing everyone who was at the Lerner party."

Her eyes flitted left and right, reading from large, clear glasses. "You were in the front room when the incident occurred?"

Lucas's head, in a square adjacent to hers, nodded.

"Yes," Mia said.

"What were you doing?"

"Just keeping an eye on things."

"Loss prevention?" she asked.

"I can't discuss client contracts."

Hodge waved a hand breezily. "Dr. Lerner told us why you were hired. Several valuable books went missing the last time he had a dinner party."

The woman's expression shifted to false concern. "You were near Tad Lee when you were both stung by an *Antipoda Lentropa*."

"We don't have those in the city," Mia said.

Lucas shook his head violently.

Anderson lifted her finger from invisible text she'd been tracing. "Excuse me?"

Antipoda Lentropa were not only nocturnal, they could also only be found in the southern hemisphere.

Mia took a deep breath. *I'm an ignorant client liaison. I'm a victim. I'm not a threat...*

"We don't have bugs in the city. The MMARVs get rid of them."

Lucas and Hodge both relaxed.

"We try," Hodge said sincerely, "but we'll never hit one hundred percent eradication. We are so sorry the MMARVs failed, and you were stung. We've transferred twenty thousand credits to your personal account for pain and suffering and lost wages. I'm sending a copy of the agreement you palmed when you left the party."

Lines of text filled the walls.

"Paragraph seven, line twelve. You are not to speak of this incident to anyone, not even your coworkers, or you'll be fined. Heavily."

Lucas held up a warning hand. He'd seen something in her expression that Hodge hadn't yet noticed. Mia took another deep breath.

"That won't be a problem. I don't want to talk about it."

"Good," Hodge replied. "Feel free to call me if you have any questions. You have my contact info." Her square faded.

"Thank you," Lucas said. "You did well. How are you feeling?"

"Tired," she said.

"Rest. I'll come by later."

"No," she said without hesitation. "Don't. I need some time to myself."

Lucas frowned as if she'd said she was going to walk to the Western Sea at noon.

"I'll call later. Please answer."

"I will."

Mia relocated to the balcony, glasses still off, and contemplated a city where illegal drugs got past scanners, people were mugged, shot, spied upon, blackmailed, framed—and criminals ran free because they were contractually forbidden from existing.

It was easier to stomach it when it was an anomaly unique to Han and its mining division, but the kids' party was in Andaman sector, and their CorSec seemed just as willing to sweep in and sweep the event under the rug. New Canberra was starting to look a lot like New Beijing, only worse because the Six had no interest in exposing weakness to each other, nor were they required to. She didn't have to go out of her way to ignore the gruesome and sensationalistic local news as she had in college, because there was no local news. No bands of intrepid reporters staked out the homes of corrupt executives or searched through dumpsters behind restaurants to find a severed finger. There were no exposés, just press releases, and justice was at best payout and an NDA—both of which she'd just accepted.

Summit might not be perfect, but everything got a whole lot worse in a world where the firm didn't exist. Those darts flew in at less than a meter off the ground—kid height. Now that she was sober and could replay the scene, when she'd crouched down to help Tad, she'd unintentionally shielded Stella, who'd been a few meters to her left and directly in the path of the dart. Stella had been the target.

Another attempt to coerce Lerner into signing the ten-year contract.

If Mikey hadn't been there to close the window, the next dart might have found its mark. If they hadn't disabled the presents, who knows what might have been brought into the house. That zebra might have galloped up to Stella and injected a lethal dose of the venom a few days from now if Lerner still refused to sign.

Summit wasn't performing flawlessly, but it was the only entity with mandate and the ability to give residents what was guaranteed in their contracts. Yes, any of the Six could revoke the charter in their sector, but that risked sending a message of weakness to their competitors. Who was afraid of a small, five-person firm that shows up at restaurants with a conversation shield or installs nanny cams? No one with an invincible army of CorSec.

Victoria wasn't the opposite of Earth in the way she wished it was, but it was still light-years better, and Summit could help make sure it didn't get worse.

She called Jason. "I'm hungry, and not very presentable."

He arrived in less than an hour. "It's me. I've got fried fish."

She'd used the time to shower. The warm water revived her—though when she ran a palm across the steamed mirror, the woman she saw was a Halloween version of herself. Dark-circled eyes, pale face, prominent cheekbones. Nothing a makeup kit couldn't fix, but she didn't want to look pretty today. The city didn't deserve it. A bruise surrounded the small scab on her shoulder where the dart had hit. *That will scar.* Her whole upper arm ached.

She pulled her wet hair into a ponytail and threw on a long-sleeved tunic and high, bugproof boots. Not a fashion statement, but they made her feel safe.

"Come in."

Jason held the bag in front of him like a shield and avoided her eyes, reverting to the jangling, ill-at-ease man she'd met so many months ago.

He unpacked and arranged the meal on the coffee table, then sat cross-legged on the floor, empty plate on his lap.

He'd remembered her favorite comfort food—butterfish rings, garlic fries, and passion fruit iced tea.

"Go ahead and start," she said, sitting across from him on the couch.

She reached for a greasy fish ring, mustering up some anticipation. If they'd been at a restaurant, it might have burned her fingers. This one was lukewarm. She bit, chewed, swallowed. The spices were off. Bland. Still, she ate. Her body needed the calories.

After enduring minutes of silence, Jason spoke. "I told Lucas about the syndrome. That's why he tried to give you the Levotrum. It's my fault. Not completely, though. I didn't know he had that pill. I just told him what I thought might be happening."

Mia dunked a fish ring in curry sauce. "I don't trust any of you anymore. It's strange that I ever did. What will you amateur psychologists do to me in the future to protect me from my own mind?"

"You know how long you were zoned out in the shower? Half an hour. Andaman was going through the whole house. The medic kept them out of the bathroom, but he couldn't keep them away forever. If they'd found you like that, they'd have taken you to the hospital, and who knows what tests they might have run and what questions they'd have asked with you hooked to a veracity detector. Lucas sent Mikey back to the office for the pill. He hoped it might jog you out of whatever hole you'd fallen into. When you finally woke up, we didn't know if you'd stay awake. All the bad things that caused you to shut down were still in your head. That's when Lucas gave you the pill. Don't blame us for not being PhDs in brain science, Mia. We were scared. If it happened once, it could happen again. Andaman would have taken you away."

Jason, no longer avoiding her eyes, drove the last point home with a crispy fry. A chunk of garlic fell to the table. He wiped it up with a finger and stuck it into his mouth. The tension broke.

"Lucas didn't tell me Andaman was searching the house," Mia said. If they'd found her, it would have been very bad. Jason was right. Some bright soul in ER who'd watched too many documentaries might have realized what a catatonic body and hyperactive brain meant.

The food in her belly formed a heavy lump.

Jason seemed to see the realization in her eyes, the shift in her mood.

"You should come in to the office. We need your help."

"With what?"

Jason crumpled the paper plates and greasy waxed paper and took them to the kitchen recycler.

"Things we can't talk about here."

"You said this apartment is secure."

"Not as secure as the office."

"Is it about the party?" she asked.

"It is."

She did want to help, but leaving the apartment felt risky. She had to, though. She knew what would happen if she didn't. A week at home to recuperate would turn into a month, and she'd give up on this place instead of trying to save it. She'd distrust everyone and find a better world in virtual reality—where she had control.

She would become her mother.

"Let's go."

"I thought you'd take more convincing," Jason said.

"Better now than never."

She shadowed Jason down the hall and out into the too-bright day. He made room when she sat next to him instead of across as she normally did, and didn't complain when she ordered the pod windows to black.

"You okay?" he asked.

"Not yet." Her conception of Victoria rocked like a wooden shed in a storm now that the foundation had been removed. "I'm not in love with this planet right now."

"It's still better than Earth."

"Better isn't good enough."

Jason didn't take the bait.

The pod stopped in front of the office, but Mia didn't get out. The path leading to the building looked longer, and the ground to the left and right wilder. It wasn't that her memory was faulty—before today, she'd focused on different aspects of the scene.

Jason slid out. "Come on. It's hot."

Right. She had to do it. The outside world wouldn't get less scary hours or days from now.

The outer door opened before Jason could palm it. Lucas stood in the hall.

"You're here."

"I am," Mia said. "Jason said you needed my help."

"Let's talk in here." He gestured to the open door of his apartment. Jason passed and hurried into the main room.

"How are you?" Lucas asked after they'd taken seats at the small dining room table. The apartment hadn't changed much in the months since Mikey had dropped Lucas on the bed after his near overdose. A few more boxes, printed maps on the wall detailing each of the Six sectors, and others showing the corporate territories, planetwide. The new clothes he'd gotten since he'd arrived hung neatly on a rack beside the black cabinet.

"Tired," Mia answered. "Of many things, but I understand why you did what you did even if I disagree. I don't think giving me a memory-erasing pill would have prevented me from zoning out in the future. That was a very peculiar situation, and one I hope will never be repeated…but it's not a memory I regret holding. Whatever happened yesterday was shock and fear, not a memory fugue."

Lucas, to his credit, didn't comment.

"Jason said you needed my help. With what?"

"I have the dart. The one that lodged in the wall didn't disintegrate."

Mia laughed, startling herself and Lucas. "Sorry. I was the only one who saw them, and there were no cameras and no proof. I didn't know if you believed me."

"Of course, I believed you. I had Mikey search the room and seal the dart in an airtight container."

"Can I see it?"

She wasn't sure why she wanted to, other than a strange need to validate what had happened after having been forced to lie about it.

Lucas produced a transparent plexiglass cube, five centimeters on a side, the dart frozen in mid-flight in the center.

She took it and cranked up the magnification on her glasses. The needle portion was thicker than she remembered from the brief glimpse before it dissolved, and dirty brown, like brackish water. The red feathers weren't feathers at all but beautifully printed whorls that grew in artificial perfection from the blunt end of the needle.

She shook the cube. The dart didn't move.

"It's a vacuum stasis chamber," Lucas said. "I didn't want to risk this one dissolving like the others. I'm not sure what triggers it. What I need," he said, extracting the cube from her fingers, "is a lab that can analyze this, discreetly. Have you heard of a place like that on Victoria?"

"Nothing we can use. Anything I've seen is tied up with Han partners. I've got another idea, though. Can that get past scanners?"

Lucas nodded. "It seems designed to do so. The medic gave me an overview of the toxins he found in your blood. All were little more than trace amounts."

"I know a research scientist on Earth. Derek Singh. He lived next door to us when I was a kid. He had a two-year grant from the University of Texas to study the effects of the venoms of Victoria's insects on cancerous tumors. That research didn't pan out, so he moved to the university's commercial applications department as a biomedical engineer. He's done well developing therapeutic drugs, some based on our insect venoms."

Lucas pulled on his glasses, air typing and scrolling through data.

"He's done more than well. He won the Apex prize two years ago."

Mia smiled. "He did. I watched his acceptance speech. He looked so uncomfortable in that tux."

"He'd help us? This…" He picked up the cube. "Is a new development in weapons technology. I've got contacts on Earth, but none I'd trust to deal with something so volatile, literally and figuratively. Dr. Singh would be ideal. Not part of law enforcement or working for a corporation… If you trust him."

"I trust him completely. He's the most ethical man I know."

They'd spoken less often the past few years, both of them busy. Derek's career path, after he gave up cancer research, had been straight as a sector road and just as smooth. He'd gone from research scientist, to department head, to Director of Commercial Development and holder of twenty-seven patents. He was married and had two kids who weren't kids anymore.

"You won't mind if I do a background check?"

"I would mind. Read all you want about him on public sites. Don't invade his privacy."

Lucas continued his perusal of invisible pages. "Public data will suffice, if you vouch for him."

"I do. I want to know what this fucking thing is and who made it and how we get the scanners to recognize it." She stared at the dart and its unnatural trajectory to nowhere.

"All this is hitting a little too close to home. Jason, Claire, and I are here because we were investigating an illegal R&D lab at Itek that was developing biological weapons," Lucas said.

It took Mia a moment to map what Jason said months ago—about pissing off executives at Itek and having to get as far away as possible—onto this new intel. And to process that Lucas was finally telling her a truth he'd been reluctant to share.

"You were investigating a lab, and then what?"

"Then everything blew up. Literally and figuratively," he repeated. "Jason, Claire, and I are key witnesses in an upcoming trial—City of New York vs. Itek. I can't give details, but suffice it to say, we're safer here than we'd be anywhere in North America."

"You're testifying against Itek?" Partners didn't do that.

He nodded, tight-lipped and grim. "I've overlooked many things during my career, but what was happening in that lab was not going to be one of them. When I worked for the NYCPD, I watched corporations eat away at the foundations of the city and couldn't stop it. I hoped I'd do better from the inside. I'm not sure I succeeded."

A document she'd seen on Lucas's screen months ago came to mind, and she recited it from memory. "To: Lucas Dunn. From: Sergeant M. Johnson. Trial date still not set."

Lucas sat up like he'd gotten a shock from the cheap folding chair. "What?"

"I told you I saw that message on your screen the day you showed me my test scores. I didn't know what it meant."

He slumped back, and the chair creaked. "I thought you were about to tell me it was on the Victoria Tribune. There's a media embargo, but it can only hold so long."

"You're in some sort of witness protection program? Why would any of the Six help the city of New York?"

"Not a witness protection program. There's no way to keep our location and identities a secret. I believe Weber agreed to host us because Itek stole a prototype solar cell from them last year. They couldn't prove it, but Itek released a nearly identical product a few months later and beat Weber to market. Given that I exposed an illegal lab at Itek and implicated partners, Weber might feel I'm an ally of sorts, or may be harboring us merely to irritate Itek."

"You never wanted to start a business here?"

"Starting a business was a necessity. Itek's lawyers managed to get all our personal assets frozen as evidence and it could be years before anything happens. New York is broke. They want us to testify but can't support us. I very much need this business to succeed."

The puzzle pieces of Lucas rearranged themselves. Again. He wasn't a drug addict quietly fired from his job. He was a drug addict who'd sacrificed his career to expose wrongdoing. He probably hadn't intended to quit Plex. He'd have been forced to when he left Earth.

"We need you," he said. "We need this business. As I said, our assets are frozen. Our apartments were sealed as evidence. We came here with nothing but the clothes on our backs and a few hundred credits from the NYCPD. If you check out, the business fails."

"I'm not checked out," Mia snapped. "I had a very bad night after being poisoned by a dart that was intended for our client's daughter. I can recreate the room for you in SusSketch if you'd like. There's no cam data, but Stella would have been hit if I hadn't crouched down."

"Are you—" Lucas cut off, seeming to reconsider his phrasing. "If you could recreate the room to the best of your ability, it might help us identify the nanny who opened the window."

"I'd be happy to, tomorrow. I'm a little off my game today."

The proof the darts existed, the idea of having Derek help, and Lucas finally opening up about why the team ended up here—all this solidity counterbalanced the shadows of New Canberra.

Mia pushed the facts up against the uncertainties and built a bulwark behind which she could…nap.

She really needed one if she were going to save the world.

Chapter Twenty Three

The *buzz-buzz* tone of an interstellar call wasn't something Mia heard often. Claire had been the only person she kept in touch with on Earth. Lucas had found someone to transport the dart and needed her to find out if Derek would be willing to analyze it.

Mia, abashed, realized it had been over a year since she and Derek had spoken. Neither of their faults—they'd been busy—but the debt she owed him meant the burden was on her to keep in touch.

"He might not answer if he's teaching a class." She sat uncomfortably in Lucas's comfortable office chair.

"I don't expect we'll get him on the first try. You want privacy?"

"Yes. I'd like to catch up before I ask for help."

Lucas nodded and closed the door as he left.

The *buzz-buzz* sounded too many times. Just when she was ready to give up, a jittery view of a street on Earth appeared—no mistaking those trees and that sky. A moment later, the scene swiveled, and she saw Derek, sweaty and smiling. She'd caught him bicycling.

"Mia! What a nice surprise! I was just talking about you."

Just like that, her anxiety vanished. Derek. A true friend and someone who knew her inside and out. It didn't matter if they didn't speak for months.

"Is this a bad time?"

He dragged the back of his hand across his forehead. "It's fine. I've got office hours, but no one ever shows up this early. Let me get out of the sun." He walked a few steps to dappled shade and leaned the bike against an unpainted wooden fence. He set the camera, which must have been on his helmet, into the bike basket.

He hadn't much changed in the last year. His smile carved deeper lines around his mouth, but his hair was still deep black and his eyes still kind and curious.

"You bike to work?" she asked, though it was obvious.

"It's the only exercise I get, other than wagging my tongue and twiddling knobs." He imitated both.

"How are Jeremy and Maya?" His daughter, born a few years after he'd left Victoria, bore a name suspiciously close to hers, but she'd never remarked on it.

"Jeremy is still working on his thesis. I'm afraid he's never going to leave school. Taking after me, I guess. Maya is in a wearable arts program in New York. She loves it."

Mia didn't ask about Della, his wife. She was a driven woman—much like Mia's mom used to be—and hadn't appreciated Derek spending time and money keeping tabs on Mia in the years after Dad died.

"And you," Derek asked. "How is Han treating you?"

"Not very well, I'm afraid. I don't work there anymore."

"Your contract ended?"

"Abruptly. My boss and I had a falling out. I'm working for a small security firm now."

Derek pressed his palms together. "Finally. I'm so glad you're out of there. I didn't want to speak badly of your employer, but I didn't have a good experience at Han, and I wished you'd had other options."

"You had a bad time at Han? You never told me that."

He shrugged. "What would have been the point? Han paid for your schooling, and you were obliged to work there for…how long?"

"Ten years." Mia's memories bubbled to the surface, and she viewed Derek from the low vantage point of her nine-year-old self. He hadn't appeared stressed or unhappy, but he was the only scientist she'd ever known, and his creased brow of concentration could have hidden any emotion.

"What happened at Han?" she asked. "You can speak freely. This is an encrypted connection."

He glanced left and right, as if a drone from Victoria might be patrolling the quiet Austin street, then leaned into the helmet cam. "First thing. They gave me the grant because I was better looking than a more qualified applicant. I'm not kidding. My quote, unquote *lab assistant* on Victoria, who happened to be a partner's son, didn't want to look at a brilliant man with a bad complexion for two years."

"That can't be true."

Derek grinned. "You see many short, pigeon-toed guys with crooked teeth and acne scars on the streets there?"

He had a point. "The partner's son told you that?" she asked.

"He did. I was up against a guy from my own lab at UT. He deserved the grant."

Derek had always been modest about his abilities, even as his awards piled up, so Mia took that with a grain of salt. "You said first thing. What was the second thing?"

"Are you sure you want to know? You've always been very…enthusiastic about Han."

"It was my career I was enthusiastic about, and that's over. I'd like to know what happened."

"Alright, though, I'm not blameless in this scenario. I was working on a side project, nothing to do with cancer research, on my own time. My first foray into therapeutic drugs and the beginning of my new focus, though I didn't know it at the time." He waggled his head back and forth. "Probably against the terms of my grant, if you were a stickler for the rules. The partner's son found out what I was up to and tried to blackmail me. He wanted me to make designer drugs that could get past HQ scanners. Otherwise, he'd tell my university what I'd been up to."

Mia sat up. "After you left, Dad had me do drawings of screens of yours I'd seen. I thought he was just giving me busywork to make me feel like I was still your lab assistant, but you knew—about me. I was smuggling your research data back to Earth."

"Of course I knew, and yes, you did. Belated thanks for my first pat-ent." He grinned and gave a thumbs-up.

That he'd known about her memory was an elephant in the room they'd both trod carefully around. The lines between Earth and Victoria they'd used to communicate weren't secure. She smiled as well, relieved to have one less secret to carry. She'd not thought about the screens of data she'd transcribed in a childish scrawl but viewed afresh…

Holy shit.

"That's the formula for Baby Janes. That was your side project? Why?"

A moment later she knew. The Registry of Extraordinary Abilities test she'd taken at age ten—the serious one where Han decided if you were eligible to be corporate property. Her father had given her a pill to help her relax, and she had relaxed. Her memories floated an arms-distance away, and she'd done well on the test but not perfectly. Derek's side project had been to save her. The commercial version of that drug, which the partner's son had clearly stolen and claimed as his own invention and released as Baby Janes…she needed to sit down. She was sitting down.

"Are you okay?" Derek asked.

Mia nodded. "Just shocked I never put two and two together. You should have told me all this sooner."

"Not while you were at Han. Not with those damned veracity detec-tors."

Mia ached to ask more questions, but she noticed the steadily rising number at the bottom of the screen—linked to a lock icon and credits symbol. *Shit.*

"Hey, sorry…I want to know more about what happened, but this connection is costing too many credits. I called to ask a favor. We need a toxin analyzed, confidentially. We're pretty sure it's made from a combi-nation of insect venoms. Bad things are beginning to happen here. Really bad. What I want to send you might be a prototype weapon that can make it past scanners and kill—disguised as a native bug."

She'd hoped for more of a reaction from Derek, but he was used to the horrors of Earth.

"I worried about that. We can stop weaponization of Victoria's venoms here because our scanners are set to zero tolerance, but there, you've got to leave a little wiggle room. The bugs are everywhere. It was only a matter of time before someone figured out how to game the system. Of course, I'll help. I can work with the lab offline. It's one of the privileges I've earned with my patents. How will you get it to me?"

"I don't know the details. My boss Lucas will be in touch." Part of the burden she'd been carrying shifted and flew through the secure connection to Earth. Derek would figure this out.

"Sounds good. I'd better get going." He waved goodbye before strapping on his helmet. "Call me this weekend on a cheaper line. I want to hear more about what you've been up to, okay?"

Mia agreed then cut the connection.

She leaned back and shut her eyes. It wasn't unusual for the very rich to have a designer drug customized for their particular chemistry, but she wasn't rich, and had counted herself lucky to have found something off-the-shelf that worked so perfectly to calm her overactive mind. Too perfectly, she'd often worried. The drug wasn't addicting but she'd leaned on it heavily throughout the years. Derek should have…she opened her eyes and took a deep breath. He wouldn't know anything about her habits and certainly wasn't responsible for them.

Focus on the positive.

Derek and her father had worked closely together to help her when she was a child, though she'd never seen them exchange more than a friendly hello. She was eager to hear the stories of how they'd collaborated.

A knock startled her. Lucas poked his head in. "You off the call?"

Shit. She'd lost time. It was twenty minutes later than it should have been.

"Yes." She jumped up from his chair.

"What did Derek say?"

"He'll do it."

"Excellent." Lucas strode around the desk and got to work on the desk screen. "I'll get in touch with him when the courier arrives. You need to inform all our current Han clients that we won't be renewing their contracts. I'm done with Han and whatever bullshit is happening in the mining division."

This would have been great news a few weeks ago, but it was still good news now.

"You put the credits Andaman gave you into the Summit account," Lucas said.

"I won't take money for perpetuating their lie."

"I will. We're going to have a big drop in income a month from now if we don't ramp up our advertising. Use those credits to get a campaign going. Target all sectors but Han."

"We won't do events in private homes anymore?"

"Absolutely not. I'll send you a revised list of services. I'd like you to work from the office for the next month or so and concentrate on rebuilding our business with a new client base. I'll take Jason or Mikey to any jobs we have scheduled."

"Sounds good." She'd seen flashes of red out of the corner of her eye as she traveled to and from work this week, and they'd left her with a pounding heart and sweaty palms. Yes, the red was there, but it was never a dart. Still, she'd limited her trips out of the apartment and felt best when she was on the couch, windows darkened.

Mia closed Lucas's door behind her and nodded to Claire, who'd just arrived. They hadn't spoken since the fateful pod ride from the kid's party, and Mia was getting tired of the strained silence. She stood in front of Claire's desk, folded her arms, and waited.

Claire's cheeks bloomed with the thumbprint of pink that signaled trouble. "Stop looking at me like that. I didn't want them to drug you. I told them not to, but you were lying in a shower and the security people kept knocking on the door, and you wouldn't wake up." She began gnawing at her thumbnail.

"I know it wasn't your idea. Lucas explained what happened. He nearly apologized."

"*I'm* not apologizing," Claire said. "It wasn't my fault. I didn't want to go to that kid's party. Lucas promised I'd never have to leave the office."

He had, yet, he'd convinced her to help. Claire was loyal. How he'd earned that Mia might never know, but having lived with Claire for five years, she knew it wouldn't have been easy.

"I'm tired of you being mad at me," Claire said, her cheeks the brightest spot in the dark room. "You've been mad ever since you started here. I didn't want to use the veracity detector on you. None of this is my choice."

Mia tried to reframe everything she'd recently learned from Lucas about the trial—assets frozen, locked out of apartments—from Claire's point of view.

Though Claire had clearly learned to manage many of the phobias she'd had in college, what she'd gone through in the past six months was enough to stress anyone, let alone someone with social anxiety, fear of travel, and need for order and a safe place to hole up at night.

"I was mad, but I'm not anymore. Let's be clear. You and I aren't trusting people. It's always been that way. Yeah, I didn't tell you about my memory, but you didn't tell me about anything. Not your family, or the names of your unofficial boyfriends, or what the hell was going on that summer in senior year when you came home after midnight every night with stacks of gift cards. I know nothing about you, except..."

Mia stopped when she tripped over the reality of what she knew about Claire. The only thing she knew about Claire…was everything. She knew whether Claire was in a good or bad mood based on the way she typed. Quick, rabbit-hop bursts when she was happy, and prolonged, relentless, pounding attacks when she was angry. She knew Claire's favorite foods—pork shui mai for breakfast at noon, sugar-encrusted cereal for dinner, both consumed with disgustingly sweet strawberry stim sodas that made her either argumentative or productive depending on a complex alignment of factors. She knew that when Claire sat slumped on the stained brown couch in the living room with tools and an eviscerated piece of tech splayed on the coffee table in front of her, that she'd had a bad day and wanted to talk.

She might know more about Claire than she knew about anyone but her mom.

"Truce," Mia said. "Let's start fresh. I don't blame you for whatever you had to do to get the business up and running. Lucas wouldn't have interviewed me if you hadn't given him data to prove I wasn't guilty of… chicken farming." She didn't want to smile, but did, and the red on Claire's cheeks fell from sirens at a crime scene to hot-shower pink.

"You didn't smuggle an illegal, memory-wiping drug onto Victoria. You're working hard to fix my records and…" Mia struggled to find something true in the mélange of emotions she felt toward Claire. "I respect you."

That seemed a good place to stop.

Claire's brow furrowed and her right hand paused midgesture, fingers splayed and half-raised as if she were waving a casual goodbye.

"I've gotten most of your records fixed," Claire said. "You might be able to get a job somewhere else now."

"Do you want me to?"

The vehement headshake surprised Mia.

"No. Someone has to do what you're doing, and I'll never get Lucas to hire anyone else."

That was true enough, yet not her problem. She could quit and get a safer job, and she might have yesterday.

"I'll stick it out a bit longer. An old friend of mine is going to analyze the dart Lucas smuggled out of the party. He'll find a clue as to who's behind this, I know it."

Mia jumped when Lucas sat two shot glasses down on her desk one Thursday evening and held up a bottle of scotch.

"To new clients."

Mia's somewhat lascivious ads, all titled, "Do you know…?" were being projected onto the sidewalks of the e-districts on Friday and Saturday nights, and asked residents in every sector but Han's if they knew what their partner/boyfriend/girlfriend/housekeeper/fill in the blank did in the apartment while they were away. Thanks to Summit, she could cite all the ways personal home security could be derailed and did so. They had dozens of new clients and uses for all the holo cams Jason had collected in the past months. She wasn't proud of these tactics, but she'd steered the business far from the quagmire that was Han's mining division.

"Not right now," Mia said. "There's some strange verbiage in Setty-Sarin's apartment leases. I need to be sure we can confiscate tech we find in those residences."

Lucas set the bottle down. "You've been productive these past weeks. Do you mind being in the office all day? You've said it's dark and oppressive."

"I've gotten used to it."

"I haven't seen you at the gym lately."

"I know all the faces on the climbing wall. Even random isn't random. It's no fun if I know what to expect."

"You could try something new. Fencing maybe? There are no presets on people."

Running a sword through one of the spoiled junior partners might be fun—if that were allowed—and she could make it to the gym.

She'd always assumed she viewed New Canberra objectively, but she'd been wrong. Imperfections jumped out like ill-trained actors in a bad stage play during pod rides to and from work. Why was everything so dusty? Armies of sweepers were tasked with keeping buildings sparkling clean, but the windows of the mid-rise apartments she passed hadn't been washed in weeks and reflected the sun as a dim, fuzzy ball. The center medians on the major boulevards between sectors were supposed to showcase reengineered Earth plants, but block after block were graveyards, the desiccated plants still colorful but stiff and dead. The people, as garish as the deceased flora, were malignant parasites infecting a world where they didn't belong, sucking credits from the soil for ten years, twenty tops, then back to "real life" on Earth. They didn't care about Victoria.

Sure, she could blacken the pod windows, and did, but all of it was still out there. Her apartment was the only place that remained unchanged, and she welcomed returning to it.

"I could try fencing," she said. "Beginning classes Thursday evenings at 7:00 p.m. Dan Reynolds, trained at Fédération Internationale d'Escrime, instructs. Bring your own foil."

Lucas shook his head. "You're not…" He scrubbed at his hair in a gesture Mia knew as frustration.

"I'm not in love with New Canberra right now," she said, guessing that Lucas was trying to give an awkward pep talk. "I thought…" She stopped before a truth slipped out. She'd never lived in the idyllic city the recruiters touted to prospective employees, the one where everyone worked and played without a care, but she knew the rules. If she kept her head down, did well but didn't excel, she'd live a long, healthy life—free from legalized slavery.

She'd kept her end of the bargain, but New Canberra hadn't.

"I thought we had the technology to keep bullshit like this from happening. No one should be able to turn off the cameras and divert drones or disable apartment privacy settings or shoot deadly darts." She pointed at Lucas. "You and the team shouldn't be here. All four of you bypassed Optima and sector security when you arrived. You're a symptom of something going terribly wrong in our system. Maybe you and the guy with the oversized glasses and the inner ear disrupter came over here on the same ship."

She'd said the last bit as a mean-spirited jab, but Lucas froze.

"Why would you say that?" he asked.

Mia scrambled for an explanation. "Everything started happening then. You arrived around the same time I was fired, right after I saw Erika with someone that looked a lot like the guy who dragged me off the sidewalk."

"It can't be him."

"Him who? It seems like you know the guy in the sketch I did."

Lucas scrubbed his hand back and forth like he was erasing something. "It isn't him. The man your sketch resembled can't leave Earth."

"Can't? Really? Do you know how many impossible things I've seen in the last six months? Privacy in the home can't be violated. Pods can't stop in the middle of the road. Inner ear disrupters can't make it past scanners. Little girls can't get their braids cut off in broad daylight. Drug addicts can't book passage on ships to Victoria."

The last sentence was more venomous than any of the creatures hunkered down in the dark holes surrounding the bar. Oddly, she didn't regret saying it.

Fuck Lucas and his back-door entry to New Canberra and the powers on her planet that were letting all this shit happen.

"He Isn't Here." Lucas's finger struck her desk hard with each word. The liquor in the bottle trembled.

Mia stared up at his anger. It was something from another world.

"You need to…" He stopped, took a few breaths. "Come back to the gym."

Lucas would handle trauma as something as simple as the face of a climbing wall. Hand here, foot there, and before you know it, you're over it.

"Sure," Mia said. "Next week."

Or, as soon as Optima replaced all those skeletal trees on Avenue A. She wasn't the one breaking a promise.

Chapter Twenty Four

Hangovers were as distinct as the drugs themselves. While Mia might not recall how exactly she felt while in the thrall of whatever she'd taken the night before, the hangovers were seared into her memory. Tequila, a whirling rollercoaster of dizziness that made her feel she was still drunk. Champagne, a brain-splitting pain as if she'd stood in the hot sun for way too long. Spark, a hyper-alertness that made it impossible to concentrate on anything. Dazzle, sick to her stomach as if she'd spent time in a badly programmed VR environment. Even her beloved Baby Janes lingered, making her recall sluggish long after the four hours the recreational drugs were all supposed to last.

On this morning, if it was still morning, she stumbled toward consciousness weighted down by symptoms from every hangover she'd ever had. A splitting headache, nausea, aching body, and a muddled brain. What had she done? She opened her eyes hesitantly. A half empty glass sat on her bedside table. Bourbon from the smell of it. Her stomach lurched.

She groaned, eased onto her side, and told her apartment to darken all windows. What instigated her overindulgence? She'd cut way down on both drinking and Baby Janes in the past month in an effort to tackle New Canberra's bullshit with a clear head. She waited for the unwelcome memories to fall into place piece by piece, a mirror breaking in reverse.

Yesterday, Friday, had been a slow day at work, and she and Jason had gone to The End in the late afternoon…and then, nothing. She couldn't think with the awful headache. She drifted back into something like sleep.

Later, thirst woke her. She sat up, dizzy, pushed the tangled sheets aside, and stumbled, head down, into the bathroom. She filled a glass with tepid water and drank it in long successive gulps. She took an analgesic patch from the cupboard and when she went to slap it on her arm, saw there was one already there.

Good thinking, past drunken self.

She peeled it off and replaced it, then leaned over the sink and splashed her face over and over until the cold water and aspirin began to steady the tipping world.

Something was starting to break through the haze. Not a memory per se…

She had the physical sensation she'd slept with someone.

She pressed her hands down on either side of the sink and slowly lifted her face to the mirror. Her skin was pale. Dark puffy circles floated beneath bloodshot eyes. A few small red marks decorated her neck. Those could be anything.

She carefully removed her nightshirt to reveal more evidence. Her inner thighs were pink, and when she rubbed them, sore. She checked her back in the mirror. Red scratches, the tally of a game she hadn't known she'd played.

What the hell did I do, and with whom?

She rested her forehead on the cool countertop and tried to think. A cocktail of Baby Janes, alcohol, and other random drugs could result in the very few hours of her life when her memory thinned and frayed. Even then, the events would come back to her slowly. Fragments.

But so far, nothing.

It was unlikely she'd done anything embarrassing in front of Jason. The End was back to its pre-partner unpopularity, and she'd certainly not have hit on any of the regulars. Had she been tempted to get in touch with Xander? She'd met him once for dinner after their night together, but conversation had been awkward, and it was clear they had nothing in common. She checked the comm record on her glasses, but she hadn't called anyone after she left Summit.

Though she never, ever, brought men back to her place, she peeked into the living room to be sure. Empty. Not just empty—neater than she'd left it. She straightened up last night? Bad sign, as it meant she'd done stimulants as well.

She went back to bed and told the house to keep the place dark and accept no calls or messages. God, she hoped she hadn't given whoever she'd slept with her contact info. As she pulled the covers over her, she noticed that she'd also changed the sheets.

Definitely stimulants.

She slept straight through to the wee hours of Sunday morning, and then got up again, starving, dry mouthed, and stinky. The pain in her head had receded to a tolerable ache. She still couldn't remember what happened. Was this what normal people experienced every time they overindulged?

Scary.

She smelled her shoulders and hair, hoping a scent might trigger a recollection, but the vanilla meant she'd showered and scrubbed thoroughly. She checked her charge log. Four bourbon and sodas, and nothing after that—not even a pod ride. She'd have to swallow her pride and ask Claire for cam data from the bar, as she'd clearly left with someone.

She'd wait until Monday to investigate; she wasn't up to it yet…

Monday, Mia dragged herself to work, still dead tired. Her head twinged when she moved too quickly despite all the pain meds she'd pressed.

Claire took off her glasses and gave Mia a strange look. "You're late."

"I know. I'm not feeling well."

"I bet," she said.

"You bet?"

"Friday night. The fight. What were you on? I've never seen you like that."

"There was a fight at the bar?"

Claire glared. "Very funny."

Mia abandoned the plan to bluff her way through this. "Please tell me what happened. I don't remember anything."

"How is that possible?"

"I don't know. I went to the bar with Jason after work, and that's it. Nothing until Saturday morning when I woke up with the world's worst hangover. Fill me in, quick." Lucas had his door shut and Jason wasn't in yet. She needed to get it sorted fast.

Claire frowned. "I was with you and Jason at the bar. I got us tacos, delivered from La Palma."

Mia shook her head, then winced. "I don't remember any of that. What happened next?"

"Some people from your old job showed up."

"From Han?"

"Yeah. Some drunk asshole knew you. Phil? He came over and made a snarky remark about chicken farming and asked if you wanted another cock. He practically put his crotch in your drink."

"Was he a tall, blond, white guy? Creepy eyes?"

"Yes," said Claire. "Really creepy. I'd keep my glasses on if I were him."

Phil. From business development. He was the one who posted the doctored photo of Mia holding a chicken. He'd asked Mia out early in her tenure. She'd declined, and he'd initiated a steady, low-grade campaign of harassment. He seemed to have a sixth sense about where the few holes in surveillance were at HQ and he'd lurk there, leering, as she passed, or accidentally bump into her as she turned a corner. If a hand happened to brush her thigh at a crowded company party, she'd turn and see the back of Phil's head as he walked nonchalantly away.

Mia had complained to Erika, who was nearly as nonchalant as Phil. *You call that harassment?* she'd asked. *You know what I had to put up with on Earth?*

The list was truly horrifying and went a long way toward explaining Erika's sharply tailored suits and aggressive stride through the executive floor hallways.

Claire continued. "You stood up and punched him in the face. Knocked him flat on his back, and then you kicked him. None of his friends tried to stop you. Lucas dragged you off him and out of the bar."

The world tilted, and Mia grabbed the edge of Claire's desk. "To where?"

"How should I know? You didn't come back."

She must have looked stricken because Claire offered a rare reassurance.

"It wasn't a big deal. The bartender kicked out all the Han people and said you'd earned free drinks for the rest of the month."

Lucas appeared in the doorway of his office.

"Was I drunk?" Mia quietly asked Claire.

"No. We'd only been there an hour or so. I figured that guy was an ex or something."

"Mia? Can I talk to you for a moment?" Lucas asked.

She shuffled toward him slowly and carefully, like she was a new arrival on a low-gravity planet.

"Are you alright? You don't look well."

"Lingering hangover."

She collapsed into the chair facing his desk. He shut the door then took his seat. "I overheard you and Claire. You don't remember what happened Friday night?"

He sat only a meter away. She forced herself to examine his neck. The hollow above the clavicle was one of her favorite spots on a man. A faint, purple, bruised mark on his.

What have I done?

"It was you, wasn't it?" Mia said.

The seconds stretched on uncomfortably as Lucas searched her eyes for something that wasn't there. His confusion morphed into astonishment.

"You don't remember."

The belay machine at the gym had malfunctioned once, and she'd fallen a few meters before it locked, bringing her to an abrupt stop and scaring the breath from her chest. She felt that way now.

Lucas turned away, jaw muscles flexing. "You took the Levotrum. You didn't throw it away."

The question was a slap that echoed through the empty spaces in her mind.

"I don't know. I woke up Saturday with a terrible headache."

Mia *had* saved it, and she must have taken it. *But why?* She rubbed her temples. The headache was still there, as was the void. The lost time.

Lucas looked at her like she was a fish bone he'd spat out. "You took a drug to forget sex with me. That's a first."

Mia teetered between embarrassment and anger. Yes, she'd had thoughts of running her hands—and various other bits—over Lucas and had shoved them away. The business was too fragile to survive serious interpersonal conflict, and her interpersonal relations always ended badly.

She stared down at the neutral gray carpet and took a breath. She'd not beat herself up for responding to a man practically everyone he brushed past wanted to fuck. The damn pheromones and crooked scar. He could star in VR porn and knew it. The scale tipped toward anger.

Lucas wasn't done. "You wouldn't take Levotrum to erase the memory of witnessing a child's near murder and almost dying yourself, and yet you'd do it now."

"My memory, my choice. I assume I had good reason."

Not only had she broken her own rule and slept with Lucas, but there'd have also been the after-sex part of the evening. Lucas had torn through the female partners at The End like a laser tunnel-boring machine. How he excavated himself from the encounters might be a bit messier.

His face hardened. "You continue to surprise me."

You and me both. How did the puzzle pieces of Friday night fit together? The bar, the fight, the sex, the Levotrum…

"Can I see the visual data from the bar?"

He turned a screen to face her and tapped in a few commands.

The bar, viewed from the interior camera above the front door, appeared. Lucas muted the throbbing music. Mia, Jason, and Claire sat in a back booth wolfing down tacos in unflattering ways. Lucas and Mikey sat in another booth consuming a liquid dinner.

Lucas fast-forwarded. Mia watched a clipped, marionette version of herself drink a not unreasonable amount of alcohol. She never took any pills or hypos from her purse. Lucas returned the playback to normal speed when a large group poured in, first-timers given how they gawked at the surroundings. The crowd converged on the bar and ordered drinks. She recognized a few faces besides Phil's. Some had been friends, she thought, but after she was fired, they refused her calls.

It still stung. Maryanne, waving a credits chip to get the bartender's attention, had gotten too high at the last company Landing Day party. Mia had helped her home, which included paying a penalty when Maryanne threw up in the pod. Hasani was one of the few who'd eat lunch outdoors with her, where they'd discuss Optima policy decisions over bean salads. She'd read Issa's entire, awful fantasy novel and given feedback over several bottles of wine, assuring her the ending was great. All that felt like what friends would do with and for each other, but apparently not.

The group from Han were boisterous and sloppy—already drunk before they'd arrived. After they were served, they moved into the center of the room and that was when Phil saw her. He pushed through the group and stopped a couple of meters away from the booth. He raised his glass and said something, then grabbed his crotch and moved closer. As Claire noted, he nearly knocked over her drink with a few exaggerated hip thrusts, meaty pink lips flapping spittle as he made the cock comment. Mia stood, pushed him away, then balled her fist and smacked his left cheek. She hadn't punched anyone since Dave Vasiliev stole her banana in kindergarten.

Phil toppled, more due to inebriation than to the inexpert blow, but what happened next disturbed Mia. She kicked him hard in the stomach as he lay on the filthy floor. She reached past Lucas to pause the image and stared at the screen. The punch, she understood. Phil had harassed her for years and seemed on the verge of laying hands on her in the bar. The kick was something else. He was on the ground, defenseless, his fake friends standing by doing nothing to stop her. The frozen frame showed her snarling, and her heavy black sandal connecting with Phil's belly. It was something from a trashy, low-budget drama.

She closed her eyes and tried to imagine being there, seeing people from Han after so long, knowing they'd read or possibly even written the lies about her, then Phil doing what he did in front of them all. She clenched her right hand and rubbed the knuckles. They ached.

She let the images flow again. Lucas jumped from the booth, grabbed her from behind and pulled her away from Phil. She fought to escape his grasp, but he picked her up as easily as if she were a bag of groceries and carried her out of the bar, keeping her kicking legs well clear of the onlookers.

Lucas switched to the view from the camera outside The End.

Lucas set her down but kept a hold on her arm. Mia yelled, and he laughed and didn't let go. She was a mess, shirt untucked and hair styled as if by a dust storm. A pod rolled up and Lucas dragged her over to it. She didn't want to get in, so he grabbed her around the waist and pulled them both in.

Lucas stopped the tape. She stared at the freeze-frame of the back of the pod. Two heads next to each other. She'd have been on his lap, the way he'd grabbed her.

Cue the sex scene—the result of an almost comical sequence of events that left her hot and sweaty and nearly undressed on his lap in the back of a pod.

Clearly, she'd snapped. Months of pretending everything was fine, trying to ignore the fact that her career had been derailed and her future was uncertain, piled on top of the growing stress of working at Summit, had finally gotten to her. Everything about that night screamed bad judgement. Even so, sex with Lucas she understood; that kick, she didn't.

"I shouldn't have done that to Phil."

"Sounds like he deserved it. He harassed you for years."

"How did you know…" Of course. She'd told him that night. What else had she said and done?

Lucas had the good sense not to answer, and they sat quietly, staring at the frame of the pod and the deep blue night sky. The silence stretched into ellipses leading to the next logical topic. She didn't know what to say. Her gaze strayed upward, back to the place on his neck. She'd betrayed herself.

Taking the Levotrum didn't undo the act. She'd done a thousand stupid things in her lifetime and managed to live with them. She'd have known the bar would have recorded her fight with Phil, and she'd be curious enough to watch.

Something had happened off camera that would have made working at Summit impossible…and she needed the job.

Their parting must have been truly ugly. Uglier than the fight at the bar. The wrong phrase from Lucas's lips could certainly have taunted her into taking the drug.

"After we…" she made a quick rolling motion with her hand. "Did you say something to the effect that we should forget it happened?"

Lucas gave her a strange, almost incredulous look.

She'd guessed right and would have been viciously angry after hearing a comment like that after sex. "Don't answer. Can we both forget? I apologize for how I acted. Kicking Phil and all the rest."

"I didn't…" He struggled to articulate and failed.

"Don't explain. I behaved inappropriately. Please don't fire me. I'm committed to the business and need to find out who's behind that dart."

"I'm not going to fire you." He seemed almost insulted.

"This isn't your fault. I thought I was feeling better but something's clearly wrong. I need some time off."

He folded his arms and drummed his fingers against his biceps. "I need you here. We're trying to build a new client base."

"I know. I just need to get out of the city for a few days."

Lucas shrugged, which she took to mean resignation.

She was nearly to the door when he spoke again. "So, the Levotrum, is it horrifying? Topiary of the soul?"

She'd said something similar to him the night of the children's party to explain why it wasn't okay to drug her. The words trickled like acid through all her weak places. Her hypocrisy. Her shame at her reliance on drugs. He'd kept what she'd said, not as a shared moment between team members after a terrible day, but as ammunition. After their night together, he'd have more to add to his arsenal. She released a breath, and it left her empty.

Seconds passed before she was able to move.

"If you ever mention anything I said the night after the children's party, or refer to our time together Friday night, I will quit. I won't stay here and be mocked."

He stood. "No…I…no. I apologize." His face was a flipboard of emotions, most of which she could identify but not map onto whatever happened between them.

She pulled the door open and stepped out.

Jason pulled off dark goggles and smiled. "How's the hand?"

The fight. Mia had almost forgotten about it. "Not good. I really don't know how to punch."

"It looked like you did from where I sat."

Mia beelined straight to his desk. "You want to go camping? Now? Get out into the wastes for a few days?"

Jason glanced from her to Lucas's office and nodded. "You know I do. I want to see some of the nature you're always going on about. What do I need to bring?"

"I'll send you a list. Meet back here at noon."

Chapter Twenty Five

Jason gazed at the dirt track meandering away from Ring 20 into the noon haze.

"There are off-road pods that will take us to a campground in the middle of nowhere with a shooting range, and you never mentioned this? This is my dream vacation."

Mia shrugged. "We live on a huge, barely populated planet. We've got something for anyone who needs to blow off steam. Undersea big game hunting in turbo submarines. 3D-printing workshops where you construct full-scale buildings then blow them up. Laser tag against teams of robots in lava tubes. I guess you never searched for recreation."

Jason snorted a laugh. "It never occurred to me. I've been on a treadmill ever since we left Earth."

"I've been on a treadmill since I graduated from college."

They stood under an awning on a plasticrete platform covered in *Beyond Safari* logos, camping supplies piled next to them. Jason had a small pack, several cases of beer, and a bin holding a dozen experimental weapons he swore wouldn't set off any alarms. Mia brought protein bars, water, coveralls, party lights, a couple of bottles of bourbon, fewer toiletries than she'd ever travelled with, and a dozen books on her glasses she'd sworn she'd read if she ever had the time.

A cloud of dust rose lazily in the distance.

"That's our pod?" Jason asked.

"I hope so." It was hot out. Mia couldn't afford the deluxe strato-shuttle option which delivered guests to the resort in half an hour. The cheaper *Adventure Seeker* package included slow ground transport.

A small, dark spot grew into a boxy unpod-like pod that jerked to a halt in front of the platform. Mia tried to puzzle out what to do next when the back half stuttered open to reveal a dusty cargo area.

Jason clapped. "We're off! I'll load."

Mia might have protested his offer, but after months of working with Jason she'd learned the mess on his desk was meticulously organized. He'd be uncomfortable if she loaded things wrong. Jason and Claire had more in common than he'd ever admit.

The odd pod squeaked or groaned every time Jason added a box.

"This doesn't seem safe," Mia said.

Jason patted the dented silver. "I feel like I'm back home. Let's get going."

The back closed as Mia hoisted her door open manually. The passenger seat was a nonadjustable slab of grey plastic. Four hours on it was going to leave her sore. She folded up her coverall, placed it beneath her for padding and buckled the safety straps.

Jason wrenched open his door and jumped in. "I've never been camping. I've never been anywhere away from people, and honestly, I don't like people much."

The vehicle being called a pod was more aspiration than fact. It wasn't mag-lev, and though the sixteen wheels beneath extended and retracted to smooth the ride, it didn't keep its promise of making passengers feel they were "floating on air."

Mia held tight to the dashboard and the grab bar, barely able to keep her head from smashing into the frame. Jason whooped with maniacal delight as they sped too fast over the rough terrain, their luggage banging as percussively as the awful music at The End. Exuberant abandon was a side of Jason she'd never seen. She liked watching him unfold from quiet worker into something bigger and bolder.

She stared out the window at the distant mountains—pale, rainbow-hued layers ground down by time and the rare rainstorm—thankful it was too noisy for casual conversation. She'd slept with Lucas. The fit man at the gym who was now a match for Mikey. The man who charmed clients and had to fend off waitstaff. The man who booked small tables and didn't move his knee away from hers as they watched data streams flow over live views of the dozens of restaurants they frequented.

What did it mean?

She found herself trying to bite her nail, but each bounce sent her thumb rocketing toward her nose. Enough. It didn't *mean* anything. Sex didn't mean anything. Humans were hard-wired to try to put bits of each other into each other. She and Lucas were human and that happened. She'd erased the memory, and Lucas would soon overwrite his with the series of voracious partners he would inevitably bed.

Four long hours later—long enough for the odd ache in Mia's chest to be replaced by an ache in her shoulder where it kept hitting the door—the pod passed through a red stone arch and pulled into a covered parking area next to a large, faux-adobe building. After her eyes adjusted to the relative darkness, Mia spotted half a dozen other beat-up pods and sliding glass doors marked "Registration."

Inside, other tired travelers wandered aisles of shelves holding a bizarre juxtaposition of products. Fresh produce, meat and seafood, hats and coveralls…and guns. Guns of every shape and size displayed in boxes as if they were shoes ready to try on.

Jason's arm shot out and stopped Mia as if she'd been about to walk off a cliff.

"Is this for real?"

"I guess so. I've never been here."

"How does it work?"

Mia pointed to a counter staffed by a man in khakis. "Ask him."

They left an hour later, Jason having spent way too much of his savings on the *Alien Assault* package, which included eight guns, cases of ammo, and three hundred drones.

"These are actual projectile weapons," he assured Mia as a bot loaded crates onto a trailer that would follow them to the campsite. "They'll only shoot the drones. If I try to shoot you, they won't fire."

"Good to know," Mia said as the bot nestled her crate of artisanal baked goods, mixers that paired well with bourbon, a pop-up pavilion, and deluxe bedding against the not-going-to-kill-her weapons and the tent and supplies that came with the campsite.

"We can camp anywhere," Jason said. "*Beyond Safari* owns the whole valley." He put on his glasses and swished his right hand. "The northeast corner looks good. No one else is camped anywhere near there. What do you think?"

Mia thought they needed to get the tent set up before the sun set. "Perfect. Let's go."

It was a slow half hour to reach the campsite. The trailer kept disconnecting, and they had to circle back around and reboot before it would recognize the pod. Finally, they ground to a halt on a nondescript patch of ground dotted with rocks and gnarled bushes. Heat distorted the desert, transforming the sandy dirt into rippling liquid. She grabbed Jason's arm before he could jump out.

"Hey! Slow down. Check the temperature before you open the door."

He looked at the instrument panel and balked. "Shit, it's fifty degrees out there."

It would only get hotter. "We need to get the tent set up, but we'll have to be careful not to get dehydrated. I'll do the bug perimeter later. If something lands on you, don't crush it. Don't move. Call me. Got it?" She and her friends had gone out into the wastes all the time in high school, and no one had ever been bitten because they'd all followed the rules.

She opened the pod door and heat slapped her back into her seat. She knew being in the wastes cleared her head, but only now remembered why. The searing sunlight made thinking of anything but the next five seconds impossible.

She dragged the pop-up dome tent to an area without too many rocks and spread it out, working slowly. Sunlight reflecting from the silver fabric forced her glasses to darken nearly to black. Once she had the tent in place, roof side up, she pounded in a few stakes, then pressed the inflate command. The metallic, quilted fabric rippled in the faint breeze as each of the hundred individual cells sucked in air, pulling the tent up into a four-by-four-meter dome. Once it was fully inflated, she pounded in the rest of the stakes. The wind was a whisper now but could kick up without warning.

Jason unpacked the rest of the gear from the trailer, and her dizziness verged on near faint as they moved it all into the dome. Fortunately, the climate control in the tent worked well, and the interior cooled rapidly. As soon as they finished and shut the door, she took the bag of DayLyte powder from her pack and peeled one of the circular patches off the front.

"Give me your hand."

Jason held out his right arm. She applied the patch, and he read the text that appeared on the small screen aloud. "Plus .75 liters water, two units DayLyte. What's that?"

She added the right amount of powder to an empty bottle and filled it three-quarters full of water. "Salts and sugars. Drink it. That patch keeps track of body and air moisture. It's so dry out here, we can lose all our water just by breathing. Red display means you're low. Yellow's a warning. Green means you're good, and the display shows an estimate of the fluids you'll lose in the next hour. Be proactive. It's almost impossible to overhydrate."

Jason took a deep draught. "Makes sense. Thanks."

The pop-up was luxurious as far as tents went—a twin bed on each side, high ceiling, and a few clear plastic windows scattered at eye level. They flopped down to rest until sunset.

Mia hadn't intended to nap, but after closing her eyes for only a moment, the circle of bright sky in the window next to her bed had transformed to deep twilight. Jason snored. The display above the tent door promised the temperature outside was a bearable 34°C.

She picked up the bag of bug perimeter stakes, quietly unzipped the inner door, sealed it, then slipped through the outer door. The sky was a beautiful dark blue tinged with purple in the west. A dozen meters from the tent she walked a circle, hammering a stake into the ground every few steps. Activating them was her favorite part. They sprang to life one at a time, the blue lights on the top of each gradually transforming from random blinking to a slow, clockwise pattern. Once they'd established contact with each other, the blue lights turned to a quick pulsing green. They'd zap anything attempting to fly or creep into the enclosure.

Next, she released the crawler, a patient little bot that would patrol the grounds of their little domain and get rid of anything within the perimeter.

Back in the tent, Jason still snored. She crouched down and examined his hand. His sticker was red, so she woke him and made him drink.

"Help me set up the pavilion?" she asked.

The pop-up pavilion by no means popped. She and Jason wrestled with poles and fabric until they had an A-frame of daisy-patterned, sun-blocking material over a bugproof floor and a sputtering but somewhat effective mist system.

"It didn't have flowers in the brochure," Mia said. "It's better than nothing. I don't want to spend all day in the tent."

He nodded, and moved all the *Alien Assault* cases under it while Mia set up folding chairs, a table, and loaded the cooler with booze, beer, and mixers.

"Shall we?" he asked.

"Drink?"

"No, shoot things."

"Can't we do both?" Mia tossed him a beer and poured a few shots of bourbon into a temperature-controlled thermos. It was okay to drink tonight. This was the long-deserved time off she'd never taken.

"Did I mention this is the best vacation ever? Thanks for bringing me along," Jason said.

"I wouldn't have done it without you." Not only because it was great to have a friend with her; camping alone wasn't allowed.

Jason unpacked a benign-looking pistol the size of her hand. "I got this one for you. I know you don't like guns, but target shooting is a game, and it won't be fun if you don't play too."

She tried without success to muster her trademark disgust, then took the proffered weapon without protest. Maybe bar-fighting Mia would be good at it.

Jason released a small, lighted drone, which flew a dozen meters away and hovered.

"I set it to *Easy*. It won't move."

Mia pointed the gun in its general direction, pulled the trigger, and heard a *p-twoo* as a bullet no bigger than a pebble flew from the barrel and landed somewhere in the endless sand surrounding them.

"You've got to aim. Like this," he said, taking her hand, raising the gun to eye level. "We don't have target assist. That's no way to learn. These are sights." He ran his finger over a u-shaped piece of plastic near the back and a nub at the front of the barrel. "Line these up with the drone."

Mia did, and when she fired again, the drone exploded. "Shit!"

"It's okay!" Jason said, laughing. "They're meant to do that. That's why I got three hundred of them. It won't be as easy when they're moving."

It wasn't, but Mia turned out to be a natural, if Jason could be believed. Her skill increased with each shot—of bourbon—until it didn't. She relaxed in a camp chair and let her pistol fall to the ground. Jason burped and tossed another empty can at the crawler.

The stars were incredible, a bright blanket that stretched from horizon to horizon. She breathed in the night. Did heat have a smell? If it did it should be this, though she had a hard time finding words for the faintly metallic aroma of the dust.

"Hear that?" Jason asked.

She listened. The clicking and snapping she'd expect to hear in an empty lot in New Canberra was absent. The evening breeze had died down and the *ting ting* of the straps hitting the poles of the pavilion had stopped.

"I don't hear anything."

"That's just it. It's so quiet it hurts. I feel like I'm wearing earplugs. I've never been anywhere like this." He stood, blocking the stars, and stretched out his arms. "It's so big. So empty. I could walk north forever and never see another human." He sat heavily and the chair creaked. "I could get used to this."

"Me too."

The feeling she'd had for the last months, that something bad was lurking just around the corner, finally dissipated. There were no corners, and no other warm-blooded creatures for kilometers. She was safe.

"I used to go camping all the time in high school," Mia said. "We'd tell our parents we were doing something safe like going to Playa Placida—that's the beach resort near town—but then we'd get someone's older brother or boyfriend to rent a skimmer and head out to the middle of nowhere. Build fires, take drugs, get drunk, have sex. Those were good times." Thanks to everyone being so high she didn't have to watch what she said.

"I don't have any good memories from high school," Jason said.

"You dropped out after a year, didn't you?"

"Yeah. I needed to get a full-time job so I could get out of the house."

"Why was that?"

Jason cracked open another beer and drank most of it before replying.

"The abridged version is that my parents were both unemployed. My dad was a stim addict, and my four older brothers took out their frustrations on me. When I, and subsequently they, realized I was gay, it got much worse. I was legally emancipated when I was sixteen and started working to support myself."

She'd pictured Jason as a child prodigy, taking a job early to stave off the boredom of the traditional educational system, not to escape abuse.

"I'm sorry."

His dismissive gesture splashed the crawler with IPA. "That was twenty years ago. Life got better as soon as I got out of there. It might have been fun to go to college, but I didn't need it for my job."

She'd read about the unintended consequences of the technological breakthroughs at the beginning of the 22nd century on Earth. Throw anything into a food chipper and something edible would emerge. World hunger was eradicated, if you could call gnawing on a gray-brown disc eating. Cheap, solar-powered water filters eliminated filth and disease. The mortality rate fell, and unemployment rose. Suddenly, the poor of the world were healthy enough to want more from life, and there was no more to be had—unless you took it from someone else. Racism, nationalism, and sexism all reemerged. It was no wonder everyone wanted to come to Victoria. Jason had a much tougher childhood than she'd had.

"Claire mentioned your dad died. You said your parents were engineers and arrived early in the colonization. What happened?" Jason asked.

Jason just revealed his painful past. Now it was her turn. Friendship was hard.

"He was bitten or stung by something. Died almost instantly." That wasn't quite true, but Jason didn't need to know the details. "The mortality rate was pretty high when the planet was first settled. A lot of it due to the bugs, much due to the gravity. It's not like every nut and bolt and tool they brought was engineered to account for that. The Six kind of reset the clock, as far as deaths go, once the city was up and running."

"What about your mom? Is she still here, or did she go back to Earth?"

"She's here." Mia took a swig of her drink. "Retired." Time to change the subject. "Your first job was at NYCPD. Did Lucas hire you?"

"No. I got in via some 'keep youths off the streets' program. I worked part-time in the weapons lab repairing and upgrading the old equipment. That's where I met Lucas. He was a special investigator in the corporate fraud department. An impossible job. The corporations had state of the art technology and our stuff was twenty years out of date. I couldn't get parts for most of it. I improvised. I've always been good with electronics. Lucas spotted my talent and brought me on full-time. It was a good job. A real challenge."

"How did you two end up at Itek?" she asked.

"Lucas saw the writing on the wall. He'd never get anything done working for the city, so he took a job with a corporation. He could fight crime from the inside and maybe finally win."

"You went with him?"

"He brought me over as soon as he could. I thought I'd be getting a cushy job at headquarters, but we got sent down to South America to do asset protection for an oil field in Venezuela. I didn't mind. I didn't particularly like New York, and I'd always wanted to travel."

He chuckled. "Boy was I naïve. I didn't know there was a civil war going on until we arrived. Mikey met us at the strataport in what looked like a tank. Our job was to keep the oil field producing, war be damned."

He never spoke about the past. If beer was the lever that opened the floodgates, she'd keep it flowing and nurse him back to health tomorrow. Hangovers in the wastes were the worst.

"How long were you there?"

"Couple years. It was a strange assignment. Exciting and boring all at once. We were constantly under siege and couldn't leave the compound. What I'd learned at NYCPD came in handy when our supply drones got shot down and I had to patch up equipment with whatever we had lying around. I never got to see the country. I spent my vacations in Barbados."

Mia had never been south of Beijing, or north, east, or west, truth be told. She'd had no budget for travel.

"Lucas's career took off there," Jason continued. "He was originally tasked with recruiting and screening staff, but soon he was running the whole operation. We managed to keep the field open and under Itek control until the war ended and Lucas negotiated a new contract with the victors. Itek promoted him and pulled him back to headquarters. He brought Mikey and me. A few months later, he was promoted to Senior Director of Internal Security for all of North America, eventually made partner, and now, this!"

He raised the can and swept it back and forth. It was too dark to read his face.

Mia took a moment, maybe longer, to consider her next words. She was drunk. The patch on her wrist had been flashing red for an hour. What she wanted to say would betray Lucas's confidence and reveal she'd lied by omission to Jason…but she was tired of all the secrets.

"Lucas told me why you're really here. You investigated an illegal R&D lab at Itek, and now you're testifying against the company. The trial might not happen for years. You came here because it was safer."

Jason groaned. "He's such an ass. I've been wanting to tell you since day one. The only reason we're safer here is because Lucas burned so many bridges in New York. I mean, sure, it was his job to stop intracompany crime, but bringing in NYCPD?"

"How did you and Claire get involved? From what I heard, you didn't work closely together."

"Lucas unofficially asked us for hardware and software assistance because he, quote, couldn't trust anyone, and that his predecessor, *dead predecessor*, had probably stepped on a landmine. Ya gotta understand, staff hiding things from the intracompany crime department was totally normal. The board of directors supported Lucas because he lowered operating costs and increased profit, but everyone else in the company was using corporate shuttles to take their families on vacation to Maui, or bringing home state-of-the-art holo projectors for *testing* and forgetting to bring them back. I was surprised he cared about whatever he'd found."

"Why? He told me he wanted to do his job but kept getting roped into representing the company at events."

Jason snorted. "I was surprised he cared about the missing resources because he was out of his mind on Plex. I dunno how much you know about that drug but it's like cocaine times a thousand. When he would call Claire and I into his office, he would have four conversation shields going, vibration dampeners on the windows, and printouts all over his desk. It was like a scene from an old conspiracy movie."

Mia's image of Lucas flickered like a flame in a strong breeze, and his silhouette shifted from hero to one of the arrogant guys at the bars in the E district, shaking with confidence and stim, not taking *no* for an answer.

Jason slid down into his chair, and she worried he'd fall asleep and she'd never hear the end of the story.

"There was a secret lab," she prompted.

Jason lurched upright. "Oh, yeah. There was some fucked-up shit happening on that floor. Claire and I helped gather evidence. I'm not sure any of us understood what we were getting into, and a day came when things went sideways. It was easy for Lucas to decide what to do, thanks to the Plex. He called his old buddies from NYCPD and led them straight through the front doors of Itek Headquarters and up the partner elevator."

"That's unprecedented."

Jason barked a laugh. "To put it mildly. Our lives blew up that night. I'm not sorry we did what we did. I hope those assholes at Itek end up in prison for life. Especially Magnussen and Richter. It's been decades since the AGE has had the chance to nail a corporation. Unfortunately, the trial keeps getting pushed out and Itek is trying to discredit us. Lucas is low-hanging fruit. Everyone knew about his drug problem. Coming here was a chance to keep Lucas out of sight, squash the rumors, and return him fit, healthy, and credible. Plus, we're banned from just about any large commercial establishment in New York. All the big corporations panicked, worried that more whistle-blowers might pop out of the woodwork, so they made an example of us. I can't go into a supermarket without an alarm going off. You've heard of no-fly lists? We're on the no everything list."

"Who are Magnussen and Richter?"

"Magnussen is an asshole."

"You said that. What kind of asshole?"

"A completely incompetent partner who did nothing but waste money. His dad was one of the founders of the company so they couldn't get rid of him. Richter was his Chief of Security. Magnussen might have dreamed up that lab, but Richter had the brains to make it happen."

Something about the way he said the name *Richter* triggered a memory.

"I made a sketch of the man who stunned me and dragged me out into the brush. You all seemed to think he looked familiar, but Lucas said he couldn't be here. Did he look like Richter?"

Jason belched a *yes*. "It did, but he wasn't granted bail. He's under house arrest in New York. The AGE may not have the resources of Itek, but they can certainly make sure someone doesn't leave their apartment building. Lucas gets updates from his friends at NYCPD. Richter is on Earth."

Mia had more questions, but she was tired, drunk, and seriously dehydrated. She'd ignored the red flashing patch for too long, and the crawler seemed to be meandering uphill despite the fact they were camped on a level plain.

"We should get inside," Mia said, rising unsteadily from her chair. "I'll pump up the humidity in the tent. That'll save us from a hangover."

It didn't. Mia woke late, patch flashing yellow, with a dull ache in her skull. A liter of water, two analgesic hypos, and a croissant later, she felt well enough to creep out to the pavilion, drag one of the chairs into the shade, and activate the mist system.

The blazing midday sun transformed the desert into a hallucination. Distant mountains shimmered in gauzy waves of heat, and the silence was broken only by the crunch of the crawler's treads as it patrolled their small settlement.

Mia leaned back, stretched, and reveled in a deep feeling of relaxation even the hangover couldn't overshadow. She'd go camping every weekend from now on. Probably best to head north next time, maybe set up right at the foot of the mountains, so by three o'clock the site would be in shadow, and she could hike or climb.

Yesterday morning's drama with Lucas was literally and figuratively out of sight and mind. Maybe not completely out of mind. Taking the Levotrum might not have been the noblest course of action, but what did a few hours of missing memories mean in the grand scheme of things? Her coworkers at Han, especially the younger ones, had overindulged in legal drugs routinely and forgotten huge swaths of time. Snippets of conversations Mia overheard in the cafeteria on Monday mornings included, "I don't know how I ended up at…" *insert name of club or friend's apartment*. Or, "I guess I bought…" *insert expensive item*, "Saturday night when I got home. No idea, but it showed up Sunday with my palm print as confirmation."

They managed to live with themselves and even laugh about it. It was all perfectly normal, and though Mia held herself to a higher standard, she'd allow herself the occasional slipup.

The seal on the outer door of the tent hissed and Jason called, voice hoarse.

"It's fucking hot out there. Come back inside. I need your help with the hydration powder."

It *was* fucking hot. The mist evaporated before it got anywhere near her face, and the wrist patch was already yellow.

Jason held the door open then sprawled onto his bed. "I can't read this thing," he said, waving his arm, "and I don't know where you stowed the water and powder."

He was clearly in worse shape than she was. Mia retrieved his dusty water bottle from the floor, mixed a batch of DayLyte, and rummaged in her bag for the analgesic patches. Once Jason was taken care of, she flopped back down on her own bed and stared up at the vermillion patch of sky in the circular window above her. The feeling of being safe in the middle of nowhere remained, and the bed was much more comfortable than the metal and canvas chair.

After waiting a respectful ten minutes, by which time the powder and patches should have done their work, she asked, "What were they doing in the lab?"

Jason groaned and rolled to face the wall. "Some kind of bioweapons research. Which would normally be totally legit as far as Itek is concerned, but they weren't using normal test subjects."

"Meaning?"

"They were kidnapping people. People with illegal implants who were off the grid. Unregistered kids. Drug addicts who refused treatment. Seniors from Staten Island. The scientists seemed to be trying to find the lethal dose of whatever they were developing without actually killing anyone, but that didn't always work out."

"You watched them kill people?"

Jason made a vague motion with his shoulder. Mia's stomach churned.

"That's a little worse than fucked-up shit."

"That's why Lucas called the cops."

Mia hadn't meant to sound accusatory, but Jason's sharp retort revealed she'd failed. What if she'd discovered something like that at Han? She'd have done nothing but tell Erika because there was no NYCPD. Optima's board agreed upon rules that would keep the planet healthy and functioning, and that was as far as their mandate went.

"What happened when the NYCPD arrived?"

"It was bedlam. Claire had downloaded as many files as she could in the weeks before—which was fortunate because those asshole scientists fried everything the moment they saw those dark blue uniforms. They all had directional, short-range data bombs, and none of them put their hands in the air until after they'd destroyed their workstations."

"The whole case depends on the evidence Claire got?"

"Not really. There were screaming people strapped in beds and syringes full of poison. Richter was waving around a machine gun—also not allowed at HQ. That's the only reason the partners didn't protest when the police dragged him off the property. None of them wanted machine guns in the elevators they rode every day, or people who could disable the sensors that were supposed to prevent weapons like that getting past the front door."

"Or the kidnapping and murder."

Jason waved a hand. "I doubt they cared about that. The people they used to legally test drugs didn't have it great either. A lot of people on Earth are desperate for credits."

Mia had seen evidence of it during her college years, but nearly everything in New Beijing had been in a state of riotous decay she couldn't decipher or control. "If Lucas had called CorSec instead of NYCPD, they'd have fired a few senior scientists and moved the lab to another location and would still be doing what they were doing. Lucas might have been on drugs, but he did the right thing."

"I might have done the right thing as well, but I wasn't consulted." Jason pulled the blanket over his head. "I need a nap. Wake me up at sunset, would ya? I want to blow things up."

"Cheers to that."

They both woke in better moods. Mia hadn't dared do a search on Magnussen and Richter on the resort's insecure network, and Jason's soft snoring lulled her to sleep, even as she tried to puzzle out what it would mean if Richter were somehow on Victoria.

After a few liters of DayLyte and a dozen drones destroyed, Jason's good spirits were fully restored.

"Shoot after you've let out a breath," he instructed. "Relax, focus, pull the trigger."

Mia faced the last light of the fading sun and did as he said. The drone exploded spectacularly.

"Woo hoo!" Jason yelled, pumping a fist into the air.

Beer and jagged bits of metal spattered the thirsty ground.

"I can't believe you're drinking again," she said

Jason relaxed in his chair. The crawler trundling by had already endured several direct hits from his empty cans.

"I'm on vacation. We've got plenty of hypos, and I can sleep until sunset. Now concentrate. You're being timed. Hit it and hit it fast."

Mia did as he suggested and obliterated the next drone in under a minute.

"You're a natural! I knew you would be once you got over your gun phobia."

Indeed. Mia tried to deny it, but she enjoyed this. Being outdoors, using her body and mind to outwit the drones—it was fun.

"Can I ask you a personal question?"

"Fire away," he said. "Get it?"

"I do. You all had to leave Earth so abruptly. I'm embarrassed I've only thought of this now, but did you leave partners behind? Claire never liked to talk about her boyfriends, so I never asked."

He waved the beer, which seemed nearly empty since it no longer spilled. "I'd say *fortunately* not, but that sounds pathetic. I wasn't involved in anything serious at the time."

"What do you think of the men on Victoria?" If being friends meant he could ask about her memory, she should be allowed to finally broach this subject. "I'm curious to know what someone who hasn't been vetted by the system thinks."

He grunted. "I think they take too many drugs. I keep getting hit on by straight guys."

"How do you—"

"Trust me, I know. I appreciate your planet's liberal views toward every flavor of sexuality, but I don't want to be anyone's guilty pleasure. Well," he amended, "I don't want to make a habit of it. What about you? What do you think of men on Victoria?"

Mia turned back to the drone, took aim, and blew it apart.

"They're well-groomed. Attractive. Career-oriented. Intelligent."

"You say all that like it's a bad thing."

She upped a level on the shooting range program, and a drone shot into the sky. "The intensive screening process you didn't have to go through means everyone who gets a contract here has a lot in common. Top of the class at some great university, awards in whatever sport or hobby they do for fun, extensive travel, expensive tastes, no real ties to any religion, socially liberal, fiscally conservative, blah, blah, blah."

"Two hundred thousand single men, and not one of them is interesting?"

"It isn't like that," she snapped. "First, I didn't get to pick from two hundred thousand men. We're strongly encouraged to date within our own sector. Second, I studied the screening procedures as part of my job. Each department and career track has a personality. They hire people who'll fit in, and I create an environment where they can thrive. You give someone a new chair in one department, no one notices. In another? It's like kicking a yellow ant nest. Everyone panics. Are we getting new furniture? I like my old chair. Are we moving? Is Matt getting a promotion? Where's his new chair? Is that in the budget?"

Jason laughed. "Really?"

"Yes. I know all the personalities, and the city is so small, I can guess who will be at what bar and why and how they'll react to me."

"What do you mean?"

"I didn't get screened either, and people can tell there's something off about me. I never get the balance right. How much am I supposed to know about the topic they mention? Too little, I'm boring. Too much, I'm intimidating. A man in a bar tries to start a conversation by telling me about a new chef in town. I know all about her, thanks to glancing at an article. I can recite a list of every restaurant she's ever worked at and the opening night menu she's planning. What am I supposed to say?"

Jason nodded slowly, finally understanding the real problem. "You can't tell them about your memory," he said.

"Of course not."

"You might not believe this, but I'm going to say it anyway. This is how dating is for everyone. You dial back parts of yourself that don't please a potential mate while also trying to *be yourself* and have a good time. You compromise. You trust someone and get screwed, you don't trust, and that fucks things up."

"It may be like that in New York but I—"

"You need to relax." Jason smashed the empty can between his flattened hands, took aim, and hit Mia in the right shoulder. "Stop overanalyzing and have some fun. You might know the personality of every employee at Han HQ, but you don't have to date those guys anymore. There are five other sectors and those corporations use different algorithms to pick their staff. Also, it isn't that strange if you know superstar chef Daniela went to Our Lady of Guadalupe elementary school and has a dog named Biscuit. We all have glasses or lenses, and we can all access that information in a heartbeat. Having a conversation isn't about exchanging data, it's about getting to know people."

"Are you saying I don't have a mate because I'm paranoid, uptight, and a bad conversationalist?"

"You're not a bad conversationalist," Jason said with a broad smile. "Here." He passed her a sweating can of beer, and though she'd vowed not to drink today, she accepted it.

"I'm also not paranoid. Let me tell you about my exes and why I didn't open up to them. It would have been like giving them the access code to my house and never being able to change it…then knowing they could walk in anytime and fuck up my life."

She divulged the sorry tale of her past boyfriends, including embarrassing details, and Jason began to chuckle almost immediately.

"You aren't paranoid," he said when she'd finished. "I wouldn't have given those guys the code to my gym locker. But you do have terrible taste in men. It's not taste though, is it? You choose men too self-absorbed or stupid or drug-addled to pose a threat to you."

"I do not."

"Yeah, you do. Your college boyfriend, a Greek sculpture come to life, but only just barely? Ouch. The intern so into gaming he almost never took his headset off. The bodybuilding lawyer with the mirror-screen apartment. The wine snob. Look, I'm not judging. I've got a list of shitty boyfriends twice as long. Hiding your ability had nothing to do with those relationships not working out, though. You picked guys that wouldn't last."

Mia couldn't muster false indignation or anger. It was true. Not that she'd stamped an expiration date on any of the men she'd dated, but she'd known they weren't the types to pay close attention to their lovers. Because of that, she could relax. Because of that, she grew bored and irritated. Thankfully, she hadn't given Jason a timeline, but the trend line headed down. She'd not had a real relationship in the past five years.

"Do you want to hear mine?" Jason asked. "They're just as bad. When I first came out I hooked up with guys who treated me like shit. We didn't go on dates where they forgot what kind of pizza toppings I liked…"

Mia grimaced. The handsome Greek ordered olives every time though she despised them.

"We didn't go on dates. We had sex in the park. Don't get me wrong. I had fun, but I was really young. It took me awhile to realize other guys went to the holos or nice dinners. I didn't have a secret…I was the secret."

"Then things got better?"

"Yeah. Not great due to the social climate, but there's a place for everyone in a city as big as New York."

Mia went into the pavilion and retrieved the half-empty bottle of bourbon. Jason was a real friend. Maybe there was a reason she didn't have many. Maybe it had nothing to do with her memory and everything to do with her mother telling her not to trust her classmates. Jason was her latest classmate, and this time she *would* say the wrong thing.

"Things aren't getting better for me. The last guy I slept with—" She'd meant to tell him about Xander, then remembered he wasn't the last, only the last she remembered. She covered the pause with a swig from the bottle. "He's really young. Zero relationship potential. I'd like to get more serious with someone. I'm tired of being on my own." Saying that true thing was harder than it should have been, what with the mother in her head repeating over and over again that it wasn't safe. She took another drink and kept going.

"I can date in every sector now, but most people won't date me. The chicken farming photos are circulating, and I'm still fired from Han. Claire's done a great job remediating my records, but she can't stop the rumors."

"There are plenty of men out there well-versed in upper-floor politics who won't believe you raised chickens. Ya gotta give them a hint of the real you, though. Otherwise, it won't make sense."

"You and the rest of the team are the only people who know the real me."

"Barely," Jason said. "Talking to you is like watching someone calculate the best way out of a burning building."

Mia laughed. It was true. She tried to escape conversations unharmed. "It's taking me a while to relax. I don't know if getting fired from Han and working at Summit is the best or worst thing that's ever happened to me."

"It might be the best. You should have seen the smile on your face the day Lucas told you to add social engineering to our list of services. You love your profession but hated Han. Do you think there was any chance things there would have gotten better? No. The more you got promoted the worse it would have become until one day, you'd be asked to optimize the flow in a research lab where they were testing drugs on unwilling interns, and you'd have no one to call."

He was right. There probably was a lab, just like the one at Itek, on the dark floors of Han HQ. Optima wouldn't and couldn't do anything about it. Now at least she could help individual employees protect themselves from the forces pressing at the edges of the employment contracts, trying to find weak places. She could do good work at Summit.

As to her personal life…she'd need to do better work on that as well.

I've been lazy.

Xander and Lucas proved it, while Jason proved she could have an honest conversation with a man…if she let herself.

Chapter Twenty Six

As the tent deflated, so did Mia's spirits. She wanted to stay longer.

They loaded all rental gear back into the trailer and began the bumpy ride back to New Canberra. Jason, who'd decided it was his job to "finish" the beer before they arrived back in town, put up with her pouting for all of half a kilometer.

"You've got to stop calling everyone that isn't you, *normal people*. It's really irritating to be lumped in with every random asshole walking the streets, and no one considers themselves normal anyway. Most people the Six hire think they're freaking geniuses, and even they have something they're secretly embarrassed about."

Apparently, they'd reached a level of friendship where Jason felt comfortable telling her how wrong she was about everything. As they bounced down the rutted road toward New Canberra, trailer in tow, Jason moved from people to the planet.

"Victoria is a science experiment gone wrong. There are no old people. All the partners move back to Earth when they hit a certain age. There are almost no kids. No one has any serious mental or physical illnesses. You've lived in a bubble of healthy twenty to seventy-year-olds your whole life. That's not reality, and it's not the reality the people you've worked with experience when they move back to Earth after their contracts are up."

Jason held the dashboard with one hand and his beer with the other, only glancing at her occasionally, as if he was piloting the autonomous vehicle and had to watch the road.

"I'm well aware of the demographics on Victoria, and I went to college on Earth."

"Yeah, but you aren't getting my point. You don't feel connected to normal people because you haven't had many *normal-people* experiences. For you, it's all about metrics and optimization and control. The only reason we're here right now is because you were attacked and don't feel safe in the city, and that's normal. I heard sirens all day and night from my apartment in New York. Drunk teens got run over by pods with out-of-date software. People died from food poisoning from a local ramen shop. Buildings caught fire because some asshole charged his bioprinter on the wrong circuit. You—" he risked raising his hand from the imaginary steering wheel to point at her, "don't routinely experience any of that."

"No one should."

"I agree, but people do, and when they do, they reach out to each other, and it doesn't matter what job title they have, or if they even have a job. We have common experiences, and that makes us empathetic."

"So, I'm paranoid, uptight, a bad conversationalist, and an un-empathetic asshole?"

"Yes," he said, a tad too enthusiastically. "You are. I'm sorry you got stunned and hit with a poison dart, but that shit happens all the time to people in New York, and afterwards they triple-lock the door and binge-watch holos for a few weeks, talk it over with their friends, and then get on with their lives."

Mia gripped her own invisible steering wheel and resisted the urge to drive Jason off a cliff.

"You're mad," he said.

"Not at you."

She wouldn't split hairs. No one on Earth had ever been hit by a poison dart carefully constructed from hundreds of insect venoms. That said, could she have had friends like Jason her whole life she could open up to? Claire knew about her memory and secured their college apartment so Mia could be safe, and Mia hadn't even noticed. Jason was right.

I am a paranoid, uptight, bad conversationalist, un-empathetic asshole.

She'd been looking at the world through the glasses her mom forced on her when she was a kid. Which reminded her—she hadn't checked in on her mom in weeks, but then, her mom hadn't checked in on her either. She never did. Neither enjoyed the other's company, nor the unpleasant memories.

"It looks like you're mad at me," said Jason.

"I'm not." She pulled herself back to the present, back to the tumbled-down mountains and dazzling morning sun. "I'm really glad we did this, and I get your point about life on Victoria making people less... resilient. Still, I'd rather Earth take inspiration from us rather than the other way around. Once Derek analyzes that dart, I'm going to make sure Optima and each of the Six get a copy of the report. They'll update the scanners, and whoever shot me will get a big surprise the next time they try to get on a shuttle."

Even if zero crime was an impossible state, she'd work toward it. Summit could work toward that as well.

Though she wasn't looking forward to returning to the city, the desert had done its magic, reminding her that humans occupied a tiny fraction of the land, and she could see as far as she wanted in any direction... If she got her head out of her ass and looked.

Gone was the rage the crazy woman at The End had unleashed on Phil. Was it possible to uncork bottled fear and anger and have it explode and disappear? The partners who yelled always had more where that came from. On the other hand, she'd heard stories of people who'd had cathartic experiences. Perhaps she'd had a breakthrough, not a breakdown. Maybe Phil deserved to be punched. Maybe she had the same low-level of violence in her that Victoria did, and she needed to accept it.

She didn't want to go back to her old life.

A year ago, she was dreadfully unhappy—overworked, trapped under Erika's thumb, pride in her work disintegrating—with no idea how to escape. Nor the will. She pacified herself with clothes, jewelry, drugs, and one-night stands, and she might have lived the rest of her life like that. Erika did.

Since then, she'd built a business from the ground up. Not many people on Victoria could say that.

As for Friday night? No one cared about the fight at The End. Mikey might tease her, but she deserved it. She wouldn't overthink the sex with Lucas. She'd fallen in his lap in a thin silk skirt. She'd been riled up. It was an animal moment. Things would be awkward for a while, but soon his recollection of whatever happened between them in the pod would fade to what she imagined all memories were like for ordinary people—worn photos on translucent paper, soon covered by more of the same.

She was good at avoiding potentially painful situations. So good she'd classified most of life as too much of a risk to take part in. The images of herself that she'd seen played on the screen in Lucas's office showed someone wound too tight, so tight they could snap, get in a fight, and sleep with whoever they ended up in a pod with.

Someone desperately unhappy and lonely.

As aggravating as the team at Summit could be, they had shown her what it was like to work *with* people, not just near them. She was starting to understand what it could be like to have friends—someday maybe a lover—who knew about her memory and could deal with it. so she didn't have to lie.

I can do this.

Chapter Twenty Seven

Lucas started when Mia tapped on his open door Monday morning.

"Is the dart en route to Earth?" she asked.

"It is. How was your time off?" He sat stiffly, one hand gripping the closed fist of the other.

"Great. Exactly what I needed."

"Where'd you go?"

"Camping. You and Mikey should…never mind. It's beautiful out there, though."

He took a deep breath and squeezed his fist harder. "We have another social engineering job, if you want to take it. It's not security related. A restaurant in Weber sector wants to add more tables without adding waitstaff."

Mia laughed. She'd charged into work this morning ready to right wrongs, but Summit would have to stay in business for that to happen.

"I've spent the last six months in restaurants. I might as well cash in on my expertise."

"You seem more relaxed."

"I haven't been on a real vacation in years."

"Should we accept the job?"

"Yes. Listen…" She forced herself into the office and to sit. "I haven't been myself since I was fired from Han, and every time I feel like I'm getting a handle on things, something happens that knocks me off track." She forgave herself for blushing but vowed it would be the last time. "I admit I've missed my career, and the paycheck, but Jason got me thinking. The violence I've witnessed might be an anomaly, or maybe it's been happening since landing day, and I've been too wrapped up in my own issues to notice. I don't trust Claire's data that no one gets assaulted or dies here because I got assaulted and Tad almost died, and none of that info is getting published anywhere. It's painful to admit my planet isn't everything I thought it was, but I give up. Reality wins. Victoria isn't perfect. It's still light years better than Earth, and I intend to keep it that way. At Summit, I'm in a position to help people deal with whatever shit the Six throw at them. At Han I'd be the one throwing it."

Lucas relaxed his hands. "You did have a good vacation."

"I'll be taking more of them. No one should spend all their time in this city. We've got…" She'd been about to spout out the exact number of uninhabited square kilometers on the planet before remembering she was a bad conversationalist and an asshole. "Lots of places to explore."

"Take long weekends whenever you need to."

"I will."

In all the ways that mattered, she hadn't slept with Lucas. The encounter wasn't a pebble in her shoe causing hurt with every step. She couldn't replay what he perhaps regretted saying. She envied—not *normal* people, that was the asshole talking again—but everyone whose memories softened over time. That's what allowed friends and lovers to stay together. The sweet forgetting and the forgiveness that took root there.

"Mia?"

"Right. Back to work."

Lucas nodded, she nodded back, and had the strange sensation they'd gone from being strangers sitting next to each other on a bus to people travelling together. Not just him, but everyone at Summit. Their motivations might differ, but they shared the goal of making Victoria safer.

Back at her desk, Mia read up on Frederick Magnussen and Gert Richter, the men behind the lab that Lucas had called in NYCPD to shut down. Yes, Lucas could probably monitor her searches and would realize Jason had told her details of what happened at Itek but fuck it.

Frederick Magnussen III's father was the CEO of Titan Mining, the Earth corporation that botched the moon mining operation, enshrouding the moon in a haze that persisted to this day. Though the company had gone bankrupt in the wake of the scandal, Magnussen senior walked away with a fortune, having discreetly unloaded most of his stock in the company when the mining operation was first announced.

Magnussen the younger attended Harvard, an institution long past its prime, but one he had guaranteed entry to thanks to family ties. There, he was involved in a cheating scandal, forced to retake an entire semester of classes, and also accused of assault, a charge he settled out of court.

He'd been made a partner at Itek as soon as he'd graduated and should have made senior partner years ago. How long would Itek keep him around if he wasn't performing? Twice divorced, his second wife successfully sued to annul their prenuptial agreement and walked away with half his assets. Rumors suggested he might be in financial trouble.

Was the secret project at the lab a risky idea that, if it succeeded, would get him bumped up to senior partner status with its associated stock grants and salary increase?

That would never happen now. Magnussen was currently on leave due to an unspecified health condition, resting in his Park Avenue penthouse. Not a whisper of this condition possibly being house arrest fluttered the pages of the gossip magazines. How had he managed that? The Itek lawyers must be extremely intimidating.

Knowing corporate politics, Itek would be looking for someone to blame. Would it be Magnussen? Given his checkered past, they might sacrifice him. And they'd certainly do what they could to make an example of Lucas and Jason and Claire to discourage future whistleblowers. Though the city of New York hoped to protect them by sending them to Victoria, being banished to another planet without any credits would certainly look like punishment to a rank-and-file worker.

While Magnussen was a long skid mark visible to anyone, Richter was a shadow on the side of the road. He'd graduated from a private university in the Cayman Islands with a degree in PhyDiSec, had a mysteriously long period of unemployment after college, and was then hired by Itek into a more senior position than he would appear to have deserved.

The few photos and fewer mentions meant he kept an eye on information that circulated about him and eliminated what he didn't like. That he'd been so successful scared her. Discov, the search engine Summit used, crawled hundreds of thousands of data repositories, and even the most mild-mannered, well-behaved nine-year-old would have a rich history. Richter had, essentially, none.

Mia stared at the photos, trying to map Richter's face onto the person she'd seen in the hallway the weekend before she was fired and onto the man who'd stunned her, but the excellent resolution of these images was a hindrance. She'd been far away in one instance, and in the dark and on drugs in the other.

While Lucas and his team circumvented certain procedures to get to Victoria, Richter was under arrest on Earth and it would be next to impossible for him to get out of his apartment and onto a shuttle and into the spaceport. Lucas was right. Richter wasn't here, but another over-zealous Itek CorSec agent was, and he'd proven to be just as dangerous.

Derek's response to their request to analyze the dart was nearly instantaneous—just over a month. It would have taken a courier three weeks to travel to Earth and presumably a day or two to set up the delivery. Derek must have dropped everything to do the analysis once it arrived.

The rainbow hailstorm of pixels on Lucas's desk screen resolved into Derek, a huge smile on his face. He was dressed in a dark suit—a far cry from the white lab coat and gray pants he'd worn every day to work at Han so many years ago. Mia had never pictured him as an executive, but he seemed comfortable in the formal outfit.

His office was a mess. Half-dead plants sat atop boxes. Floor to ceiling shelves groaned under the weight of instruments and printouts and sculptures that looked like they might be awards.

"I'm sorry to have to get right to business but I've only got ninety minutes of encrypted calling in my budget each month. I'll give you a quick overview of the report I sent in case you have questions." Derek looked at the screen he held. "I worried about these venoms being weaponized, and it looks like that's what we have here. Is it a problem on Victoria?"

"Hasn't been until now," Lucas replied. "Not many people die here for any reason."

"Glad to hear it. This weapon would work as you surmised, Mia, all the toxins acting in concert to extinguish life, none lethal on their own. What you might not guess is that these venoms are synthetic…and made on Earth."

Mia said, "Made on Earth?" at the same time Lucas said, "Synthetic?"

"Yes. None of your Six are happy about this. They hoped to keep a monopoly, but samples of nearly every type of arthropod venom have made it back here. I'm glad they did," he said, waving to his shelf of might-be-awards. "I couldn't have done any of this without them."

"How do you know they're made on Earth?" Lucas demanded.

Derek chuckled. "They're watermarked, of course. It's quite simple to embed permanent watermarks into synthetic genes. Amino acids are used to comprise binary bits. I won't go into the details. I only do that when I'm trying to get out of a conversation at a cocktail party. More importantly, watermarks are required, so I can tell you that all these compounds came from the Martell Corporation in Barbados."

"Martell. Why do I know that name?" Lucas stared into the distance, massaging his chin.

"No surprise you've heard of them. They're infamous," Derek said. "In addition to its legitimate business dealings, Martell sells billions of dollars a year of highly regulated products to a local veterinary college. A very small veterinary college."

"A venom laundering scheme?" Mia asked.

"Yes, but more than venom. Anything and everything that can be synthesized."

"Of course," Lucas said. "Martell." He drummed his fingers on the desk. "They sell to corporations as well."

"Corporations, scientists, criminals…anyone who can afford it," Derek confirmed. "I'm ashamed to admit I've placed an order from time to time. It's so difficult to get what I need through the university. It takes months and a dozen signatures, or I can get it overnight from Martell."

"Do you know who bought the toxins in the dart?" Lucas asked.

"No idea. The watermark is on everything they sell."

Part of Mia was relieved. This blight on Victoria *was* imported from Earth and could be deported.

Wait a second…imported from Earth?

She stood, startling Derek and Lucas. "Can you send us the report?"

"I already did. Lucas has it."

A knock sounded on a wooden door in faraway Austin. Derek looked left.

"I should go. I've got a meeting with the department chair. We can chat again if you have any questions after you've read the report. Mia, call me even if you don't. We need to catch up."

He gave a mock salute and disconnected.

Mia spoke as soon as he did. "What the hell is going on? Did Martell sell venom to Itek? Is that what they were using in that lab?"

Lucas slid his chair back, retreating from her accusatory finger. "What are you talking about?"

"The illegal R&D lab you were investigating at Itek. Did they buy venom from Martell?"

Lucas was probably trying to recall what he'd told her, but he had an ordinary memory and would be stumbling around conversations they'd had like a traveler in an unfamiliar hotel room at midnight. She'd save him some time.

"Jason said it was a drug testing lab and that they'd been grabbing people off the streets and injecting them with something. Was it synthetic insect venom?"

"I don't know. We didn't understand the data we collected. We aren't scientists."

"You don't need a PhD to read the name *Martell Corporation* on a list. Has Sergeant Johnson told you anything?"

"No. If this ever goes to trial, I'll be hooked to a veracity detector. NY-CPD and AGE don't want me disqualified as a witness. I've no idea what they've culled from all the information Claire collected."

Mia pulled on her glasses. "Why haven't you forwarded the report? I want to see it."

"I don't want that data in your head."

"It doesn't matter if I see the formula. This shouldn't be a secret. Derek can send the dart to the NYCPD investigators in case it matches something Itek was working on in the lab. Plus, we need to get the data to Sergei at The Center so he can recalibrate his sensors. He can forward it to Optima without saying where it came from so the strataport scanners can be updated as well."

"Slow down. Derek had to break apart the dart to analyze it, so there's nothing to send. I agree with you in theory that it would be good to let Optima know but—"

"Every time something bad happens, you have a reason why we can't tell the authorities."

"There are no authorities here."

"I'm going to send the report to Sergei. He can get it to the right people."

"What if he gets it to the wrong people, and they start manufacturing the toxin? I'm not sending you the report. I'll decide how to handle this."

"No, you won't," she said. She pulled open the door and strode into the main room.

Lucas followed.

"Everyone," Mia said. *Everyone* at the moment consisted of Jason, Claire, and Lucas. "You've all got admin privileges on our system. I'm the only one who doesn't and hurt feelings aside, it makes it hard for me to do my job. I've been waiting for the magical day when you'd grant me access as a symbol of trust. Still waiting."

Jason put down the stunner he'd been assembling.

"What's even more ludicrous is that Lucas believes he has the power to deny me access to a file." Mia gave him a level stare. "You want me to be myself and not hold back? Fine."

Claire had an extremely complicated password, but over these many months Mia had inadvertently gotten a glimpse of bits of it until the pieces fit together to make the whole. She'd never used it until now.

She typed it quickly, then triple-tapped to put her glasses into 3D mode. The password was just the first step, granting access to the real security feature—the object orientation room.

The room was pure Claire. A small living room, shades drawn, a board game on the coffee table, a carton of wontons, three cans of stim soda, a battered couch strewn with blankets. She'd observed Claire making the same synchronized movements day after day, and now she was in the place where the motions mattered.

Mia sat—Claire was always sitting—and held out her arm in the same position she'd seen Claire do and reached forward until her fingers brushed the chopsticks sticking from the Chinese takeout.

Yes. Here. The gestures flowed from that point.

She grasped the chopsticks and used them to pick up a small pewter figure of a warrior. She set him on the other side of the board, laid the chopstick on either side of him, then…what was Claire doing when she clenched and raised her fists?

Ah…the blanket.

She pulled the plaid wool blanket to her chest. The room vanished and a list of files appeared. *Success.* She sent them to display on the large screen above the hallway door that normally cycled through images from the security cams.

"Get out of there!" Claire yelped.

Mia hurriedly made herself an admin before Claire could boot her. With a few swipes, she found the mail server and Lucas's account, located the message from Derek, opened the report, paged through it, and sent it to herself. She was about to log out when a name jumped out at her. Erika Brunhoff. The message was from last week.

What the hell?

Lucas and Jason exchanged a guilty glance.

"Why is Erika mailing you?"

"She's a client," Lucas said.

"You've got to be fucking kidding. She—"

"She gave me documentation not just about which records of yours were altered, but copies of the records before their alteration. Thanks to this, Claire has been able to restore almost everything. We planned to present you with a clean bill of health once she finished."

Why did things have to be so complicated? Couldn't she just hate Erika, enjoy this moment where she was proving she couldn't be held back, and revel in her new admin powers?

"Why did she hire us?"

"Same as all our clients. Privacy in her home. She's definitely been targeted. The ADM Jason installed is working overtime."

"We've never had a Han client outside the mining division."

"Our business is all word of mouth. Brunhoff wouldn't have known we'd existed if it wasn't for you."

True. What did it mean? Was spying endemic in all divisions of Han?

An awkward silence followed.

I just hacked Claire's impenetrable room, granted myself admin powers, and retrieved a document Lucas didn't want me to see. Erika is a client and helped undo the harm she'd inflicted upon me...

"We need to restructure this business," Mia said, surprising everyone including herself. "Lucas shouldn't own Summit. We're all equal players. This has to be a partnership and decisions made by consensus. We've just gotten the dart composition report back from Derek. I'd like to give it to Sergei at The Center so he can train the front door scanners to recognize it, and I'd like him to pass the data on to Optima. It won't be traced back to us. I'll make sure of it. All in favor?"

Mia raised her hand. Jason's went up immediately after. Claire folded her arms.

"I'm sorry I broke into your account, Claire. I swear I've never been in it before, and I won't go in again, but you've all been sloppy around me. I could have logged in as Jason as well. If you don't want me to remember something, don't let me see it. For now, will you agree that people need to know there's a new type of weapon on Victoria?"

Her scowl didn't lessen, but she nodded.

"Great," Mia said. "I'll take care of it. Also, we should start having weekly staff meetings. I'm pretty sure that up until now, everything's been decided by Lucas and Mikey after a sparring match at the gym."

Jason snorted. "I second the co-op and staff meeting ideas. I don't know why we're all pretending like we still work at Itek and Lucas is our boss. We brought *you* here," he said, indicating Lucas with a taut finger. "You could barely walk when we left Earth. Mikey had to pretend you were drunk. I've been more instrumental in building this business than you have. None of us is ever going to work for a major corporation again. I'd like to have *business owner* on my resume."

Lucas, to Mia's surprise, seemed more bemused than angry. "I agree. We should restructure. It will make it easier for Mia to take over when we leave. Do you mind if I keep my office? Or should we take turns?"

"You keep it," Mia said. "We're happy where we are."

Mia hadn't intended to publicize the plans she'd been mulling over, but Lucas's refusal to let her see the dart report flipped a switch. Why had she played by his rules? The title of *Partner* bewitched her even though he didn't hold it anymore.

Jason gave her a thumbs-up and a big smile once Lucas retreated and shut his door a bit too loudly. "I don't know where that came from, but you're my hero."

"We all need rescuing, and I haven't been doing my part."

"You know what?" Jason stood and lifted his chin. "I'm staying. We can run the business together. Fuck Earth. I'll show up to testify if the AGE pays for round-trip passage, but I'm coming back. I don't have a job there. I hate my family, and I'm banned from most retail establishments in New York City. My last boyfriend dumped me for one of my previous boyfriends. Yeah, I left all my tools in my apartment, but I've already got most of what I need here."

Claire stripped off her glasses. "I don't want to go back either, not even to testify. I'm never getting on a starship again. Those were the worst three weeks of my life. The burst drive fired up every hour and made my stomach flip, and the ship was too crowded. It's true New Canberra is essentially a shopping mall—but at least it's spacious. Only four hundred thousand people on the planet? Yes, please. I like my apartment here. No one wants a below-ground unit so I'm paying half what I was in New York, and it's twice the size."

Mia had never been to Claire's apartment—never even wondered where it was. Was that login screen her real place?

"Are you two serious? You want to stay and run the business together?" Mia felt lightheaded, as if she'd just done a stim and stood up too fast.

Claire shrugged. "I live here now. I found a group of gamers who are worthy opponents. I can get anything delivered at any hour. It isn't considered odd that I never want to go outside. The connectivity is great, and trying to hack into the Six undetected could be my life's work. I'll have some of my stuff shipped here after the trial, but overall, I'm good."

Mia glanced at Lucas's door. He wasn't good and wouldn't stay. Being a partner at Itek meant a top-floor penthouse, handcrafted furniture, closets full of bespoke suits, a vacation home, and God knew what else. She could flip through pages of Earth-made luxuries and imagine what Lucas owned and what it must be like to have all that waiting back there while he lived on Victoria in a garage. *Slumming.* Maybe that's what he'd call it. Maybe his night with her had been slumming it as well…

Fuck Lucas and fuck all the partners who considered people and even a planet something to chew up and consume to fuel their own ambitions. She'd make this business work.

Chapter Twenty Eight

Mia sat with Sergei on the top of the world, sipping vodka.

A domed lounge crowned the pinnacle of the shell that was The Center. The view was spectacular—the glittering headquarters' towers ringed the dark parkland, lights sparkling in the waves of rising post-sunset heat. On the rare days the space wasn't rented out and Summit did a meeting onsite, Sergei would send her a thumbs-up message, and she'd make an excuse to the team after they finished and meet him by the service elevator behind his office.

"This place is never free on a Friday night. What happened?"

Mia reclined on the purple velvet Didion sofa—shoes off, of course—and held her glass out for a refill. Sergei obliged. They were only a quarter of the way done with the vodka, and Sergei always insisted they finish the whole thing—though he did most of the drinking.

"The partner decided to go to Novus instead for a ski weekend. So, now we get to eat and drink his cocktail party."

Shrimp on ice, tiny quiches, charcuterie from France, and a dozen other hors d'oeuvres were artfully arranged on the low coffee table the couch wrapped around.

"You should have let me invite the team. We can't eat all this."

"Your pretty boss with his nose in the air? The big man looking at me like he wants to fight? The nervous technician who doesn't look at me at all? I don't like them. I am sorry you have to work with them."

Mia laughed. Lucas felt the same way about Sergei and disapproved of her spending time with him in a way that pleased her. She'd tried to explain he was the uncle she'd never had, and Lucas had raised an eyebrow and shaken his head. *Keep your stunner close,* he advised.

Sergei undid his tie and knocked back the shot. "What a week I had. Thank you for that toxin data. We had two alerts this week. I can't tell you who," he said as Mia half raised herself from the couch. "They were not happy, but you can't argue with the front door. She doesn't let you in, that's that. No explanation needed. They can pretend it was a mistake. Say they took Nightshade earlier, and it's still in their system. No one judges." Sergei tapped the side of his head. "I judge. Those people can't book rooms here in the future. We are always full."

"Did you get in touch with your colleague at Optima?"

"Yes, finally. You understand I had to wait until she came here for another reason. Her group booked a meeting last week. I gave her the data and implied that our scanner had discovered it. They are retraining their AIs and letting the Six know as well. This weapon won't be used again."

Mia relaxed. "Thank you. I'll sleep better tonight."

"Can I ask how you discovered it?"

"I discovered it in my shoulder," Mia said.

Sergei scowled. "You should not be working at Summit Security. They are idiots. Come, work for me. I'll find a place for you. We can use a social engineer."

Mia hand poised above the shrimp, paused. "Really?"

"Of course! I know you ran into trouble at Han, but your old boss—Brunhoff—she is here all the time. Scheming. I see it in her eyes. I don't trust her. You, I trust."

The Center would be the perfect venue for Erika. Mia remembered how she behaved at HQ events—scanning the room for cameras, conversation shield at the ready, leading whoever she was trying to chat up to the only corner of the room with a bit of privacy. Now that she had all she wanted here, what would she do?

"Thanks for the offer. I'm committed for the near-term, but after that? Our charter could be revoked, the Six might decide private security is a bad idea… Who knows? Let's talk more when I'm not drunk."

Jason and Claire were gung ho about running Summit with her, but what if the Itek case was settled out of court? What if they got a fat settlement and were no longer banned from retail establishments? What if Claire grew nostalgic about the vintage board games she had tucked under her bed?

"Of course. This is Friday night. We are off work and don't talk business. We drink."

Sergei held up his glass, and she met it with a clink.

"He offered you a job? What did you say?" Lucas looked up from the screen he'd been reading from.

Mia suppressed a smile. She hadn't intended to tell Lucas about the offer, but when he'd officiously instructed her to retrieve equipment from Han clients whose contracts were expiring, something in her snapped. He was still "figuring out" how to restructure Summit without losing the charter, still giving orders, and she was still mired in petty tasks.

Sure, they'd had a few more social engineering jobs, but they'd been nothing more than literally arranging tables and chairs on a restaurant patio or playing with sound and light to keep guests from lingering in a corridor. Nothing at the scale she was used to. She needed time to build that side of the business.

"I told Sergei not now. I want to see how this plays out."

"Why are you smiling?" Lucas asked.

She grinned because he was annoyed at Sergei for giving her options and underlining her worth. "Oh, it's just, be careful what you wish for. I wanted things to calm down, to have a normal job, and now I've got it. Our new clients are so dull."

They were. The clients from sectors other than Han weren't being spied upon. The appliance data monitors never got strange signals. There were no holo cams hidden in bedrooms, no bugs in the carpet. Everything was just as it should be—as it was promised in the contracts and the brochures.

"You seem…better. You've been climbing?"

"Yes, outdoors. There's a group that maintains a face below that restaurant outside of town, 360 Degrees. After 2 p.m. it's in shade. They've got a laser system that zaps all the bugs and a MMARV onsite to deal with anything that flies in while we're climbing. It's a lot of fun. You should—" she caught herself. "You should try it once you're a level five. If you're still doing the wall?"

"I am. I'm a three now."

"That was fast. You're a natural."

"I…is it a rule that you have to be a level five?"

"It is. Liability issues."

He lingered by her desk, an awkward silence stretching. This happened from time to time, and Mia waited it out. Whatever he wanted to say, he never did say it, and Mia understood why. She'd created so many rules around What Must Not Be Mentioned—everything from her memory to the sex—that he was probably worried if he asked the time in the wrong tone of voice, she might storm out the door. Now, thanks to Sergei, she had somewhere to storm to and they both knew it.

"The equipment," he finally said. "I'm having Jason pick up most of it, but some of our clients don't want to give it up. They won't return his calls. I need…" he waved a hand. "Diplomacy? A friendly face?"

"You've got a friendly face, sometimes."

He actually smiled. "These are clients you've met. They'll let you in. If we don't get this equipment back, we can't sign new contracts."

A few months ago, she'd have refused to go into Han sector, but everything seemed back to normal now. Erika was a client and had no reason to speak ill of her or Summit. Claire had remediated all Mia's falsified records, so anyone trying to find proof of the allegations against her would be at worst puzzled and at best, assume there'd been an error.

"I'll try," Mia said. Lucas nodded, lingered for another awkward few seconds, then went back to his office.

The first name on the alphabetical list, Dezzie Adeyemi, was one of their first clients and one she suspected had sold something that wasn't his.

She called him—best to try that before banging on his door—and it was a long minute before he answered. He looked like he'd just woken up, though it was late afternoon.

It took him a moment to place her. "Mia. From Summit Security. What do you want? Did my payment not go through?"

"It went through fine. Your contract is up, and we need to get our conversation shield back."

"I forgot I had it. I'll bring it with me to Unlimited tonight if you want to stop by and pick it up. You know where that is?"

She did. It was in Setty-Sarin sector—not Han, fortunately. The game bar was infamous for its unbearable noise—explosions, gunshots, roaring engines, death metal music—and patrons screaming to be heard above it all. She hadn't been there in years and was sorry to learn it was still in business. She agreed to meet him at 8 p.m.

Dezzie sat by himself at a small table. He'd been there for a while, she guessed, from the three empty glasses beside the pint he was currently downing. That was a lot of beer for someone his size. He didn't get up.

"Hey. Want a drink?" He spoke slowly, speech slurred.

"No thanks. I'm on my way to the gym."

He made no move to hand over the conversation shield, and his morose expression begged a polite inquiry.

She sighed and sat in the chair next to him. "Everything okay?"

"No. I got transferred."

"To another division?"

"I wish. To a mining project in the intemperate zone. They need staff and…" He fished around in his pocket, pulled out the conversation shield, and turned it on. Not that they needed it in this din.

He leaned in. "I was forced to volunteer for it. I don't want to go."

"How were you forced?" Mia asked. Most people's contracts included a clause about working conditions and location, so you didn't have to worry about signing up for an office job then ending up on a fishing boat.

Dezzie began to shred a wet napkin. "You know how I hired you to watch out for me at that meeting? I didn't tell you what was really going on. I sold that man a list of Han parts suppliers. I didn't think it was a big deal. Anyone in the company can access that information. A few weeks ago, I got a message listing all the rules I'd violated. Selling trade secrets, transporting private company data across sector lines. The sender said I was a criminal. If I didn't volunteer for the project, they'd tell my supervisor what I'd done and I'd lose my job and pension. I head south tomorrow." He paused, a tragic look on his beautiful, young face. "I don't know where I'm going or how long I'll be gone. I don't want to go to the intemperate zone. It's not safe."

The gears in Mia's head spun madly. A dangerous project no one would willingly sign up for. Scientists, monitored in their homes for no apparent reason. Dr. Lerner's family threatened so he'd sign a new contract…

"Did you offer the list of parts suppliers, or did that man reach out to you?" Dezzie didn't seem the type to mastermind the sale.

He struggled to remember. Staccato bursts of machine gun fire seemed to break his concentration.

"I didn't know the guy. He sat down next to me at a bar, and we started talking about gaming. I told him how much I wanted the new Zibo game chair. That's two years' salary for someone like me. He said he needed some information from Han, nothing secret, and if I got it to him, he'd transfer enough credits to me for the chair. I was skeptical, but when I heard what he wanted, I said yes."

"How could anyone prove it was you that gave it to him?"

"I didn't realize everything I download from work has my ID embedded in it. And that PDS…I erased it before I put the supplier list on it, but I guess I didn't fully erase it. I'm not a tech."

"If you'd told us you wanted to transfer data anonymously, we could have helped."

"I know," he muttered.

"Has anyone else you know been recruited for this project?"

"I have no idea. I signed a really strict NDA, and I'm not supposed to discuss this with anyone, even coworkers. I think a few others from my group might be going because they've been handing off their project work."

Did he realize he was discussing it with her?

He hiccupped. "I don't want to go. They say our communications will be limited while we're there, but I'm afraid we might be completely cut off. The PM told me I should set up all my bills for automatic payment for the next few months 'just in case.' I can't be offline for months! I'm in the semifinals in my game league. My mother is furious. She thinks I'm going to Earth for vacation and trying to avoid visiting her. My roommate will take over my bedroom, I'm sure of it. I probably won't have a place to live when I get back."

This is what I've been waiting for.

The team at Summit had been running their hands over a dark shape for months, unable to determine its true size or nature. Excitement lifted her from the chair.

"I'm sorry Dezzie, I've got to go." She snatched up the conversation shield. "Don't drink too much."

He blinked at her, eyes unfocused. "What? Wait. Is there something I can rent from you so I can get on the network wherever I am?"

"If Han doesn't want you to communicate with the outside world, they can make sure you don't. Be safe and give us a call when you get back. I'm sure everything will be fine."

She wasn't sure everything would be fine but it wouldn't help Dezzie to know it.

She hurried out, caught a pod back to the office, and banged on Lucas's apartment door.

"What's wrong? You okay?" He surveyed the hall, stunner in hand, shirt unbuttoned.

"I'm fine. I learned something from Dezzie."

Lucas set down the stunner and began to button his shirt.

She stepped away and focused on her bag until he was dressed. "You want to meet in your office?"

"Here's fine." Once his shirt was safely back in work configuration, he gestured for her to enter.

The large room was more lived-in than the last time she'd seen it. Almost messy. A detailed map of the city was tacked to the wall above an equipment-strewn table where a small projectile weapon lay in pieces, soldering gun smoking beside it. Remnants of actual, from-scratch cooking lay scattered on the counters of the kitchen nook—smashed cloves of garlic, onion skins, an empty pasta box, dirty knives and pans. The partially unmade bed had clearly held only one person last night, the right side neatly tucked in.

Lucas cleared his throat. She ceased gawking.

"What did you find out from Dezzie?" he asked.

She took a seat at the kitchen table and poured out everything she'd learned and added her own speculation that their client's houses had been bugged to gather blackmail material.

"Our clients don't have much in common other than working in the same division, and that's because you need all kinds of people to run a big mining project. Scientists, engineers, administrators. And you can't force anyone to work in the intemperate zone. That's in everyone's contract. No one came to Victoria to live in a tent out in the middle of nowhere."

Lucas picked up a screen and ran through the Han client list, nodding. "It makes sense. If Han wants to move an innovative product from prototype to production without anyone leaking project details or selling critical info to a competitor, they'd set up a completely secure facility outside the city. Itek routinely locked down whole floors for months. No one left the building or communicated with the outside world until the product launched."

He took a deep breath and let it out, relaxing back into the chair. "This is good news. It explains why things have quieted down over the past few months. We were interfering with their recruiting, and that phase is over. The project is starting. We might be in the clear. This calls for a toast."

He grabbed a bottle of scotch and two glasses from a makeshift bar on a bookcase and poured a healthy serving into each. "I know you aren't a fan but it's all I've got. To surviving."

He lifted his glass.

Mia picked up her own. "I think we should aim a little higher."

Lucas smiled. "We should." He raised his glass a few centimeters more toward the ceiling.

Mia took a drink after they clinked glasses. Scotch still tasted like dirty socks. "What happens next?"

"Dezzie and his friends work like dogs for a few months in some newly built office park in the middle of godforsaken nowhere, and soon thereafter, Han announces they've found a way to change granite into gold, or sand into a superconductor. Dezzie gets a bonus, and no one complains about being blackmailed or the unsafe working conditions."

"It shouldn't be hard to figure out who's in charge of this."

Lucas made a noncommittal head wag. "I know that by 'in charge' you mean the person controlling the person who fired the dart. It doesn't work like that. A partner comes up with a product or process that will make credits. The work needs to take place in the intemperate zone. She hands the list of the staffing needs to a senior director and says to make it happen. Some people can be nudged with a bonus or promotion, but others refuse. That's when other tactics come into play."

"Tactics?"

"Yes, tactics like hidden holocams and dragging people off roads and poison darts. Tactics that I worked hard to stop when I worked at Itek and," he waved his hand to indicate the room, "here's my reward. I don't mean to be cavalier. I know you want to find out who harmed you. I'm more interested in making sure it never happens again."

"It will help to know what happened this time."

"Agreed."

"You can't drag X number of people from the city and not have lovers and spouses complaining. Dezzie told me everything after two beers. The project will be common knowledge by end of week."

"That it's happening, yes, but details, no. This is something big. The care Han is taking to staff this reminds me of that mineral mine in Venezuela. One of my first jobs at Itek was to secure it."

"I thought you were protecting an oil field."

"Oh, we were. More importantly, we were also safeguarding a coltan mine. Coltan is a mineral you might not have heard of, but it's refined into a metal known as tantalum which is used in the circuitry in guidance control systems in smart bombs. It's worth far more than oil."

"Did Jason know about that? He was with you."

"Of course not. Almost no one knew. There was a civil war raging around us. Both sides wanted control of strategic resources, including oil fields, but there were hundreds of oil fields and ours wasn't the highest producer. Had they known what was really in the ground, we'd have been slaughtered."

"Do you think Han found a valuable mineral here?"

"If they did, there'd be no reason to hide the mining of it. Han owns their land, and they can do what they want, as long as it doesn't have an impact on planetary health."

"Doesn't it seem like more than a coincidence that thugs from Itek were developing dangerous drugs and weapons, possibly with supplies from Martell, and then a dart with venom made by Martell shows up here?" Mia took another sip. The scotch tasted a bit better.

"If Dr. Singh is buying from Martell that means everyone is. All corporations and governments have their own thugs and bioweapons labs. This isn't an Itek incursion. We'll keep an eye on whatever Han is doing in the desert. As you said, it'll be common knowledge by the end of the week. In the meantime, we need to get our equipment back before our former clients vanish. How far down the list are you?"

"Just Dezzie."

"Can you do Tanaka next? Jason can't get ahold of her, and she has an ADM, a dozen conversation shields, and God knows what else. You've got her private number. Call her tomorrow."

Mia glanced at her glass. Empty. Lucas's was as well. Liquor and frank conversation—she craved more of both, but what was she still doing here? She'd delivered the news and needed to leave. Now.

She stood abruptly, and the metal chair shrieked as it slid across the concrete floor.

"Thanks for the drink. I've got to go."

"To the gym?"

Mia's mind, normally full to overflowing, was blank. She had no plans. Lucas, mercifully, gave her a pass.

"It's been a long week. Call Tanaka on Monday. I'll do some more research on this mystery project, and we can regroup Monday afternoon."

Mia was out the door and down the hall before he finished the sentence.

Chapter Twenty Nine

Is this birdsong or a bad connection? Mia puzzled over the screeches coming from her screen. "Ms. Tanaka? It's Mia, from Summit Security."

The blackness of blocked video jerkily resolved into blue and green squares, then a scene from a dreamy tropical vacation advertisement. Tanaka lay on a chaise longue in a red and white hibiscus print swimsuit, a turquoise pool behind her, palm trees swaying above.

"Mia! I'm so glad you called."

Between the shrieks of the birds Mia heard the crash of ocean waves. "Where are you?"

Tanaka laughed. Her severe haircut had devolved into a messy shag.

"Hawaii. Big Island. My family has a place here."

She was tan and relaxed, nothing like the tense partner Mia had last spoken to.

"You're on vacation?"

"Nope. We moved back. Best decision ever."

"I thought you had—"

"I had contractual obligations I needed to fulfill in order to fully vest my stock, blah blah blah." Tanaka opened and shut her fingers like a cranky bird talking. "Fuck them. It's only money. I've got plenty of that already."

A child careened in from the left side of the frame and did a cannonball into the pool.

Children on Earth could jump so much higher than those on Victoria. Mia tore her attention from him. "You have some equipment of ours that I need to get back."

Tanaka nodded. "We had to leave it connected so we could get away safely. I'll send you access codes for the flat and let the staff know you'll be by. The equipment will still be there. The flat is leased until the end of the year. As a matter of fact, enjoy the place. Have a party, move in, whatever you want. Honestly Mia, if you hadn't disrupted that meeting, I might not be here now. That project—" She took a sip from a glass of what looked like iced tea. "Was there fallout from Summit doing the meeting for me?"

When Mia didn't answer Tanaka removed her sunglasses and stared up at the screen. "What happened?"

Mia gave a noncommittal shrug. "A lot of not very good things, but most of them have nothing to do with you. Can I ask you something?"

Tanaka glanced at the pool, where the young boy screamed and splashed.

"I might not be able to answer."

"I understand. Do you know anything about Han employees being pressured to volunteer for a mining project in the intemperate zone?"

Tanaka scowled. "I suppose that's one way of putting it. Stay as far away from that as you can. Don't ask questions, don't get in the way. Very few people know the scope of the project, and I sacrificed a pile of stock options to ensure I wasn't one of them. They were trying to get me to invest, and that meeting was when they planned to share the details—and likely threaten me and my family if I didn't buy in. After Jason came to my home and showed how they were using my appliances to spy on me, I knew we couldn't stay. I picked the kids up from school and had my husband meet me at the Regency Hotel in Weber sector. We hired movers to pack our things, and we were on the next ship back to Earth." She put her glasses back on. "That's all I can tell you. I wish—"

Her frown transformed into a beaming smile. "We left some furniture and other things in the apartment. It'd cost more to ship it back than to buy it again. You can have any of it. Keep it, sell it, do whatever you want. Consider it a bonus."

Tanaka shrieked when the boy, soaking wet, leapt onto her. "Theo! Get off! Momma's working."

He turned toward the screen and stuck out his tongue.

"Mia, it was great catching up, but I've got to go. I'd say call again soon…but don't. You understand?"

Mia nodded. Tanaka cut the connection.

Paradise vanished.

Mia froze when the elevator doors opened onto Tanaka's apartment, ignoring Jason's mutter of complaint and Lucas's query.

Tanaka hadn't left some of the furnishings, she'd left nearly everything. Only a few dented places in the carpet indicated a piece had been removed. Mia moved slowly toward the centerpiece of the room—a low-slung, L-shaped Abruzzo sofa. Yes, it had a few juice stains and she had to brush off bits of orange crackers before she sat, but it was an Abruzzo. Handcrafted in Italy. Plush velvet in stunning, jewel-like greens and blues. Worth at least twenty thousand credits even in the shape it was in. She closed her eyes and caressed the fabric.

"I want this."

"It's all yours," Lucas said.

Tanaka had sent a hastily written but official transfer of ownership for the contents of the apartment along with the codes to enter. Mia had expected to find a few inexpensive oversized pieces that wouldn't be worth shipping back to Earth. Instead, she was surrounded by a treasure trove of carefully curated modern and vintage furnishings.

She leaned forward and placed her hands reverently on the glass-topped coffee table.

"This is a Noguchi."

Lucas, bemused, stood above her. "I know. I have one. I didn't think you cared about furniture. Your apartment is so spare."

"I do care. I can't afford well-made things that feel as good as they look. I can see everything," she made the swirling motion Jason used to indicate her memory, "but I don't remember touch."

"Memories never change, but every time you touch, it's new."

She looked up sharply. The way Lucas said it sounded like he was quoting her, but she'd never said that.

"Let me guess," Jason said, setting his black bag on the table with a clunk. "Everything in here is made by a designer and worth buckets of credits."

Mia jumped up and grabbed the bag. "That's right, so keep your tools on the floor."

"Yes ma'am."

Mia followed him to the master bedroom, tastefully decorated in gray and tan, and tried to absorb the scope of the gift Tanaka had given her. The charcoal angora Monique Voss throw blanket draped across a modernist walnut and leather Artzi chair smelled of vanilla. Mia wrapped it around herself even though it was quite warm in the room.

"You're acting very strange," Jason said as he began disconnecting the ADM in the walk-in closet.

"I'm not going to grow old and die in a tent in the desert," Mia said, collapsing into the chair, which was more comfortable than it looked. "They confiscated my retirement account when they fired me from Han. I might be the first person to grow old on this planet, and we've got no safety nets. If I sell all this furniture and make some smart investments, I get to live indoors and eat when I'm a hundred."

"You really think all this stuff is worth that much?"

She threw off the blanket, eager to explore the rest of the place. "I'll let you know."

Two hours later, giddy with excitement and relief, Mia had an inventory of the contents of the twelve-room apartment. She'd keep the Abruzza sofa and Noguchi coffee table and offered the rest of the team their pick of the less valuable furniture. Mikey wanted the huge king bed from the master suite, Jason, the sturdy oak table in the breakfast nook, and Claire, the beat-up couch in the playroom and a strange standing lamp that looked like it was made of stacked vertebrae.

Mia found Lucas in the study, lounging in apparent rapture in a Corona Automated Comfort Plus desk chair. It was worth quite a lot, even used.

"I used to have one of these," he said.

"You can have this one. The desk as well."

"I'd feel like I was snatching food from your future mouth."

Mia hadn't realized he'd overheard her.

"Don't worry about it. I feel like *I'm* stealing. Thank God Tanaka and her husband had a taste for expensive, hard-to-ship furniture."

Jason walked by the open door holding a pile of pale purple towels. "You're sure I can have these? And the sheets?"

"Absolutely. I can't resell those."

"Don't you want them? Six-hundred thread count Egyptian cotton. They're like silk but better."

"Leave me one set."

She eased herself down into the comforting folds of a sheepskin-covered K.D. armchair. Worth five thousand credits—if she didn't spill anything on it between now and when the consignment dealer arrived next Wednesday. "We don't have Santa on Victoria but I feel I woke from a dream and it's Christmas morning."

"You don't want to keep more of it?" Lucas levered himself upright.

"Of course I do, but I'm going to be moving as soon as my lease ends and it won't be to a big place."

"You love your apartment."

He said this with an odd certitude though Mia knew for a fact they'd never discussed the subject.

"I love the view, and I can get that in another sector on a ring further out at half the price. I don't want to live in Han anymore."

"Probably for the best. Weber…"

Lucas may have been about to suggest she move there, then realized he knew nothing about the real estate market.

"You like to cook," she said. "Take anything you want from the kitchen, aside from the bamboo-handled sushi knives." Tanaka must have forgotten she'd brought the antiques with her to Victoria, or she'd have grabbed them along with her kids. The set would fund a quarter of Mia's retirement.

"I wouldn't mind having the pans and…"

He slumped his shoulders, rubbed his head, and looked away. Embarrassment. Mia had only seen it a few times on him and wasn't sure how to respond.

"I can't sell the small appliances. I might take the blender. You can have the rest."

"I'd like the spices. I can't find most of them here. Tanaka must have brought them with her from Earth."

"Of course." Why was he embarrassed? Ah—they were used. The equivalent of picking food off someone else's plate in a fancy restaurant. Something a partner would never conceive of doing. "Help yourself to anything but the knives."

"Thanks. I will."

The chair assisted as he rose, lifting the seat and the armrests. "I'm relieved you got this windfall. If things settle down now that this secret Han mining project is up and running, we can build our business in the other sectors and give ourselves a raise."

"We can talk about that during the next team meeting."

Her low salary, which just hours earlier had felt like a weight dragging her slowly toward financial ruin, was now little more than an irritation. Tanaka's gift gave her time and space to breathe and plan. She would be okay.

Chapter Thirty

Erika sat ramrod straight in what Mia considered Lucas's booth at The End, smoking a stim cigarette. Her hands shook. No surprise, given the six spent plastic tubes scattered around her empty martini glass.

Mia watched for a few moments before approaching. She'd almost ignored the screen when she'd seen the ID, but Erika had provided accurate copies of all Mia's documents, pre-alteration. Thanks to that, Claire had remediated all the records, and Mia's official past was back to what it should be. The burning hate she'd felt for the woman had burned itself out, leaving a cold, ashy void.

Erika was even more undone than the last time Mia had seen her, though you'd have to know her well to recognize the signs. Sloppy drunk was Erika under a bit of stress. This rigid, expensively dressed woman with perfect hair and perfect makeup was Erika in extreme crisis mode. The regulars gave her a wide berth—none of the tables near the booth were occupied.

Mia caught the eye of the bartender and raised an invisible glass to her lips. He nodded then gave Erika a disapproving glare.

Erika started when Mia slid into the booth. She'd been trying to spear an olive in the martini glass with the toothpick it'd fallen from.

"I didn't think you'd come."

Mia shrugged. "I almost didn't."

"I'm in trouble." Erika reached up as if to smooth her hair then forced her hand back to the dirty table. "You…Summit, I mean, helped secure my apartment but it wasn't enough. Someone went back to Earth to dig up dirt on me."

"Back up. I don't know why you hired us. I didn't even know you were a client until recently. What's going on?"

Erika tried to shake a single cigarette from the pack and three spilled onto the table. Two rolled off the edge and fell to the ground. She made no move to pick them up.

"You want to know why I fired you? There wasn't supposed to be anyone on the 187th floor that night. When the elevator doors opened and I saw someone working on the lighting at the end of the hall, I prayed it wasn't you. I wanted it to be someone else's problem. Then you sent your report, and we were both fucked. Thank God I had secure encryption between the two of us, or we'd both have had an extreme allergic reaction to shellfish and been one of the few dozen people who've died on this planet." She picked up the cigarette that hadn't fallen and pressed it to life.

"That man—" Mia began.

"There was no man. You didn't see anything. You were fired for a completely unrelated reason. Awkwardly, yes, because you couldn't be sent back to Earth. Stop resenting me and appreciate the fact that I saved your life."

The bartender set Mia's double bourbon and soda down with a clunk and retreated before Erika could ask for another martini. Mia did some quick math. Stunned and dragged into the brush, plus being hit by a poison dart, plus Tanaka forfeiting more than five hundred million credits in stock equaled Erika's story likely being true.

"Was he there because of the mining project in the intemperate zone? Our clients at Han were being pressured to volunteer for it," Mia said.

Erika stabbed at the table until the menu appeared. "There is a project, it's called Topsoil, and it's not in the intemperate zone. It's in the uninhabitable latitudes, and they want me there."

While the intemperate zone was dangerous, the uninhabitable latitudes were off-limits to anything but robots. Victoria's ozone layer was onionskin thin at the equator, and even brief exposure to sunlight guaranteed skin cancer. The inland temperatures would kill a human in less than an hour. No human workers could legally go there, even if they volunteered.

"They can't make you," Mia said.

"They can if they have my birth certificate."

There was only one reason this could matter. "You're over eighty?"

Erika took a long drag on the stim cigarette, and the tip glowed bright blue. "Eighty-four. Seventy-three on my official ID. I shaved a few months off my age whenever I got the chance. Some asshole broke into physical data storage at UCLA and stole the BioKey my mother and I palmed when she brought me into this world. Not this world. The one I want to go back to."

"You can't go back on a burst drive ship. You could have an aneurism."

"Two percent chance. I don't know which ball-less insurance agency decided eighty was the cutoff." She finally located a martini on the table menu and pressed "2" for quantity. "You know how I feel about Victoria. I hate the gravity and the heat and having cocktails with the same damn people year after year. I want to go home. If that asshole gives my birth certificate to Optima, I'm stuck on this sunbaked dog turd of a planet for the rest of my life."

Mia's reflexive defensiveness flared and retreated. She, too, didn't want Erika on Victoria for the next forty years.

"What's this project about, and why do they want you?"

Erika flicked her stim cigarette as if it had an ash. "No fucking idea. They asked me to help with recruiting. That's what you saw that night. Them bringing me in to help staff up the project. I've got a network and dirt on everyone. It was supposed to be completely aboveboard after the employees signed the waiver and the NDA, and I was supposed to be reassigned to the Santa Monica office, still on partner track. That's when things went sideways, and I called Summit to secure my apartment."

Erika's two martinis arrived—half the volume of what a regular would receive—and John spilled more when he set them down. She didn't seem to notice, grabbing one and gulping it down. Mia took a sip of her bourbon, drawn in by the story and mapping it onto Summit's clients.

"Rumors are flying," Erika said. "Everyone in the mining division knows their colleagues are involved in something top secret but no one can figure out what. They don't know it's in the uninhabitable latitudes, of course, but the fact that it is raises more questions. If Han is developing a new technology, they could set up a lab anywhere in their territory and lock it down…unless they're doing something that violates the charter. It's hard to do remote scans at the equator, so they can probably get away with more. There's only one reason they want me there. They want me complicit in something extremely illegal."

Mia nearly spit out her drink. "Are you kidding? You've spent your whole career breaking the charter. The recruiting? With hidden holocams?"

Erika help up one, steady finger. "Contractually allowed. Trust me, I did my homework."

"What about poison darts?"

"We never threatened anyone with physical harm."

"No cutting off little girl's braids? Shooting poison darts into a kid's party?"

Erika shook her head. "Absolutely not. Violence yields unpredictable results. People will say anything if they're in physical danger. I can get what I want by finding out what they're trying to conceal or what they want." She gestured toward the blue jumpsuit-wearing patrons of the bar.

Mia's revulsion resurfaced. "I don't know what you want from us. Summit provided you the privacy you needed to blackmail a whole team of people that is now being shipped off to a place no human should be. I don't care if they send you as well."

Erika gripped her wrist and Mia jerked away.

"You didn't save my life. You put me in danger, and you're still doing it," Mia said.

"I didn't know what I was getting into. Everything has been unraveling since I agreed to help Larissa. Don't pretend you don't know me. We've both got each other's numbers. I want to be partner and get back to Los Angeles, and you don't want anyone to know about your implant."

"My implant?"

Erika leaned forward. "Yes. I've been dying to know where you got it and how you managed to keep it from the scanners all these years. It must be from New Beijing, but something able to record and store data like what you've got would've ripped through the industrial espionage community and been detected a few months in. Who installed yours? Some genius college boyfriend who had second thoughts about selling out? That's my theory. He'd be rich if he'd had the balls to monetize his invention."

Mia's confusion gave way to a few moments of blind panic. Of course, she'd screwed up more than a few times in the decade they'd worked together, but Erika never seemed to notice. She only cared about results, not the myriad details leading to them. She'd flip to the back page of Mia's carefully written reports and give a curt nod or shake of her head.

Erika smiled. Mia knocked back her drink.

"I knew it. How does it work? Does it connect to your glasses, or do you have implanted lenses as well?"

Erika's mistaken assumption was too close to the truth for Mia's comfort, but did Erika have any real leverage over her?

No. Erika was in a much worse position. She was over eighty, someone had her birth record, and if they shared it with Optima she'd never be allowed to go back to Earth. She'd probably be in breach of contract with Han as well and likely lose her pension. Mia didn't have an implant, and Erika wouldn't have any hard evidence to support her theory. Still, she didn't want Erika calling attention to her unnatural ability to recall facts.

"I agree that you need to get back to Earth. I'm just not sure how Summit can help."

Erika picked up the second martini. "Ideally, I'd like the BioKey destroyed, but I don't know where it is or who has it. I received an anonymous threat, and UCLA confirmed it's missing. I don't dare bring it up with Larissa in case it's not her. Trust me, I get the irony. This is exactly the kind of thing I did to the others to get them to sign up."

"Can you stall?" Mia's social engineering brain spun up. "When are you supposed to leave?"

"Next week."

"You need to get badly injured, extremely ill, or check into rehab. Anything that officially prevents you from travelling for a few months."

Erika laughed. "I knew you'd have a clever idea. You always do. I don't need to be seriously ill; I just need a doctor to say I am, and a hacker to falsify my medical records. I've got both."

Of course she did.

Erika relaxed, leaning back into the booth and unbuttoning the top button on her neck-high shirt. "We were a good team. You'll deny it, but we were."

Mia signaled to John, who nodded. "You need to leave now."

Erika sighed. "No need for drama. I've got to get going. My life-threatening illness isn't going to happen all on its own. Maybe you'll come visit me in the hospital?"

"Only if you take that opportunity to pass on anything you learn about Topsoil."

"That's fair. Extra info if you cry?"

"Goodbye, Erika."

She sidestepped John and click-clacked her way out of the bar, pausing to give Mia an exaggerated wink before stepping out into the bright sunset light.

"Sorry about that," Mia shouted to John, who'd been watching them as he wiped glasses. "Don't worry, it doesn't signal another partner invasion. She isn't one of them."

Taylor, her high school friend whom she hadn't seen since she visited his office months earlier, arrived half an hour later, Optima-blue blazer folded carefully over one arm. She hadn't taken him up on his offer to meet the old gang for drinks, so she appreciated he'd agreed to come today. He seemed to recognize the song blasting from the low-end speakers and nodded in approval.

"What's this about?" he asked, sliding into the booth. "You said official business."

"It is. We provide security for this bar. The whole place is shielded. This booth especially."

"I get it. We can speak freely. I need a drink. Setty-Sarin fired up a new desalinization plant and set off air quality monitors a hundred kilometers away."

"I've had a not-so-great day too, and that's why I called. Thanks for coming."

Taylor seemed much more at ease than when she'd visited him at his office. He ordered a pint of South Sea Ale and drank a quarter of it in a few deep gulps as soon as it arrived.

"Ah! Much better. Is it really safe to talk?"

"Yes."

"You're probably wondering about the MMARVs. The rip in the fabric…I think that's what you called it. I had my friend look into it, and we did get hacked. Not only were they able to control the MMARVs, they trained the AI to ignore the holes in coverage and disabled our alerting system. Once we knew what to look for, we found more instances of these rips." He sliced a flattened hand across his throat. "It's chaos in the cybersecurity division. Nothing like this should have been possible. People are getting demoted. Thanks for bringing it to my attention."

"Do you know who did it?"

Taylor shook his head. "So far no idea."

"I'm glad Optima is taking this seriously. That isn't what I wanted to talk about today, though. Something unethical and probably illegal is going on at Han. I don't know if Optima can do anything about it, but I'll feel better if someone outside Summit knows it's happening. You might be more inclined to believe me, now that my story about the MMARVs checks out."

"Is this going to require me nudging a colleague in another department to look into something?"

"Maybe? I don't know. For now, hear me out and treat this as confidential info."

Three beers, two bourbons, and one hour later, Mia had given Taylor an abridged version of what she knew of the Topsoil project, the dubious tactics used to staff it, and that it might be taking place somewhere in Han's uninhabitable latitudes.

"You see the problem. We've got clients who were blackmailed and can't or won't speak up about it, and an extremely unreliable source telling me they all might be smuggled into the uninhabitable latitudes. Is that even possible?" Mia asked.

"I suppose it is if you have a very long tunnel, or convenient holes in satellite surveillance, but it doesn't make any sense to send people there instead of robots. I'm guessing your unreliable source heard a rumor and panicked. The project taking place in the inhospitable zone is more plausible. I know several of the Six have *secret* research labs down there. Having an air-gapped facility with nothing within a thousand kilometers is a level of privacy and security Earth companies can only dream of. Of course the Six are going to develop products in a place where spying is impossible. I'm sorry for the poor saps that get stuck down there, but they'll get paid. That's why they all come here, isn't it?"

Indeed. Erika didn't want to be locked down in a secure facility no matter where it was. Far from restaurants, upscale shops, and most importantly, her plastic surgeon. Erika knew Mia would be more inclined to help if her life were in danger instead of her looks. Mia cursed herself for falling for another one of Erika's tricks. Though, playing at having a serious illness might curtail the woman's shopping as much as being south of the equator would.

"That said," Taylor continued, "I'm curious. Han shouldn't have needed to blackmail anyone into signing up. I'll keep a lookout for any unusual particulate matter in Han sector, as this is a mining project, in theory. I'll also ask my friend to look into any rips in the fabric of our satellite surveillance coverage."

Mia felt more than saw Lucas enter the bar.

"Shit. My boss. He wouldn't want me talking about this."

Taylor laughed. "You haven't changed. You're terrible at keeping secrets. Hey."

He waited until Mia looked back at him. "You're allowed to have a drink with an old friend from high school. It doesn't matter where I work."

An old friend. Did she have an old friend? *What a nice thought.*

"Join us at the tiki bar next month. I told everyone I'd seen you, and they want to catch up. We're all better than we used to be. I swear."

Lucas passed the booth, giving her a small nod and Taylor a quick once-over.

"I will," Mia said. She meant it. She had a past and needed to repair the parts that were salvageable and abandon those that weren't—and the wisdom to know the difference. She'd give Taylor and the others a chance.

Chapter Thirty One

"Any activity by our vanished Han clients?" Lucas asked from his office.

The query was likely directed at Claire, who of course couldn't hear with her earbuds in place. Mia transcribed the question and passed it on. Claire straightened and replied.

"No financial transactions other than automated payments. None of them eat out or buy groceries, ride pods or make calls to Earth. None have entered or left their apartments. I've got a bot analyzing satellite images of the inhospitable and uninhabitable zones, looking for changes like new structures, roads, piles of dirt, unusual thermal signatures, but I've found nothing that could be Topsoil."

"I didn't think you would. Keep watching though."

"I do have good news. The attacks on our network have stopped. Here's this month compared to last." Claire replaced the satellite imagery on her screen with the network-monitoring dashboard.

Mia had never paid much attention to it but even her untrained eye could tell that last month there'd been a hundred times the traffic.

"It's been my full-time job to keep us from being paralyzed. Sunday, the attacks stopped," Claire said.

Jason whistled. "That is good news. Maybe we'll finally be able to experience whatever passes for a normal workday here. What time do you want to head over to The Center, Lucas?"

"I'm coming, too," Mia said.

"Don't feel obligated, either of you," Lucas said to Mia and Claire. "I could use your help, but I promised you wouldn't have to work outside this office."

"I haven't seen Sergei in ages, and the lounge is free tonight. I'm going to meet him there after the job," Mia said.

Lucas's mouth twisted as if he'd eaten a bad sand-dab claw, but he quickly recovered. "What about you, Claire?"

"I'd rather not, but I've been trying to hack into The Center for months. Maybe I'll have more luck if I'm inside."

"Great. This is a tech-free Weber meeting. Thing is, none of the attendees know it. They'll get through screening at the front door of The Center, and we'll have a secondary screening outside the meeting room. The organizer is afraid no one would surrender their expensive toys to the AI, but hopes they'll comply if we keep them in locked bins right outside the room."

Mia was looking forward to the event. Lucas—accustomed to charming his way to whatever he wanted—never got the perks from Sergei that she did. That pleased her to no end. When she was along, Summit always received a free upgrade to the most secure room—if it was available.

The most secure room *was* available, and Sergei handed her the access card with a wink and a bow. Nestled in the very center of the spiral, it was a ten-minute walk from the front doors. Lucas didn't like that there was only one way in or out. However, it would be a ridiculous place to try anything criminal, as getting there required passing a hundred other rooms and as many cameras and sensors.

"Why didn't we rent a cart?" Claire grumbled, as she lugged her unwieldy black box around the seemingly never-ending looping hall.

"Our equipment doesn't leave our hands," Lucas said, as he ran his down the faintly luminous pink wall.

Summit had a generous two hours of set-up time before the attendees arrived. Claire began to assemble the doorlike scanner frame they'd last used at the birthday party. Jason attached BabelBoxes to the outside walls to ensure no conversations from the inside could be deciphered.

Mia checked to be sure the meeting room next to theirs was empty and device-free. The door handle didn't budge. These doors were solid, stronger than the walls around them.

She called Sergei. "Hi there. Can you unlock 1B?"

"It is unlocked," he replied.

"Maybe it was, but it's locked now." She demonstrated for the cameras.

Lucas, overhearing her, walked over and tried the handle—as if Mia didn't have the strength to press it down. He didn't notice her glare.

"Can you unlock it again?" Mia asked.

She and Lucas stood back and watched the brushed-aluminum handle.

The lock whined. Nothing happened. It whined again. After a few more increasingly high-pitched squeals, the lock gave the familiar *thunk* she was used to hearing.

Lucas pulled the door open.

The room wasn't empty. A man and a woman sat at the round conference table. Three bulky figures leaned against the wall behind them, likely bodyguards.

The lights were dim, and an incredibly complicated holographic schematic floated above the table. Mia couldn't tell what it was, though it seemed to be four different views of the same machine or factory.

For a moment no one moved, then the woman slammed her hand down onto the table. The diagram disappeared, and the room lights brightened.

Mia was about to apologize for the interruption when she realized she was face-to-face with Han partner Larissa Mills. The man next to her was Frederick Magnussen, thick-lipped partner from the Itek corporation.

The one Lucas caught running the secret lab.

The one who should be on Earth under house arrest.

One of the guards drew a weapon, which shouldn't have been possible to get into the building, and stepped forward.

"If it isn't Lucas Dunn. Why won't you stay in your corner and let the big boys play?"

That voice. That mouth. It was the man who stunned her. And the face was that of Richter, also from Itek, also involved in the lab, and also under arrest on Earth.

Lucas slammed his open palm against Mia's chest and knocked her to the side. She stumbled and fell to her knees in the hallway. A flash of light that streaked past his head and blew a chunk out of a nearly indestructible wall across the hall. He leapt behind the door and slammed it shut. A whooping alarm sounded, a bright red light pulsed above the door, and heavy deadbolts slid into place.

A neutral voice spoke. "Unauthorized weapon discharge, room 1B. Please clear the corridors. Security is en route." The message repeated.

Mia scrambled to her feet, heart pounding.

Lucas pressed his back against the door and yelled, "Sergei! Room 1B isn't empty. There are five people in there and at least one has a laser pistol. Keep them inside."

Claire and Jason rushed from the room next door.

"What's going on?" Jason asked, examining the smoking hole in the wall.

Lucas made sure the door was locked then grabbed Mia's arm and steered her toward the others. "We leave. Right now."

Claire opened her mouth, then shut it when she saw Mia's wide-eyed expression. She grabbed her case. Jason detached one of the BabelBoxes.

"Leave them," Lucas ordered.

They set off at a jog down the long, curved corridor, Jason taking Claire's case when she began to lag behind.

"Lucas, the man that made the comment about big boys, he was the one that stunned me," Mia said.

Lucas halted. "What?"

"I'm sure of it. I'd know that voice anywhere."

"Fucking Richter. One more reason…" He began to jog again.

As they got closer to the lobby they slowed and threaded their way through uneasy Center clients milling in the hall. The alarm was distant but audible, and no one was sure what to do.

Sergei stood at the front desk, data glasses on, hands flailing. Virtual screens surrounded his coworker, and the icy blonde receptionist who usually eyed Lucas like he was deep-fried dew fish frantically fielded questions she couldn't answer. Mia knew how they all felt, since—and it sounded hollower every time she said it—*things like this don't happen here.*

Lucas tapped Sergei's shoulder.

Sergei pulled off his glasses. "I don't know who's in there. We have records. Everyone is accounted for. The room is empty as far as the system is concerned, and we can't scan it." He waved his hand at one of the screens. "The only way we can tell there are people in there is from the air filtration system data. Oxygen consumption and carbon dioxide production. I don't know what to do. All I have is stunners. I can't fight them."

"Were we the only ones in that area?" Lucas asked.

Sergei nodded.

"Don't do anything, or you'll end up with dead guards. How could they get in here?"

Sergei shrugged. "It should be impossible."

"Then they can get out in the same impossible way. Let them."

Sergei weaved an elaborate pattern with his fingers and hands, and the alarm ceased.

Lucas took Mia's arm and propelled her out the front exit. It was an apparently normal day outside. The conference center lay relaxed in its watery bed, staring at the world with unblinking reflective eyes. He pulled her to the curb, hailed a pod, and turned her to face him. "You know who the other man was?"

She nodded.

"Don't say anything. We need to be in a safe place before we discuss this."

Claire and Jason joined them.

Lucas drew in a deep breath. "We need to go to Frontier."

Claire's eyes widened. Jason looked sharply at Lucas then back at the building.

"No questions. Jason, you and I will go to the office first. We probably have fifteen minutes before they get out of there and decide what to do. Mia and Claire, go to Frontier now, separately. Take your time. They'll try to trace our path later, so be careful. Claire, as soon as you get there, remove any data we have on our office node."

"What is Frontier? I don't know where it is," Mia said.

A pod pulled up and Lucas opened the door with one hand, gesturing with the other. An address in IVS sector flashed onto Mia's glasses.

"Don't go right there. Go somewhere else and change pods. Walk the last kilometer or so. I don't want any pod trips logged to that address."

He pulled out his wallet and flashed a random credit voucher over the reader then tossed it to her. They weren't anonymous per se, but gift credits under someone else's name passed from hand to hand, sold for more than their face value, and were rendered untraceable over time. It was the closest thing Victoria had to cash.

He slammed the door, and the pod rolled leisurely down the tree-lined drive that was the only way in or out of the conference center. New Canberra's placid exterior irritated her. Shouldn't there be some indication of the random violence that just occurred? Someone shot at her, again, and meanwhile everyone picnicked on the lawn, played games, kissed…

She wanted to scream at them.

Just before the pod merged onto Ring One, another pod passed hers, headed to The Center. In it were two men—both wearing nearly illegal face-covering glasses.

She called Lucas.

"What?" he answered immediately.

"A pod with two suspicious-looking guys just passed me—and no other pods are turning up Center Drive. You won't be able to catch one before they arrive."

Lucas's breath quickened, and she heard muffled footfalls on grass.

"Thanks for the warning. We're heading into the park. We'll catch a pod on Ring One in Setty-Sarin Sector."

Mia struggled to recall a map of IVS sector—a sign that she was truly stressed. She directed the pod to take her to Pandemonium, a huge indoor-outdoor mall not far from the address Lucas gave her. Always crowded, it had numerous entrances above- and belowground. She kept an eye on the pods around her on the ring road, but all held happy shoppers and irritated businesspeople.

The pod dropped her at the west entrance—a triple-paned glass door at the base of a faux Egyptian pyramid—and she quickly lost herself in the crowd. Once inside, she ducked into Night Shots, a store she'd loved when she was a teen. Amazing it was still in business. Dark, loud, and obnoxious. The perfect place to hide. She nestled into one of the big armchairs as holo dancers began to file past, dancing in jerky unison while sporting the flashy sparkling outfits the store was known for.

She tried to collect herself; to separate confusion from fright. Everything had happened too fast for her to make much sense of it. Her heartbeat—which had matched the frantic beat of the drums when she first sat—slowed.

Magnussen and Richter should be under house arrest on Earth. Instead, they were on Victoria and clearly involved in the Topsoil project. Why? *If Han needed dirty work done, who better to hire than two men who had proof they couldn't be here...*

A particularly earsplitting string of notes pulled her from her reverie.

She needed to get to Frontier. She puzzled over the address Lucas had given her. The D on the end didn't make sense. 240, 3E-D. She queried the city map, and a network of spidery lines she'd never paid much attention to popped into focus. The D stood for delivery, and a jagged alley ran all the way from E to F Street behind the stores on Ring Road 3.

She was close to where E hit Ring 3, so she'd walk. She used the credits voucher to buy a very different shirt than the one she was wearing, replacing formfitting white with something billowy and blue. It might not help much but it seemed like a good idea. Lucas had already made sure the team's glasses were untraceable.

She exited the mall from the door closest to the alley, turned right on E, and walked quickly under cover of the shade awnings. Twenty meters away, she found the alley. She'd seen these narrow openings and assumed they were delivery areas for one or two stores, not through streets.

She entered hesitantly and walked slowly down the narrow, quiet canyon. Pipes and buildings rose straight up on either side of her, the sky a thin blue squiggle far above. The road jigged and jagged, tracing the backs of the businesses. A few pods passed, holding freight not people.

After half a kilometer, she came to a wide, gray metal door with a worn sign that read, *240-D. Deliveries only—Frontier.* The state-of-the-art palm reader and retinal scanner embedded in the wall to the right was definitely Jason's work. She pressed her hand on the glass and gazed into the scanner. A surprisingly solid *clunk* sounded, and the door slid forward a few centimeters. She pulled it open. Stairs led up into dimness. Uneasy, she stepped inside, grasped the handrail and slowly climbed upwards.

At the top of the stairs a light snapped on, revealing a large, dingy storage room. To the right, metal shelving units held dusty boxes of dried beans, cans of tomato sauce, metal bowls, and a pile of red-and-white checked tablecloths. To the left, a small room with a bare concrete floor, oversized metal sink and a non-smart toilet. A set of swinging doors, small round windows in each, stood directly in front of her. She pushed one open and peeked in.

Old-fashioned fluorescent lights stuttered to life with a flicker and buzz. Mia gazed at what must be the ghost of a restaurant dining room, dead silent, the air stale and still. The name, Frontier suddenly made sense. Rusty farming equipment hung on the railroad tie spikes—shovels, pitchforks, as well as other tools she couldn't identify. Booths ran along one side, tables and chairs thrown haphazardly on top of them. The room was bizarrely bisected by a convex wall/ceiling that cut through at a forty-five-degree angle, bulging inward as if she were under the bottom quarter of a giant wooden beach ball. More tables and chairs, along with piles of boxes and crates, crowded the corners.

She tried to orient herself. What would be on the other side of this place on the main street? Giverny, a French restaurant themed on Monet's water lilies. All the tables sat on rising terraces circling a giant pond. They'd renovated the older restaurant and built right on top of it. Surreal.

To her left was a door. She tried it, but her hand on the palm reader did nothing.

Now what?

She'd been too busy moving to truly panic and needed to keep that momentum. She went back into the storage room, a marginally less creepy space than the half-lit dining area, and paced, waiting to hear from the team.

A few minutes later the bolt on the front door thunked, and Claire clomped up the stairs. She dropped a heavy black bag onto the floor and leaned glumly against the wall, dragging a wrist across her damp forehead.

"Did everyone get out of the park okay?" Mia asked.

"Yeah. We had to walk a kilometer, but no one bothered us."

"Why did Lucas tell us to come here? What is this place?"

"Our satellite office. A place we could meet if we were ever in trouble. As to why we are here, I have no idea. Who was in that room at The Center?"

"Is it safe to talk here?"

"Of course."

"Richter, Magnussen, and a Han partner, Larissa Mills. They were looking at a schematic of some kind of machine."

Claire's eyes widened. "That's impossible! Richter and Magnussen can't be here. They're under house arrest on Earth."

"I'm one hundred percent certain Richter was the one who dragged me out into the brush and also the man I saw at Han HQ right before I was fired. And he was definitely the man in the room today."

"We're dead." Claire grabbed her bag, knuckles white.

"No, we're not," Mia said. All the attacks against her suddenly made sense. "They could've killed us anytime. They proved that. Whatever Richter and Magnussen are up to, if anything happened to you or Lucas or Jason… They'd be prime suspects, and the NYCPD would investigate and discover they're gone."

"That might have been true before, but now you and Lucas know they're here. They'll definitely want to kill you both before someone hooks you to a veracity detector." Claire paused. "Actually, Jason and I aren't a threat. We'll be fine." The conclusion seemed to buoy her spirits. "I need to get our data moved over." She slammed, bag first, through the swinging doors, which flapped wildly in her wake.

Claire was right. She and Lucas were in serious danger unless he could convince his friends at NYCPD to confirm their suspects were still under house arrest. Mia stilled the doors then followed Claire into the formerly locked room.

The eight-meter square windowless cube was antiseptic compared to the rest of the place. Bright white paint and excessive lighting made her feel as if she were in a hospital operating room. Claire opened a plastic crate, extracted several PDS units, and stacked them on a plastic folding table.

"Do we have a veracity detector?" Mia asked.

"Not here."

"Can you have Jason pick up the one you have at the office? The sooner Lucas and I get verified info back to Sergeant Johnson, or to whoever is in charge of the case, the sooner we don't get murdered."

Claire sighed but did a quick airtype. "Just caught him. They were about to leave."

"Can I help unpack?" She wanted to stay busy.

"Unfold the tables and chairs and unpack all that." She waved at the orange crates in the back. "That's Jason's stuff. He won't mind if you touch it."

Mia did, gradually reconstructing a pared-down version of Jason's work table.

They both jumped when the double doors slammed open nearly an hour later. Lucas, Jason, and Mikey trod heavily into the white room, each laden with overfull bags. They dropped them and returned with another load. Jason set Mia's travel backpack at her feet.

"We stopped by your apartment and got some clothes for you. Sorry, I don't know what goes with what. I grabbed a couple of everything—plus your bourbon."

"Lucas," Mia began. "We need to send Sergeant Johnson veracity detector data—"

"Already done. Thanks for the reminder that we have one."

Lucas disentangled himself from straps and lowered everything he carried to the ground. "He believes me, and the data is good, but it's going to take time to get a warrant. We'll have to stay out of sight until Richter and Magnussen are off the planet."

"What makes you think they'll leave?" Mikey yelled from the dining room. "Han isn't going to admit they're here, not after they went to all the trouble of busting them out of house arrest. If I was looking at the jailtime they're facing, I'd stay, and there's no legal precedent for extradition."

Mikey was right. The momentary elation—as quickly snatched away—drained the last of her adrenaline, and she sat heavily in one of the plastic folding chairs.

"It's not all bad," Lucas said. "Mitch can confirm they spoofed their tracking devices and are no longer under house arrest. They'll forfeit bail, and AGE can pressure Optima to ship them back. Maybe the damn trial will finally get started."

"It is all bad," Mia said. "Based on what Ms. Tanaka implied, most of Han doesn't know what's going on. There's no one for Optima to pressure. We're more of a threat than ever. There's no downside to killing us."

Claire gasped.

All attention shifted to her screens, which displayed interior and exterior views of the Summit Security office. A pod branded *Bernal Building Repair* idled out front. A ladder leaned against the building, top rungs resting below one of the porthole windows—now a gaping black hole. Inside, a man and a woman carelessly emptied draws and cabinets and threw anything that looked like it might store data into bags. The woman knocked the cactus on Mia's desk to the floor to gain easier access to the big screen.

"What the hell?" Mia cried. "They can't do this! It's broad daylight. Weber security will be there any second."

Lucas shrugged. "Maybe, maybe not. If they can halt the MMARVs and turn off the cameras like they did when you were stunned, they'll have the time they need. Or perhaps we have a contract with Bernal Repair to fix that broken window and do some interior renovations."

"Can you set off a sonic cannon?" Mia asked Jason. "They're ruining everything."

"I could," he mused.

"No," Lucas said. "Did you wipe the office data, Claire?"

"I did, and installed all latest viruses and tracking software. With any luck, we'll be in their system soon."

The man and woman ransacking the office suddenly stopped, responding to a signal only they could hear. They hefted their heavily loaded bags and crunched through the debris. A few moments later, they were gone.

"I'm sorry we lost that equipment, but we may know a lot more about this project soon," Lucas said. "You don't keep any work files at home, do you Mia?"

She shook her head.

"Do you have any relatives on Victoria?"

She almost said no, then forced herself to admit the truth. "My mother."

"We should check in on her."

She sucked in a breath and held it—her animal brain reacting to the idea that someone was in danger. Then, the stench from the familiar compost of emotions rose, and she grimaced.

"She'll be fine. She never goes out, and there are enough locks on her door to secure a bank vault."

"We can hack into the security cameras in her building. What's the address?"

Mia reluctantly sent it to Claire. "She doesn't know anything about my day-to-day life. We don't have to—"

Everyone was going to see Annette. Mia pressed her palms to her already flushed face.

Claire cycled through the cameras. An exterior view first. The building Mia had grown up in was nice back in the day but was now a bit of an eyesore. Next, the interior hallway. Empty. Finally, the apartment itself.

The living room held the only interactive wall in the apartment, and from there, the team saw everything. Mia's stomach churned. Annette lay flaccid in a data chair in the center of the room, arms encased in the sensor-rests, head completely enclosed in an immersion helmet. Any exposed flesh was pale and puffy like overly risen dough. Her white legs, crisscrossed with blue varicose veins, jutted out of incongruously jaunty red shorts.

Surrounding her was an intricately-constructed mandala of spent silver hypos, orange straws from SuperSmoothie cups, carefully folded dirty napkins, packs of Chinese mustard sauce, clear water bottle caps, and against the far wall, two-meter high towers of take-out boxes from the only restaurant she'd order from—East West Kitchen.

Annette used to worship science. Now this was her altar. The art she'd constructed meant she'd fired the housekeepers Mia hired—again.

Mikey gave a long, low whistle. "That's—"

Lucas cut him off. "Enough. Is she alright? Claire, can you get bioreadings?"

"She's sedated." Claire looked to Mia.

"Blue Belles. A recreational drug." Mia tried to keep her voice even.

Claire looked back at the screen. "I've established a secure link. You can talk to her."

"Ask if anyone has tried to contact her," Lucas said.

Mia came forward reluctantly and leaned into the camera.

"Annette," she said loudly. The pale body didn't stir. Mia cranked the output volume. "Annette," she repeated firmly. The woman twitched then freed her arms and pulled off the helmet.

"Why are you yelling? I'm right in the middle of excavating an Egyptian tomb." Her eyes were red-rimmed, bleary. She'd dyed her hair a few months ago, and the inch of gray roots made the jet black appear disconnected from her head.

"Has anyone called and asked about me?"

Annette lowered the helmet as if to replace it, then paused. "Some man friends of yours…yes…I think that was today. What did they want?"

"You have to tell me what they wanted. I wasn't there." She failed to keep annoyance from her voice.

Annette's brow furrowed. "They wanted to talk to you. Something about work. Where do you work? Han? I told them you'd be there. Right?" She glanced at the window, presumably to confirm that it was indeed daytime.

"Yes, I'm at work at Han."

Annette put the helmet back on. "I need a new laundry service." Her muffled words were hard to decipher. "Spring Rain didn't fold my shirts right, and now I can't wear them." She nestled her arms back into the rests and returned to the game.

Mia stood, pushed past Mikey and Lucas, and banged through the swinging doors into the storage room. She paced, glasses on.

Multiple traumatic events had transpired in the past few hours, but interacting with Annette was by far the most upsetting. Mia hadn't visited her since Landing Day. The panic she used to feel when she stepped into the apartment had subsided to discomfort and disgust over the years. Annette's prideful refusal to see a therapist, return to Earth to be with her brother, or admit she'd essentially kept Mia prisoner for years made mother-daughter visits awkward.

Dad had begged her to take care of her mother in the moments before he died—and she'd done her best. The imprisonment had been psychological, not physical. The Six weren't prepared for children and had no official policies. If a PhD mechanical engineer wanted to home-school her daughter, that was her business, so Mia had spent fourth through eighth grade making sure Annette ate, washed, and didn't overdose. Once Annette was down for the night, Mia would don coveralls and go out exploring. Probably not the best time to do it, given that the deadliest insects were nocturnal, but the coveralls lived up to their bugproof promise, and she'd survived.

Derek urged her to rejoin her classmates for high school, and Mia did, unsurprised that personalities hadn't changed much since fourth grade, and relieved that the online classes she'd taken more than prepared her for freshman year.

Annette was deep into virtual worlds by then and rarely surfaced. Mia did what she could—buying advanced game chairs with muscle stimulators and massagers, hiring caretakers to make her shower and eat—but nothing helped. Annette was a ragged hole in her soul, draining energy. When Mia would take a certain cocktail of stimulants and depressants, she'd vividly imagine returning to the apartment to find her mother dead—and would feel nothing but sweet relief. At least for a few hours. Then the guilt returned.

Jason peeked into the storeroom.

"You okay? It was rude of us to barge in like that."

She scowled. "I'm not okay. My contract with Summit doesn't have a clause about spying on my own mother."

"Claire should have kept the image data on her glasses."

"She should have. You don't know what it's like to have a mother like that on a planet like this." This sane, perfect world had no place for those who crashed against it and shattered.

He took a step into the room. "I know what it's like to have terrible parents. I wouldn't want Claire poking her nose into my folks' place in Queens. Don't worry. It doesn't reflect badly on us. We aren't like them."

She opened her mouth to tell him her mother was nothing like his drug-addicted, unemployed mom and abusive father then stopped. His empathy seeped into the cracks of the façade she was desperate to maintain, and it tumbled down. She stumbled into the bathroom and slid the mechanical bolt to the left with a *thunk*.

Her mother looked all right on paper. Officially, she was retired. She still had her patents, title, and a PhD from Stanford. Mia didn't mind being the daughter of that person and worked hard to ensure that no one ever saw the wreck Annette had become.

Jason knocked softly on the door. "You okay?"

"I'm fine." She leaned against the door and shut her eyes. The team hadn't just seen her mom. If they had any sense at all, they'd also seen Mia was a hypocrite and a snob. She did think residents of Victoria were superior to those of Earth. She'd been taught this since birth. They were smarter, healthier, wealthier, better educated… She could list a hundred superlatives and unfortunately sometimes did.

When she and Jason were out in the desert, and he shared stories about his family, she'd pitied him, relieved there weren't low-class people like that on Victoria.

But Jason said "us." People with awful parents. The wound in her, the one her mom never allowed to heal, ripped open a bit more. Jason's parents were high-school dropouts, and her mom had a PhD, yet Annette was no better than them, and Mia wasn't better than Jason, or Claire, or anyone from Earth.

Ever since Mia started this job, she'd been confronted with flaws in the city and herself and struggled to categorize them as anomalies. Some part of her held onto the fantasy that she was still a social engineer, making a good income, and New Canberra was safe. Her team members were competent, but not as clever and smart as she was.

In reality, she was an underpaid client liaison, a job anyone fresh out of high school could do. New Canberra was perfect on paper, but despite constant efforts to keep the city in an ideal state, once it moved from the computer-generated holo to plasticrete and metal, disintegration started. A person with the perfect resume, too, could crack and crumble. Lucas and the team knew something she didn't want to acknowledge—that Victoria would probably be very much like Earth in another forty years.

She wanted to save the place—but had it ever wanted to save her? She'd been under attack since the day she was born, first by the Registry, then by her own mother, then by petty classmates, by Erika, and now by some evil cabal within Han.

Fuck this shit. Nothing was perfect, it never had been, and she wasn't going to be able to fix it no matter how much social engineering she did.

She splashed her face with cold water. She couldn't stay in the only bathroom forever, much as she'd like to. She dried off then fumbled in her purse for a Baby Jane. She didn't want to face Jason. He'd been a good friend, and she'd stayed aloof. She could have told him about her mother that night in the desert when he'd confided in her about his past. Instead, she nodded and said the right things and kept her secret up there with her on her pedestal.

I'm an asshole.

As soon as she felt the warmth and the loosening from the drug, she put her glasses back on and went out.

"Are you okay?" Jason asked.

She tried to smile. "I'm fine. Thanks for understanding what that meant."

"Trust me, I wouldn't want my dad up there on-screen." One edge of Jason's mouth quirked up. "Unless he was…" He made a small ball shape with both hands. "A pile of ashes about this big inside an urn."

He freely spoke of her secret desire for her own parent. The Baby Jane propelled her forward, and she hugged him.

He wrapped his lanky arms around her and held tight. "It's okay. This has been a crazy day. We need to get a few more things finished up and then we can relax and…" He let go and picked a can up from a nearby shelf. "Eat red beans?"

She wiped her eyes, composed herself, and followed Jason through the double doors. No one appeared to have noticed her absence, and the image of her semicomatose mother was hopefully long gone from everyone's minds.

Lucas stood on the far side of the room in conversation with someone on his glasses.

"Mitch. It's Lucas. Did you get the veracity detector data? Magnussen is on Victoria with Richter." A pause. "Yes, I'm sure. Look at the data. I was two meters away from them and Richter took a shot at me." Another pause. "I know you have orders not to harass them, but you won't be. They aren't there. I swear on my old badge." He listened. "I realize that. He might be here about a joint project with Han called Topsoil. Partner named Mills is involved." Pause. "Why do you think they tried to shoot us? Check it out. I can't do much digging from here without raising flags." After a few minutes, Lucas nodded. "Thanks. Yes, we have a place to lay low, but I wouldn't feel comfortable staying here for more than a week or two. The faster you can establish they're gone and forfeited bail, the sooner we're out of danger. We can't prove they're here, but you can prove they aren't in New York." Pause. "Okay, thanks. I'll keep in touch." Lucas took off his glasses and rubbed his face. He didn't look happy.

"Well?" Mikey asked.

Lucas shook his head. "I'm not sure the data from the veracity detector will be enough to get a warrant."

"Sergei can get evidence," Jason said. "Their DNA will be all over that conference room."

"Which they surely wiped before they left," Mia said.

"We have to figure out what's going on. Mia, I'd like you to…" Lucas stalked over and pulled off her glasses. "Damn it. You're high."

He seized her purse and dumped the contents onto a plastic table.

"Hey!" She caught a lip compact headed toward the floor.

He rifled through the objects and found the Baby Janes.

He held the silver package up to her face as if he were brandishing a knife. "You do not get to take these. We are in crisis mode, and I need your help. Do you understand?"

She made a desperate grab, but he shoved them deep into his front pocket. She nearly lunged for them.

"I need those."

"I need your brain fully functional," he retorted. "I'll see you back here in four hours. Go clean up some of the booths in the dining room. We'll be sleeping in there."

Mikey gave her a wink. "I'll get 'em back for you," he said in a loud whisper.

She left the overly bright room with relief. *Fuck Lucas and his urgency.*

He told Mitch they'd be here for a week or two. That was enough time to figure things out. If it weren't for the Baby Janes, she'd still be locked in the bathroom watching a bad slideshow—of her mom, Richter, the flash of light, the hole in the wall—and too stressed to do whatever Lucas expected of her.

Cleaning was the perfect job. Anything physical on Baby Janes was a joy.

She surveyed the dining room. The wallpaper was a repeating pattern of what looked like fern leaves, gold on a crimson background. What was left of the ceiling—a triangle that the beach ball hadn't smashed—was embossed tin tiles. Was that an actual pitchfork? She walked to the wall where it was mounted and ran her fingers over the rusted metal. It'd be worth something if it was from Earth. As would the horseshoes, whips, and leather saddle. She came upon a small army of sweeperbots huddled forlornly half a meter from a charging station, passage blocked by a fallen chair. She moved it aside and scooted them close to the station with her foot, and their green charging lights blinked on.

What about the booths? The sweepers couldn't reach those. She'd have to move all the crap piled on top of them and dust them by hand. She took a long, deep breath and stretched her arms wide. She'd had a very bad day, but now it was calm and quiet, and she had something to fix that she *could* fix.

Chapter Thirty Two

Mia must have dozed off because she awoke to someone persistently flicking her cheek with a fingernail.

"Are you sober?" Lucas leaned over her.

"Stop. Yes," she croaked as she pushed herself upright on the booth bench where she'd been napping. Her mouth was dry and stale and her shoulders ached. She took off her glasses and rubbed her face.

The sweeper bots were hard at work transforming the room. The floor was real wood, a dark walnut purposely distressed with dents and burns. If she could find some spare lights in the storeroom to replace the flickering ones, the place would be habitable.

Lucas sat down next to her and gestured to a fresh glass of water. "Drink up. I've got work for you."

It was as close as they'd been to each other since, well, in a while. He'd taken off his vest and rolled up the long sleeves of his slate-gray shirt to above the elbows. His fingernails were dirty, something she'd never seen, and his brow bore four serious lines between the eyebrows, not the usual two.

"Sorry?" she asked. He'd been talking, and she hadn't heard.

"Can you recreate the plans we saw in the meeting room at the con-ference center?" He set a large screen and stylus in front of her.

She ran her fingers through her snarled hair. "I think it was four views of the same thing."

"Pick one. I'll send it to Mitch and see if he can find out what it is. I don't want Claire doing an image match query from here. If your drawing is at all accurate, we might trigger an alarm."

If her drawing was accurate. "As long as he can do it confidentially. If it is some new Han tech, we could be guilty of IP theft." Ironic that, if they weren't careful, they'd flip from victims to perpetrators.

"Of course."

"It's going to take a while." She examined her memory of the machine. "Maybe a day or two. It's like a miniature city."

"Just do the most important parts."

"I need to do the whole thing. We don't know what's important and what isn't. I don't want to leave out the defining widget."

Lucas nodded. "Alright. The whole thing. The sooner the better though."

"Did you and Mitch work together at NYCPD?" she asked.

"He was my boss. We kept in touch after I left. I called him when I realized the only way to kill the Itek project was with NYCPD's help. He led the raid."

He seemed about to tell her more but stopped himself.

"Why would Magnussen come here?" she asked. "It was a big risk."

"He didn't think he'd get caught, or maybe planned never to return. Perhaps he's brought something to Mills worth more than his bail."

"The thing we saw plans for?"

"Maybe. Let me know if you need anything."

He slid from the booth, sidestepped a few sweepers, and returned to the white room.

Mia stared down at the blankness she'd fill with memories, then opened a drafting program and started with the top left corner of the view that had been closest to her. The task, thankfully, required her full concentration and left no energy for worry.

She worked until her eyes burned, just past 2 a.m., then went to the bathroom to refill her water glass. Jason, Lucas, and Claire were silently busy in the bright room. Mikey leaned back in a chair propped against the door to the alley, eyes closed, snoring softly.

She'd either need a stim or a nap, and shaking hands meant a shaking stylus, so she opted to sleep. Lucas might not approve but she was near the end of her rope.

Six hours later, Mia woke with a start. A sweeperbot clanged repeatedly against a metal garbage can, one of its wheels caught in an extra deep grove. Jason lay one booth over, arm flung across his face to block out the light, his deep sleep undisturbed by the racket.

She freed the machine, then rifled through the bag Jason had packed for her, relieved to find a toothbrush, hairbrush, and lotion. She crept past the bright room quietly. Lucas and Claire were still at work. After cleaning up as best she could in the bathroom, changing into a fresh shirt, then slicking back her hair into a tight ponytail, she felt almost normal.

She completed the drawing to the oddly restful sounds of Jason's restless sleep. He muttered, rolled from side to side without falling off the narrow bench, leather squeaking under his weight. Mia stood, surveyed the screen from a few different angles, then nodded in approval.

She'd done it. Perfect.

She slid the thin gray slab under her arm and returned to the white room. Claire typed on a real keyboard—a sign of real fatigue. Lucas bent over one end of the longest foldout table, examining what she took to be 3D satellite images of the equatorial region.

Mia tapped his arm. "Tell her to take a break. She'll go until she falls over."

Lucas glanced up, irritated, his face relaxing when he focused on Claire. He stretched, back cracking. "I might need a break as well. Claire."

She didn't respond.

"Claire. Stop."

"I've almost—"

"We're good for now. Take a nap. I'll wake you in six hours. I want you in top form."

Claire took a breath, as if summoning an argument, then collapsed back into the chair. "I need to pee." She picked up a gray-and-orange checkered backpack and left the room.

Mia set the screen down onto the warped plastic table, Lucas's maps floating above until he wiped them away. "I finished the first one."

He stared at the intricate plan, eyebrows raised, mouth open as if to speak. His reaction would have given her ego a boost, if his being flabbergasted meant anything other than he still doubted the power of her memory.

There's more where this came from, she wanted to say. *You want the New Beijing subway map? The Han employee directory?* She rubbed her forehead, trying to stave off a headache.

"Good work," he managed after a moment of silence. "I'll send this to Mitch."

Mia pulled up a chair and sat. "What's the plan? We hide out here until Mitch proves Richter and Magnussen skipped bail, and then we're safe?"

"To be honest…"

Mia frowned. Those might be her three least favorite words, as it meant the speaker wasn't always.

"I don't have a plan. I never imagined this scenario. Yes, I suspected we might need to go to ground between the time the trial date was announced and when we caught a shuttle home. That'd be when Magnussen would have the least fucks to give and might try to have us assassinated out of pure spite. This." He pointed to the drawing. "Topsoil, Magnussen and Richter being here… I don't know what it means. I do know Ms. Mills isn't going to be happy we've seen her with two felons. Clearly, she facilitated our office being raided. What next? Rumors about Summit Security? Anonymous posts? A formal complaint from Han to Weber about our business practices? It's going to get ugly."

"Erika might be able to help keep us updated on what's in store for us. We met at The End a few weeks ago, and I helped her with a problem. You probably know that. You keep tabs on everything that happens at the bar."

"I do. I have no audio, but you seemed to have reached agreement on something, and she left happy."

Mia hadn't told Lucas about the meeting. Erika hadn't exactly sworn her to secrecy, but being over eighty on Victoria was unprecedented. Erika might be the first and only person to be that old on this planet.

She filled him in on their discussion.

Lucas, clearly as tired as Claire, perked up as the story unfolded. "She thinks you have an illegal implant? Good." He'd pulled up Claire's chair and sat across from Mia. "No one could work with you for a decade and not realize there was something unusual going on. Why would she help us, though? We can't get the BioKey back."

"They're pressuring her to work on-site. Wherever Topsoil is taking place, if it's a locked-down facility, Erika won't be able to handle it. She's very high-maintenance. I suggested she have a horrible accident or life-threatening illness that would prevent her from going. She was very enthusiastic about option two. She seems to have a doctor in her pocket."

Lucas laughed, a been-awake-too-long guffaw. "Good idea. Stay in touch with her. Anything she can tell us about Topsoil or any attempts to undermine Summit will help."

"You should get some sleep as well. I can keep an eye on," Mia indicated the room, "anything you need me to. I had a great nap. One more thing. I need my Baby Janes. I'm not getting high when I take them, I'm getting a break from the pressure of memory. It isn't healthy for me to spend too much time in the past—like I just did when I recreated that schematic. It makes it hard to stay in the now. You know my brain is finicky."

Lucas looked startled, as if he'd set a glass too close to the edge of a table and realized it could teeter and fall. He may have been recalling a memory she didn't have—her comatose in the Lerner's shower.

He stood, pulled the bubble pack from his pocket and handed it to her. "You should have told me."

"I tried." A twelve-pack, one gone. That should last a week or two if she were careful.

"I will take a break. Keep an eye on the Summit office cams. I hired repair crew to fix the window, so don't panic if you see Davis Construction out front." He leaned down and typed on the table. "I'll send Mitch your drawing—with an NDA as you suggested—and see if he can find out what it is. See you at noon."

He'd need more than four hours sleep to recover, but no point in arguing. She considered the Baby Janes. She wouldn't take one now. Mitch would have some tall bureaucratic hurdles to jump to convince a judge that Lucas's veracity detector data was real, which meant they'd be here for longer than a week.

Later that evening Lucas called everyone into the dining room. Mia had been in the storage area organizing the food left over from the former restaurant—an astonishing array of canned beans—and the dehydrated camping rations she'd found in one of Summit's boxes. None of it looked appetizing. She should be hungry, but her body seemed to be in a holding pattern that any change might interrupt and send her spiraling down, so she stuck with water.

Mikey had cleaned out another booth—now they all had their own areas to sleep—and arranged the least damaged chairs into a semicircle in the center of the room. Lucas stood in front of those, pacing, a screen under his arm. She and Jason were the only ones seated. Claire slouched in her booth, and Mikey stood guard by the double doors.

Lucas stopped, held the screen in front of him, Mia's drawing of the machine displayed.

"Firstly, thank you, Mia, for the excellent work. Mitch sent the drawing out to some of his trusted contacts and received a reply from a friend of his at Astrys, an asteroid mining company."

He played the message without audio. A thin, friendly-looking man in a plaid shirt sat frozen behind a messy desk. Lucas fast-forwarded to a section he'd marked. The man pointed to Mia's drawing then pulled up another that looked very similar but with a scale indicator. The thing was massive–twenty meters wide, fifty long, and thirty high.

"He believes what we have is a plan for a modified asteroid ore extraction and processing machine. Modified in that the one in our diagram appears to be repurposed for use on a planet with gravity, probably for surface strip mining as opposed to tunneling." Lucas pointed out the differences between the two machines. "Asteroid mining machines bore straight down; ours has cutting rotors on the front and a control room on top. The squares along the bottom might be all we can see of massive treads, meaning it's mobile."

Mia took a closer look at the screen. "In one of the other views… maybe a back view, there are things I thought were large panels, but they might be treads as well."

Lucas continued. "He doesn't think anyone would actually build this. Even the most conscientious mining operations can't fully contain the dust generated during the grinding; it's too fine. Using one on a planet would be a disaster. The slightest breeze would create a cloud that would take days to settle, if it ever did. If you were to mine a small area, you could enclose the site, but then why use this behemoth? This is meant to chew through a lot of material fast."

"Han couldn't use this on Victoria, unless they found a way to deal with the dust, or there were caverns in the uninhabitable zone big enough to fit that thing." Mia said. "Either way, this doesn't make any sense. Han has more ore than they can handle. There's no reason to increase production with that monster machine, though if they wanted to and could do it safely, it wouldn't have to be a secret. They own the land."

"The Six limit metal exports to Earth to keep prices high, don't they?" Lucas asked.

"They limit export of just about everything."

Lucas rubbed at the stubble on his chin. "If Itek had a big project planned, they might want to bypass the price fixing and go direct. Set up a deal with Han. Provide them with this machine and have the material sent to Earth. That'd be against the charter, wouldn't it, Mia?"

"Absolutely. The other five would fine Han back to landing day. Itek would need personnel from Han to run the project. Itek employees couldn't come to Victoria en masse, and a tourist visa is only good for one month," she said.

"They'd have to find people who'd keep the secret. The best way to ensure that is bribery or blackmail," Jason said.

"Our clients. All in the mining division." Mia said.

"Makes sense to me," Mikey rumbled. "Magnussen risked a lot by coming here. Richter was clearly helping in the recruitment efforts. That machine is part of Topsoil. They'd have to build it here, and if they found a way to solve the dust problem, that would open up whole swathes of the uninhabitable latitudes for easy, cheap mining. Han would have a huge head start with that technology. Maybe there's some kind of add-on you didn't see. A big vacuum cleaner bag on one end of it."

Though Mikey had proven he wasn't the oaf he appeared to be, it still surprised Mia when he made a well-thought-out point.

"Optima and the other five won't be happy about this," she said. "It'd be legal but walking right up to the line…chewing up land like that."

"Good reason to keep the prototype a secret," Mikey replied.

"I'll have Mitch dig deeper," Lucas said. "Only a few companies make machines like this, and they haven't made many. It shouldn't be hard to find out if a custom order was placed in the last few years, probably by a nondescript holding company. Even if they plan to assemble it here, they'd still need the parts."

"Tanaka," Mia said. "Her company made asteroid mining machines. Han bought them and owns all their IP."

"True," Lucas said, "but if this is an off-the-books project, they might use Tanaka's plans to contract with a variety of suppliers, so none of them could piece together what they were actually building."

"Slow down everyone. We don't know if any of this is actually happening," Jason said. "We have a few puzzle pieces we're jamming together, trying to make them fit. All I care about right now is having Mitch prove Richter and Magnussen skipped bail. I want a powerful person on Earth to pressure the Six to do a DNA search for them here on Victoria. I want them hauled back to Earth in chains and I want to go back to work and never have to worry about those assholes haunting us again."

Mikey held up a beer. He'd brought beer?

"I'll drink to that. I don't give a shit about Topsoil or our former clients. I care about this team and Summit Security. Fuck everything else."

Mia wished she had a glass to raise with him. He chuckled, ducked behind the pile of chairs, and emerged with two more beers—which he handed to her and Jason.

"You think I'd build a bolt-hole without beer and tequila? I've got enough booze for us to stay drunk for the next month."

"We won't be here for a month." Mia looked to Lucas for confirmation.

"One day at a time," he said, which wasn't reassuring. "We wait to hear back from Mitch."

The news was not good. Mia could tell even from hearing only one side of the conversation. Lucas paced and nodded, walking from the bright white office to the dim dining room and back. Every time he said "right" or "that makes sense," Mia's hand strayed to the Baby Janes in her pocket. She kept them with her in case Lucas changed his mind and decided she was a critical asset that must be alert at all times.

"Good idea. I forgot he was there. You're right about Victoria. We can't stay hidden. Not for the months it'll take to get that thing up and running. Thanks, Mitch. Talk to you later."

He removed his glasses, expression dark.

By this point the team had all gathered in the dining room, following Lucas as his pacing narrowed to the space in front of the empty chairs.

Jason shook his head. "Not again."

"What did Mitch find out?" Mikey asked.

"Not much. His polite inquiries to the asteroid mining machine makers were ignored. They have contracts and NDAs and won't disclose anything without a warrant—which he'll never get because any purchases were probably legal."

"What about Richter and Magnussen?" Jason asked. "We sent veracity data."

Lucas shook his head. "We're running outdated software. Everyone is on 11.8.47 and we're on 11.8.33. It's inadmissible in court."

"This is bullshit." Jason stood and held a rigid finger in front of Lucas's face. "I am not running from these assholes again. Upgrade the software and send a new statement and get them off this planet."

"There's a firmware upgrade we can't get," Claire said. "I've tried. Earth doesn't trust veracity data from Victoria. The best we can do is 11.8.34. What did you mean when you said we can't stay hidden?"

Lucas took a deep breath. "Mitch can't get a warrant to check on Magnussen and Richter unless there's hard evidence they've left home. We can't provide it, but we've seen them and know they're here. We're a threat. It may take a few days, but the powers that be at Han will locate this hideout. Mia, time to cash in on the favor Erika owes you. Find out what she's heard about Summit."

Claire set up a secure line for Mia in the white room. Erika answered immediately. She was lying in bed, her arm encased in a white plastic sheath, ominous red lights pulsing. Monitors on the wall behind held data and line graphs.

"Where are you?" Mia asked.

Erika reached her free hand to a side table, tapped something, and a conversation shield hiss filled the room. "Omni Hospital. Oncology ward." She smiled and winked—likely the first time that phrase and expression had been paired. "Don't worry. They caught it just in time. I should be fine, but I've got to come in for treatment once a week for the next few months."

"Have you heard any rumors about Summit?" Mia asked. No need to express concern for Erika's faux illness.

"Unfortunately, yes. One of your former clients claims you've collected unencrypted data from their residence. Weber allowed Han to investigate. So far, no hard evidence but everyone's a bit put off by your team's disappearance."

That would explain the raid on the office.

"Han plans to circulate an internal memo strongly advising employees not to use your services. It doesn't help that you were let go under questionable circumstances and are now working in another sector. That just isn't done here."

"Do you think we'll lose our charter?"

"I doubt it. The contracts your clients sign protect you as well as them. Han would have to prove you collected, stored, and misused data. That'd mean showing data to Optima, and we both know they don't have it."

One of the screens behind Erika began to chirp. She glanced up at it.

"I almost forgot. I'm not going to respond well to one of the medications. That'll mean a slowdown in treatments. I won't be able to do any rigorous work for at least six months. I've got to go. Keep in touch. I appreciate—"

A thin young woman in a white bodysuit slid into the frame. "Ms. Brunhoff needs to rest." She waved a silver-nailed hand and the feed ended.

"This might be an off-the-books project but they have enough sway to get corporate to investigate us," Jason said. "Not a good sign."

"I told you, a place with only one exit was a bad idea," Mikey said. "We should head down to South Shore. I met some people there who might be able to help us out."

"No. We need to get further away from Topsoil, not closer," Lucas said.

With no other cities on the planet, that meant camping or boating. "How long will we have to lie low?" Mia asked.

"Until Han announces the project was a success, or the personnel come back, or Mitch sees Magnussen standing on his balcony," Lucas said.

Claire was incredulous. "Months. I heard you say months. What are you proposing? We go live in a cave somewhere? I can't do that!"

Claire was not a fan of nature.

Lucas held out his hands. "Victoria was a refuge for us because Itek wasn't here. Now it is, with the resources of Han."

"What do you mean, Victoria *was* a refuge? Where are you proposing we go?" Mia asked.

He looked to her as if for confirmation, but she had no idea what he was about to say.

"To Novus."

That caught her off guard. The others were even more confused.

"The hotel by the strataport?" Claire asked. "How is that safer?"

"No," Lucas said. "The planet. We can get passage on an Earth-owned transport ship and won't show up on any New Canberra passenger manifests. Tony Espinoza from NYCPD moved to Novus about ten years ago. He's a city administrator there and can keep us off official records and help us find a place to stay."

Claire stood so quickly her chair fell over backwards. "I'm not going."

"Claire," Lucas began.

Two small, bright red spots on her cheeks signaled fury. "I'm not going to another planet. I'm finally getting my life in order here."

Jason scowled. "I can't believe this is happening again. We're running out of planets, Lucas."

"Thank you for pointing that out." Lucas rubbed his temples. "We don't have a choice. We aren't safe here. How long have we got, Mikey?"

Mikey's expression shifted from blankly amicable to coldly intelligent. "We have sixty, maybe seventy hours before the other sectors allow Han access to scan for genetic trace materials and review camera data. Negotiations are probably going on now. It will take a few business days to work out the details. This isn't information the Six like to share, but everything here has a price."

Mia wasn't sure whether to be terrified or excited. She'd always wanted to visit Novus. The next planet out from the sun from Victoria fascinated her, and from what Jason told her months ago, the team would have chosen to hide out there if there'd have been any way to make money—which there wasn't. The scant four thousand residents wouldn't need security.

"You'll like it," she told Claire. "It's the opposite of here. No shopping malls. No rules. They've banned corporations, and everyone is just winging it."

She ran through the literature she'd read and the holos she'd watched, trying to find something that would appeal to Claire. "The weather is a huge improvement. Sixteen degrees tops in the dead of summer. Big role-playing game community. Old school. Dice, figurines, the real deal."

"It was our first choice," Lucas said. "We all agreed but couldn't make it work financially. You voted yes."

Claire sighed capitulation. "I never wanted to come here."

"I know you hate space travel," Lucas said, "but it won't be a burst drive ship. None of us enjoyed that."

"We have a place to stay on Novus?" Mikey asked.

"Yes. Mitch will handle the details. I don't want to communicate with Tony until we land. In fact, I'd like us to go online as little as possible from now on."

Mia tried to picture how the next three months might play out compared to what she'd imagined…and realized she hadn't imagined anything. She'd been living day to day with no expectations other than merely surviving. There was no escaping the gravity of Victoria, was there? She loved her home planet, but it had crushed her and kept her from climbing as high as she might. There was nowhere she could be herself.

Novus was nowhere.

"What do you think?" Lucas asked her.

"It's a good plan. The sooner we leave the better."

Lucas frowned, as if suspecting sarcasm, but found none in her direct gaze.

"I'm surprised you're okay with this. If you truly are, I could use your help in creating a false trail. Han has to think we're somewhere north, camping. Work out a scenario. We'll rent the equipment, so make it real."

"I can do that."

She imagined a dream getaway—two months exploring the caves of the Sienna Mountains. She'd visited a few times. The theoretical trip would have to avoid the popular sites like the crystal palace, but there were thousands of caves and passages, and it was impossible to scan for life signs through the thick rock.

Perfect.

Throughout the day, she overheard Lucas and Jason making discreet inquiries to find out if any Earth ships going to Novus would take unofficial passengers. Claire was glasses down doing who knew what, seeming to be in a much-improved mood.

Mia presented her camping scenario to the team that evening. She tried to make everyone sit in the semicircle of chairs. Mikey laughed and stayed by the swinging doors. Claire took off her glasses but didn't leave her booth. Lucas stood behind Jason—the only one who'd actually sat.

Mia held up a big screen. "This would be the best hideout slash adventure ever."

She showed maps of trails through tunnels and caves three hundred meters underground, sunken lakes, and a detailed supply list with explanations by each item. For a few minutes she forgot they were in trouble. Even Claire showed interest in the strange rock formations they weren't actually going to see.

"Good work," Lucas said. "Claire, Jason, Mikey, make this happen. Buy the supplies then have them disappear. Rent a skimmer. Destroy it."

Mikey nodded confidently. He'd worked under Lucas at the oil field in Venezuela back in the day. Maybe their current situation wasn't so different.

Lucas addressed Claire. "I want you to use the same care to keep this secret that you are using to obscure our real plan, understand?"

Claire's fingers flew into motion.

"Is there anything else I can do to help?" Mia asked.

"Not now," he said. "I'll let you know if I need anything. Stay offline."

It was too early to take a Baby Jane—she'd need it to sleep after today's brain drain—so she went back to her booth and ran through all she knew about Novus. As a child she'd been fascinated by the planet's dramatic landscapes. The mountains—formed by volcanic activity and crashing tectonic plates and chiseled by glaciers—were jagged black protrusions ripping through pastoral green valleys, waterfalls tumbling down their steep sides. She envied all its water features—huge rivers, steaming milky-white lakes, sky-blue hot springs, geysers. Victoria had no aboveground water other than the ocean, which she did love to visit, but it was little more than a blue smudge from New Canberra. The exuberantly active landscape of Novus made Victoria look lazy and dead.

Relations between Novus and Victoria had always been cool. The Associated Governments of Earth hadn't really wanted the planet; they'd just wanted to keep it from the Six. To make doubly sure the Six never secured a toehold, the AGE enacted strict anticorporation laws and equally strict protections of individual property rights. The planet was an AGE protectorate, but independent.

Travel to the planet wasn't forbidden, but Optima kept a low-key, negative ad campaign running. Novus wasn't safe. Transportation and communications were unreliable. If you were injured, there was no hospital. Shopping was dismal and culture nonexistent, with no museums or galleries, and the few restaurants didn't rate even one star from the most generous reviewers. Crater City was voted least interesting city in the solar system year after year, a tired running joke. An eccentric Earth billionaire financed an exclusive ski resort in the perpetually snowy north, but it was understood that if you couldn't afford your own medic and shipboard clinic, you shouldn't go.

Barely four thousand people lived on the planet, the majority of them in or around Crater City, which was—surprise—in a large crater two kilometers in diameter and about one kilometer deep. The AGE threw a dome over it, erected a large solar array and some wind turbines to provide power, then left the settlers on their own. A flat five percent income tax supported infrastructure for the planet and slowly paid back the AGE for the dome and power.

How did Novus residents earn a living? Half did nothing, retirees surviving on pension checks from Earth. Others fished or did fishing-related work such as canning or refining biodiesel from fish waste. A handful ran small businesses. The potential for geothermal power was great but no power plants had been built. Per capita income was a horrifyingly low twenty thousand AGE MUs, worse even than Earth's.

Though glaciers covered a sixth of the planet, the weather was relatively balmy in the equatorial region—up to twenty degrees Celsius in the summer and never below one or two in the winter. Oddly, that wasn't where Crater City was located. She wondered why they chose to place the city at such an inhospitably high latitude.

"Mia, Mikey." Lucas called.

She joined the rest of the team in the white room.

"Good news. We have transport to Novus. We leave tomorrow," Lucas said.

So soon? It'd been fine to fantasize about leaving Victoria, but actually leaving was another matter. She wasn't ready. "What kind of transport?" Mia asked.

"Freighter."

"So, no burst drive."

"Correct," he said.

Claire's fingers slapped her virtual keyboard. "The trip will take five weeks!" Her voice ricocheted against the shiny walls.

"Four," corrected Lucas, "and we'll have our own cabins, and there will be no other passengers. It wasn't being cooped up that bothered you. It was the burst drive. It nauseated all of us."

Claire took a deep breath, opened her mouth to launch a complaint.

Lucas held up a hand. "You don't want to be here when Richter breaks down the door a week from now."

Silence.

"Right," Lucas said. "Claire, transfer funds to Mitch. He'll pay the freighter for our passage. This transaction *must not* be traced back to us."

While Mia didn't enjoy being trapped in the cramped confines of the restaurant, leaving the next day felt rushed. Lucas's elaborate plan to get the team to the strataport unnoticed and his assurances that "everything would be fine" convinced her everything wasn't fine.

She packed and repacked the bag of clothes Jason brought from her apartment, puzzling over his selections and imagining how she'd get by with so few garments for four weeks, then wondering what she'd do once they arrived on Novus. She'd never searched for retail there and couldn't go online now to check. Petty worries to be sure, but ones that kept her from thoughts of traversing the most surveillance-heavy city on three worlds to make it to the strataport without Topsoil's forces intercepting them.

At midnight, Lucas clapped his hands. Three sharp raps. Mia had never heard him clap before, and it clearly wasn't his style.

"Everyone, get some rest. Mia, Mikey, and especially Jason and Claire. I need you focused."

None of them had managed to get much sleep since they'd arrived, and tempers were growing short. Jason and Claire had gotten into a spat earlier in the day over which equipment was essential and Mikey had to intervene.

"I need everyone sharp tomorrow. No mistakes," Lucas said.

He came to Mia's booth, sat across from her, and spoke softly. "No Baby Janes, okay?"

Mia covered a neatly folded pile of black silk panties with a pair of gray linen pants. "No Baby Janes, no sleep."

"You probably don't realize but you're slow after you take those, long after they've supposedly worn off. Mikey has a stash of tequila here. How about a drink instead? Won't that help?"

"Better than nothing."

"Shots for everyone," Mikey bellowed as he reached behind a pile of chairs and fished out a liter bottle of tequila—half empty.

The dinner crowd at Giverny, the restaurant above, seemed to be thinning, the incessant thumping and clacking of shoes, both heavy and delicate, subsiding to solo patters. Lucas went to the supply room and returned with four shot glasses.

"Jason?" Lucas asked.

"I'll take that in my beer." He held out a glass bottle and Lucas poured generously, then filled three of the shot glasses.

Mikey knocked his back and slammed it down on the table. "Another."

"I was going to do a toast," Lucas said, frowning as he refilled Mikey's glass. "Claire, I know you don't drink, but join us."

Claire sighed, took the empty glass, and stood next to Mia in the loose circle.

Lucas still had on the shirt he'd worn to The Center, and he and it looked decidedly worse for wear. He held the shot glass up, careful not to spill as he'd filled it nearly to the brim.

"To the best team I've had the privilege of working with, and the only people I'd trust with my life. Who I *have* trusted with my life," he corrected. "Let's use the trip to Novus as a chance to relax. It won't be luxurious, but it'll be the first time we won't have to look over our shoulders in…" he rubbed his free hand through his already disheveled hair, "I don't know how long. Onwards and upwards."

He raised his glass higher, and Mikey clinked it, sending half the tequila cascading to floor. A sweeperbot rushed out to clean the mess, and everyone laughed. Mia touched her glass lightly to Jason's beer bottle then drank her shot in one gulp, hoping Lucas would let her have a refill. He did but refused her request for a third.

She might be able to sleep.

She couldn't. When the sun rose in the invisible east, she'd managed only a few hours of rest—evidenced by dreams of being crushed.

Mikey had passed out immediately and snored loudly. Claire tossed and turned and muttered, the red leather of her booth squeaking under her weight. Jason and Lucas slept quietly or did a good job of faking it. She suspected the latter, as she'd seen faint lights playing on the pile of chairs, evidence someone was using a virtual keyboard.

At 6 a.m. she gave up pretending and padded quietly into the bathroom, lightheaded and weary. She washed and changed into fresh clothes. She'd soon be face-to-face with residents of Victoria and needed to blend in. Funny…she already considered herself something different, more and less attached to the planet than they were. Native born but not chosen.

A tap on the door brought her back. She'd been drifting.

"Sorry, I'll be right out."

Jason, hollow-eyed in the unflattering overhead light, nodded as she exited.

"That fucking restaurant is so loud. Did you hear when they knocked over what sounded like all the cutlery at two a.m.?"

"I did. How about when the pond pumps came on at four a.m.?" Mia asked.

"This whole place started to vibrate. I'm not sure I want to go to Novus, but I definitely don't want to stay here."

Everyone else was up by now.

"Mia," Lucas said. "Can you put this place back into the same state it was when you arrived? A decent scanner will reveal we were here, but not for how long. If it doesn't appear we stayed the night, whoever is looking for us will assume we picked up equipment and left the city—especially if they find out about our camping plans."

Mikey helped her recreate the state the dining room had been in when she'd arrived, tossing chairs back onto the booths and tables with ease. Mia refilled the sweeperbot's cleaning fluid reservoirs and set them all to sanitizing mode. The rest of the team packed equipment, arguing over what to bring and what to leave. Lucas insisted no one bring more than they could carry.

When all was ready, everyone assembled in the storage room by the front door. The alley outside Frontier was patrolled by MMARVs, but infrequently.

Claire watched live camera views. "We've got thirty minutes now, if the pattern holds."

"Let's go," Lucas said.

Chapter Thirty Three

The plan was simple. They'd leave one at a time in five-minute intervals and travel in separate pods to the strataport. Mikey arranged for a student from his dojo to meet them at the end of the alley, hail a pod, direct it to the strataport, pay with an untraceable credit voucher, then get out. Mikey would go first, Lucas next, then Claire, Mia, and Jason.

Mia wasn't a fan of the one-by-one plan. It didn't feel right to separate the team, but Lucas insisted he and Mikey needed to get there first, locate the shuttle that would take them to the freighter, bribe the captain to turn off any cameras, and get the majority of their gear loaded so they could leave as soon as possible.

The fact that bribes were needed made Mia uneasy. Clearly everything hadn't been "taken care of" by Lucas and Mitch.

"No communications unless it's an emergency," Lucas said. "Claire has set up special links between us, text only."

Mikey left, carrying the heaviest of the gear—two oversized cases even he strained to lift. The briefly open door let in a breath of fresh air and the diffuse glow of daylight. No one had showered in days. Did she stink? Mia dropped her nose to shoulder and breathed in. Not yet. She might not draw attention to herself by nervous actions, but any New Canberran would notice bad personal hygiene. Of all the trends to sweep the city, natural body odor had never been one of them. She should have checked on Mikey.

"You okay with this and your pack?" Lucas held out a sturdy gray crate.

Mia reached for it and for an awkward moment their fingers touched. She grabbed the crate, tested the weight.

"I can carry more. I've been climbing twice a week."

Lucas lowered his voice. "I'm sorry we can't all go together, but it isn't safe." He took the crate back from her, this time deliberately encasing her hands in his. "The pods won't pass through Han sector. We'll be fine."

"The more often you say that, the less fine I feel."

He'd shaved off the stubble he'd worn since they arrived—recently, based on the thin line of soap by his right ear—and his breath smelled sweetly unfamiliar. The secret hideout held different toiletries than he normally used.

Jason glanced over, saw their hands locked and gave Lucas a glare that could've melted plasticrete. Mia pulled away.

"We're being hunted," Lucas said, oblivious of anyone but Mia. "Actively. Keep your glasses and hat on."

"I know the plan. I'm not going to stop and shop."

He gave her a strange, penetrating look that reminded her of the day he'd first interviewed her, when he was deciding whether she was a victim or a thief. What was he trying to decipher today?

"Be careful," he said.

"Time for you to go, Lucas," Jason said. "We need to keep to the schedule."

"Right. All clear, Claire?"

"Yes."

Jason pulled open the door, and Lucas disappeared into the light.

"You're next Claire. Five minutes," Jason said.

She stood stock still amidst the remaining bags.

"Claire." Mia said. "Put on your hat."

"I can't walk down that alley. It's nearly a quarter kilometer to the road."

Claire feared being on her own outdoors. In college, it took Mia almost a year to notice Claire never went anywhere without someone. Only when Claire snapped at her during summer break, "Aren't you ever going to do laundry?" had she realized Claire was waiting for her to go to the student laundromat.

Clair had changed so much in the last ten years Mia had assumed she'd outgrown that.

"Does that mean you took a pod all the way here when you arrived?" Mia asked. "Lucas didn't want any pod trips logged to this address."

"Fuck." Jason said when Claire didn't reply. "You did. What the hell were you thinking?"

Claire shifted her weight from foot to foot.

"I can't go by myself," she whispered.

"I'll go with you," Mia said.

"No, you won't." Jason said. "Two of us together increases the chances of facial recognition ten-fold."

Mia put on her backpack and picked up the crate of equipment. "The plan is to get to the strataport unnoticed. Claire will panic if she has to walk down that alley by herself, and she's carrying PDSs loaded with confidential data. I'll get her into a pod and then wait in the alley until mine comes."

"I don't like this," he said.

"Neither do I," Mia said. "I especially don't like that none of you bothered to tell me we had a hideout. If you had, I'd have been able to stash some of my stuff here and not have to spend the next four weeks in my least comfortable underwear. And I might have had some input on this location, which is wrong for so many reasons—only one of which is that it's absurd to expect Claire to walk four hundred meters by herself."

Mia put on a sun hat, slung her bag over her shoulder, and picked up the case. "Come on Claire, let's go."

Claire nodded.

Jason opened the door. "For what it's worth, no one asked my opinion, either. Be careful."

"We will. Pull down your hat, Claire." It was lucky that sun protection was perfectly ordinary attire and the best possible way to avoid facial recognition.

Mia stepped out into fresh air and daylight. No direct sunlight made it down the narrow canyon of the alley, but it was so much brighter than Frontier she had to darken her glasses. A driverless delivery pod whizzed past.

She walked briskly down the street, hugging the left-hand side. Claire had hacked into as many of the alley cams as she could, freezing a frame from before the team started their exodus. Claire followed so closely her case banged against Mia's back when Mia stopped in the shadows a dozen meters from the ring road. A yellow pod sat to the right of the alley, the passenger door held open by a thin, blond teen in a Bulldog Gym t-shirt. That was where Mikey taught and the sign that the kid worked for him.

Mia flattened herself behind a large air-conditioning duct then pushed Claire forward. "Go."

Claire walked hesitantly to the pod. "Johann?" she asked, and he nodded.

Mia cursed silently. None of them were supposed to speak. Voice recognition on a busy street was a pretty unlikely scenario, but still a risk.

Claire fumbled her case then herself into the pod, and a moment later she was off.

Johann hadn't noticed his next customer was already here and paced away, engrossed in his glasses. A few minutes later, he hailed another pod, ran the credit voucher over the scanner, and held the door open. Mia hurried across the sidewalk, levered the case in, then settled into a backward-facing seat—a better vantage point to see if she were being followed. She visualized the various routes the pod might take, hoping it stayed on the busy inner rings.

"Strata—" Johann started to say, when he was jerked back and away and fell sprawling onto the sidewalk.

The pod rocked as Richter slammed down onto the seat diagonally across from her. "Where to, Ms. Julian?"

She shrieked and pressed the *open* button on the door near her, but it was on the traffic side and locked for safety. Johann picked himself up from the sidewalk and backed away.

"Shut up," Richter said in a quiet, reasonable tone. "I know how these stupid eggs work. You scream again, and a MMARV shows up. Before it does, you'll be dead from some very toxic venom."

He pulled what looked like a pen from an inner breast pocket and pointed it casually at her belly.

"Optima got wind of our first formula, but we've improved it since then."

Mia sat very still. "What do you want?"

"Where are you going?"

His breath was as foul as spoiled fish. He wore the same oversized glasses he'd worn the night he stunned her, as well as the same sneer—but his suit was rumpled and stained. Had he been physically hunting for them all this time?

"Home," she said automatically. Shock and surprise gave way to panic. She fought to stay in the present moment. Memories of Richter flashed across her field of view. Him at The Center. Him in the black pod, pointing a weapon at her. The horror of it happening again.

"Home, then where? Where's Lucas?"

He didn't know they'd all been hiding out together, and that meant everyone else was safe. She tried to text the team. No response.

Richter must have a transmission jammer.

Johann gaped as the pod pulled away.

Call someone, she willed him.

Her story was fake, but the tears were genuine. "I don't know. I don't know where any of them are. Lucas threw me in a pod after we saw you at *The Center* and told me to meet him at a shop called Pandemonium, and then never showed up. I got a nap room at the mall to sleep and kept checking back in at the shop, and he still never came. I wanted to go home, but Lucas told me not to scan my hand anywhere, so I convinced that waiter to pay for my pod ride."

She couldn't judge his reaction. All she could see was her own pale, tear-streaked face reflected convexly in his glasses and the hard set of his mouth.

He let the pen droop—slightly. "I'll ask again when you're hooked up to a veracity detector. It makes sense that Lucas wouldn't share information with anyone he hired from this planet." He passed a credit voucher over the pod's scanner and directed it to take them to an address in the Han sector manufacturing district.

Shit. She knew that area. More robots than people.

"I want Lucas, not you," he continued. "I wasn't allowed to go after him directly until he interrupted our meeting. Ms. Mills was not happy to be seen in my company. Help me find him, and all you'll lose is your job—which I don't think you'd mind, given the hazards of this one." He poked a thick thumb into her right shoulder. "Bullseye."

The dart had left a scar there, black in the center, a red ring around it.

"You shot me." She'd meant it as a question, but the words came out as a definitive statement.

He laughed. Not the evil laugh she'd expected, but something you'd hear after the punchline of a good joke.

"I did. You got between me and my target. Is that going to happen again today?"

That he'd admitted he'd done it frightened her more than the weapon he held now. He wasn't going to let her go.

The pod turned onto Ring 3 in the entertainment district of the IVS sector.

"Damn it. Not this street," Richter shook his head and gestured, but the pod continued its leisurely roll around the wide ring, sidewalks busy with shoppers taking advantage of the relative cool of the morning.

This isn't a pod he can control, Mia realized, and that meant she could. She had to act now while they were still in a well-populated place.

Holo ads followed the pod, and when a naked woman blowing flower petals distracted Richter, she flashed her hand over the scanner.

"Mia Julian, registered technician 84207934," she blurted out.

Richter's head snapped back. "What did you say?"

"Acknowledged," the pod replied.

She braced herself. "Diagnostic mode. Test emergency brakes."

The pod slammed to halt in the middle of the road. Richter flew forward. His head hit the front window hard enough to crack the plastic, and he slumped—out cold.

Pods flowed smoothly around the stalled pod as if they'd expected this maneuver.

She opened the now unlocked door.

What next?

She couldn't leave the case. Everything in it had been deemed essential. She pushed it out onto the road and threw her pack on top. Once she was safely out as well, she paused as a thought struck her. Against her better judgment and all common sense, she tugged on the right side of Richter's jacket until she could reach into the pocket he'd pulled the weapon from.

There it was. A small gray rectangle of metallic glass etched with a round circle containing an open book, star above it, the words "Let there be light" and "UCLA" below. Almost certainly the record of Erika's birth. She shoved it into her pack.

Passing pods slowed and informed her that she was not in a passenger zone.

She needed to get going but not until she took care of Richter. She mentally paged through the pod diagnostic manuals she'd studied months ago until she found the perfect solution.

"Bio hazard 772943." She spoke loudly then slammed the door. The windows changed to mirror and multiple bolts slid into place. Contagious illness. The pod sped away to deliver an infectious, possibly dangerously deranged patient to the nearest hospital, which in this case was in the IVS sector. Richter *would* be deranged when he arrived, and once the emergency personnel sedated and scanned him, they'd discover he wasn't a legal resident or visitor, and they'd find the pen full of deadly venom. IVS security would assume he was a spy. Optima would be called in. Especially if they had a heads-up.

She threw on her pack, picked up the case, and walked to the sidewalk, passersby giving her strange looks. Pods didn't let people out in the middle of the street. She smiled tightly, nodded, and took refuge under a bakery's deep awning.

First things first. Call Taylor.

Taylor took way too long to answer. "I can't talk now. I'm in in a meeting."

"I found the man who tore the hole in the fabric of MMARV coverage. His name is Gert Richter. He works at Itek, an Earth corporation. He's been accused of murder and attempted murder and is supposed to be awaiting trial in his apartment in New York. He's here."

Taylor, who'd been voice only, turned on his camera. "What are you talking about?"

"This is the guy who assaulted me. The guy who created a weapon out of a perfect blend of bug venoms The Center alerted you to. I locked him in a pod, and he's on his way to Verity Hospital in IVS sector. Oh, and the next generation of that venom weapon is rolling around the floor of the pod, and it can get past our scanners… Again."

Taylor blinked, then gestured and typed. "I see the pod. It's marked biohazard."

"That's him. I need to go. I'd give you more details, but I trust you to figure it out. Later, Taylor."

How long had this all taken? Was Jason safely on his way, or had another guard been waiting for him? She texted the team.

Richter was waiting for me outside the alley and got in my pod. I'm safe now. Is everyone okay? What should I do?

After a few heartbeats, Lucas replied.

We're all safe and en route. Where's Richter?

Unconscious and on his way to a hospital, she replied. *He doesn't know where I was headed or where you are.*

Stay put. Johann will come to you.

She kept her head down and pretended to examine the croissants in the window.

A few minutes later, she saw Johann's reflection in the glass. He crouched half in, half out of a pod. She threaded through the shoppers to meet him.

"I'm sorry," he said. "I didn't know what to do."

"It wasn't your fault," she assured him.

"I'm only a yellow belt."

"You did great."

He smiled shyly, loaded the crate into the pod, paid the fare to the strataport, then retreated with an apologetic bow.

She mirrored the windows and scanned the crowds on the sidewalk to see if anyone was paying attention to her. No one seemed to be. The pod navigated the streets, moving further from the center of the city. By Ring 10, Mia was sure she hadn't been followed.

She took a breath, the first in what felt like an hour. Had she really taken care of Richter? Taylor said heads had rolled due to the MMARV hack. He'd take what she told him seriously—and having a pen full of venom wouldn't help Richter's case.

She traced the outline of Erika's BioKey, safely stored in the front pocket of her pack. She'd let her know she had it…soon. Maybe after the team arrived on Novus.

The pod picked up speed as traffic thinned. The familiar city looked strange now that she was leaving it. Even perfect memory couldn't stop emotion from clouding her perceptions, and odd features jumped out from the buildings she passed. Asymmetrical rooflines, tall, locked gates, dark recessed windows—did she even know this place?

After the pod cleared Ring 20, Mia shut her eyes, and her pounding heart gradually slowed. Thank God the strataport was twenty minutes from town. She needed time to collect herself. As tempting as it was to call the team, she'd already drawn too much attention to herself.

Would they still be able to go ahead with the plan?

Yes. Richter didn't know she'd been with the team and seemed to believe her story, nodding as she sobbed out an explanation of how she'd been abandoned at the mall. He also didn't know where they'd been hiding, or he'd have led a raid on Frontier. She'd probably been caught by a street camera as she lurked in the alley after delivering Claire to the pod, and he'd literally come running.

Richter wouldn't be able to escape the pod before it arrived at the hospital. He'd been out cold when she took Erika's birth record from his jacket, and the hospital was less than five minutes away. The staff there would be prepared for a patient with an infectious disease. Medical drones would enter the windows and sedate and treat Richter before the doors opened and any humans got near him. Optima would arrive on scene.

Han can't cover this up.

Terrifying as it had been, things were better now. They were safer.

The pod slowed in the heavy traffic near the strataport. Though Victoria had only one real city, small settlements popped up near fishing or mining operations, research facilities dotted the planet, and the strataport served all of them, as well as Sunrise Station, the orbiting space dock.

Mia sat up and eyed the scene for anything suspicious or unusual. All was well.

The pod slid to a stop under the huge overhang shading the main entrance. Security cameras dripped from the eaves, and Optima guards patrolled the sidewalks. It would be impossible for anyone to abduct her. She repeated that mantra as the pod politely alerted her that she'd reached her destination.

Not quite yet, she wanted to reply. *I have about two hundred million kilometers to go.* She adjusted her hat, opened the door, and submerged herself in the crowd.

The passenger terminal was a long, low building with an arched ceiling and white, filigreed, plasticrete walls of a vaguely Moorish pattern. Hundreds of frosted skylights lit the interior to blown out, overexposed brightness. The air-conditioning was aggressive—designed to please new arrivals from Earth. Mia shivered. She hated being cold. A thousand voices blended to form a gently rolling ocean of white noise, punctuated by an occasional shrill laugh or shout. Bits of music filtered out from ad kiosks.

Mia lurched through the throng, the heavy crate making speed and grace impossible. She'd probably passed many of these people on the streets of New Canberra, but here, on the beginning of a trajectory to somewhere else, they were strangers. Everyone was anxious, on a schedule, dragging unwieldy baggage, trying to get from point A to point B without the pod's ability to avoid collisions.

She pulled up the strataport map on her glasses and followed the red line it projected through the travelers to the freight terminal. She left the chatter and laughter behind as the ethereal airiness of the passenger area gave way to stark gray plasticrete. No skylights here—and the temperature began to climb. Giant roll-up doors opened to the outside, and the air-conditioning fought to maintain the cool and lost. Workers in grubby coveralls directed bots loaded with tools. Caterpillar-like carts of expensive and exclusive Earth goods—she recognized the logos—crawled down the center of the corridor.

The red line stopped at Bay 10. Just outside the open door, Mia saw Lucas, Mikey, Jason and Claire standing in the beating sun beside a pile of rugged plastic cases. She nearly burst into tears again. They'd all made it. The anxiety that had propelled her all these kilometers and the final few meters vanished and she stopped, dropping the case.

Lucas caught sight of her and jogged over.

"Are you okay?" He grabbed her shoulders and held them too tightly.

"I'm not," she said. "If I had a normal brain, I'd have seen him coming and locked the pod door. Instead, I was visualizing the route."

"This wasn't your fault. If Richter doesn't want to be seen, he won't be seen. He's a professional. How did you get away?" He spoke quickly and stared at her like she'd just emerged without coveralls from an empty lot at midnight, right after the deadly spring stick bugs had hatched.

"I'm a certified pod technician," she said quietly. "You remember how I studied after I was stunned? I know how to control them in diagnostic mode—in theory. I'd never tried, but it worked. I slammed on the brakes and knocked Richter out, then had the pod recognize him as an infectious patient and take him to a hospital in IVS sector."

"You're certain?"

"Yes. I called my friend Taylor at Optima and let him know who Richter is and that he was the one that hacked the MMARVs. That was a big deal at Optima. He'll be ID'd and deported. Han can't cover it up."

Lucas shook his head. "I thought we'd lost you and instead, you saved us. Fill me in on the details later. We need to get going." He loosened his death grip on her shoulders and took her arm, pulling her toward the others.

"He's the one that shot me. He more or less admitted it."

"Of course he did. That's his style. Women and children first."

When they reached the team, Mikey gave her the gentlest shoulder punch yet. "How'd you get away? Used the old noggin, eh?" He tapped his head.

Jason circled her with the device he used to scan apartments. "No bugs on you. Nothing transmitting but glasses. You okay?"

"I am," she said, though truthfully, she was feeling a bit shaky. The competing waves of hot and cold air felt like they were physically pushing her back and forth.

"We've got to move," Lucas said. "Seal the crates and get them on the shuttle."

A small, slate-gray craft sat sullenly on the black tarmac thirty meters from the roll-up door. Its name, *THE AXIS*, was nearly indecipherable thanks to the burns and scrapes mangling the text. It would, hopefully, carry them safely to the freighter.

"Claire, Mia, get on board. We'll stow the equipment and join you shortly."

Victoria didn't care what tourists brought to Novus, so the screening on this end was nonexistent—even though most of Victoria's recreational drugs were illegal there. That was Novus's problem.

The morning sun blazed, and The Axis shimmered like a hallucination. Claire tried to hurry but her bag was so heavy all she could manage was an awkward lurching shuffle.

"I can get that," Jason offered, but she ignored him and clanged up the steep metal stairs.

Mia grasped the railing and yelped, pulling her hand quickly away. Too hot.

Claire, at the top of the stairs, turned left and right, trying to jam herself through the small opening without unstrapping the bag, adding more dings to the scarred exterior of the craft. Suddenly successful, she disappeared with a clatter and a curse.

Mia waited until the banging subsided, then climbed and hunched to enter.

The small cabin held just twelve seats, six on each side of a narrow aisle. Claire, all the way in the back, tried to jam the very large bag into the very small overhead bin.

"Maybe just strap it into the seat next to you," Mia suggested. She dumped her own pack in a seat nearer the front and helped Claire loosen the seatbelts to accommodate the lumpy bundle of what seemed to be hundreds of data storage units.

Once Claire's baby was safe, Mia stowed her own bag and strapped in. It'd been a while since she'd been on a shuttle. Three years ago, she dated the younger brother of a junior partner. Big brother rented a shuttle to drift above the dateline in order to be the first to ring in the New Year. The shuttle was more penthouse apartment than transportation, and competition to be the first to declare Happy New Year was fierce. Several hundred shuttles coasted back and forth along the longitudinal line, aggressively jamming each other's GPSs and using collision-avoidance systems to bump each other into the past or future. Mia had stopped paying attention once she found the globules of Dom Perignon floating in the observation deck.

The metal bin she sat in now was the dumpster that penthouse would have jettisoned its empty bottles into. The cracked black imitation leather of the seat stank of food and sweat. The emergency exit instruction card had clearly been used to hold a drug that required a heat source to activate. If Mia needed to learn to inflate a flotation device, she'd be out of luck. That panel was a charred hole. She'd have been squeamish about touching any of this, if she wasn't just as dirty.

She leaned forward, elbows on knees, and shut her eyes, taking a moment to relax. To breathe. To acknowledge they'd soon be safer.

Claire's complete silence eventually roused her. What was she doing? Mia looked back. Claire gripped the armrests and stared resolutely at the seat in front of her, jaw tight. Mia wasn't in the mood for dealing with

Claire's phobias, not after having been kidnapped and threatened with a deadly weapon, but walking through the strataport on her own was probably as terrifying to Claire as Mia's ordeal had been to her.

"You okay?" Mia asked.

Claire glared at the seatback. "I hate this." She took off her glasses and wiped her eyes roughly with the back of her hand.

Mia had never seen her cry and resisted an urge to go back there and give her a hug. It would only make things worse.

"I just got my apartment here the way I like it. Now we're leaving again, and I've got nothing, again." Claire sniffed and rubbed her nose with the sleeve of her jacket.

"You have your data and your glasses. That's what matters most, isn't it? We won't be gone long. Novus is beautiful. We'll sightsee for a month and then head back."

Claire scowled. "Maybe you can give me a Baby Jane so I can forget my life sucks."

Mia had rarely felt a physical need to slap someone. She balled her hands into fists and turned away. From the window she saw Lucas and Mikey pushing a loaded cart toward the rear of the shuttle. Jason headed to the stairway, canvas bag over his shoulder. He clanged up the staircase and dropped into the seat behind her.

"The real Summit Security team just boarded a research boat headed for the North Pole," he said. "I'd rather be with them than in this rust bucket."

"What? I thought we were going camping," Mia said.

"We're doing both. We set up a more easily discoverable plan—the boat. The camping trip is our *secret* plan. No one will figure out where we really are. I hope."

The shuttle shifted to an accompanying *thunk*. The crates, loaded, cargo door, shut. Mikey squeezed through the hatch and ratcheted himself into the front seat, knees pressed into the wall panel.

"Here we go again, huh? Stick with Lucas and you'll see the galaxy."

He chuckled, and she could almost hear Claire frown.

Lucas entered and pulled the door closed behind him, turning the locking bar to the horizontal position. His shirt was sweat-stained, his face damp.

"No other passengers?" Mia asked.

"Technically, there are no passengers on the shuttle at all. Just spare parts for the fish freighter," Lucas said.

This must be costing quite a bit. Much of the hard-earned business account would be depleted by the time it was over. Mia couldn't be too upset; those savings were saving their lives.

Claire spoke up. "Did you say fish freighter?"

Lucas took the seat next to Mia. "I did. Don't worry, it won't smell. The fish are frozen, and the freighter is picking up fish from Novus, not delivering them."

Mia had heard about fish freighters. The crews—all from Earth—were reputed to be the worst in the industry. Drug addicts, criminals, anyone who couldn't get a proper job.

An intercom crackled and buzzed, interrupting the complaint that Claire was clearly about to deliver.

"Buckle up and prepare for takeoff," said a gravelly male voice. "We'll be leaving in five minutes."

Mia checked her buckles again. They were worn, and it was tough getting them to stay latched. She examined the rest of the shuttle more critically. The plastic wall panels were cracked, most ceiling tiles were missing completely, and the carpet down the aisle was frayed. The armrest next to her was broken off. Hopefully the engines were in better repair.

"Don't worry," Lucas said, leaning close across the too-narrow aisle and resting his hand on the unbroken armrest. "They're all like this. Crappy on the inside but structurally sound. The Six don't want shuttles blowing up and raining debris on New Canberra."

Logical but not comforting.

He laughed. "You just hacked a pod, knocked out my arch enemy, and told Optima where to pick him up. The rest of this day is going to be easy."

She doubted it.

Chapter Thirty Four

The Axis lurched and rolled forward on electric power, main engines not yet engaged. It taxied past the freight terminal and onto the long straight black runway, the flat blue line of the ocean dead ahead, then stopped. A low rumble started and rose to a high cyclical whine. Everything began to shudder. The overhead bin holding Jason's duffle popped open, and the bag fell to the floor. He grabbed it and shoved it under his seat. Claire stared around in alarm. Mia didn't like take-off and landing and liked it even less on this rust bucket.

The shuttle abruptly leapt forward and gained velocity at an atrocious rate, the force pressing Mia deeply into the stinky black seat. Her head shook so badly she could barely see. The landscape blurred, and the shuddering lessened only slightly when the wheels left the ground. The shuttle banked and New Canberra swung into view, quickly shrinking to a small gray circle in a sea of tan dirt and sand. The sky darkened to deep blue, then to black. Day transformed to starry night. The shuddering subsided, and shoulder straps restrained her now weightless body. She reached into her pocket for the rubber band she'd almost forgotten to bring and pulled her lion's mane of hair into a ponytail.

The fifteen-minute trip to Sunrise Station seemed to take only moments. While New Canberra was a well-tended garden, Sunrise Station was a tangle of weeds. Originally meant to serve only as a dock for shuttles and freighters travelling to and from Earth, the station now included a hotel, restaurant, shopping mall, hospital, and university research center. In the city, four decades of evolving taste and technology could be gracefully blended with updated facades, but the additions to Sunrise Station hung exposed, embarrassing reminders of the past. The Bella Vista Hotel was the worst. Attached to an original, stark metal docking arm, the orange ball was a ridiculous eyesore. Architecture from the teens was bad all over, but up here there was no way to justify the expense of a remodel.

Only a handful of ships were docked today. One stood out—a sexy executive flyer, bright silver and brand-new. A few trips back and forth to Earth would leave the hull scratched and pitted like those of the crafts around it. Was this Magnussen's ship? Could he bribe the right people to transport him and Richter to it? Probably. They'd be back on Earth before Mitch could get a warrant to confirm they hadn't skipped bail, and that would be fine. Mia just wanted them gone.

They powered past the station and into open space. The freighter had already detached from the dock and hung a few kilometers away, ready to head to Novus.

If a bulldozer scraped up the contents of a wrecking yard and dumped everything into a compressor, the resulting square of smashed metal that emerged would closely resemble the ship that lay ahead of them. Purely functional objects could be beautiful, but this freighter wasn't. Its job was simple. Transport fish from Novus and return with supplies for the homesteaders, over and over again. The name, printed crudely on the side, read *THE ALBATROSS*. That was auspicious.

The shuttle matched velocity with the behemoth and shot out magnetic grapples that latched onto the side of it, roughly outlining a dented door. Mia's perspective shifted abruptly—Victoria suddenly looming above instead of below. Her stomach fluttered as she tried to deal with being upside down. Or right side up? Zero G was awful.

The freighter door jerked open, and a white tube snaked toward them, clanged against the side of the shuttle, and hissed. Once the hissing stopped, Lucas unbuckled and floated to the door. A green light above it lit up. He braced himself, wrenched the bar, and pushed it open.

The passenger tube was a vertiginous swirl of white plastic ringed with handles, swaying in a nonexistent breeze. Mia held her breath. The tube should be double walled. How was it attached to the shuttle? The outer shell—dented as it was—couldn't possibly hold a proper seal. Passenger ships running between Victoria and Earth connected to Sunrise Station with solid, magnetic gangways. The idea that only a millimeter of fabric separated her from space increased her nausea.

Cold air swirled around the cabin.

"We have to go through that?" Claire asked.

"This isn't safe," Mia said.

"It isn't going to get safer if you sit here longer," Lucas replied. "Get moving. Mikey and I will deal with the bags you brought onboard."

Better get this over with. If she didn't get some gravity soon, she was going to throw up. Mia unbuckled, grabbed the handle on top of the seat in front of her, and propelled herself into the tube.

She'd gone in too fast and at the wrong angle and hit the side of the tube.

Fuck.

Would that knock it loose? Was she going up or down or across? Her brain couldn't decide, and her stomach flipped. She willed herself to see the way forward as across, though when Jason emerged from the shuttle, he was upside down, and that didn't help. He turned out to be surprisingly adept for someone who couldn't possibly have done this before, gracefully launching himself and flying to the far end of the tube. He poked numbers on a keypad, and a door opened inwards with a groan.

"Mia, come here." He held out a hand, the other grasping the rim of the freighter's door.

She pressed tentatively against the damp, spongy tube wall with her own hand and floated the last few meters to him. He corrected her course and landed her safely in what must be an airlock.

"Now you, Claire," he called.

Claire stood ramrod straight, arms crossed. Mikey laughed, grabbed her waist, and pushed her from the shuttle. She squeaked but his aim was good, and Mia caught her when she floated into the airlock.

"You okay?" Mia asked.

Claire shook her head. "Shut the door."

"Go on," Lucas yelled. "We'll catch up."

Jason pulled himself into the two-by-two-meter chamber and studied a faded but serious-looking set of all-caps instructions.

"Orange is down," he declared as he pressed a large green button, and the door creaked shut.

A synthetic voice warned, "Fifty percent Victoria gravity returning in thirty seconds. Place your feet on the orange floor and hold on to the yellow handles."

Mia looked around in a panic. Their feet floated above dingy gray. A few moments of comedy ensued as they all reoriented, Claire nearly giving Jason a black eye in her frantic attempts to rotate 180 degrees.

A chime sounded just as Mia grabbed the handles, and her organs fell back into place. Maybe not the same places they'd been in on Victoria. She burped.

"Sorry. I'm not good at this." She burped again.

As soon as the red light over the inner door turned green, Jason wrestled it open. Stale, damp, fishy air enveloped the three of them.

Claire held a hand over her nose and mouth. "Lucas said it wouldn't smell."

Mia's nausea returned. It wasn't the mild bouquet of fresh sushi but the stench of a rotting carcass. They stepped into a junction of corridors leading straight, left, and right.

"Where do we go?" she asked.

A man in a filthy gray jumpsuit appeared at the end of the center corridor, walking backwards and dragging a tank.

"Where are the passenger quarters?" Jason called.

The man gestured back down the hall then disappeared into a doorway without any further instructions.

"Lucas," Jason said as he settled his glasses. "We need a map. This ship isn't talking to me."

The interior of the place was as ugly as the outside and excessively well-lit, revealing gray-green walls and flooring smeared with streaks of dark-brown goo. Fish blood? Where were the sweepers?

"Okay," Jason said. "This way." He pointed left.

Mia followed, keeping to the center of the corridor, Claire close on her heels. The ship was huge, and she was thoroughly disoriented by the time they traversed a maze of left-right-left turns and arrived at a section with numbered doors.

Jason paused and ran a finger through the air. "This is it. Claire, you're in five, Mia, you're in eight. I'm in fifteen. I'll send the door codes." A four-digit number flashed in the corner of her view area. "Lucas will send a ship map. We'll regroup once they've unloaded our cases."

The door to her cabin was solid metal with rounded edges, straight out of a 20th century submarine movie. The lock was mechanical. She pressed the code on the raised buttons, and it clunked and swung inward.

Twin-size bunk beds hung on the left wall of the tiny room. A small porthole was set into the wall she faced, a desk and chair directly beneath. A sink, mirror above it, jutted out from the wall on her right. A prison cell had more charm. She slid the metal bar that served as a door lock into place. The heaviness of it pleased her. While every crew member likely knew the code to her room, they'd not get past that medieval marvel.

The air is better in here. She found the climate control panel and dialed down the heat. Her stomach began to settle. She leaned her forehead against the coolness of the porthole, stared at the bright splash of stars, and took long, deep breaths.

The ship's engines, until now a quiet vibration underfoot, suddenly grew louder. The whole cabin thrummed with a bass rhythmic throbbing, more a feeling than a sound. Though she felt no movement, the stars shifted and spun, and Victoria filled her vista.

This is really happening. I'm leaving.

New Canberra was nothing more than a tiny dark spot in a crinkled sea of tan and gray. The engine's rumbling volume increased, and they began to pull away. New Canberra shriveled and disappeared. Soon she could see the whole continent and the Eastern and Western Sea, then both poles and the wisps of clouds circling there. After a few minutes, she could barely distinguish tan from blue. The planet shrank, consumed by the black space growing around it, until it was nothing more than a bright ball.

She waited for the angst. For the tearing. She was leaving her world. Her pretty apartment. The deserts. The blood-warm sea.

The angst never came.

She'd spent her entire life running from something. The REA, her mother's suffocating need, boyfriends who thought she was a know-it-all, Erika's manipulations, and finally, Richter and the greedy assholes behind Topsoil.

She'd never run *to* something.

Novus had been little more than fiction to her until now, but it had always been a story with a geyser- and volcano-filled happy ending. *And I'm going there.*

Plus, she felt honest-to-God safe on this shitty ship. Claire and Jason would scan every square inch of it, and there'd be no one on here but the Summit team and the creepy crew. She could relax. Really, truly relax.

It was the vacation she'd never taken, and it started right now.

She took the pack of Baby Janes from her pocket and considered taking one, then rejected the idea. These were all she'd have for the next few months. She'd save them for a real need, and right now she was so tired she would and could nap—no meds required. The blanket on the lower bunk was scratchy, but the texture fascinated her fingers and lulled her to sleep.

A knock on the door startled her awake.

"What?" she croaked, mouth dry.

"It's Lucas. I have your pack and need to scan your cabin."

She groaned and forced herself out of bed. The mirror revealed a mess of a woman—hair a crazy tangle and a big crease down the side of her face. No one needed to see that.

She drank from the faucet. "Later," she yelled to the closed door. "I'm resting."

"Alright," Lucas said. "I'll leave your pack outside the door and check your cabin after dinner. We'll meet in the mess hall at 6 p.m. The ship runs on Novus time. Claire sent out a ship map."

"Got it."

"Good. See you soon. I'm in seventeen if you need anything."

She was glad he'd woken her. The nap had revived her, and she examined the cabin with lazy optimism. The place was going to be home for weeks so she might as well make the best of it. She unbarred the door, pulled it open half a meter, and grabbed her bag before anyone could see her.

She unpacked, again marveling at the garments Jason had chosen for her. He clearly didn't have sisters. She hung the mismatched garden of floral prints from the top bunk. The riotous colors of her shirts and pants and dresses overpowered the dull green.

Once the decorating was done, she untangled her hair. By some miracle, Jason had packed her favorite brush. Normally she had to coax the gentle waves into existence; here, with low gravity and humidity, her hair was wild. She looked like a cast member from "Moon Madness," the short-lived reality show about the moon colony. She washed her face and changed into a clean yellow tank top and a daisy-patterned skirt—the most subtle outfit she could piece together. It was nearly time for dinner, and the opportunity for the team to grill her about the encounter with Richter. He was already a thousand kilometers away in reality, and by some miracle, in her memories as well. She wanted to keep this calm, not relive the trauma.

Minutes later there was another knock at her door.

Shit, it was already 6:15. She'd been daydreaming. She pulled back the deadbolt to find Lucas staring down at her with disapproval.

"I was worried about you, but I see you've medicated yourself into oblivion, again."

"I've not," Mia said. "You can check the pack. I fell asleep."

Lucas furrowed his brow. "You look relaxed."

"I am, and I'd like to stay that way. I'm not ready to talk about what happened in the pod. It's done and we're gone."

Lucas also relaxed, the furrow vanishing. "I understand, and we'll never talk business in public areas of the ship regardless. Only in our cabins, and only after we've secured them."

"In that case, I'll join you."

"You should probably put something on over that." He gestured toward her top. "The crew is comprised entirely of men from Earth, and they spend months at a time on the freighter. There are no cameras to force people to behave."

No cameras. Good news in that no one from Victoria could log in and spy on them, but bad news in that Phil from business development had taken advantage of the tiny slivers of unsurveilled space at Han to harass her. *What might happen here?*

"Don't worry," Lucas said. "None of us will go anywhere alone, and we have stunners."

She picked a violet, zip-up jacket from the fabric-festooned bunk and put it on.

"I look like a freak," she declared. "I wish you'd have been the one to pick out my clothes."

Lucas laughed. "You might not like what I'd have picked, either. Come on, the mess is only open until seven."

He'd changed as well, maybe even showered. His attempt to hold the door open meant she had to sidle awkwardly past, her chest brushing his.

She'd taken only a few steps down the corridor—hoping to bury the awkward moment in movement—when the throbbing of the engines turned to a hiss. The ugly, gray-green floor tilted up toward her. Her vision turned white and then to nothing. She opened her eyes to an out-of-focus view of the ceiling. Lucas knelt beside her, one hand on her forehead, the other on her wrist. He spoke but she couldn't hear. Eventually, his moving lips formed sounds, then words.

"Don't try to get up. When did you last eat?"

She blinked hard a few times and took a deep breath. The three fuzzy lightstrips above her sharpened and merged into one. "I have no idea."

"You didn't eat at all at Frontier, did you?"

The days in that strange, windowless, carved-out section of the past blurred together. She'd drunk many glasses of water, but the dehydrated rations and dusty canned kidney beans had held no appeal.

"I don't think I did."

His dark expression made her reluctant to admit it but… "I wasn't hungry."

Lucas frowned. "I should have paid more attention."

"It isn't your fault. I'm not a cat. You didn't have to open a can for me."

"I'm in charge of the team, and people aren't themselves in those kinds of situations, especially if they aren't used to them. I was responsible for our physical safety, and food is part of that. You might have fainted in the strataport. Security would have come, and then what?"

Cold rivets pressed painfully into her back. "Can I please get off this floor? It's disgusting."

Lucas rose and offered his hand. She took it, stood unsteadily, and didn't complain when he put his arm around her waist for support. A thousand kilometers from Victoria, and he still smelled like lemonbush.

"I'd rather you didn't try to walk to the mess hall. I have some protein bars in my cabin."

She stumbled along beside him down the hall. He punched in the code at cabin seventeen. She saw it before she could think to look away. His cabin was identical to hers but crammed with many of their equipment crates. He steered her to the lower bunk and handed her a colorfully wrapped bar.

"Eat that. I'll get you something to drink."

He came back a few minutes later with a red can festooned with stars. Galaxy Cola. Never heard of it, but it was ice cold and the best thing she'd ever tasted. He returned with another before she could ask, and she finished it just as quickly, taking gulps between bites of the protein bar.

Lucas sat at the table, watching her. Why so intently? Did she look like she was about to collapse again?

"How are you feeling?" he asked.

Mia set the empty can on the floor. "Good. You were right. I didn't realize I was hungry. I was so focused on our situation. Thank you." She leaned forward, ready to get up and return to her own cabin, but Lucas put a restraining hand on her shoulder.

"Not yet. Have another protein bar."

Mia didn't argue. While she did feel better, good was a bit of an over-statement. The dizziness had receded but not vanished, and she didn't want to faint again.

Lucas pulled the top case off the pile. "The Scotch better be in here."

He unclasped the lid, peered in, and smiled as he pulled out a bottle and a stack of rugged plastic cups. He filled one halfway and took a long drink before he sat back down.

"We had quite a day."

Mia nodded, mouth full.

He leaned back, visibly relaxing, though she could see it was a strug-gle to find a comfortable position against the metal wall.

"We made it. By some fucking miracle, we all made it," he said.

He held up his glass for a toast, and she clinked the empty soda can against it. He'd doubted they would? She pictured his worried face as he told her to be safe when she left Frontier.

"How's your cheek? You're bruised," he said.

She pressed her fingers against the sore spot. "It's fine. Lucky we've got such low gravity. I'd have a concussion if this happened on Victoria."

The soda and the protein bar began to make their way into her sys-tem, and a feeling of well-being trickled through her.

"You look better. You're getting some color in your face. In addition to the purple. Let me take a look at that." He crouched in front of her and took her chin in his hand, turning and tilting her head up to the ceiling light. His hand was rough and warm. He slid a finger down the side of her face. "I don't think we need to ice this. Anything else hurt?"

She shook her head.

He dropped his hand to her leg. She blushed. He noticed. The con-cern in his eyes changed to something like affection. "That's amazing."

"What?" Mia asked, feeling her face grow warmer.

"After a week like this…"

He kept his hand on her thigh a moment longer then retreated to the chair and refilled his glass. He hesitated, then took another cup off the stack and offered her a much smaller pour.

She took it, surprised he'd let her drink after she'd just passed out, but alcohol was calories, right? Scotch, for the first time, tasted amazing, the smokiness driving away the fishy smell she'd been unable to escape.

Lucas focused on the cheap cup filled with expensive liquor, swirling it as he spoke. "You're a hard woman to know. You don't expect much from other people…not help or anything else. You and your ocean and Baby Janes."

Mia froze, then gulped down the rest of the booze. Suddenly too warm, she shrugged out of the jacket.

He cleared his throat. "There's something I need to tell you about that night. About what happened after you got in the fight."

"We agreed not to talk about this."

He held up a hand. "Things have changed. I'm not your boss anymore. I suspect that power dynamic made you uncomfortable, but since then we've restructured the business. Plus, we're here." He gestured at the ugly cabin. "We're going to have to work together in close quarters for the next few months without being uncomfortable. We can't continue to avoid each other or this subject."

"I haven't been avoiding you. I work in the office, and you work offsite with clients, and I haven't been going to the gym because I joined that outdoor climbing group—" Mia's words tumbled over each other.

"I know, but I'd like the chance to clear up some misunderstandings. I won't bring this up again after today."

She glanced around the ancient, rusted cabin, desperate to find an escape hatch. "We don't have a conversation shield."

Lucas shook his head. "We don't need one." He clanked his cup against the chipped paint of the metal wall in a mock toast. "No signals get through this. I checked. Welcome to your first taste of real privacy. We'll be lucky if this ship has air pressure monitors. It certainly doesn't have surveillance drones or hidden cameras."

She grimaced. "Fine." She held out the cup and he refilled it, nearly to the brim. A bad sign.

He folded his arms and drummed the fingers of his right hand against his bicep. "You seem to be under the impression that we fought.

We didn't. After our…night together," he cleared his throat, "I suggested we shower, and afterwards I'd make a midnight snack. You…"

He let out a breath. Mia held hers.

"You shut down. You said you knew what happened next. Something about a parade of expensive women. You demanded I leave, so I got dressed and left."

"What do you mean, I asked you to leave? Where were we?"

"Your apartment."

She remembered waking up with clean sheets and noticing she'd straightened up the living room. Her mental picture of the evening contorted. She never brought men to her place.

"I'd assumed it happened in the pod," she admitted.

She could picture it so clearly. She'd been wound up after the encounter with Phil. Lucas pulled her into the pod, she'd struggled against him, their bodies mistaking energy and friction for passion. She'd been on his lap, facing him in the last of the still images she'd seen. Minutes later, it would have been over. She'd pull her skirt down and tuck in her shirt, retreat to the far side of the small space, and ask the pod to take her home. Undignified, but accidental, even understandable given the circumstances.

"It did, the first time." He smiled into his scotch.

What the hell? She'd invited him in, and they'd done it again? And Lucas offered to cook? "This isn't clearing the air. It's making me uncomfortable."

"You need to hear this. It wasn't me that suggested we forget what happened. It was you. You practically pushed me out the door." He leaned back in the chair and gave her a strange look. "A man with less self-confidence might have considered that and the memory-wiping drug a bit of an insult."

He held up his hands in response to her open-mouthed astonishment. "We were having a good night until you decided it was over. You need to know that and get rid of whatever fiction you've manufactured to fill the void you created. I wasn't the bad guy in this scenario, and I'm tired of your sidelong glances and quiet air of having been wronged."

She stared at the cabin floor, utterly flummoxed. Had she been acting like the stoic victim of Lucas the Seducer when, really, she'd been the one calling the shots that night?

She took a gulp of the scotch, and it burned. She'd cast the scene with a fictional, villainous Lucas, combining bits of him from when he was ill, sarcastic, and short-tempered, and adding a dash of the predator she'd watched pick up women at The End. That man had sex with her, and when they were done, hacked away any affection she'd felt with blunt, cruel words. He had certainly not offered to cook her breakfast.

That Lucas hadn't been real, but the Mia he described certainly was. How many breakups had she orchestrated with a similar script? Man gets too friendly, feels too comfortable, tries to take things to the next level, and she shuts it down. Shuts him down. Tells herself she knows what happens next. In every future, the man betrays her.

This time she'd betrayed herself. "I did imagine the worst."

"You've seen me at my worst," Lucas replied, "but it wasn't that night."

Mia focused on a rusty rivet on the wall across from her and thought about the flawed version of herself Jason had called out when they were camping in the desert. She was uptight and untrusting and chose men specifically for their lack of serious relationship potential. Part of her felt she owed Lucas an apology, but she couldn't do it, not sincerely, given she had no memory of what transpired. She could, however, respect Lucas for broaching a subject he was also uncomfortable about, and for calling her out, quite politely, for being an ass.

"You'd have to have said something very nice for me to get that angry."

He laughed, and the tension in the room vanished. "I may have. Too bad we aren't allowed to talk about this, or I'd tell you what set you off."

She glanced up, and his lingering smile and slightly raised eyebrow invited her to imagine a compliment so heartfelt it had thrown her into a rage.

She took a deep breath. "I'm hungry. Is the mess still open?"

Lucas glanced at a screen on the table. "We have fifteen minutes. If we hurry, we can make it."

He stood. When she didn't get up right away, he must have mistaken her hesitation for continued unsteadiness, because he held out his hands. They were steady. She thought back to the day they met and how his hand shook, his pallor. Victoria had been good for him.

There was no way around him, so she took his offered hands, and he pulled her up—too forcefully. He was strong, and the gravity was weak. She stumbled into him, and they ended up against the wall and froze there, hands clasped at chest height, looking at each other in surprise. He began to loosen his grip, but she didn't let go.

Her perspective flipped. Upside down changed to right side up.

Lucas had been avoiding her. She'd rarely seen him in the past months but thought nothing of it. They were busy. She ran through a typical work-day and what she remembered, reframed, seemed almost comical. Lucas catching his own pod even when sharing made sense. Never calling her into his office. Avoiding the main room when she worked late. Sending messages instead of meeting face-to-face. He'd been acting like…

Like I broke up with him.

She didn't go to The End often after the incident, but when she did, she saw Lucas focused on drinking and little else. Women were still around, and Mikey still went after them, but Lucas sat brooding.

Pieces of the past slid around and reordered themselves. The void from the Levotrum cast a long shadow, obscuring her perception of Lucas from that night forward. She hadn't been physically avoiding him, true, but mentally, she'd quarantined him based on a fictional scene she'd written. Something happened that night that scared her so badly she'd panicked. Lucas knew the real reason she'd taken the Levotrum—he'd been there. He'd been gracious enough not to shove the truth into her face…until now.

Because right now she was a badass who'd knocked his mortal enemy out cold and sent him into Optima custody. That woman could handle the facts about a night of good sex and her own skittishness.

She couldn't look up.

Lucas freed one of his hands and trailed his finger down the bruise on her cheek, ending at her chin. He lifted it gently.

She finally raised her eyes.

His gaze held no irony, no challenge, just a hint of a question. She hadn't conquered the thing in her that found him attractive. She'd compartmentalized and mocked it and all the *normal* people that drooled over him. His good looks wouldn't have been why she invited him up to her apartment after their first go-around in the pod.

He was a puzzle she wanted to solve.

She thought about him even when she wasn't thinking about him.

Famous Lucas. Drug addict Lucas. Hero Lucas. Barely alive Lucas. Charming Lucas.

Ever since he got back from the clinic he'd been steadily and relentlessly building himself and the business. He was ambitious, intelligent, curious, and driven. She'd witnessed this during their hundreds of hours together. So many hours. So many evenings at too-small tables after a client engagement when it made sense for Lucas to buy her dinner because they'd worked late. So many "let's take the long way" pod rides around the city so Lucas could learn more about the place. His sudden interest in climbing. The way he held her hand so hard after she'd been hit by the poison dart that when she couldn't feel anything else, not even the burning stones under her back, she could still feel his hand.

Maybe he wanted to solve her as well.

She must have smiled because Lucas's questioning eyes brightened. He leaned forward and kissed her like he'd just made it to the top of the climbing wall, climbing blind.

The kiss blew through her like a hot wind in the wastes. She smelled him and tasted him and something cracked open that she wouldn't be able to shut. She understood why she took the Levotrum.

She broke away to suck in a breath.

Lucas looked at her with an openness and anticipation and fire she'd never seen in him before. Nothing like how he looked at the women in the bar. He slipped his hands beneath her shirt and pulled her in and kissed her even more intensely, running his hands up and down the bare skin of her back. She buried her lips against the place on his neck where she'd seen the small blue and purple mark the day after she'd forgotten. He tasted of salt and Lucas. She pressed hard against him, feeling all of him meeting all of her. He breathed heavily as he pushed her away and used his now free hands to strip off her tank top.

She fumbled with the too many buttons of his shirt, but he pulled it up and over his head, saving her the time and trouble. They came together, mouths hot, hands frantic. The smooth skin of his back was interrupted by the scars she'd never seen. A relief map of a life she knew so little about. She wondered if she'd left a mark—last time. She had the urge to scratch, to make herself a part his life that he could never erase. But she had done the erasing, not him.

He gave a crooked smile and took her face in his hands. "I missed you."

They kissed again, bare chests pressed together. The dizziness she'd experienced in the hall was nothing compared to this. She was back on Victoria on a hot summer night in a pod driving around Ring 20, her head out the window, speed and hot wind, stars and darkness.

She broke from the kiss. "We should lie down."

"We should."

He backed her down onto the little bunk and deftly removed her skirt then stripped off his pants, unselfconscious with his nudity.

"You won't forget this time," he said.

"I don't want to," Mia replied.

The twin bed should have been too small, but it wasn't. The poles holding the bunk above, the wire mesh supporting the thin mattress, and the metal walls of the ship were the boundaries of a playing field—and they played.

Lucas had an advantage in the game—memories of their previous night together. His familiarity with her body unnerved and thrilled her.

"You like this," he whispered as he pressed into her, deep then shallow, deep then shallow, waves on an endless beach. She shut her eyes and drowned under him, having him and wanting him all at once.

She muffled her cries of pleasure. Her analytical brain, never silent, informed her it was safe to scream, to yell. They were in a metal box hurtling through space *away* from Victoria. It would take some time for that to sink in, though.

Abruptly, Lucas slowed, trying too late to prolong the moment. A gasp transformed into a groan. A shudder passed through him, and he dropped to her chest, head buried in her hair, full weight on her, heart pounding. She held him until it slowed.

Time passed. Sweat cooled. Lucas eased off her and rested on his side, pulling her to him. They lay face-to-face, legs entwined.

Lucas smiled and brushed back the damp tendrils of her hair. "You can see why I had trouble pretending nothing happened."

She nodded and closed her eyes. She felt as good as she'd felt in years, maybe ever. This was the sex she'd dreamed of but never actually experienced. Lucas knew her. He knew how she moved and anticipated where she'd put her hands and body as she negotiated his surfaces, and worked with her to get to a place they both wanted to go—together.

This wouldn't and couldn't be a moment trapped in amber like the rest of her memories. The 98% accurate *Visual Generalist* had been crushed by smell, touch, taste, and the sound of Lucas's ragged breathing as he let go and trusted she'd be there to catch him.

She breathed him in and relaxed, banishing thought and memory, as in the present as she'd ever been.

She didn't realize she'd fallen asleep until she woke, disoriented. She was in bed, covered by a sheet and blanket. Lucas sat at the desk, shirtless, in loose pants, a screen in front of him and a plate of food next to that.

She sat up, flustered. He smiled, calm and content.

"How long have I been asleep?" She tried to find some clue in the stars, but they sparkled cheery and unchanging.

Lucas glanced at the screen. "About four hours. I got you something to eat."

Shit. Had she snored? The twinkle in Lucas's eyes said she had. She grabbed her tank top off the floor and pulled it on, then stumbled the few steps to the small sink and splashed water on her face, trying to wake up.

"Oh my god." The image in the mirror was a fright. Her sweat-soaked hair had dried in bizarre tufts, parts flat, parts sticking out in clumps. Her cheeks were red, pupils wide.

Lucas came over, slipped his arms around her and caressed her belly, one hand slipping up to give her breast a proprietary squeeze. He gazed over her shoulder at their reflection. A hint of a smile flittered on one side of his mouth, and he bent over and kissed her neck.

"You're beautiful. Come, eat." He pulled her from the mirror and offered the chair.

She pulled on the daisy skirt, then sat.

The fish pasta dish had gone cold, but she was ravenous and set into it frantically. Lucas sat on the edge of the bunk and watched, bemused. She wolfed it down in less than five minutes.

"That was good. Thanks." A silence followed, and the reality of where she was and what she'd done hit her. Anxiety crept up from the soles of her feet, bare against the cool metal floor, and she shivered.

"You're cold."

"No." Nervous, but she wouldn't admit it.

The sex with Lucas glued together feelings she'd worked hard to keep separate, and their combined weight unbalanced her. This new thing was more than admiration, respect, lust, and the rest. It had a name she wasn't going to say.

She felt that same helpless falling feeling as zero G, and her stomach turned sickeningly. "Can I have some scotch?"

Lucas reached forward and took her hand. "Why do you look sad?"

She was the queen of the one-night stand but wouldn't be able to bear it if that was all it had been. She gave an unconvincing grin and examined the empty pasta plate.

"I'm not sad, just not awake, and I ate too fast."

He kept hold of her hand. "This ends differently this time. You can't throw me out. We're in my cabin, and you don't want to forget, do you?"

Mia shook her head.

"I'd like to give this a try." He hesitated. "Give us a try. If you're interested. It's been a while since I've had anything that wasn't casual, and I'm not easy to get along with, but you know that already."

She glanced up and he was still there, not withdrawing, not angry. Her panic receded. She took a deep breath and tried not to sound antagonistic. Either one of them could break this so easily.

Please, let it not be me again.

"I want to give us a try, too." She pulled his hand to her mouth and kissed it. "But not on this freighter with everyone on top of each other. I'd like a personal life separate from the team and the job. Us being together is going to affect the team. Jason will be angry at me for trusting you. Claire…" Mia gritted her teeth and shook her head. "She doesn't like change, and she's very loyal to you. Mikey will never stop teasing me."

He shut his eyes and leaned his forehead against hers. It was a strangely vulnerable position, almost more intimate than the passion. They sat like that for a long minute.

He raised his head and opened his eyes. The calm was gone, the steel back. "You're right. It will happen, just not here. We won't be shipboard entertainment for Mikey and Jason and Claire. When I start with you, I'm not going to stop." He leaned in and kissed her long and hard then pulled away. "No more. Not now. We're being hunted. I need to get the team safely settled on Novus, and then we can consider our next moves."

As much as she wanted to curl up in bed with him, if they spent nights together, the relationship wouldn't stay secret long. Their bodies would betray them. Even now she resisted the urge to reach out and stroke the stubble on his cheek. Their relationship had to stay professional until Topsoil played out.

The trip to Novus was going to be the longest month of her life.

"I should get back to my cabin," she said.

"Yes," Lucas said without conviction.

She found the rest of her clothes and finished dressing. How had one shoe ended up under the bed and the other on top of a crate?

"Could you make sure no one is in the hall?" she asked.

He peered out the door. "It's clear."

He stood aside.

She leaned in as she passed, not for the kiss he expected, but for a long deep inhale. Lucas was a scent she could wear forever.

"Thanks for everything." She squeezed his hand then hurried away.

She thought she'd seen him from every angle and could spin him around like a holo in her mind, but he was always new. How could one person be so different every day? She glanced back.

He stood in the doorway, shirtless, tan, his loose off-white linen pants hanging low on his hips, hair messed; a spark of life against the dull gray-green paint of the ship. She had to turn away. He was too vibrant to stay put in the drawers of her mind.

"Mia…" he called softly as she padded quickly away. She didn't dare turn back. Waiting for him wasn't going to be easy, and the less she saw of him looking like that, the better. The Topsoil project absolutely, positively needed to be wrapped up by the time they touched down on Novus so they could do what they just did again.

She punched in the code to her cabin door and once safely inside, slid the metal bar into place with a satisfying *clunk*.

Safe.

She made her way to the porthole and located the dimming dot that was Victoria. Not the view she wanted. The map Lucas had sent earlier indicated a gym in the bow of the ship. Would it have a porthole as well?

Mia pulled on a shapeless jacket and crept back out into the hall. No crew members lurked. She followed the yellow arrows her glasses cast on the filthy floor. Ten minutes later—the ship was big—she arrived at a door with the word *GYM* stenciled on it. She wrenched at the handle. It screeched open. She looked left and right quickly but no predatory crew members emerged from the shadows.

The equipment—out-of-date resistance machines, barbells, and dumbbells—hadn't been used in quite some time, based on the fine dust that had settled over everything. She might be able to work out here without being harassed.

Beyond the machines was what she'd hoped for—six porthole windows with a view of where they were headed. She wiped the nearest clean with her sleeve, and a thousand stars resolved from fuzzy balls to sharp, bright sparks.

"Which one is Novus?" she whispered, and her glasses interpreted it as a query. A microsecond later a pale blue circle surrounded one of the sparks in the dead center of the window. It seemed to grow larger as she watched.

Just over a year ago, she'd been fired from Han, disgraced on social media, and unable to find a new job. She'd taken the tram to 360 Degrees to meet Claire and gotten a bird's-eye view of the rings of New Canberra. The city and all its petty machinations seemed insignificant compared to the vast wilds that surrounded it, and that had calmed her. Still, she'd remained bound and bounded by those rings.

She'd been looking down, not up.

Novus. No rules. No Registry of Extraordinary Abilities.

Maybe no career opportunities, but thanks to the sale of Ms. Tanaka's furniture, she had enough credits to jumpstart a business. Not security or social engineering, of course, but the planet had so much untapped potential. With Lucas's charisma, Jason's technical skills, and Claire's coding genius, they could get something going. She couldn't imagine what yet, but something. Mikey likely wouldn't stick around. The median age or residents was seventy-six and the ratio of men to women heavily weighted to men.

She smiled and let her forehead rest against the chill porthole glass. Dare she imagine a future on Novus? At Summit, she'd only used her imagination to visualize worst-case scenarios. Not just at Summit, it'd been like that her whole life.

What had Jason said? *Talking to you is like watching someone calculate the best way out of a burning building.*

He was right. She spent most of her time anticipating danger and trying to avoid it, not picturing a better future or even enjoying the moment.

For the next few months, she'd do both. She had credits, a team she could count on, a lover, and a whole new planet to explore.

Imagine that.

Six

A note from the author

I started writing this book over ten years ago in Iceland in a small notebook I bought from a corner store. A combination of jet lag and the exotic locale spawned an idea and I hurried to catch my thoughts before they escaped.

I wrote and wrote, revised and revised, and declared this thing done numerous times before realizing it wasn't. I set the book aside and published a prequel novella, *The Perfect Specimen*, which allowed me to plant a stake in the ground of this world and start sharing it.

So many people supported me in the creation of this place and these characters. Thank you all. This wouldn't exist without you.

And to those of you who suspect you have a novel in you but are not sure how to get it out, start writing. Take your time, be patient with yourself, respect your characters, and trust your readers. The book you write will be someone's favorite and it deserves to exist.

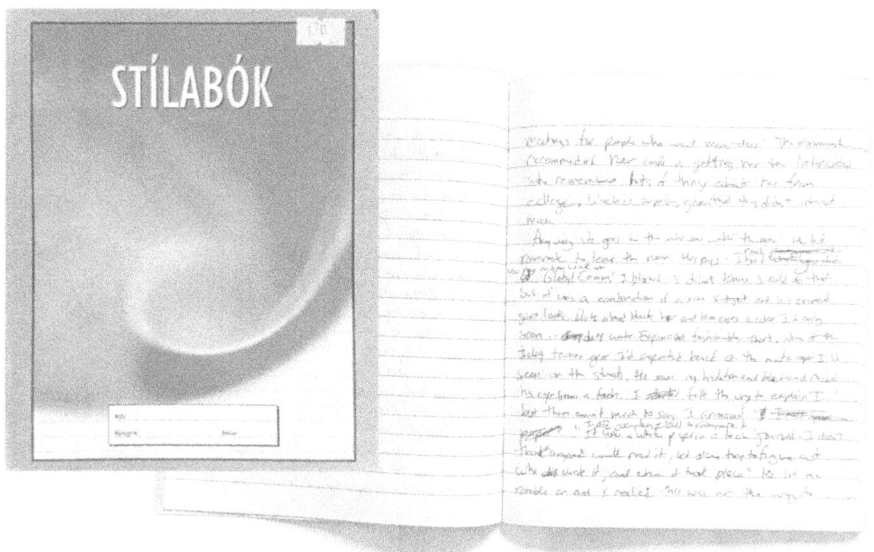

About the author

M. Luke McDonell is a San Francisco-based science fiction writer and visual designer. Her five-minutes-into-the-future fiction explores the effects of emerging technology on individuals and society. Her short stories have appeared in numerous publications, and her novellas, *The Perfect Specimen* and *The Bear Box,* have garnered rave reviews from readers.

When not writing, she serves as the creative director of SomaFM, which features over 30 unique channels of listener-supported, commercial-free, underground internet radio.

Learn more at mlukemcdonell.com, and listen at somafm.com.

THE PERFECT SPECIMEN

The prequel to *Six,* by M. Luke McDonell

Dr. Derek Singh is sure that one of planet Victoria's millions of venomous insects holds the key to destroying cancerous tumors–and jumpstarting his stalled career.

Unfortunately, the traps he sets each night capture nothing but dust, and his competitive colleagues don't share the venom they've collected. The clock is running down on his two-year grant and he's making no progress.

When his young neighbor–one of the few native-born children–finds out he studies "bugs," she is eager to bring him all the specimens he needs. Derek worries she'll be bitten or stung, but soon discovers Mia is in danger from a far larger predator–the corporation that funds him.

"Great read. Speculative fiction at its best."

"Brilliant, inventive story, beautifully descriptive language, and amazingly well rendered characters."

"Vivid prose and intricate characters pull you through a science-fiction world of surprising complexity and depth."

THE BEAR BOX

by M. Luke McDonell

In the aftermath of a tragic accident, Yosemite National Park blocks access to WorldNet, hoping visitors will focus on the natural wonders that surround them instead of virtual entertainment.

Seventeen-year-old Anika gets an unexpected break from the intrusive monitoring of the cuff she's worn since birth. She finally has the chance to bend some rules, but so do the rest of the visitors to the valley.

What happens when guardrails and safety nets vanish? It's a weekend of firsts...and lasts.

"Both very enchanting and very ominous. McDonell's writing is vibrant and precise in this can't-put-it-down coming of age story."

–Peter Delacorte, author of *Time on My Hands* and *Levantine*.

"Great, troubling, thought-provoking story. McDonell balances our utopian ideals/fantasies with the very real dystopian costs of our technical obsessions, and has a knack for realistic predictions of how our current technical fads can turn into tomorrow's blinding addictions, all using highly relatable heroines and heroes."

www.ingramcontent.com/pod-product-compliance
Lightning Source LLC
Chambersburg PA
CBHW072000110726
47910CB00005B/1601